JULES VERNE'S
LIGHTHOUSE ™

D1473448

Shadowline

image

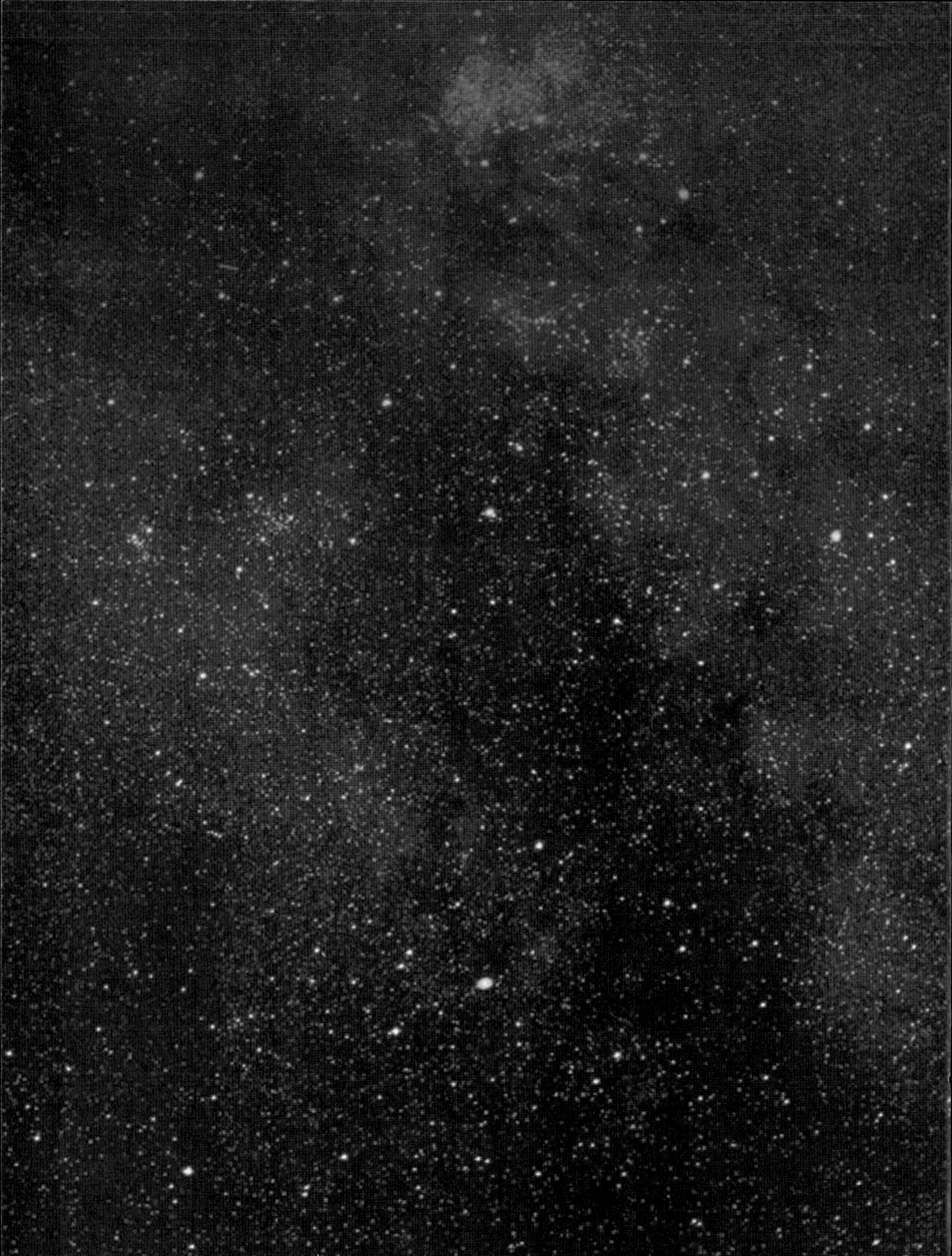

FIRST PRINTING: OCTOBER 2021

ISBN: 978-1-5343-1993-6

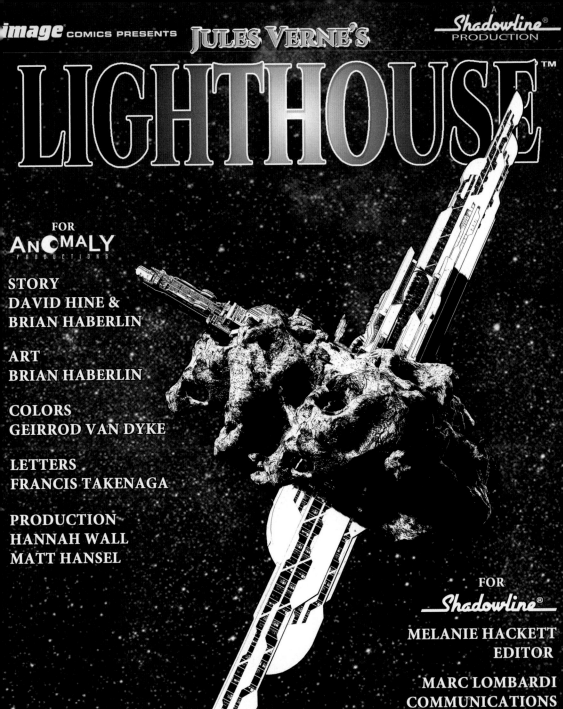

image COMICS PRESENTS

A Shadowline PRODUCTION

JULES VERNE'S
LIGHTHOUSE™

FOR
AN○MALY
PRODUCTIONS

STORY
DAVID HINE &
BRIAN HABERLIN

ART
BRIAN HABERLIN

COLORS
GEIRROD VAN DYKE

LETTERS
FRANCIS TAKENAGA

PRODUCTION
HANNAH WALL
MATT HANSEL

FOR
Shadowline®

MELANIE HACKETT
EDITOR

MARC LOMBARDI
COMMUNICATIONS

JIM VALENTINO
PUBLISHER

ERIKA SCHNATZ
PRODUCTION

IMAGE COMICS, INC. • Todd McFarlane: President • Jim Valentino: Vice President • Marc Silvestri: Chief Executive Officer • Erik Larsen: Chief Financial Officer • Robert Kirkman: Chief Operating Officer • Eric Stephenson: Publisher / Chief Creative Officer • Nicole Lapalme: Controller • Leanna Caunter: Accounting Analyst • Sue Korpela: Accounting & HR Manager • Marla Eizik: Talent Liaison • Jeff Boison: Director of Sales & Publishing Planning • Dirk Wood: Director of International Sales & Licensing • Alex Cox: Director of Direct Market Sales • Chloe Ramos: Book Market & Library Sales Manager • Emilio Bautista: Digital Sales Coordinator • Jon Schlaffman: Specialty Sales Coordinator • Kat Salazar: Director of PR & Marketing • Drew Fitzgerald: Marketing Content Associate • Heather Doornink: Production Director • Drew Gill: Art Director • Hilary DiLoreto: Print Manager • Tricia Ramos: Traffic Manager • Melissa Gifford: Content Manager • Erika Schnatz: Senior Production Artist • Ryan Brewer: Production Artist • Deanna Phelps: Production Artist • IMAGECOMICS.COM

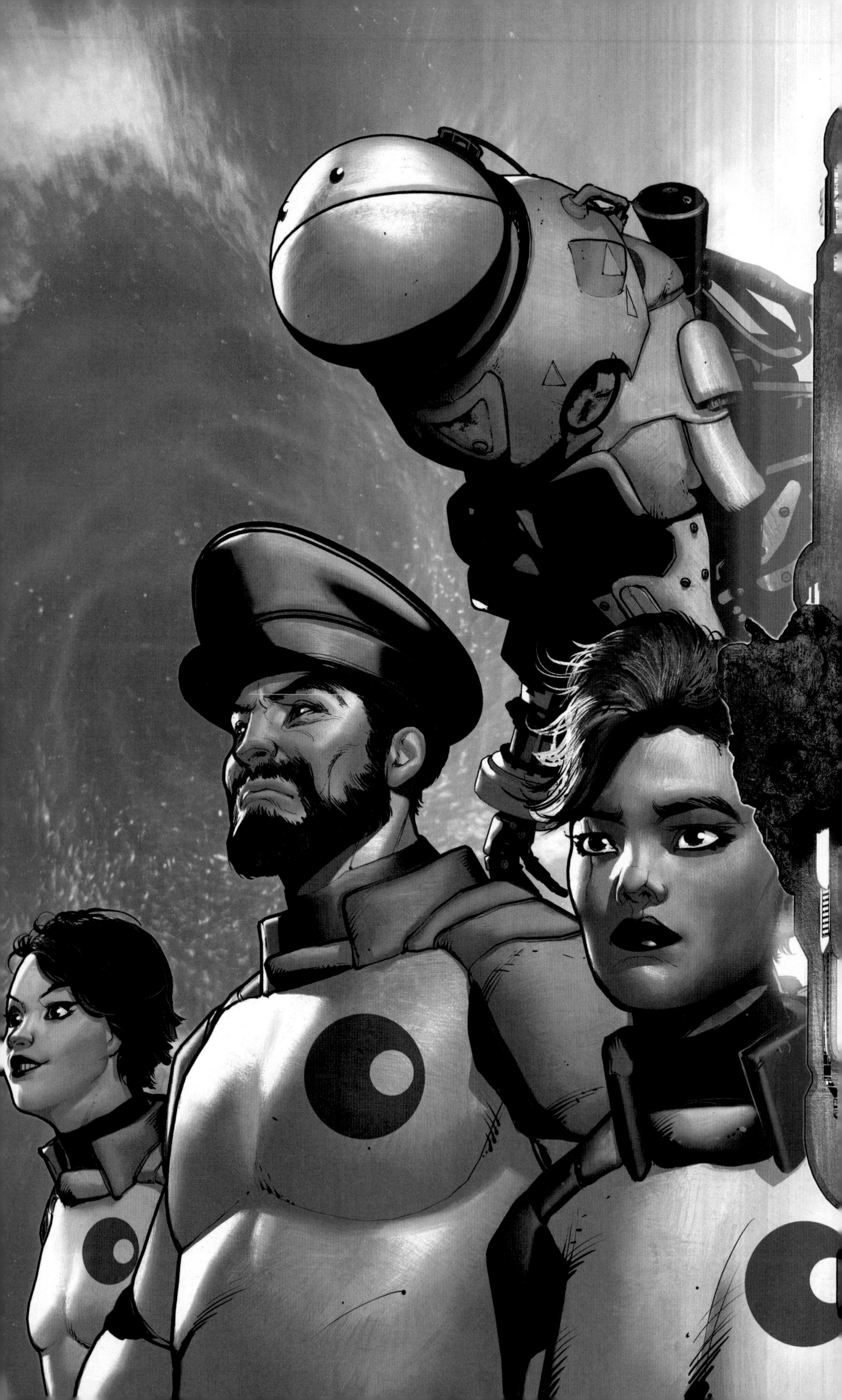

Issue #1 Cover A

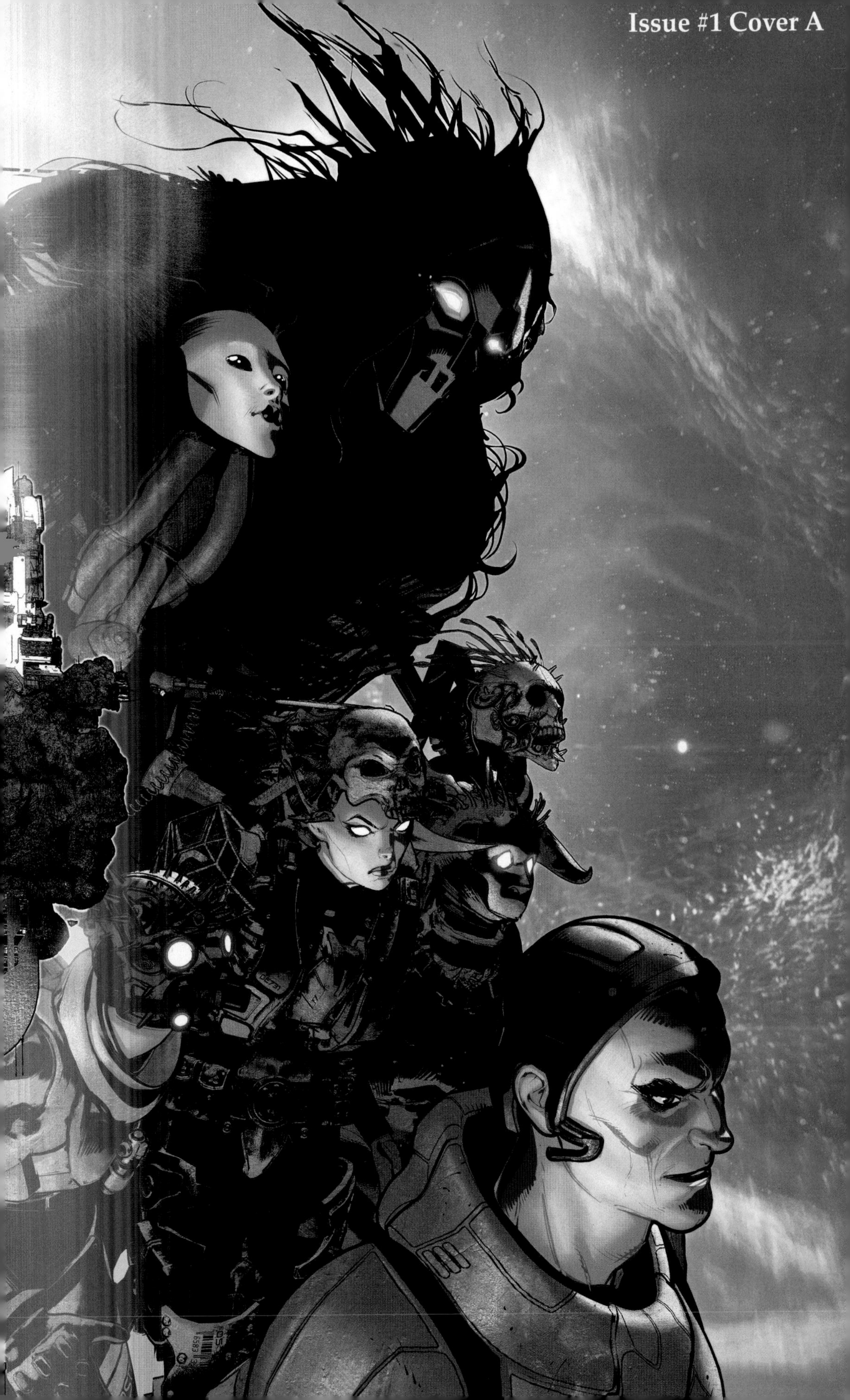

Issue #1 Cover B

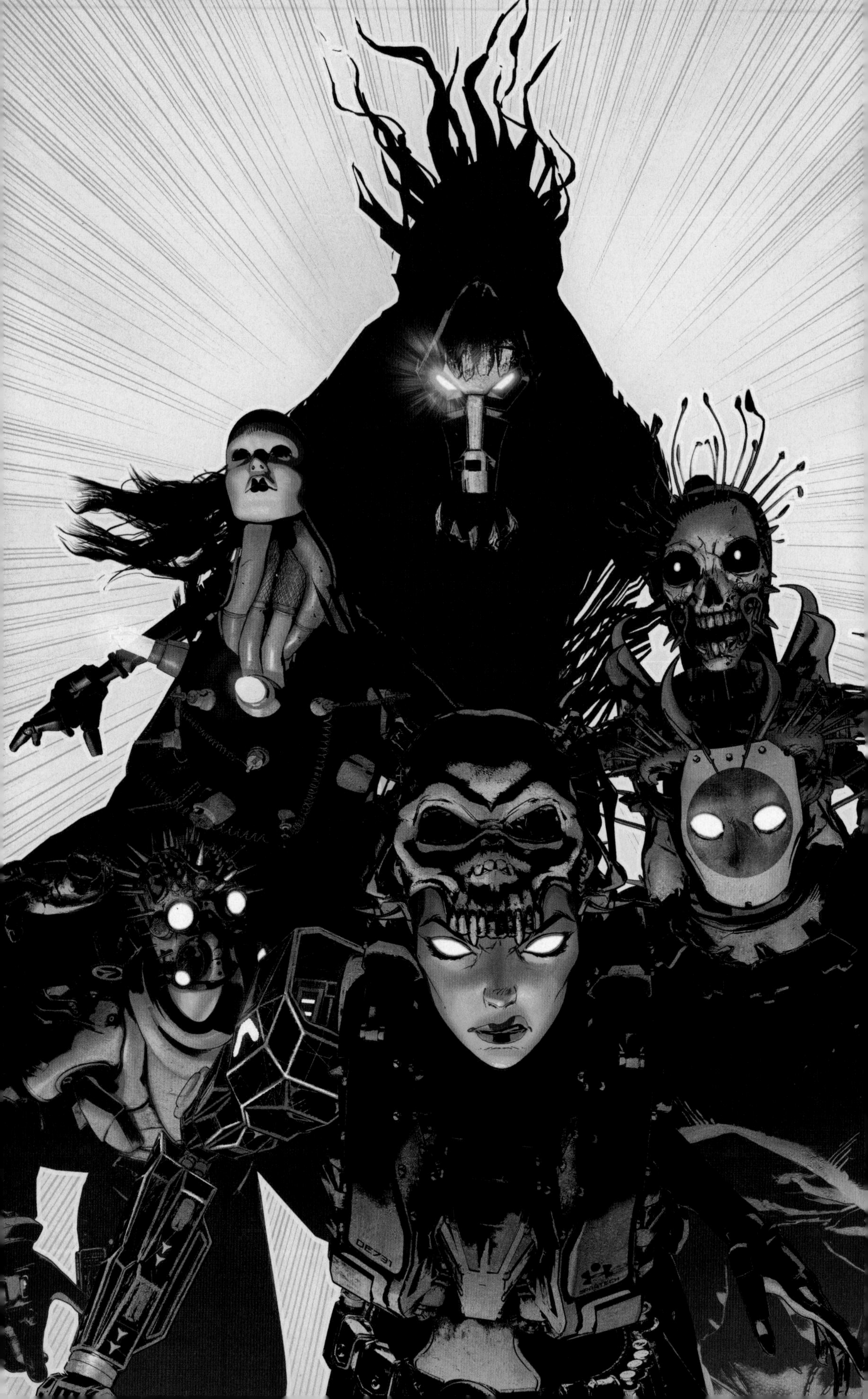

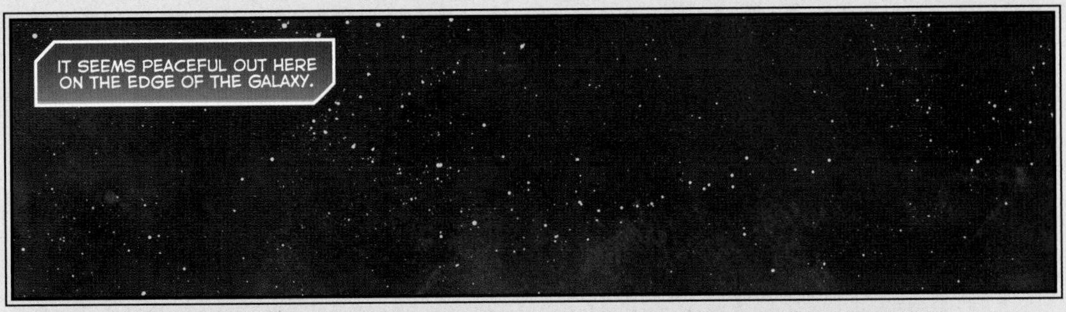
IT SEEMS PEACEFUL OUT HERE ON THE EDGE OF THE GALAXY.

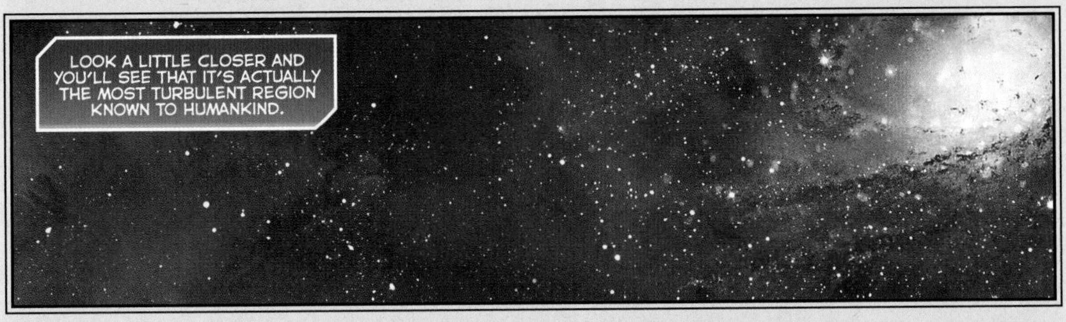
LOOK A LITTLE CLOSER AND YOU'LL SEE THAT IT'S ACTUALLY THE MOST TURBULENT REGION KNOWN TO HUMANKIND.

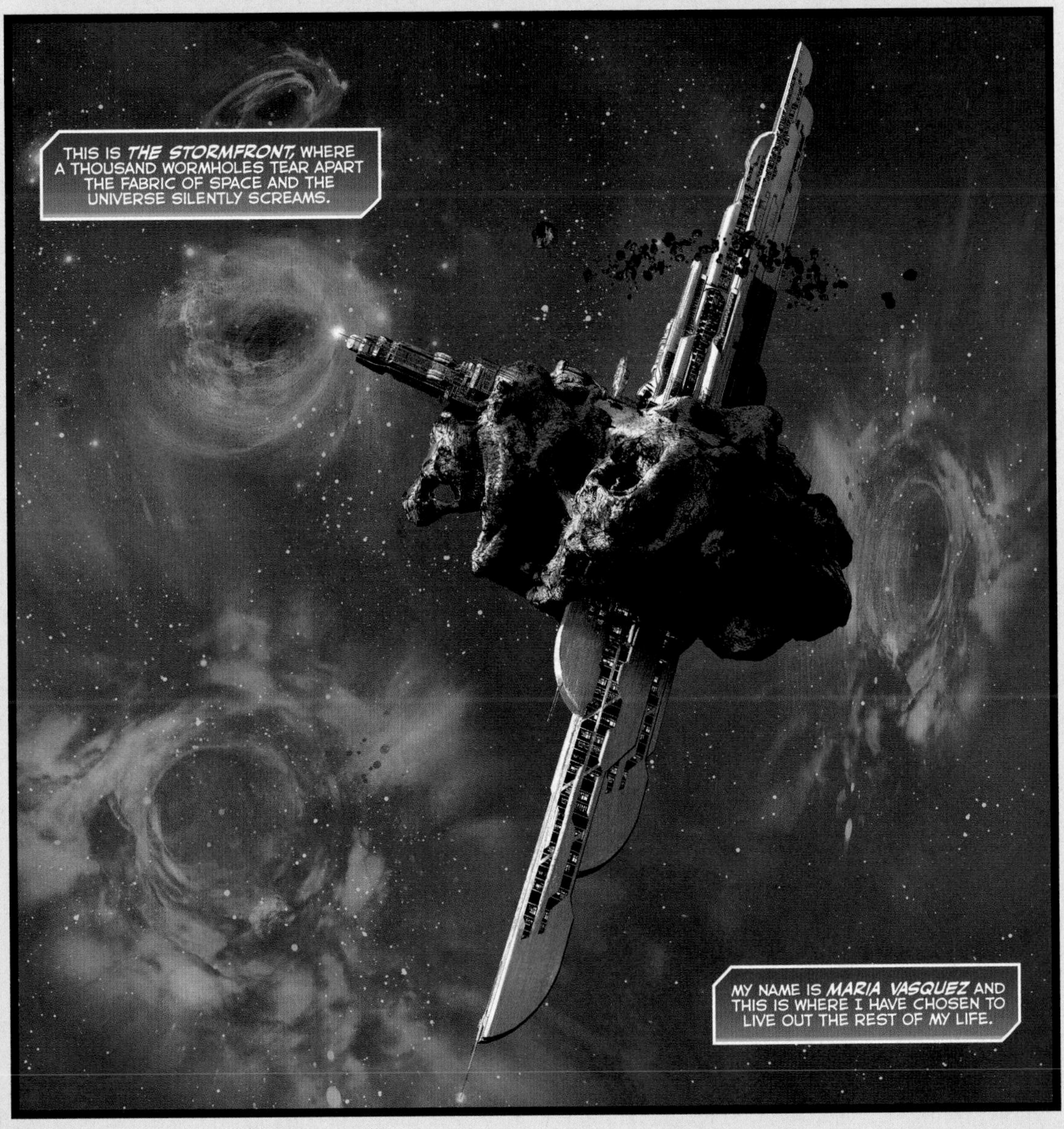
THIS IS *THE STORMFRONT,* WHERE A THOUSAND WORMHOLES TEAR APART THE FABRIC OF SPACE AND THE UNIVERSE SILENTLY SCREAMS.
MY NAME IS *MARIA VASQUEZ* AND THIS IS WHERE I HAVE CHOSEN TO LIVE OUT THE REST OF MY LIFE.

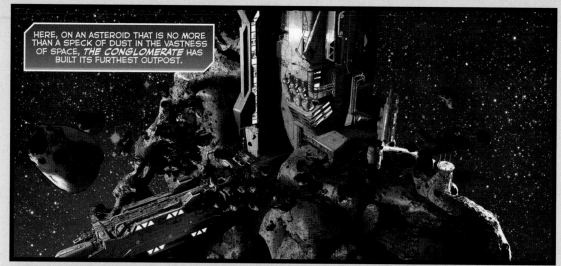

HERE, ON AN ASTEROID THAT IS NO MORE THAN A SPECK OF DUST IN THE VASTNESS OF SPACE, *THE CONGLOMERATE* HAS BUILT ITS FURTHEST OUTPOST.

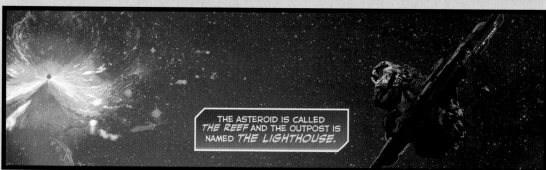

THE ASTEROID IS CALLED *THE REEF* AND THE OUTPOST IS NAMED *THE LIGHTHOUSE*.

ONCE, CENTURIES AGO, ON THE BIRTH PLANET, *EARTH*, A LIGHTHOUSE WOULD GUIDE SHIPS THROUGH THE HAZARDS OF AN OCEAN OF WATER.

OUR FUNCTION IS MUCH THE SAME. WE SHINE A DIGITAL LIGHT TO GUIDE VOYAGERS SAFELY ON THEIR WAY.

WITHOUT US, THE GRAVITATIONAL FORCES WOULD REDUCE THE SHIP AND ALL WHO SAIL IN HER TO A CLOUD OF QUARKS AND ELECTRONS IN AN INSTANT TOO BRIEF TO MEASURE.

LOOK LIVELY, SHIPMATES, LET'S SEND THESE VOYAGERS SAFELY ON THEIR WAY WITH THEIR SKINS INTACT.

CONFIRM COORDINATES TO—

FOR THE LOVE OF NEPTUNE!

HOW AM I SUPPOSED TO CONCENTRATE ON MY CHARTS WHILE YOU'RE MAKING THAT CURSED CATERWAULING—

LET THEM BE, CAP'N, FELIPE'S GETTING BETTER ON THAT THING EVERY DAY.

AND YOU HARDLY NEED TO CONCENTRATE ON CHARTS OR ANYTHING ELSE. THE LIGHTHOUSE DOES EVERYTHING AROUND HERE WITHOUT ANY HELP FROM US.

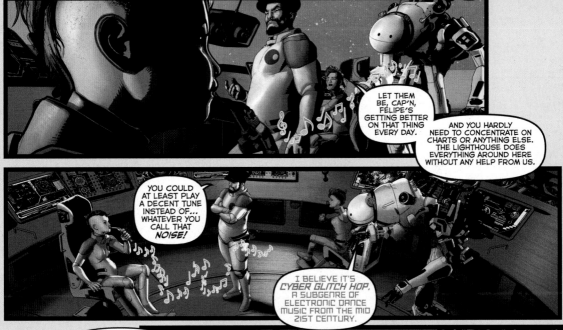

YOU COULD AT LEAST PLAY A DECENT TUNE INSTEAD OF... WHATEVER YOU CALL THAT *NOISE!*

I BELIEVE IT'S *CYBER GLITCH HOP,* A SUBGENRE OF ELECTRONIC DANCE MUSIC FROM THE MID 21ST CENTURY.

YOU NEVER CEASE TO AMAZE ME, *MOSES.* YOUR RESERVOIR OF KNOWLEDGE OF THE MOST UTTERLY POINTLESS TRIVIA IS TRULY BOUNDLESS.

THANK YOU, MISTRESS VASQUEZ...

...AND I BELIEVE IT MAY BE THE APPROPRIATE TIME TO HIT THE 'EXECUTE TRANSIT PHASE' BUTTON.

ON IT.

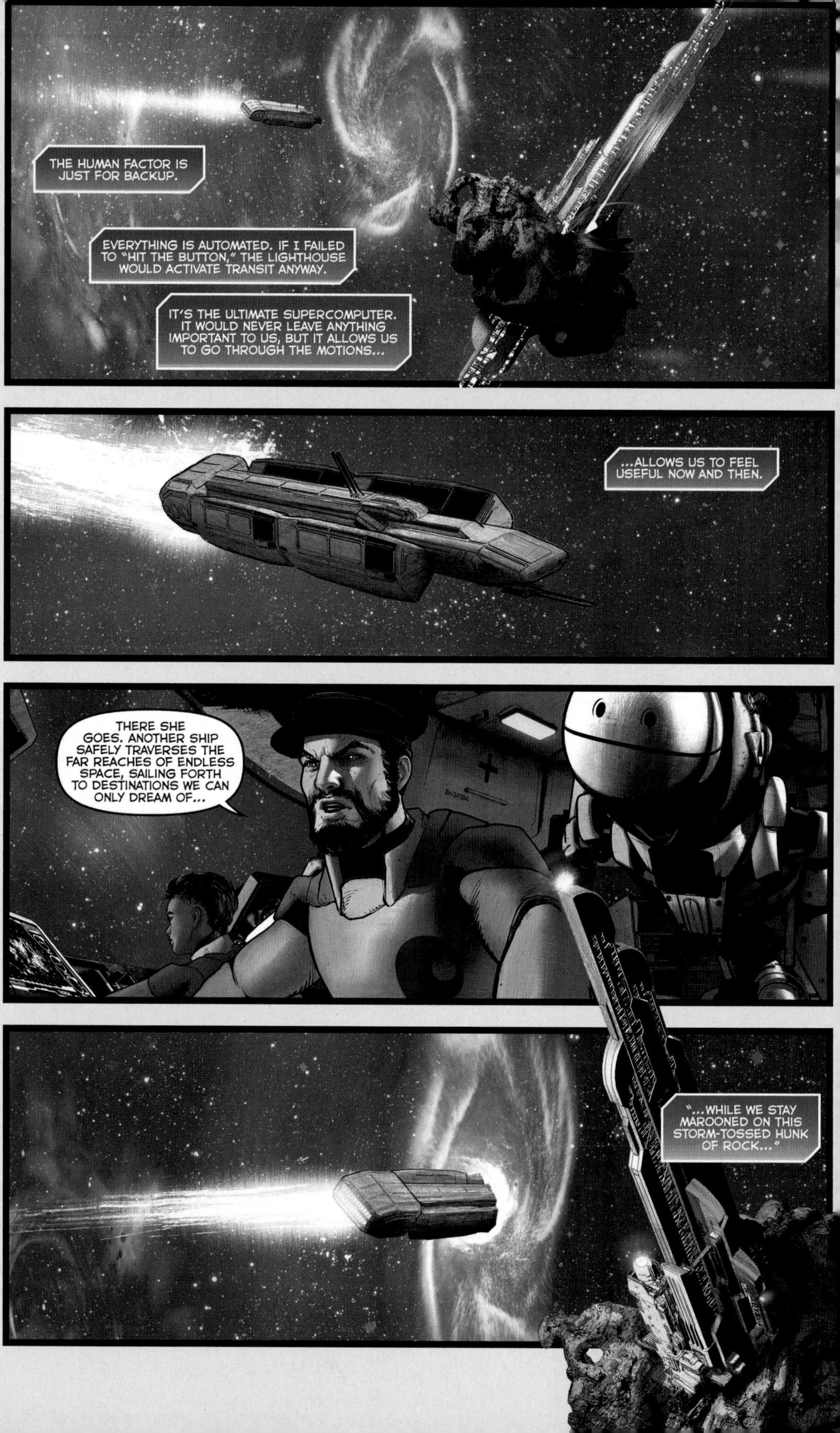
THE HUMAN FACTOR IS JUST FOR BACKUP.
EVERYTHING IS AUTOMATED. IF I FAILED TO "HIT THE BUTTON," THE LIGHTHOUSE WOULD ACTIVATE TRANSIT ANYWAY.
IT'S THE ULTIMATE SUPERCOMPUTER. IT WOULD NEVER LEAVE ANYTHING IMPORTANT TO US, BUT IT ALLOWS US TO GO THROUGH THE MOTIONS...
...ALLOWS US TO FEEL USEFUL NOW AND THEN.
THERE SHE GOES. ANOTHER SHIP SAFELY TRAVERSES THE FAR REACHES OF ENDLESS SPACE, SAILING FORTH TO DESTINATIONS WE CAN ONLY DREAM OF...
"...WHILE WE STAY MAROONED ON THIS STORM-TOSSED HUNK OF ROCK..."

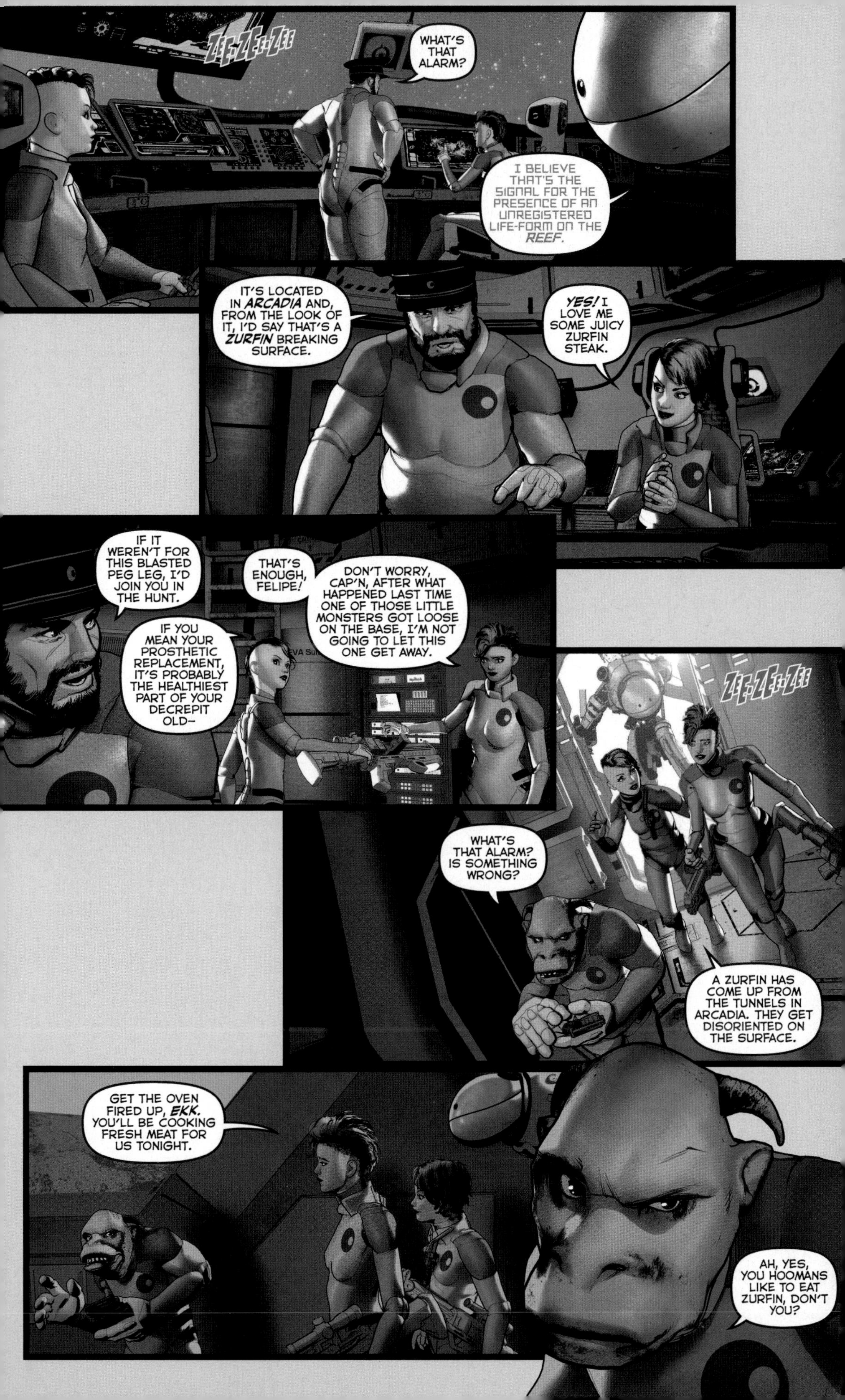
ZEE-ZEE-ZEE
WHAT'S THAT ALARM?
I BELIEVE THAT'S THE SIGNAL FOR THE PRESENCE OF AN UNREGISTERED LIFE-FORM ON THE *REEF*.
IT'S LOCATED IN *ARCADIA* AND, FROM THE LOOK OF IT, I'D SAY THAT'S A *ZURFIN* BREAKING SURFACE.
YES! I LOVE ME SOME JUICY ZURFIN STEAK.
IF IT WEREN'T FOR THIS BLASTED PEG LEG, I'D JOIN YOU IN THE HUNT.
IF YOU MEAN YOUR PROSTHETIC REPLACEMENT, IT'S PROBABLY THE HEALTHIEST PART OF YOUR DECREPIT OLD–
THAT'S ENOUGH, FELIPE!
DON'T WORRY, CAP'N, AFTER WHAT HAPPENED LAST TIME ONE OF THOSE LITTLE MONSTERS GOT LOOSE ON THE BASE, I'M NOT GOING TO LET THIS ONE GET AWAY.
ZEE-ZEE-ZEE
WHAT'S THAT ALARM? IS SOMETHING WRONG?
A ZURFIN HAS COME UP FROM THE TUNNELS IN ARCADIA. THEY GET DISORIENTED ON THE SURFACE.
GET THE OVEN FIRED UP, *EKK*. YOU'LL BE COOKING FRESH MEAT FOR US TONIGHT.
AH, YES, YOU HOOMANS LIKE TO EAT ZURFIN, DON'T YOU?

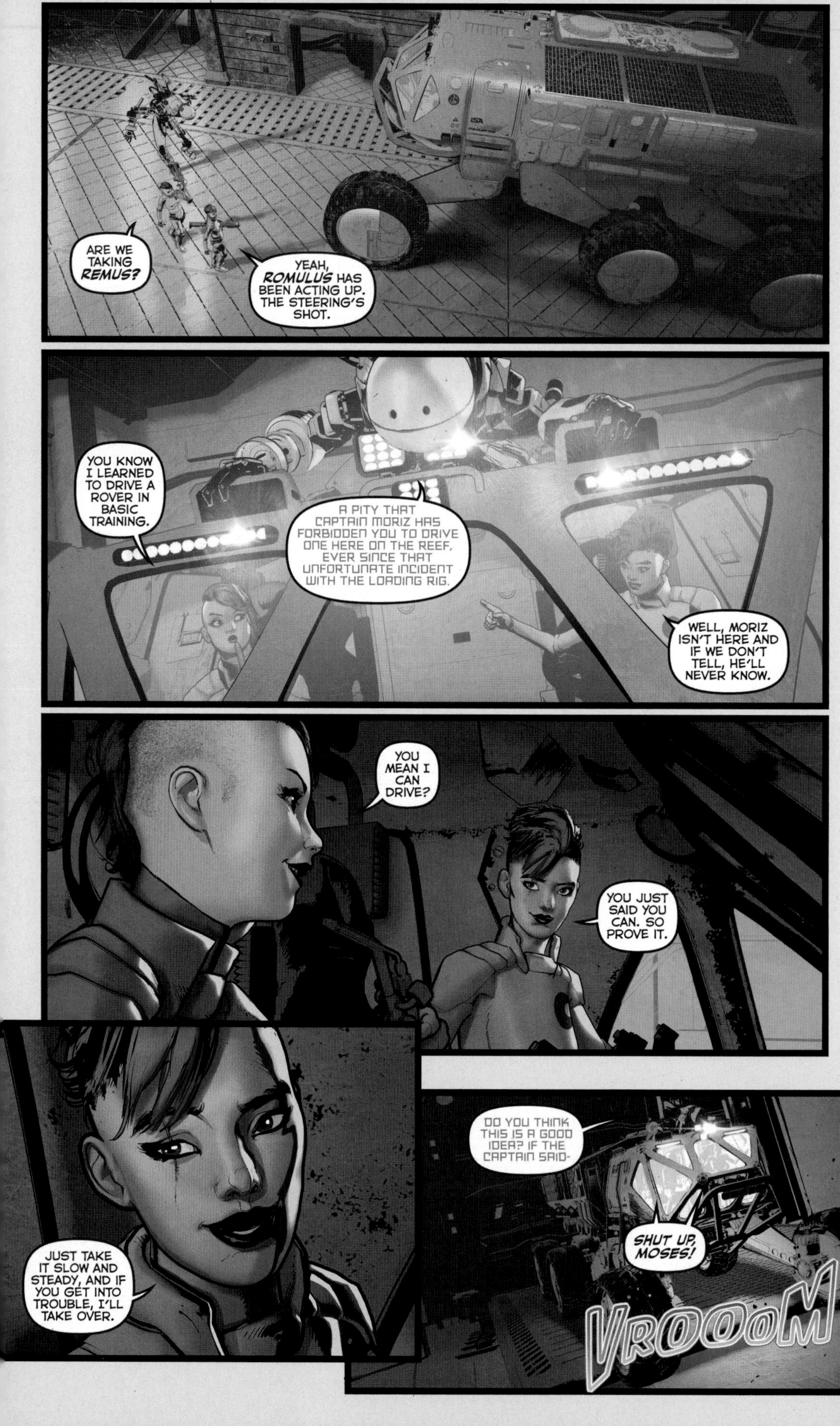
ARE WE TAKING REMUS?
YEAH, ROMULUS HAS BEEN ACTING UP. THE STEERING'S SHOT.
YOU KNOW I LEARNED TO DRIVE A ROVER IN BASIC TRAINING.
A PITY THAT CAPTAIN MORIZ HAS FORBIDDEN YOU TO DRIVE ONE HERE ON THE REEF, EVER SINCE THAT UNFORTUNATE INCIDENT WITH THE LOADING RIG.
WELL, MORIZ ISN'T HERE AND IF WE DON'T TELL, HE'LL NEVER KNOW.
YOU MEAN I CAN DRIVE?
YOU JUST SAID YOU CAN. SO PROVE IT.
JUST TAKE IT SLOW AND STEADY, AND IF YOU GET INTO TROUBLE, I'LL TAKE OVER.
DO YOU THINK THIS IS A GOOD IDEA? IF THE CAPTAIN SAID-
SHUT UP, MOSES!
VROOOM

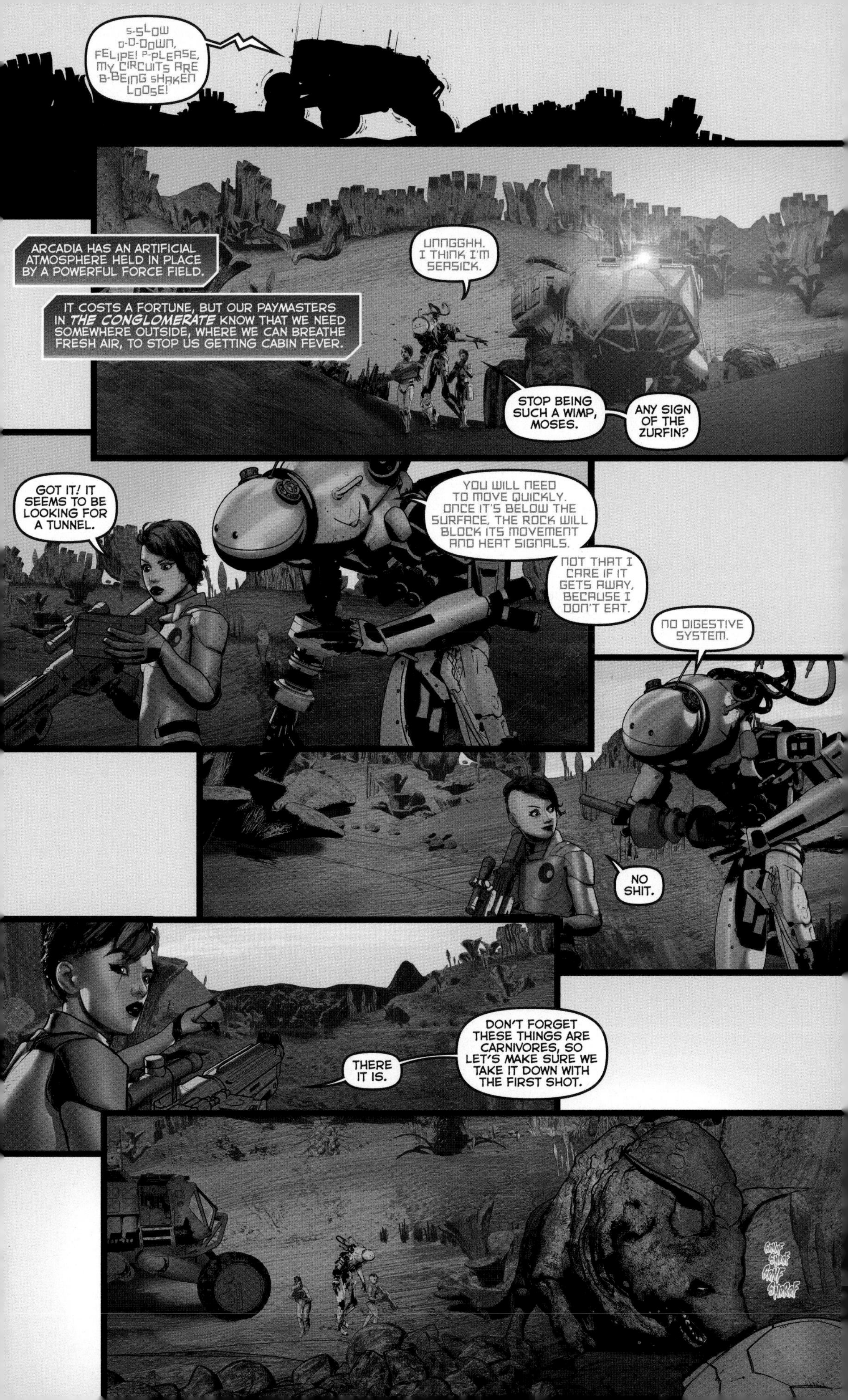

S-SLOW D-D-DOWN, FELIPE! P-PLEASE, MY CIRCUITS ARE B-BEING SHAKEN LOOSE!
ARCADIA HAS AN ARTIFICIAL ATMOSPHERE HELD IN PLACE BY A POWERFUL FORCE FIELD.
IT COSTS A FORTUNE, BUT OUR PAYMASTERS IN *THE CONGLOMERATE* KNOW THAT WE NEED SOMEWHERE OUTSIDE, WHERE WE CAN BREATHE FRESH AIR, TO STOP US GETTING CABIN FEVER.
UNNGGHH. I THINK I'M SEASICK.
STOP BEING SUCH A WIMP, MOSES.
ANY SIGN OF THE ZURFIN?
GOT IT! IT SEEMS TO BE LOOKING FOR A TUNNEL.
YOU WILL NEED TO MOVE QUICKLY. ONCE IT'S BELOW THE SURFACE, THE ROCK WILL BLOCK ITS MOVEMENT AND HEAT SIGNALS.
NOT THAT I CARE IF IT GETS AWAY, BECAUSE I DON'T EAT.
NO DIGESTIVE SYSTEM.
NO SHIT.
THERE IT IS.
DON'T FORGET THESE THINGS ARE CARNIVORES, SO LET'S MAKE SURE WE TAKE IT DOWN WITH THE FIRST SHOT.
SNRRF
GRNF
SNRRF

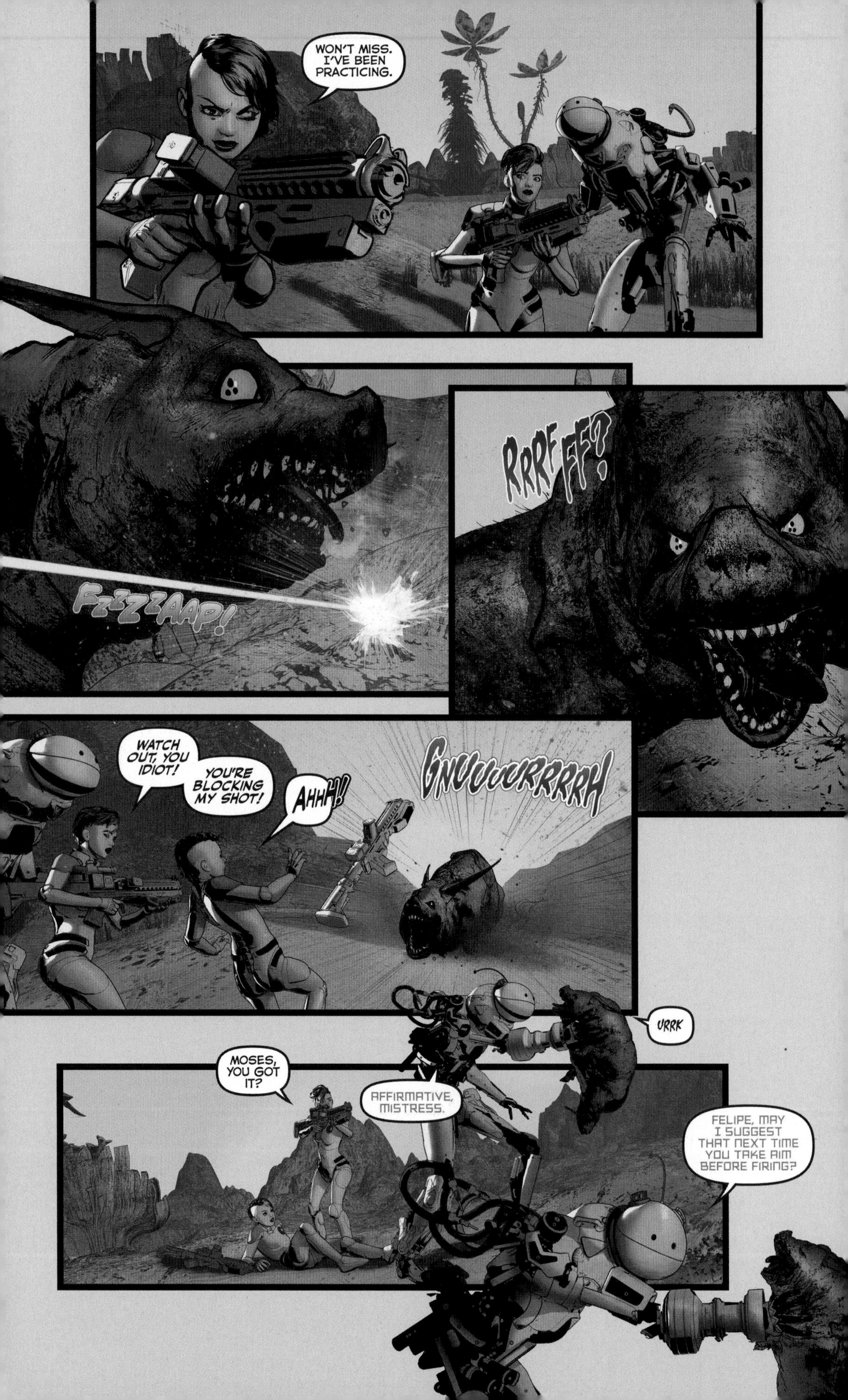
WON'T MISS. I'VE BEEN PRACTICING.
FZZZZAAP!
RRRFFF?
WATCH OUT, YOU IDIOT!
YOU'RE BLOCKING MY SHOT!
AHHH!
GNUUUURRRRH
URRK
MOSES, YOU GOT IT?
AFFIRMATIVE, MISTRESS.
FELIPE, MAY I SUGGEST THAT NEXT TIME YOU TAKE AIM BEFORE FIRING?

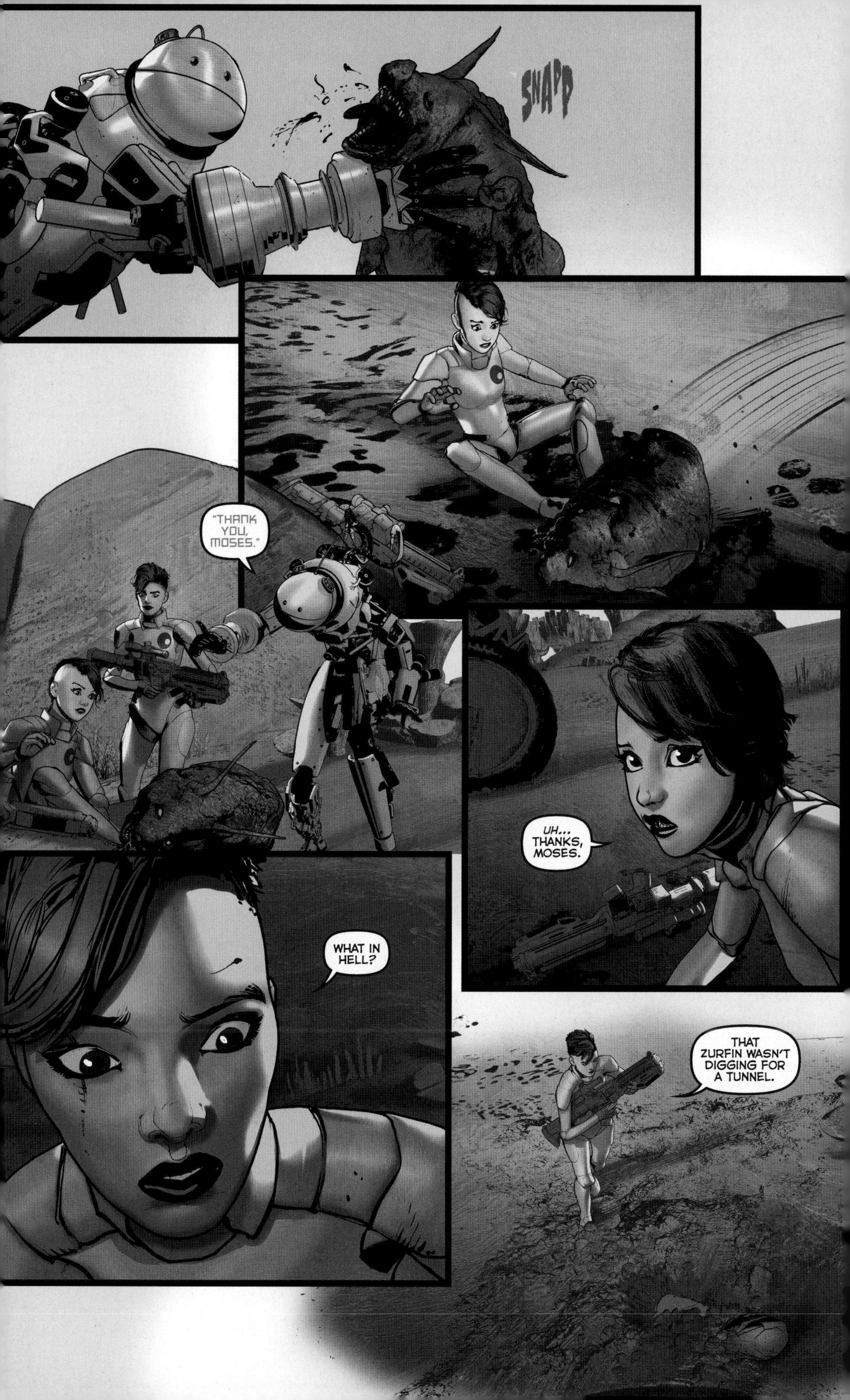
SNAPP
"THANK YOU, MOSES."
UH... THANKS, MOSES.
WHAT IN HELL?
THAT ZURFIN WASN'T DIGGING FOR A TUNNEL.

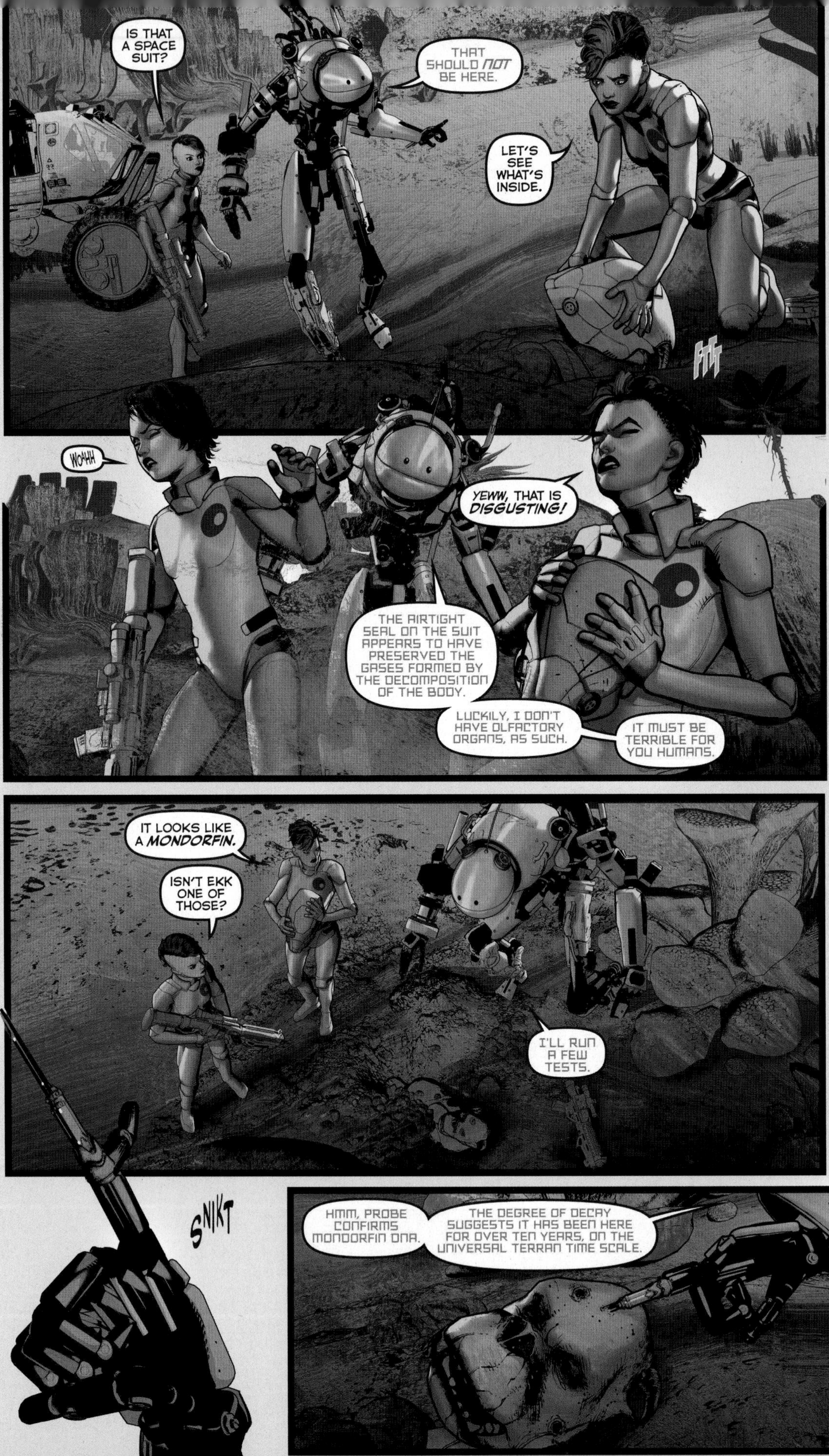
IS THAT A SPACE SUIT?
THAT SHOULD NOT BE HERE.
LET'S SEE WHAT'S INSIDE.
FFT
WOAHH
YEWW, THAT IS DISGUSTING!
THE AIRTIGHT SEAL ON THE SUIT APPEARS TO HAVE PRESERVED THE GASES FORMED BY THE DECOMPOSITION OF THE BODY.
LUCKILY, I DON'T HAVE OLFACTORY ORGANS, AS SUCH.
IT MUST BE TERRIBLE FOR YOU HUMANS.
IT LOOKS LIKE A MONDORFIN.
ISN'T EKK ONE OF THOSE?
I'LL RUN A FEW TESTS.
SNIKT
HMM, PROBE CONFIRMS MONDORFIN DNA.
THE DEGREE OF DECAY SUGGESTS IT HAS BEEN HERE FOR OVER TEN YEARS, ON THE UNIVERSAL TERRAN TIME SCALE.

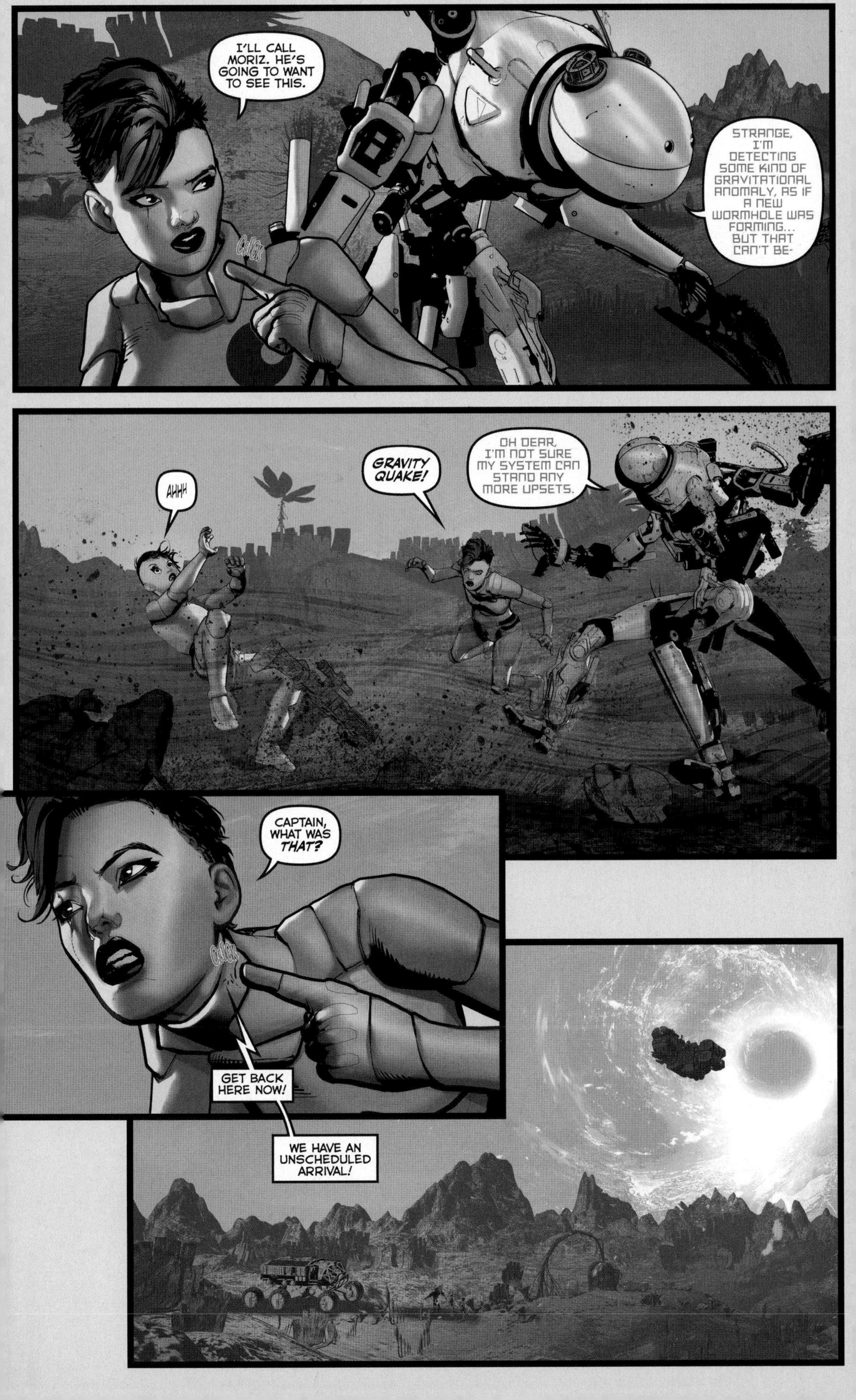
I'LL CALL MORIZ. HE'S GOING TO WANT TO SEE THIS.
STRANGE, I'M DETECTING SOME KIND OF GRAVITATIONAL ANOMALY, AS IF A NEW WORMHOLE WAS FORMING... BUT THAT CAN'T BE-
AHHH
GRAVITY QUAKE!
OH DEAR, I'M NOT SURE MY SYSTEM CAN STAND ANY MORE UPSETS.
CAPTAIN, WHAT WAS THAT?
GET BACK HERE NOW!
WE HAVE AN UNSCHEDULED ARRIVAL!

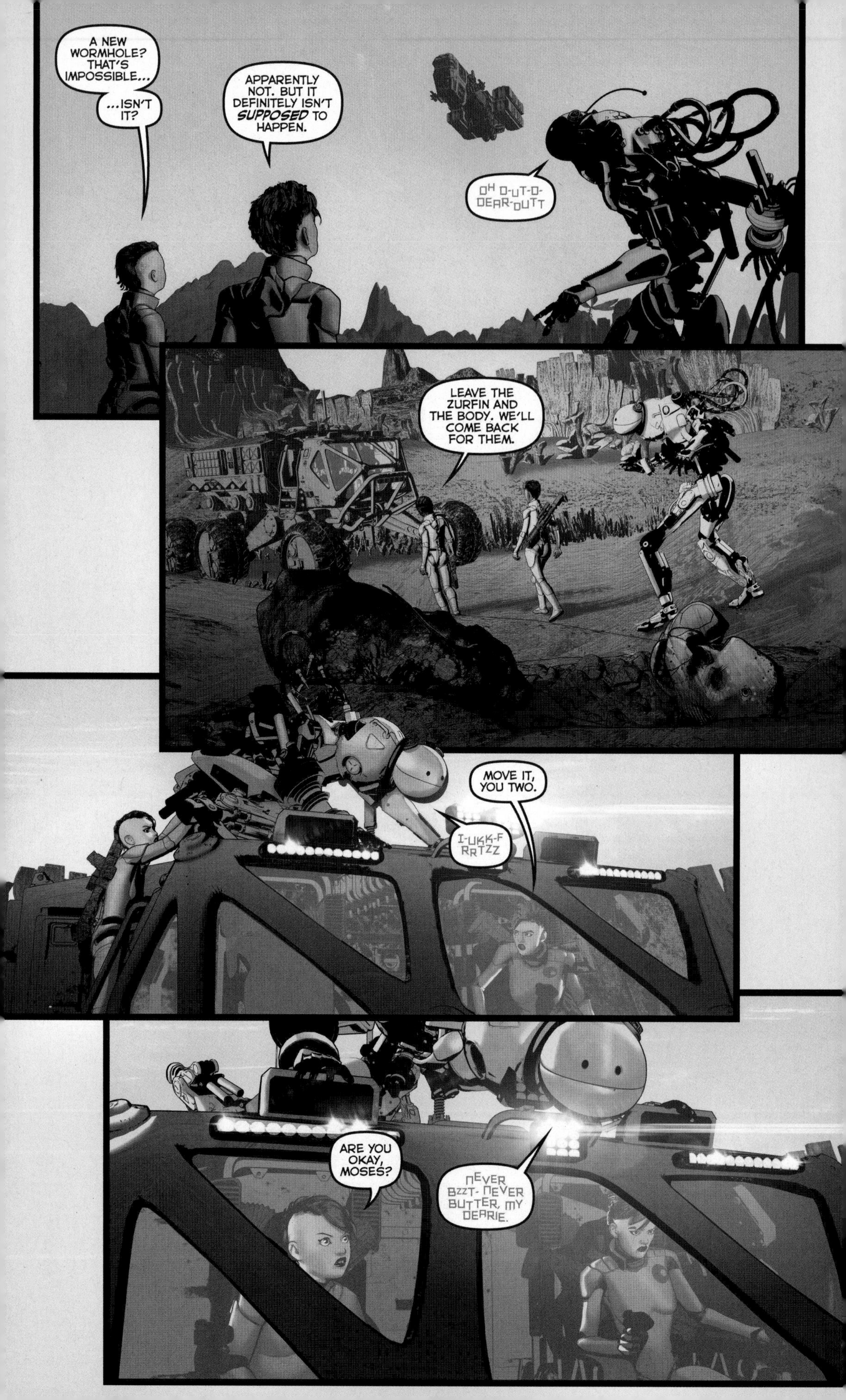
A NEW WORMHOLE? THAT'S IMPOSSIBLE...
...ISN'T IT?
APPARENTLY NOT. BUT IT DEFINITELY ISN'T *SUPPOSED* TO HAPPEN.
OH D-UT-D-DEAR-DUTT
LEAVE THE ZURFIN AND THE BODY. WE'LL COME BACK FOR THEM.
MOVE IT, YOU TWO.
I-UKK-F RRTZZ
ARE YOU OKAY, MOSES?
NEVER BZZT- NEVER BUTTER, MY DEARIE.

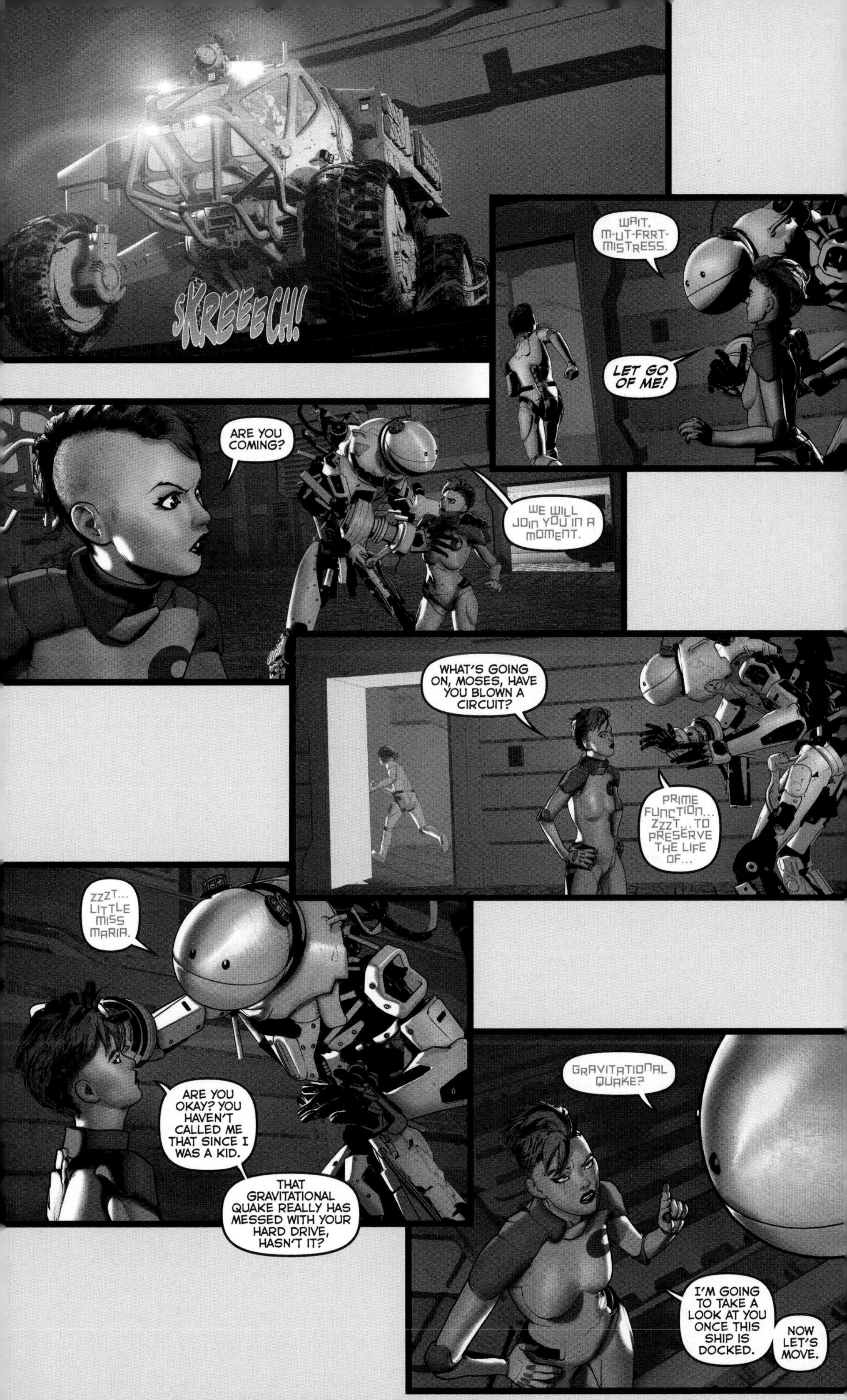
SKREEECH!
WAIT, M-UT-FRRT-MISTRESS.
LET GO OF ME!
ARE YOU COMING?
WE WILL JOIN YOU IN A MOMENT.
WHAT'S GOING ON, MOSES, HAVE YOU BLOWN A CIRCUIT?
PRIME FUNCTION... ZZZT... TO PRESERVE THE LIFE OF...
ZZZT... LITTLE MISS MARIA.
ARE YOU OKAY? YOU HAVEN'T CALLED ME THAT SINCE I WAS A KID.
THAT GRAVITATIONAL QUAKE REALLY HAS MESSED WITH YOUR HARD DRIVE, HASN'T IT?
GRAVITATIONAL QUAKE?
I'M GOING TO TAKE A LOOK AT YOU ONCE THIS SHIP IS DOCKED.
NOW LET'S MOVE.

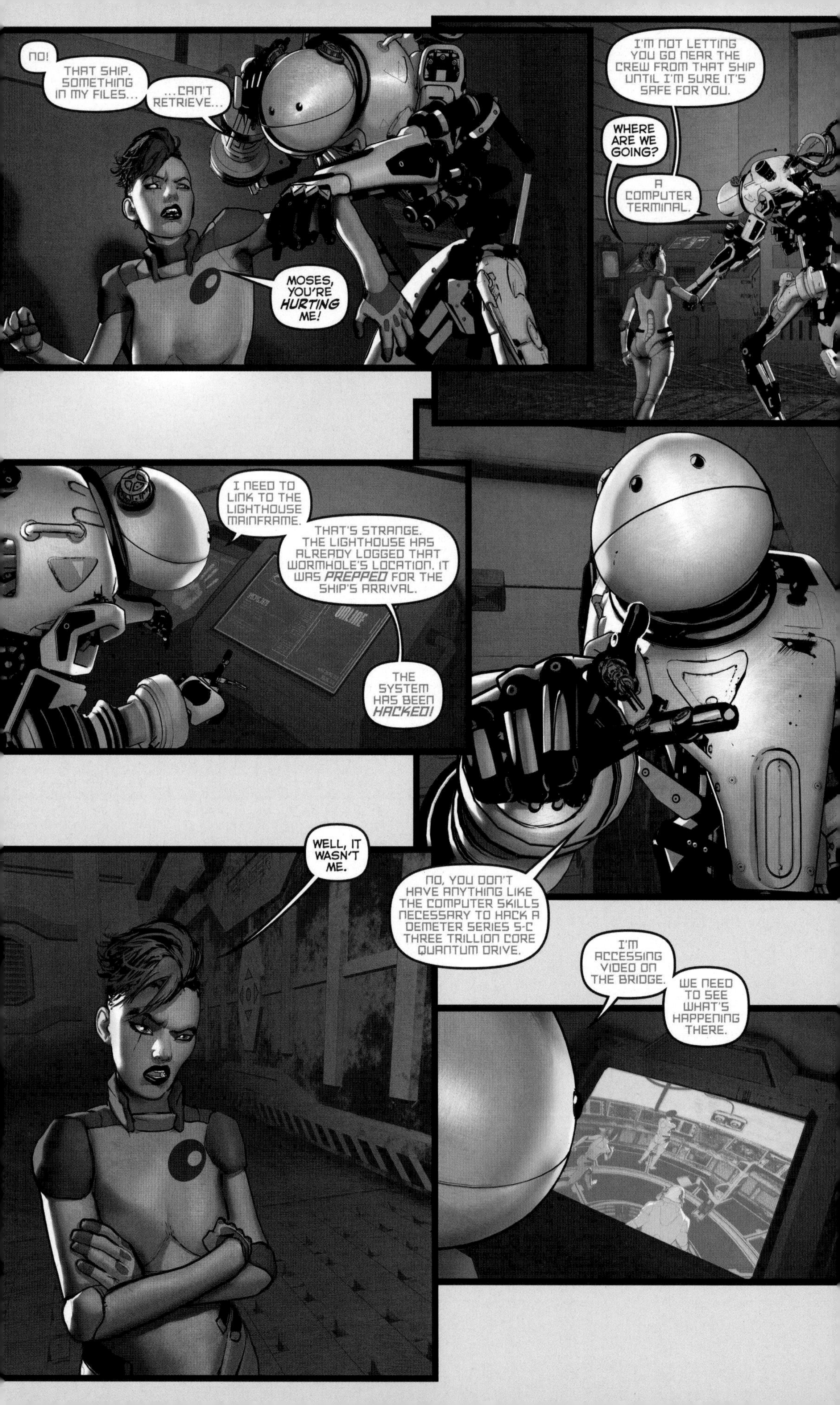
NO!
THAT SHIP. SOMETHING IN MY FILES...
...CAN'T RETRIEVE...
MOSES, YOU'RE HURTING ME!
I'M NOT LETTING YOU GO NEAR THE CREW FROM THAT SHIP UNTIL I'M SURE IT'S SAFE FOR YOU.
WHERE ARE WE GOING?
A COMPUTER TERMINAL.
I NEED TO LINK TO THE LIGHTHOUSE MAINFRAME.
THAT'S STRANGE. THE LIGHTHOUSE HAS ALREADY LOGGED THAT WORMHOLE'S LOCATION. IT WAS PREPPED FOR THE SHIP'S ARRIVAL.
ONLINE
THE SYSTEM HAS BEEN HACKED!
WELL, IT WASN'T ME.
NO, YOU DON'T HAVE ANYTHING LIKE THE COMPUTER SKILLS NECESSARY TO HACK A DEMETER SERIES 5-C THREE TRILLION CORE QUANTUM DRIVE.
I'M ACCESSING VIDEO ON THE BRIDGE.
WE NEED TO SEE WHAT'S HAPPENING THERE.

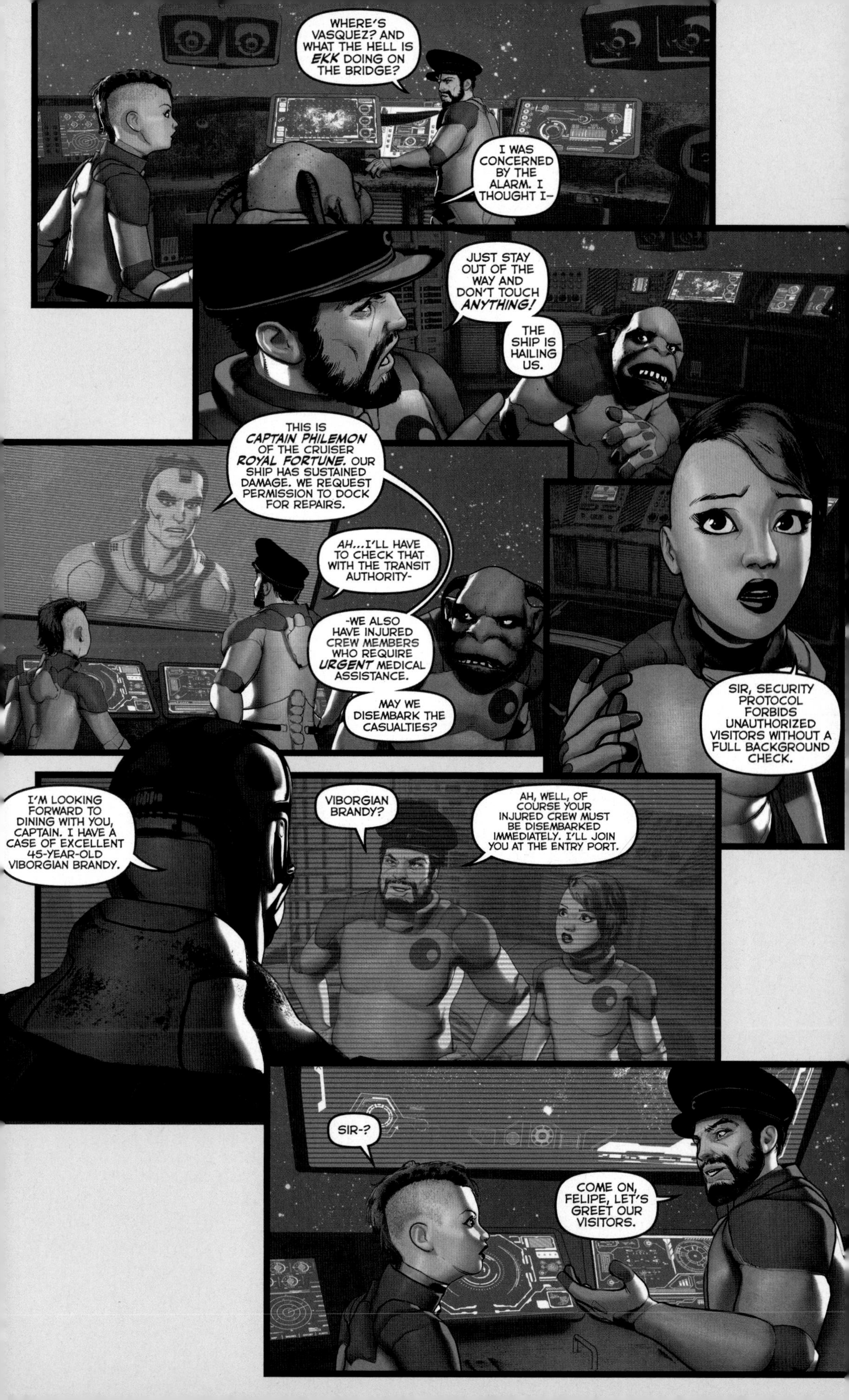
WHERE'S VASQUEZ? AND WHAT THE HELL IS EKK DOING ON THE BRIDGE?
I WAS CONCERNED BY THE ALARM. I THOUGHT I–
JUST STAY OUT OF THE WAY AND DON'T TOUCH ANYTHING!
THE SHIP IS HAILING US.
THIS IS CAPTAIN PHILEMON OF THE CRUISER ROYAL FORTUNE. OUR SHIP HAS SUSTAINED DAMAGE. WE REQUEST PERMISSION TO DOCK FOR REPAIRS.
AH...I'LL HAVE TO CHECK THAT WITH THE TRANSIT AUTHORITY-
-WE ALSO HAVE INJURED CREW MEMBERS WHO REQUIRE URGENT MEDICAL ASSISTANCE.
MAY WE DISEMBARK THE CASUALTIES?
SIR, SECURITY PROTOCOL FORBIDS UNAUTHORIZED VISITORS WITHOUT A FULL BACKGROUND CHECK.
AH, WELL, OF COURSE YOUR INJURED CREW MUST BE DISEMBARKED IMMEDIATELY. I'LL JOIN YOU AT THE ENTRY PORT.
I'M LOOKING FORWARD TO DINING WITH YOU, CAPTAIN. I HAVE A CASE OF EXCELLENT 45-YEAR-OLD VIBORGIAN BRANDY.
VIBORGIAN BRANDY?
SIR-?
COME ON, FELIPE, LET'S GREET OUR VISITORS.

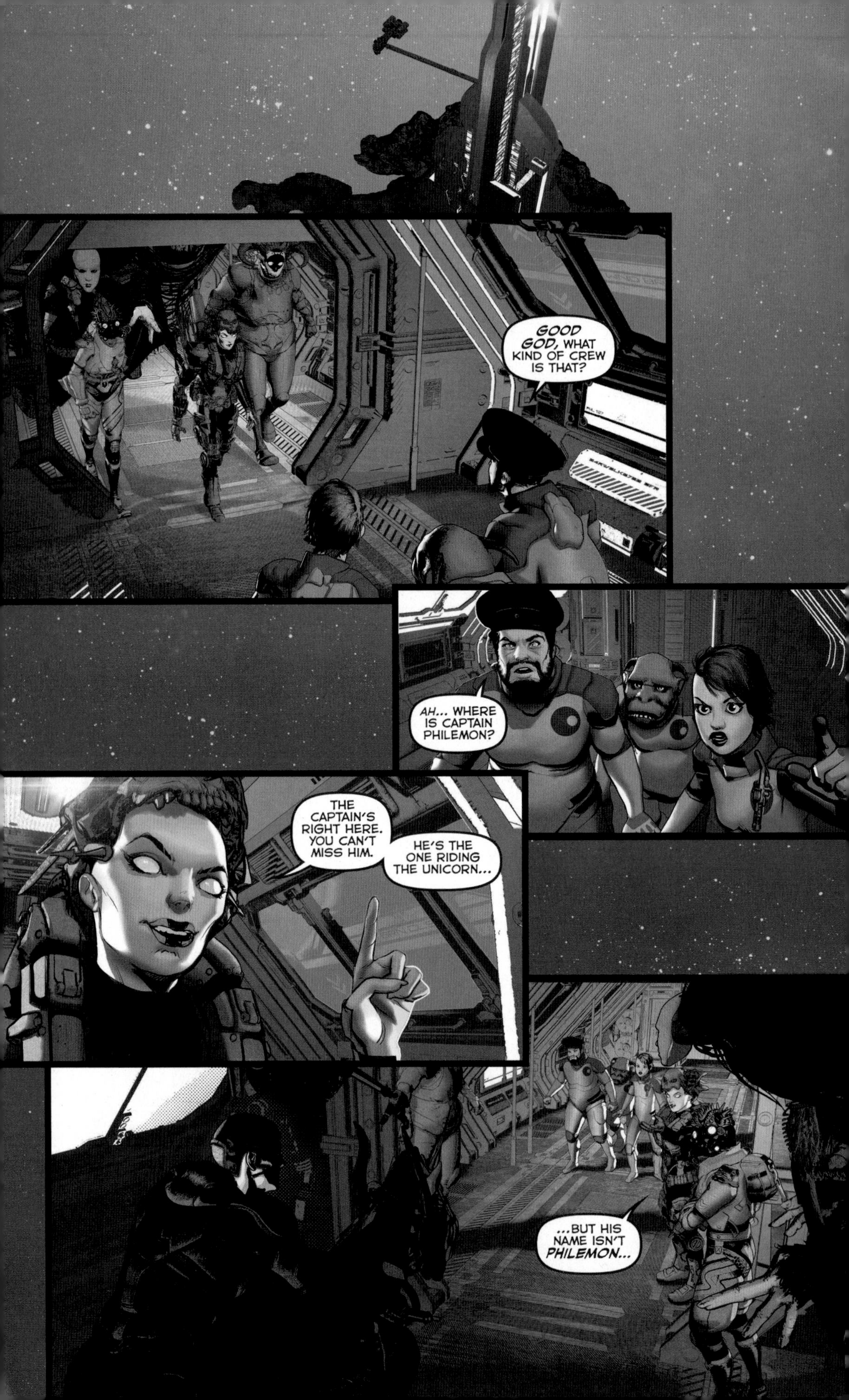
GOOD GOD, WHAT KIND OF CREW IS THAT?
AH... WHERE IS CAPTAIN PHILEMON?
THE CAPTAIN'S RIGHT HERE. YOU CAN'T MISS HIM.
HE'S THE ONE RIDING THE UNICORN...
...BUT HIS NAME ISN'T PHILEMON...

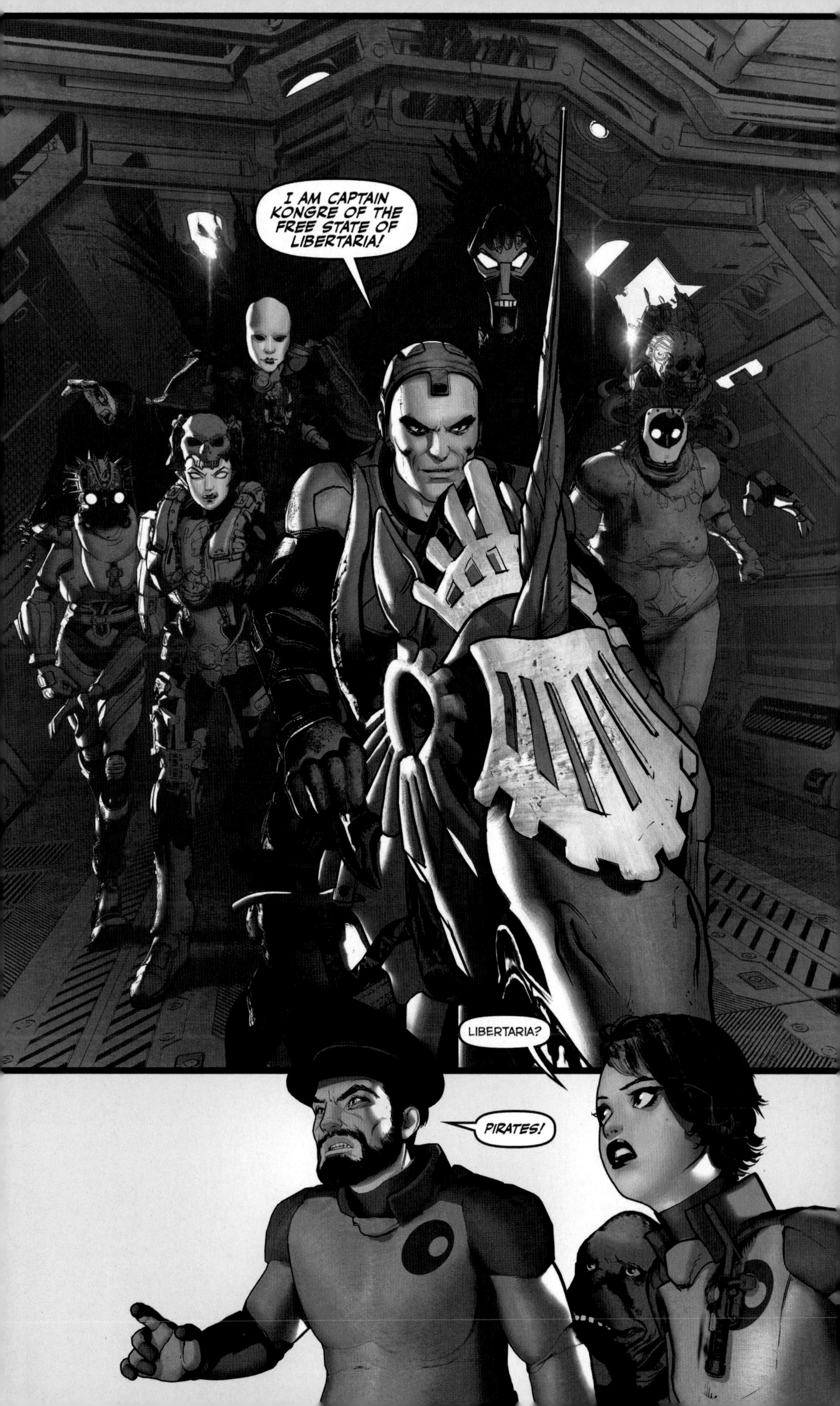
I AM CAPTAIN KONGRE OF THE FREE STATE OF LIBERTARIA!
LIBERTARIA?
PIRATES!

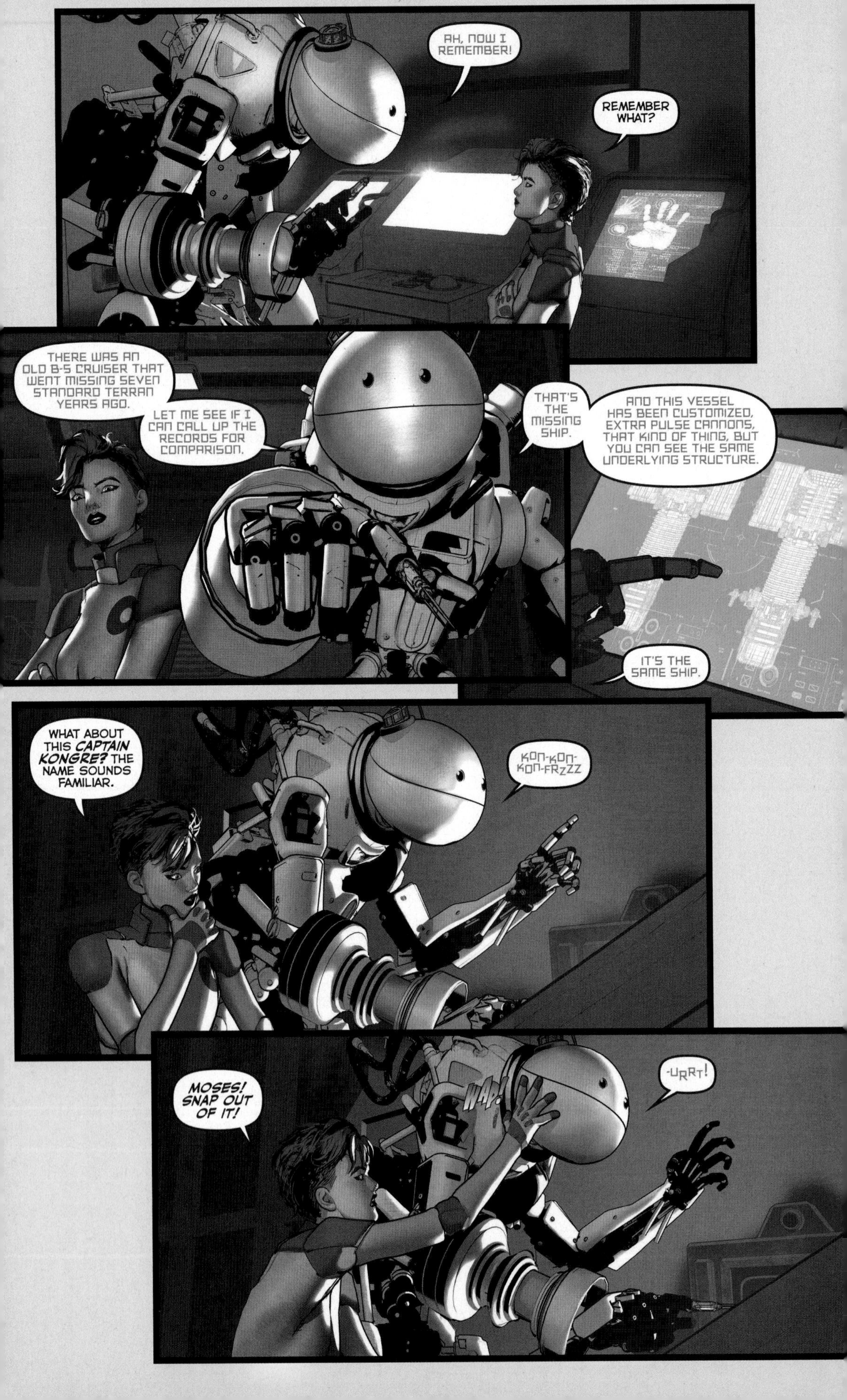
AH, NOW I REMEMBER!
REMEMBER WHAT?
THERE WAS AN OLD B-5 CRUISER THAT WENT MISSING SEVEN STANDARD TERRAN YEARS AGO.
LET ME SEE IF I CAN CALL UP THE RECORDS FOR COMPARISON.
THAT'S THE MISSING SHIP.
AND THIS VESSEL HAS BEEN CUSTOMIZED, EXTRA PULSE CANNONS, THAT KIND OF THING, BUT YOU CAN SEE THE SAME UNDERLYING STRUCTURE.
IT'S THE SAME SHIP.
WHAT ABOUT THIS *CAPTAIN KONGRE?* THE NAME SOUNDS FAMILIAR.
KON-KON-KON-FRZZZ
MOSES! SNAP OUT OF IT!
WAP!
-URRT!

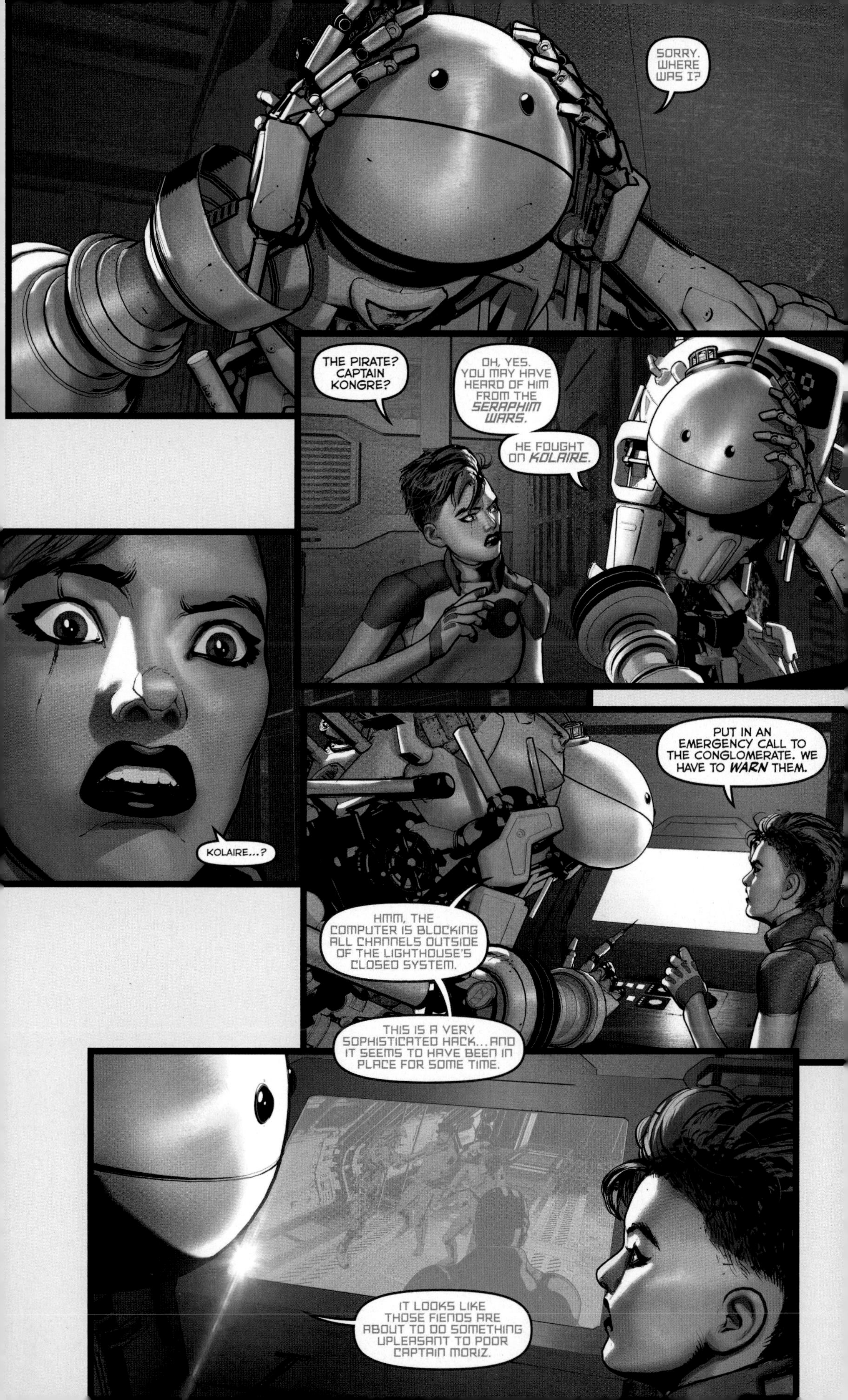
SORRY. WHERE WAS I?
THE PIRATE? CAPTAIN KONGRE?
OH, YES. YOU MAY HAVE HEARD OF HIM FROM THE SERAPHIM WARS.
HE FOUGHT ON KOLAIRE.
KOLAIRE...?
PUT IN AN EMERGENCY CALL TO THE CONGLOMERATE. WE HAVE TO WARN THEM.
HMM, THE COMPUTER IS BLOCKING ALL CHANNELS OUTSIDE OF THE LIGHTHOUSE'S CLOSED SYSTEM.
THIS IS A VERY SOPHISTICATED HACK...AND IT SEEMS TO HAVE BEEN IN PLACE FOR SOME TIME.
IT LOOKS LIKE THOSE FIENDS ARE ABOUT TO DO SOMETHING UPLEASANT TO POOR CAPTAIN MORIZ.

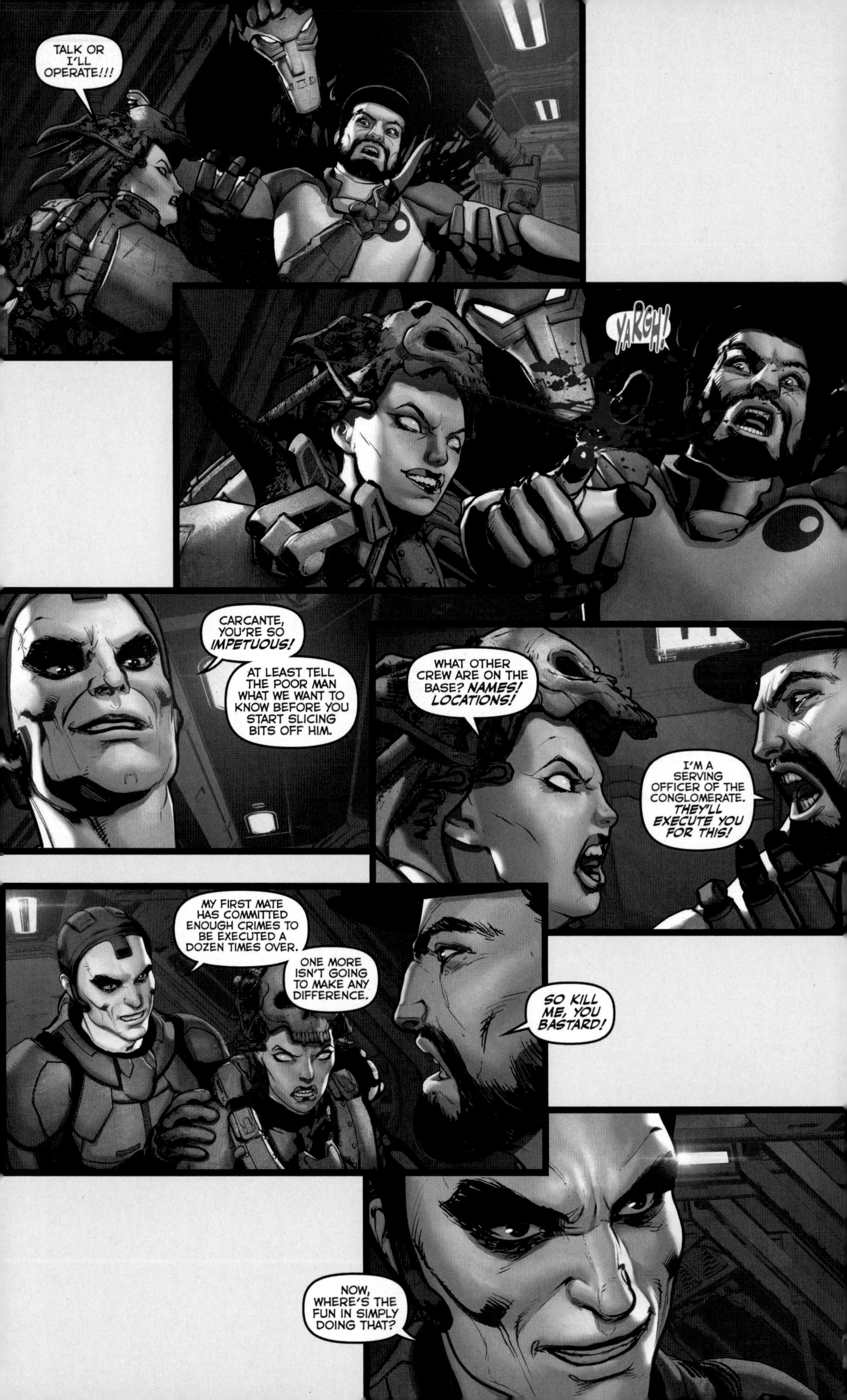
TALK OR I'LL OPERATE!!!
YARGH!
CARCANTE, YOU'RE SO *IMPETUOUS!*
AT LEAST TELL THE POOR MAN WHAT WE WANT TO KNOW BEFORE YOU START SLICING BITS OFF HIM.
WHAT OTHER CREW ARE ON THE BASE? *NAMES! LOCATIONS!*
I'M A SERVING OFFICER OF THE CONGLOMERATE. *THEY'LL EXECUTE YOU FOR THIS!*
MY FIRST MATE HAS COMMITTED ENOUGH CRIMES TO BE EXECUTED A DOZEN TIMES OVER.
ONE MORE ISN'T GOING TO MAKE ANY DIFFERENCE.
SO KILL ME, YOU BASTARD!
NOW, WHERE'S THE FUN IN SIMPLY DOING THAT?

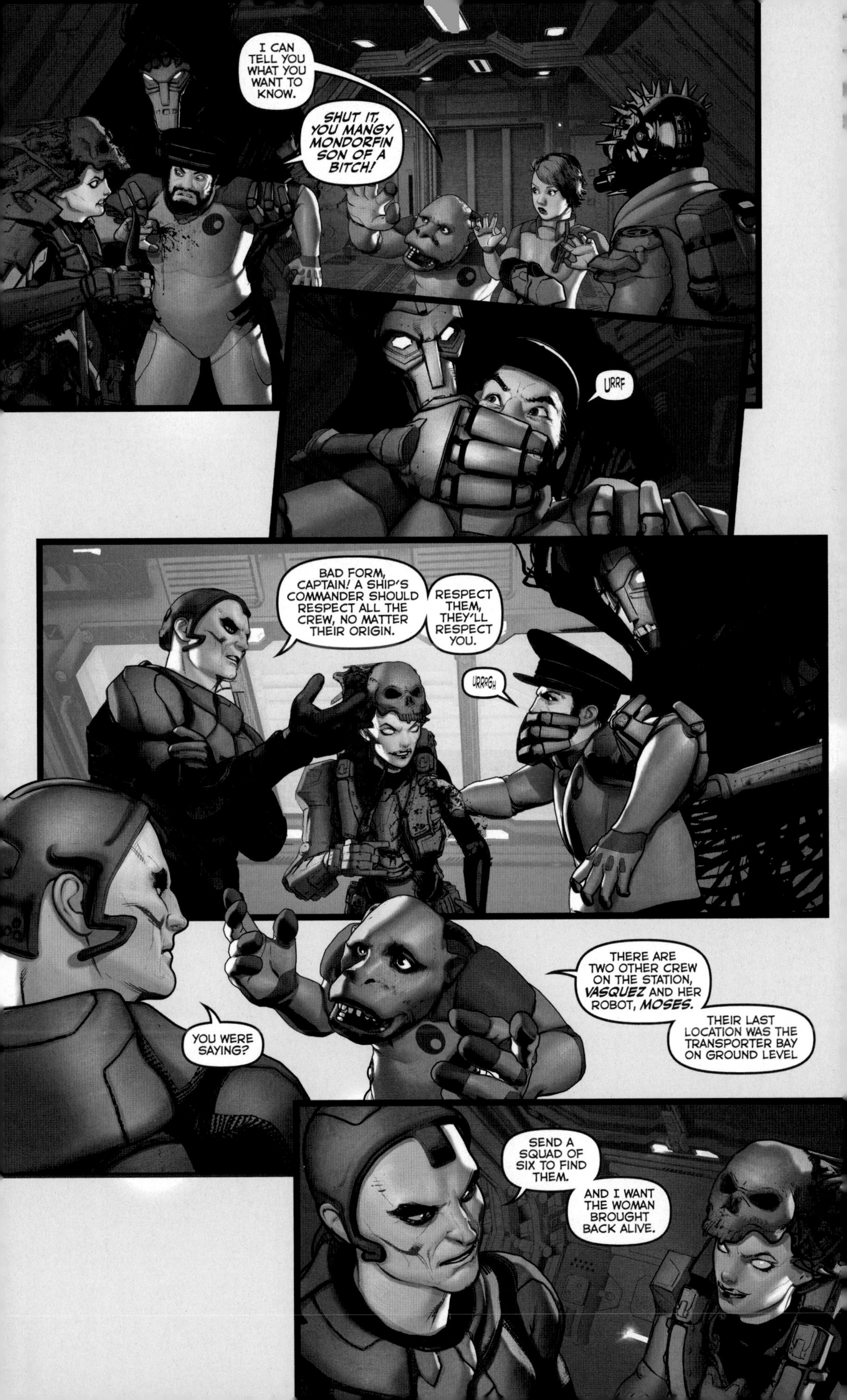
I CAN TELL YOU WHAT YOU WANT TO KNOW.
SHUT IT, YOU MANGY MONDORFIN SON OF A BITCH!
URRF
BAD FORM, CAPTAIN! A SHIP'S COMMANDER SHOULD RESPECT ALL THE CREW, NO MATTER THEIR ORIGIN.
RESPECT THEM, THEY'LL RESPECT YOU.
URRRGH
YOU WERE SAYING?
THERE ARE TWO OTHER CREW ON THE STATION, *VASQUEZ* AND HER ROBOT, *MOSES*.
THEIR LAST LOCATION WAS THE TRANSPORTER BAY ON GROUND LEVEL
SEND A SQUAD OF SIX TO FIND THEM.
AND I WANT THE WOMAN BROUGHT BACK ALIVE.

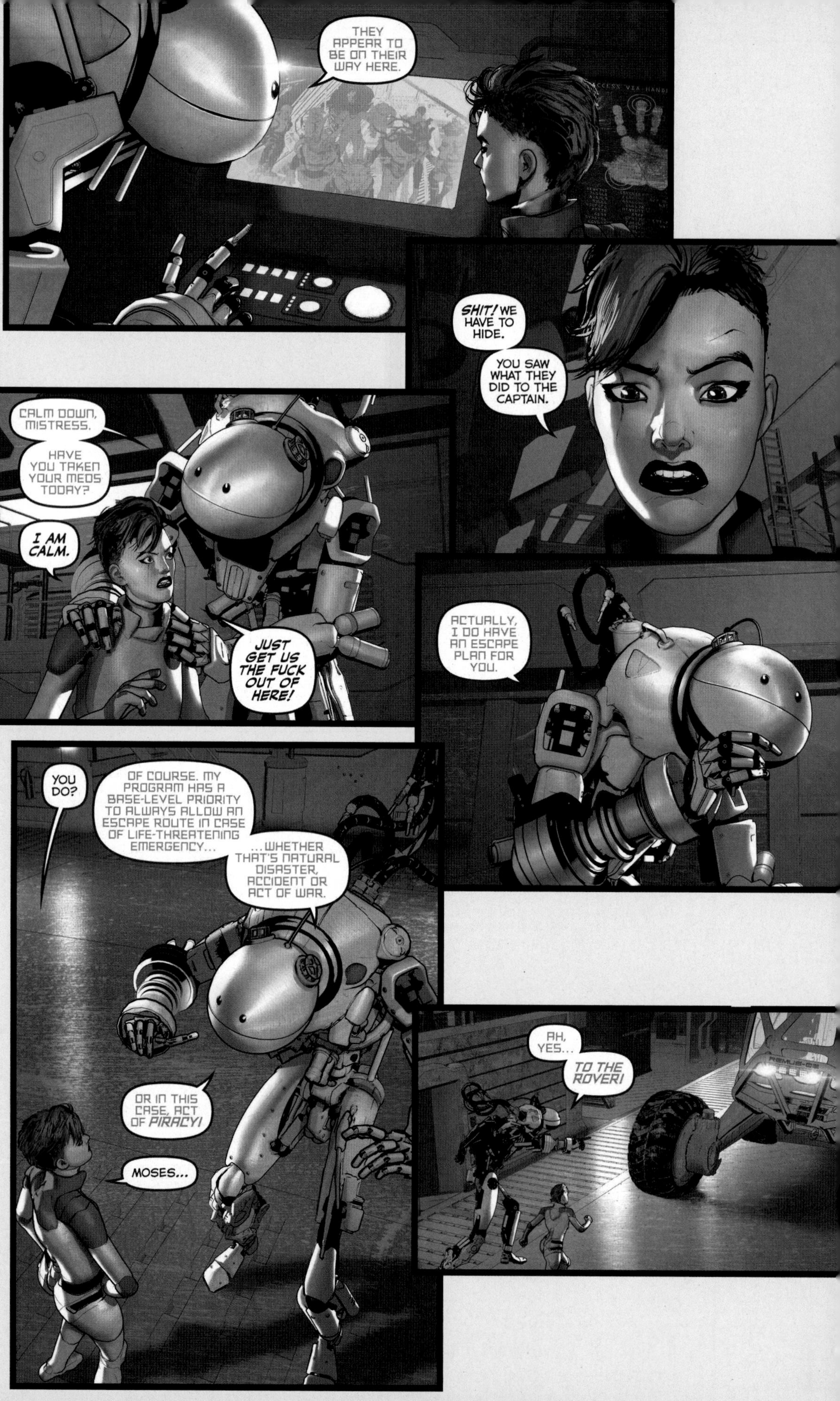
THEY APPEAR TO BE ON THEIR WAY HERE.
SHIT! WE HAVE TO HIDE.
YOU SAW WHAT THEY DID TO THE CAPTAIN.
CALM DOWN, MISTRESS.
HAVE YOU TAKEN YOUR MEDS TODAY?
I AM CALM.
JUST GET US THE FUCK OUT OF HERE!
ACTUALLY, I DO HAVE AN ESCAPE PLAN FOR YOU.
YOU DO?
OF COURSE. MY PROGRAM HAS A BASE-LEVEL PRIORITY TO ALWAYS ALLOW AN ESCAPE ROUTE IN CASE OF LIFE-THREATENING EMERGENCY...
...WHETHER THAT'S NATURAL DISASTER, ACCIDENT OR ACT OF WAR.
OR IN THIS CASE, ACT OF PIRACY!
MOSES...
AH, YES...
TO THE ROVER!

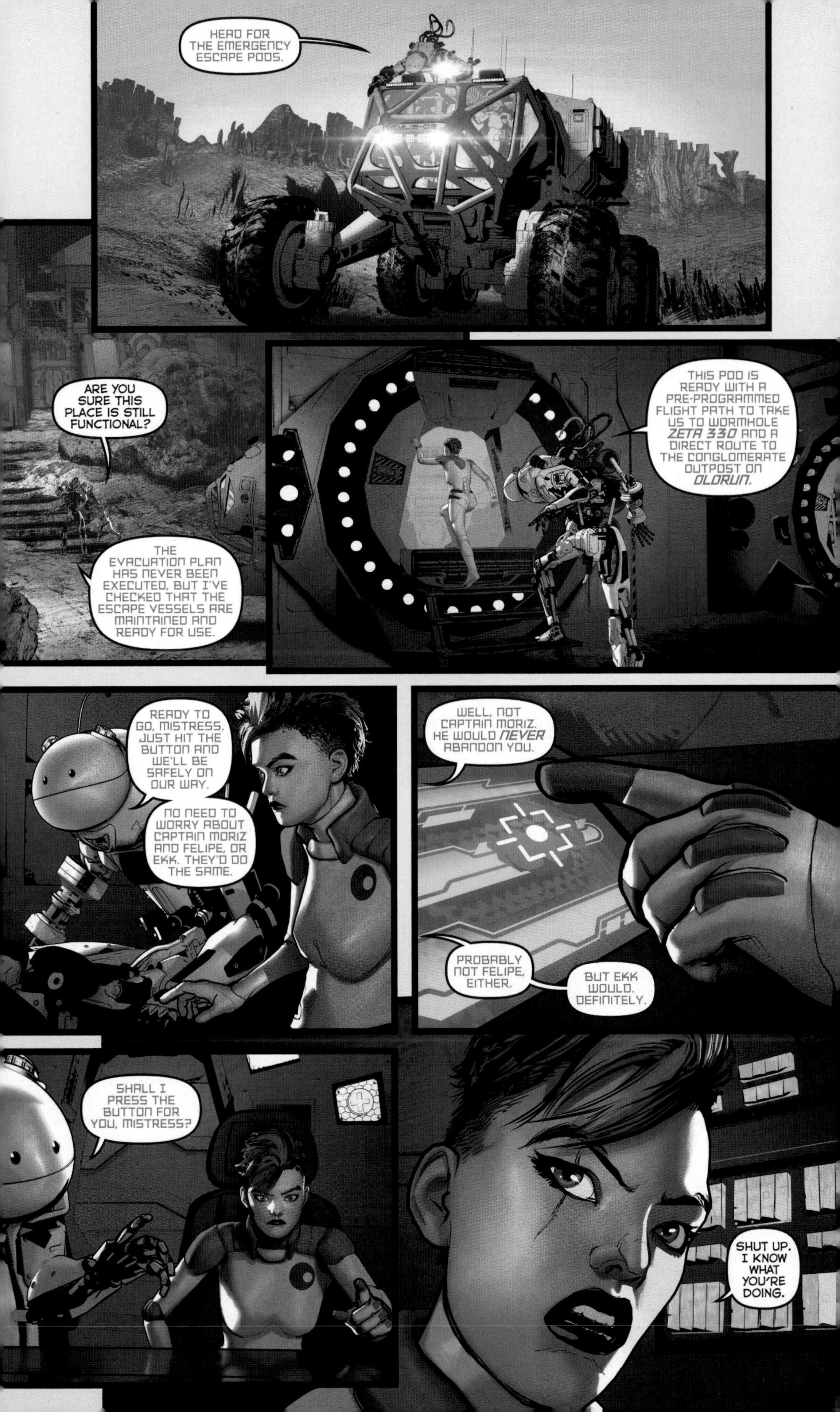
HEAD FOR THE EMERGENCY ESCAPE PODS.
ARE YOU SURE THIS PLACE IS STILL FUNCTIONAL?
THE EVACUATION PLAN HAS NEVER BEEN EXECUTED, BUT I'VE CHECKED THAT THE ESCAPE VESSELS ARE MAINTAINED AND READY FOR USE.
THIS POD IS READY WITH A PRE-PROGRAMMED FLIGHT PATH TO TAKE US TO WORMHOLE ZETA 330 AND A DIRECT ROUTE TO THE CONGLOMERATE OUTPOST ON OLORUN.
READY TO GO, MISTRESS. JUST HIT THE BUTTON AND WE'LL BE SAFELY ON OUR WAY.
NO NEED TO WORRY ABOUT CAPTAIN MORIZ AND FELIPE, OR EKK. THEY'D DO THE SAME.
WELL, NOT CAPTAIN MORIZ. HE WOULD NEVER ABANDON YOU.
PROBABLY NOT FELIPE, EITHER.
BUT EKK WOULD. DEFINITELY.
SHALL I PRESS THE BUTTON FOR YOU, MISTRESS?
SHUT UP. I KNOW WHAT YOU'RE DOING.

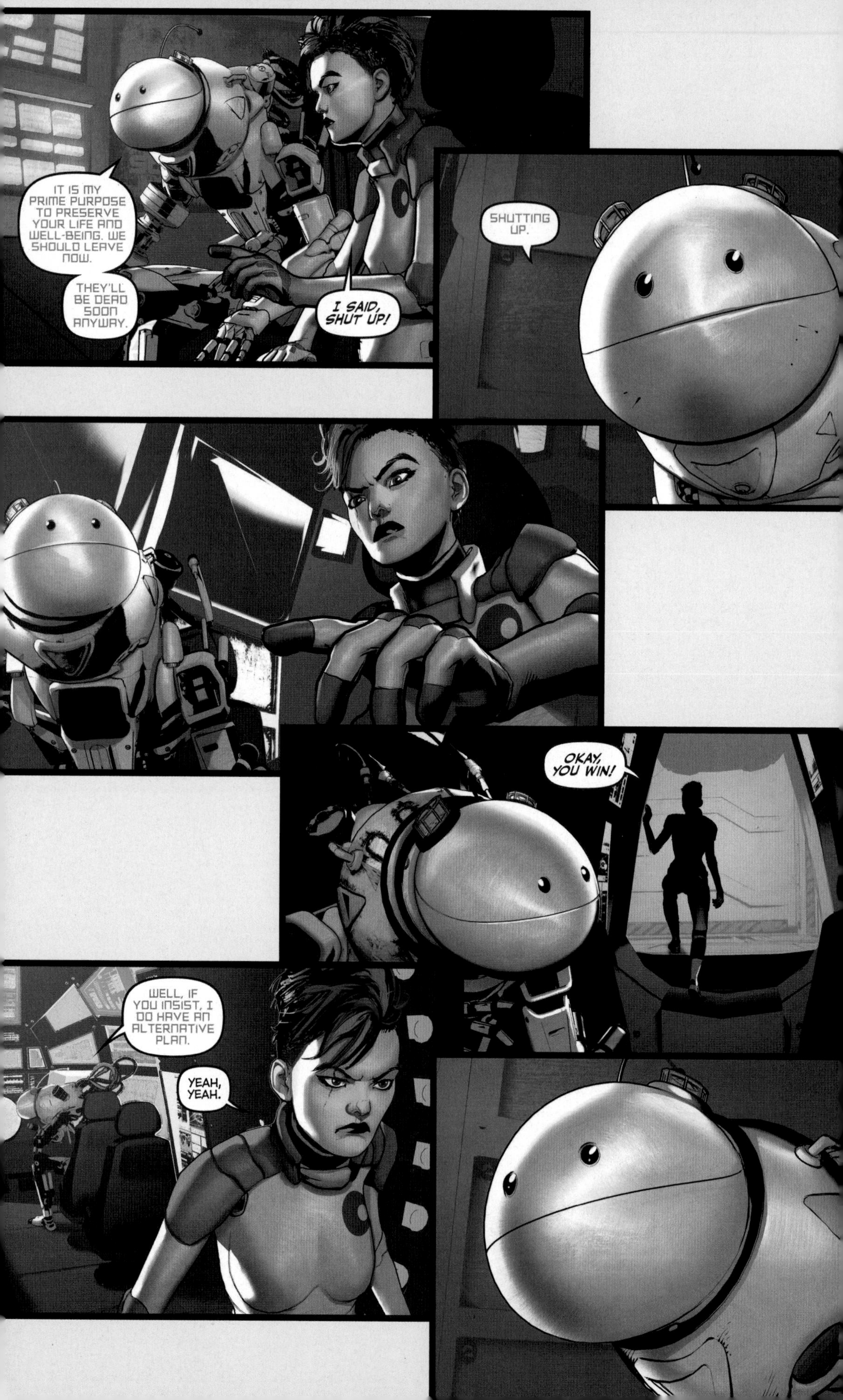
IT IS MY PRIME PURPOSE TO PRESERVE YOUR LIFE AND WELL-BEING. WE SHOULD LEAVE NOW.
THEY'LL BE DEAD SOON ANYWAY.
I SAID, SHUT UP!
SHUTTING UP.
OKAY, YOU WIN!
WELL, IF YOU INSIST, I DO HAVE AN ALTERNATIVE PLAN.
YEAH, YEAH.

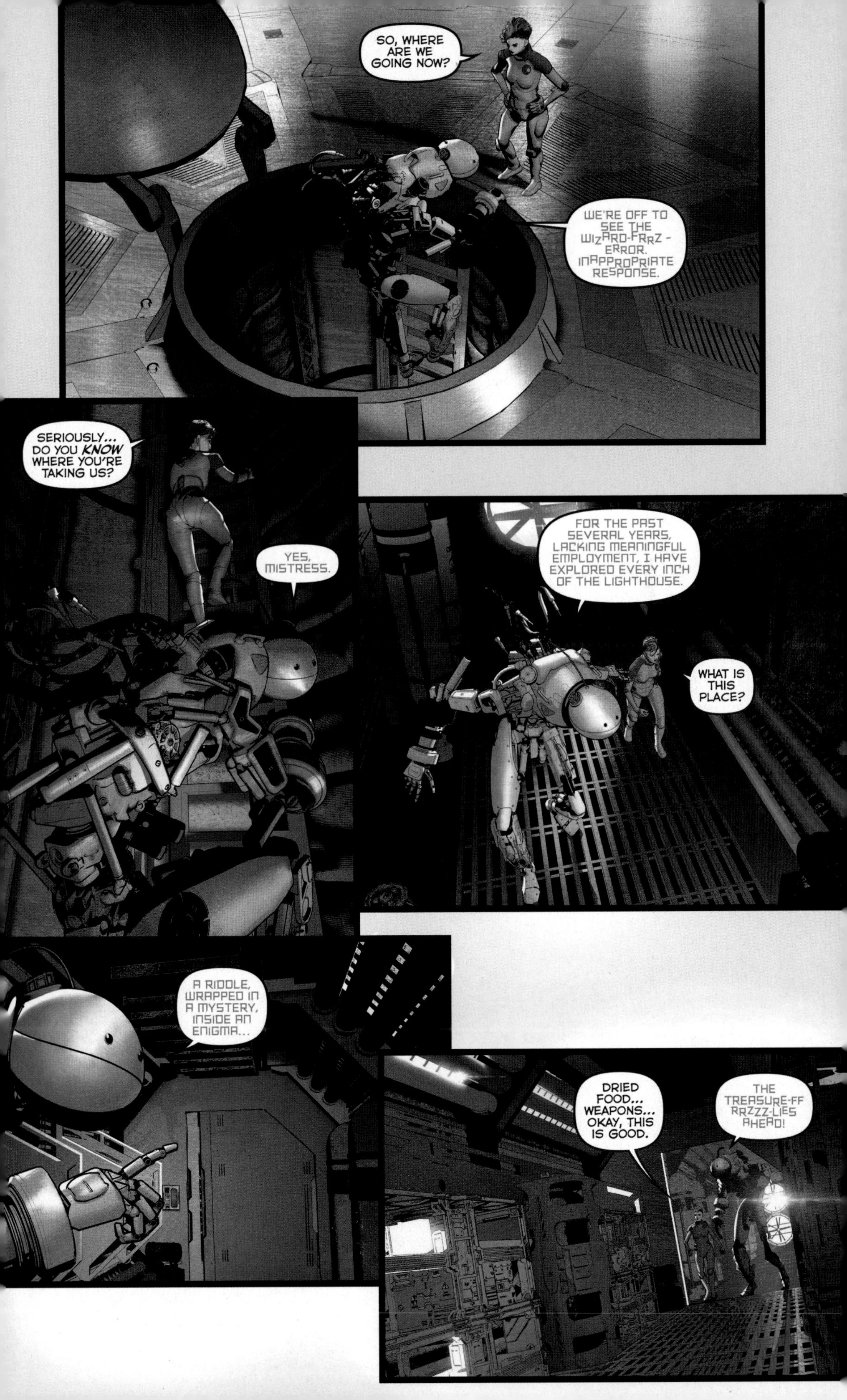
SO, WHERE ARE WE GOING NOW?
WE'RE OFF TO SEE THE WIZARD-FRRZ - ERROR. INAPPROPRIATE RESPONSE.
SERIOUSLY... DO YOU *KNOW* WHERE YOU'RE TAKING US?
YES, MISTRESS.
FOR THE PAST SEVERAL YEARS, LACKING MEANINGFUL EMPLOYMENT, I HAVE EXPLORED EVERY INCH OF THE LIGHTHOUSE.
WHAT IS THIS PLACE?
A RIDDLE, WRAPPED IN A MYSTERY, INSIDE AN ENIGMA...
DRIED FOOD... WEAPONS... OKAY, THIS IS GOOD.
THE TREASURE-FF RRZZZ-LIES AHEAD!

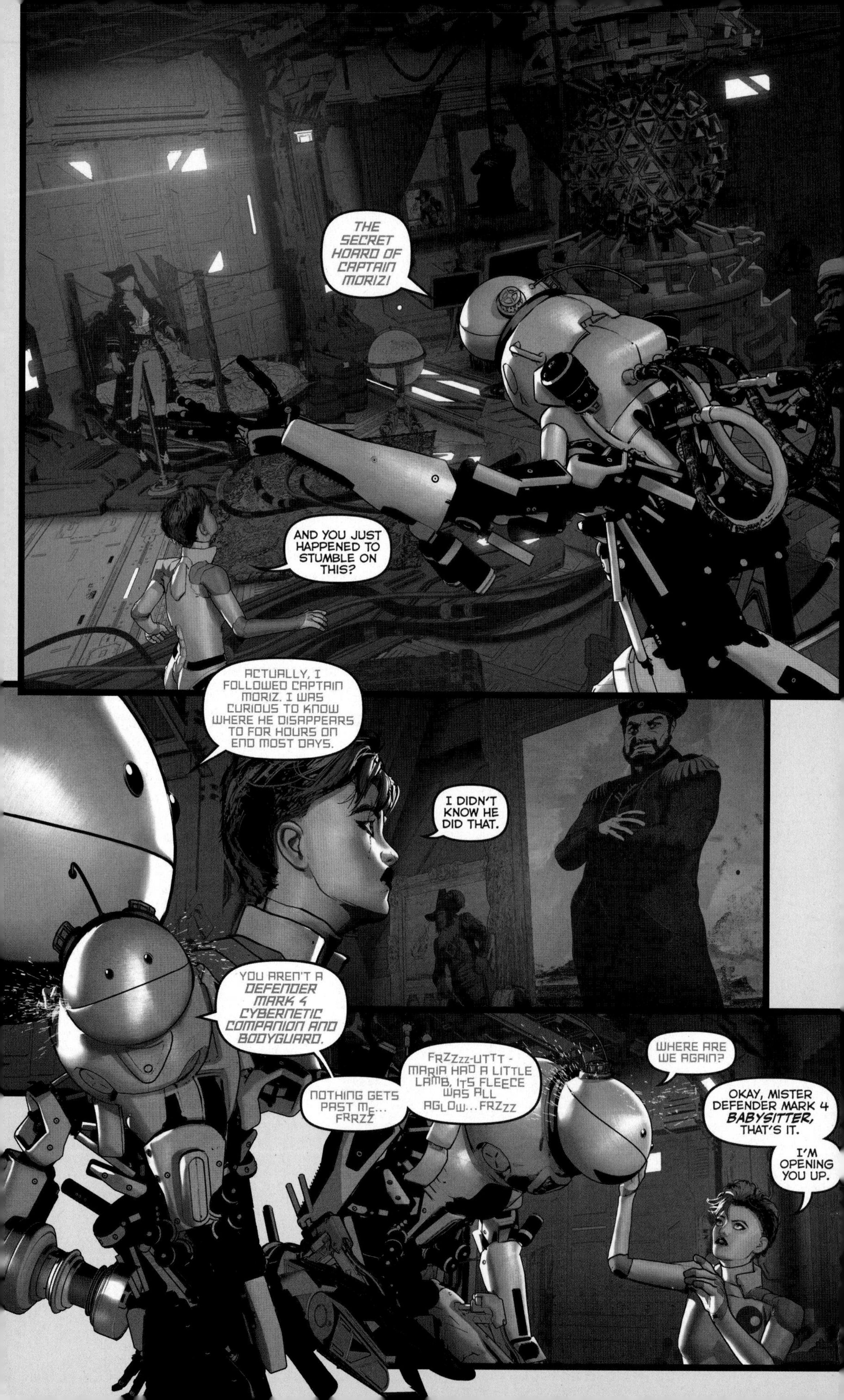
THE SECRET HOARD OF CAPTAIN MORIZ!
AND YOU JUST HAPPENED TO STUMBLE ON THIS?
ACTUALLY, I FOLLOWED CAPTAIN MORIZ. I WAS CURIOUS TO KNOW WHERE HE DISAPPEARS TO FOR HOURS ON END MOST DAYS.
I DIDN'T KNOW HE DID THAT.
YOU AREN'T A DEFENDER MARK 4 CYBERNETIC COMPANION AND BODYGUARD.
NOTHING GETS PAST ME... FRRZZ
FRZZzz-UTTT - MARIA HAD A LITTLE LAMB, ITS FLEECE WAS ALL AGLOW... FRZZzz
WHERE ARE WE AGAIN?
OKAY, MISTER DEFENDER MARK 4 BABYSITTER, THAT'S IT.
I'M OPENING YOU UP.

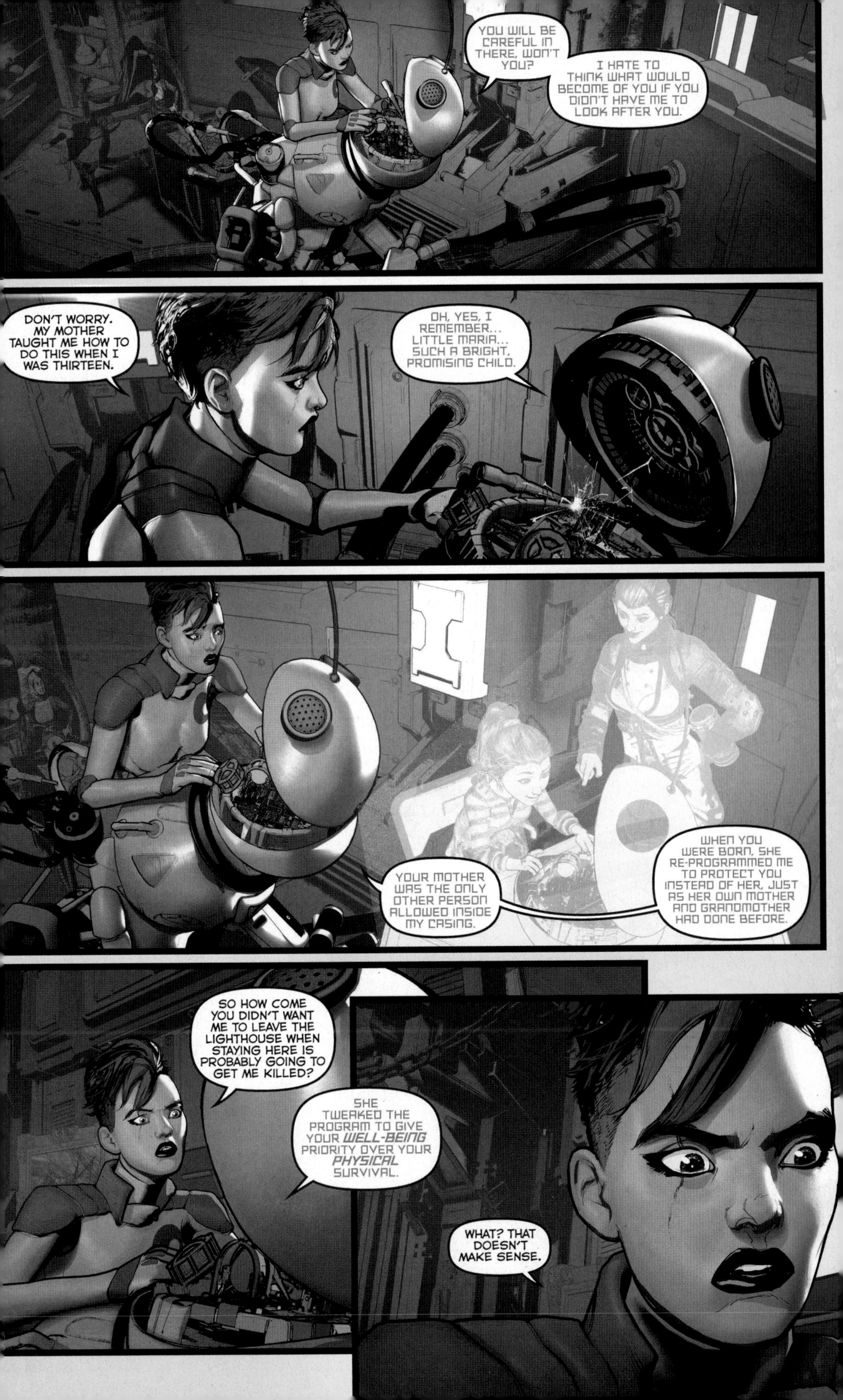
YOU WILL BE CAREFUL IN THERE, WON'T YOU?
I HATE TO THINK WHAT WOULD BECOME OF YOU IF YOU DIDN'T HAVE ME TO LOOK AFTER YOU.
DON'T WORRY. MY MOTHER TAUGHT ME HOW TO DO THIS WHEN I WAS THIRTEEN.
OH, YES, I REMEMBER... LITTLE MARIA... SUCH A BRIGHT, PROMISING CHILD.
YOUR MOTHER WAS THE ONLY OTHER PERSON ALLOWED INSIDE MY CASING.
WHEN YOU WERE BORN, SHE RE-PROGRAMMED ME TO PROTECT YOU INSTEAD OF HER, JUST AS HER OWN MOTHER AND GRANDMOTHER HAD DONE BEFORE.
SO HOW COME YOU DIDN'T WANT ME TO LEAVE THE LIGHTHOUSE WHEN STAYING HERE IS PROBABLY GOING TO GET ME KILLED?
SHE TWEAKED THE PROGRAM TO GIVE YOUR WELL-BEING PRIORITY OVER YOUR PHYSICAL SURVIVAL.
WHAT? THAT DOESN'T MAKE SENSE.

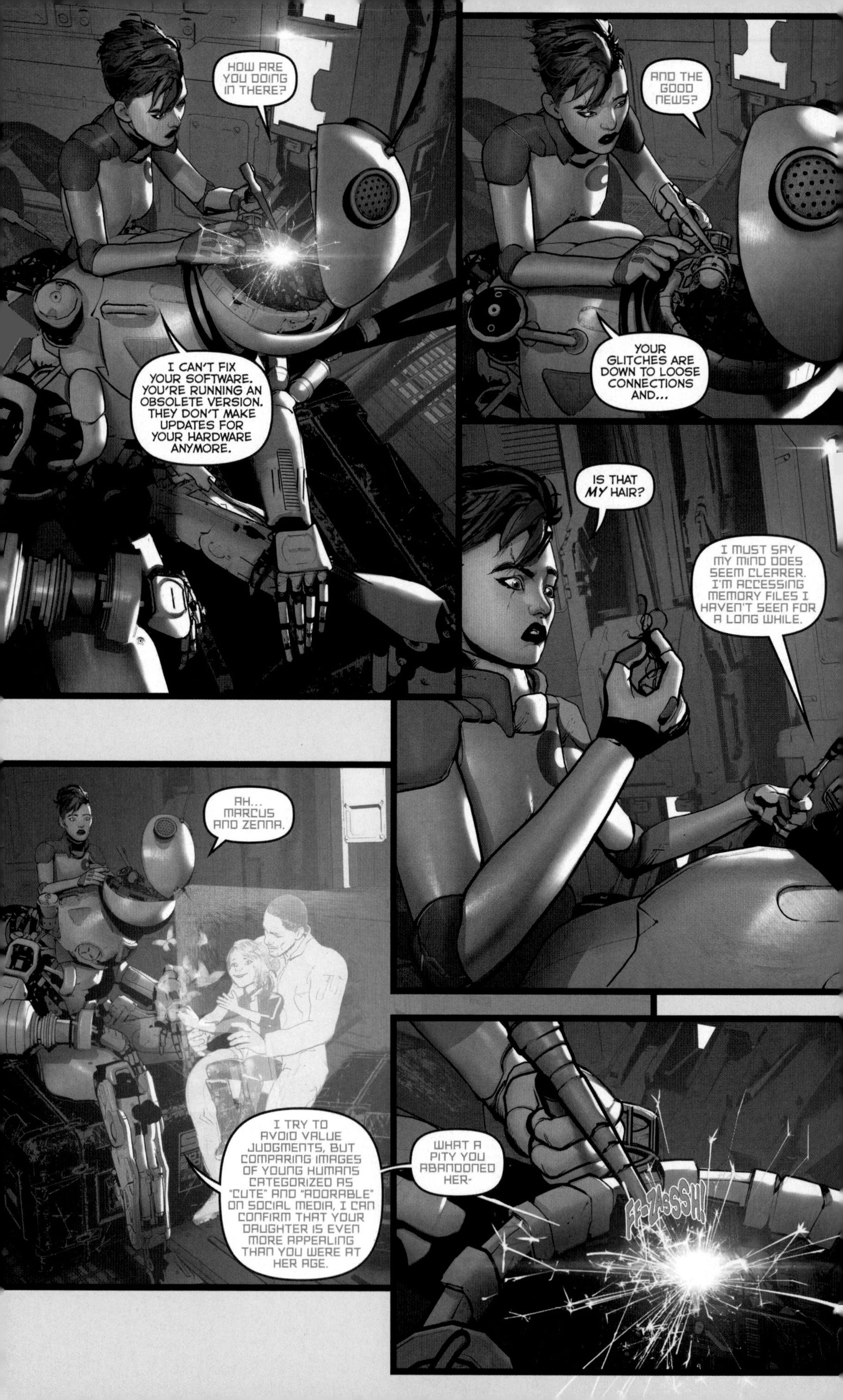
HOW ARE YOU DOING IN THERE?
I CAN'T FIX YOUR SOFTWARE. YOU'RE RUNNING AN OBSOLETE VERSION. THEY DON'T MAKE UPDATES FOR YOUR HARDWARE ANYMORE.
AND THE GOOD NEWS?
YOUR GLITCHES ARE DOWN TO LOOSE CONNECTIONS AND...
IS THAT MY HAIR?
I MUST SAY MY MIND DOES SEEM CLEARER. I'M ACCESSING MEMORY FILES I HAVEN'T SEEN FOR A LONG WHILE.
AH... MARCUS AND ZENNA.
I TRY TO AVOID VALUE JUDGMENTS, BUT COMPARING IMAGES OF YOUNG HUMANS CATEGORIZED AS "CUTE" AND "ADORABLE" ON SOCIAL MEDIA, I CAN CONFIRM THAT YOUR DAUGHTER IS EVEN MORE APPEALING THAN YOU WERE AT HER AGE.
WHAT A PITY YOU ABANDONED HER-
FF-ZASSSH!

MOSES!

OH GOD! I'M SORRY. MY HAND SLIPPED. IT WAS AN ACCIDENT.

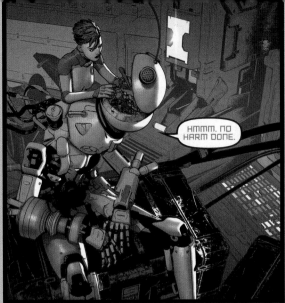

HMMM. NO HARM DONE.

I KNOW YOU WOULD NEVER DELIBERATELY HURT ME, ANY MORE THAN I WOULD HURT YOU.

THOUGH I DO RECALL NOW THAT YOU HAVE FORBIDDEN ME TO EVER MENTION YOUR HUSBAND AND CHILD...

...OR THE REASON YOU LEFT THEM.

PLEASE DON'T.

IT'S GOING TO BE HARD TO AVOID THE SUBJECT. YOU HEARD THE PIRATES. THEY FOUGHT IN THE SERAPHIM WARS. THEY WERE ON *KOLAIRE*.

FOR FUCK'S SAKE, MOSES!

ALL RIGHT. I'LL SAY NO MORE.

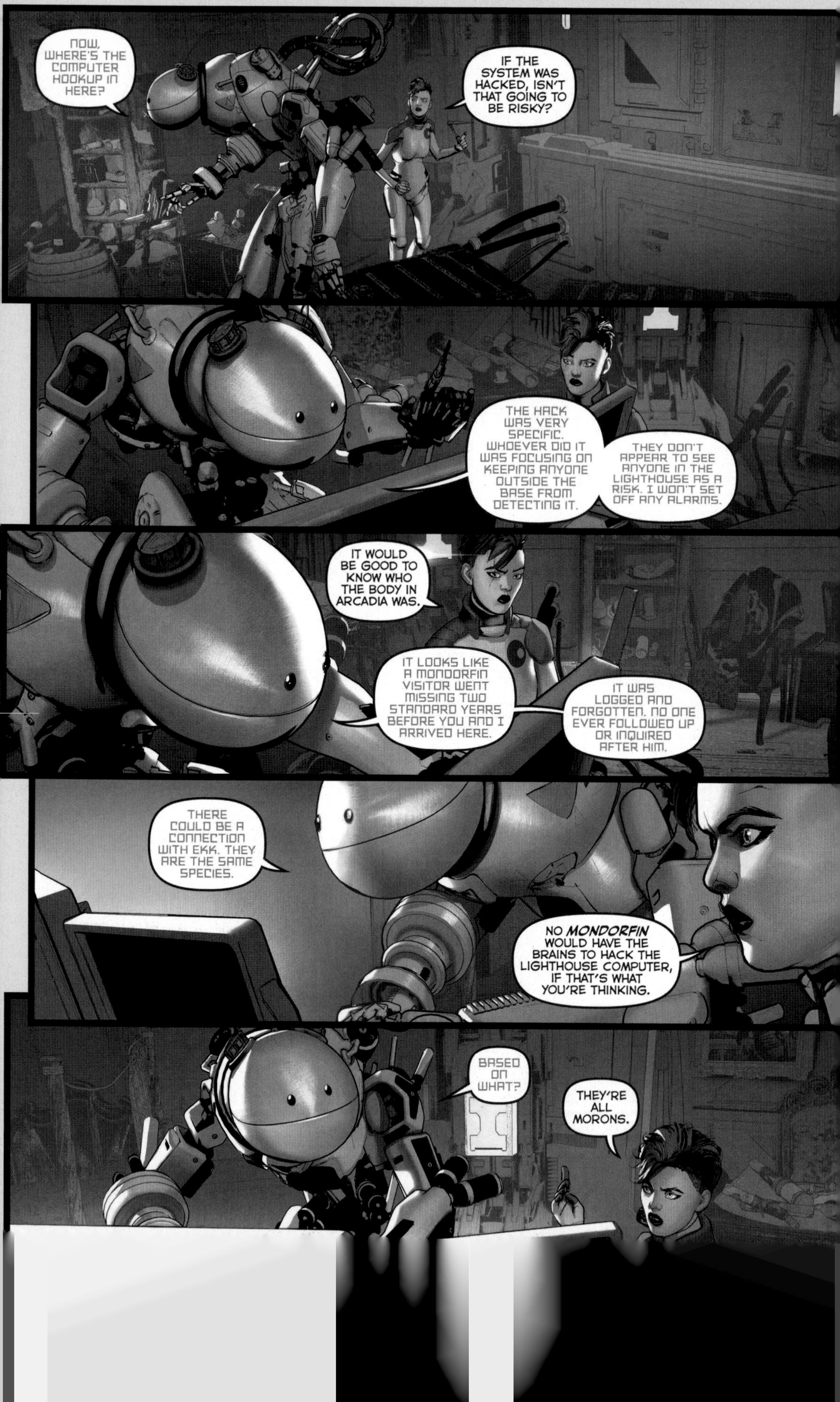
NOW, WHERE'S THE COMPUTER HOOKUP IN HERE?
IF THE SYSTEM WAS HACKED, ISN'T THAT GOING TO BE RISKY?
THE HACK WAS VERY SPECIFIC. WHOEVER DID IT WAS FOCUSING ON KEEPING ANYONE OUTSIDE THE BASE FROM DETECTING IT.
THEY DON'T APPEAR TO SEE ANYONE IN THE LIGHTHOUSE AS A RISK. I WON'T SET OFF ANY ALARMS.
IT WOULD BE GOOD TO KNOW WHO THE BODY IN ARCADIA WAS.
IT LOOKS LIKE A MONDORFIN VISITOR WENT MISSING TWO STANDARD YEARS BEFORE YOU AND I ARRIVED HERE.
IT WAS LOGGED AND FORGOTTEN. NO ONE EVER FOLLOWED UP OR INQUIRED AFTER HIM.
THERE COULD BE A CONNECTION WITH EKK. THEY ARE THE SAME SPECIES.
NO *MONDORFIN* WOULD HAVE THE BRAINS TO HACK THE LIGHTHOUSE COMPUTER, IF THAT'S WHAT YOU'RE THINKING.
BASED ON WHAT?
THEY'RE ALL MORONS.

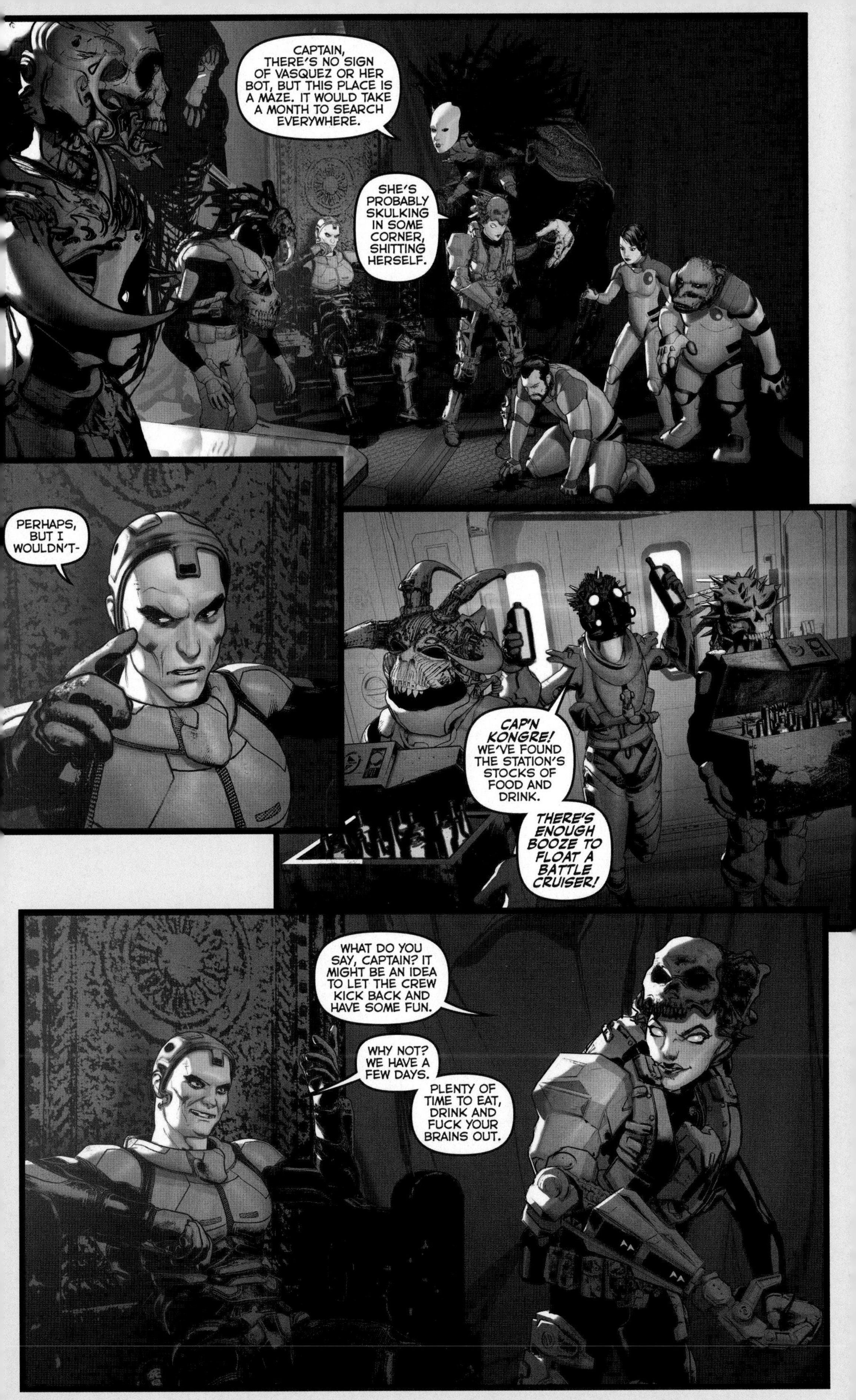
CAPTAIN, THERE'S NO SIGN OF VASQUEZ OR HER BOT, BUT THIS PLACE IS A MAZE. IT WOULD TAKE A MONTH TO SEARCH EVERYWHERE.
SHE'S PROBABLY SKULKING IN SOME CORNER, SHITTING HERSELF.
PERHAPS, BUT I WOULDN'T-
CAP'N KONGRE! WE'VE FOUND THE STATION'S STOCKS OF FOOD AND DRINK.
THERE'S ENOUGH BOOZE TO FLOAT A BATTLE CRUISER!
WHAT DO YOU SAY, CAPTAIN? IT MIGHT BE AN IDEA TO LET THE CREW KICK BACK AND HAVE SOME FUN.
WHY NOT? WE HAVE A FEW DAYS.
PLENTY OF TIME TO EAT, DRINK AND FUCK YOUR BRAINS OUT.

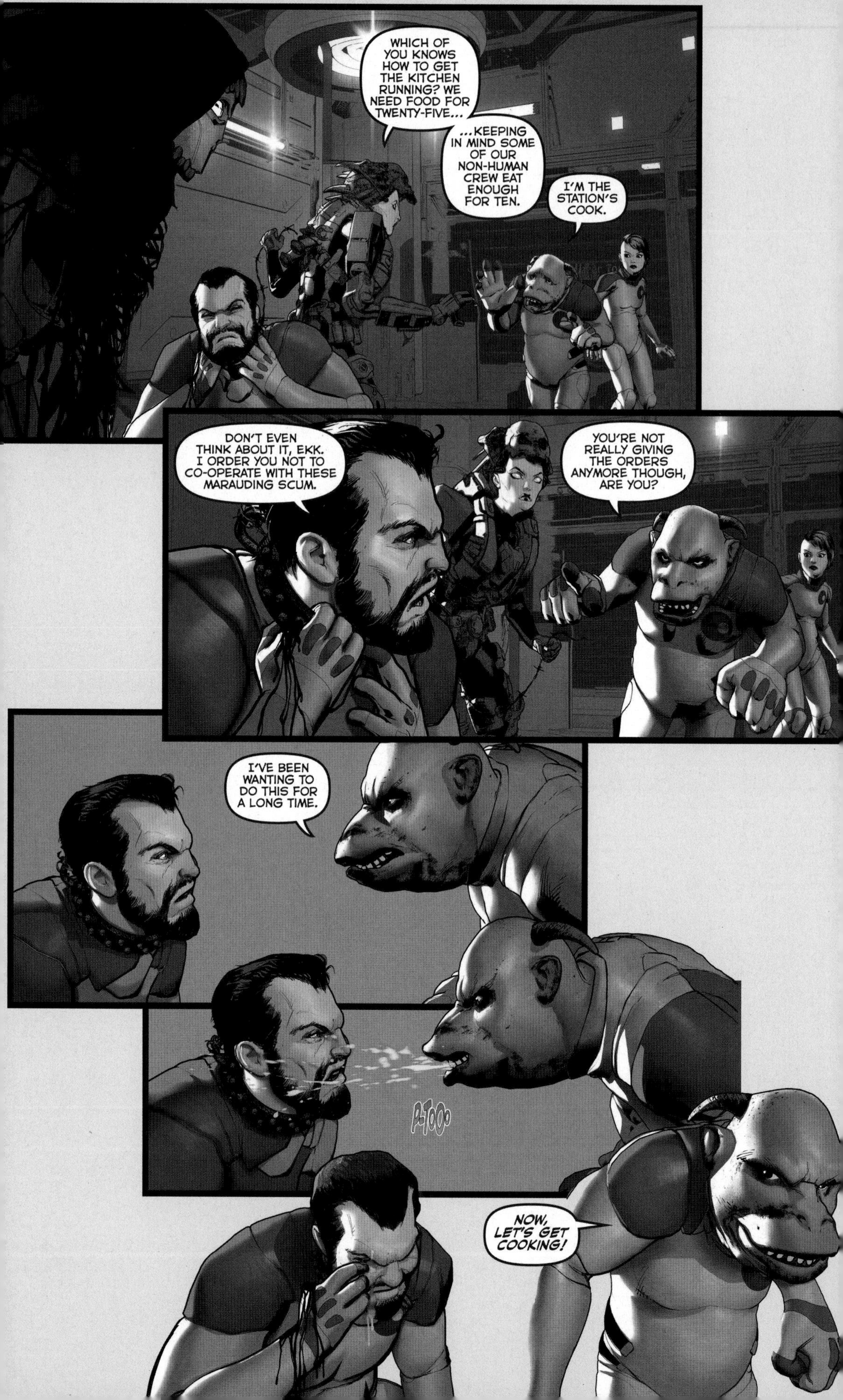
WHICH OF YOU KNOWS HOW TO GET THE KITCHEN RUNNING? WE NEED FOOD FOR TWENTY-FIVE...
...KEEPING IN MIND SOME OF OUR NON-HUMAN CREW EAT ENOUGH FOR TEN.
I'M THE STATION'S COOK.
DON'T EVEN THINK ABOUT IT, EKK. I ORDER YOU NOT TO CO-OPERATE WITH THESE MARAUDING SCUM.
YOU'RE NOT REALLY GIVING THE ORDERS ANYMORE THOUGH, ARE YOU?
I'VE BEEN WANTING TO DO THIS FOR A LONG TIME.
P-TOOO
NOW, LET'S GET COOKING!

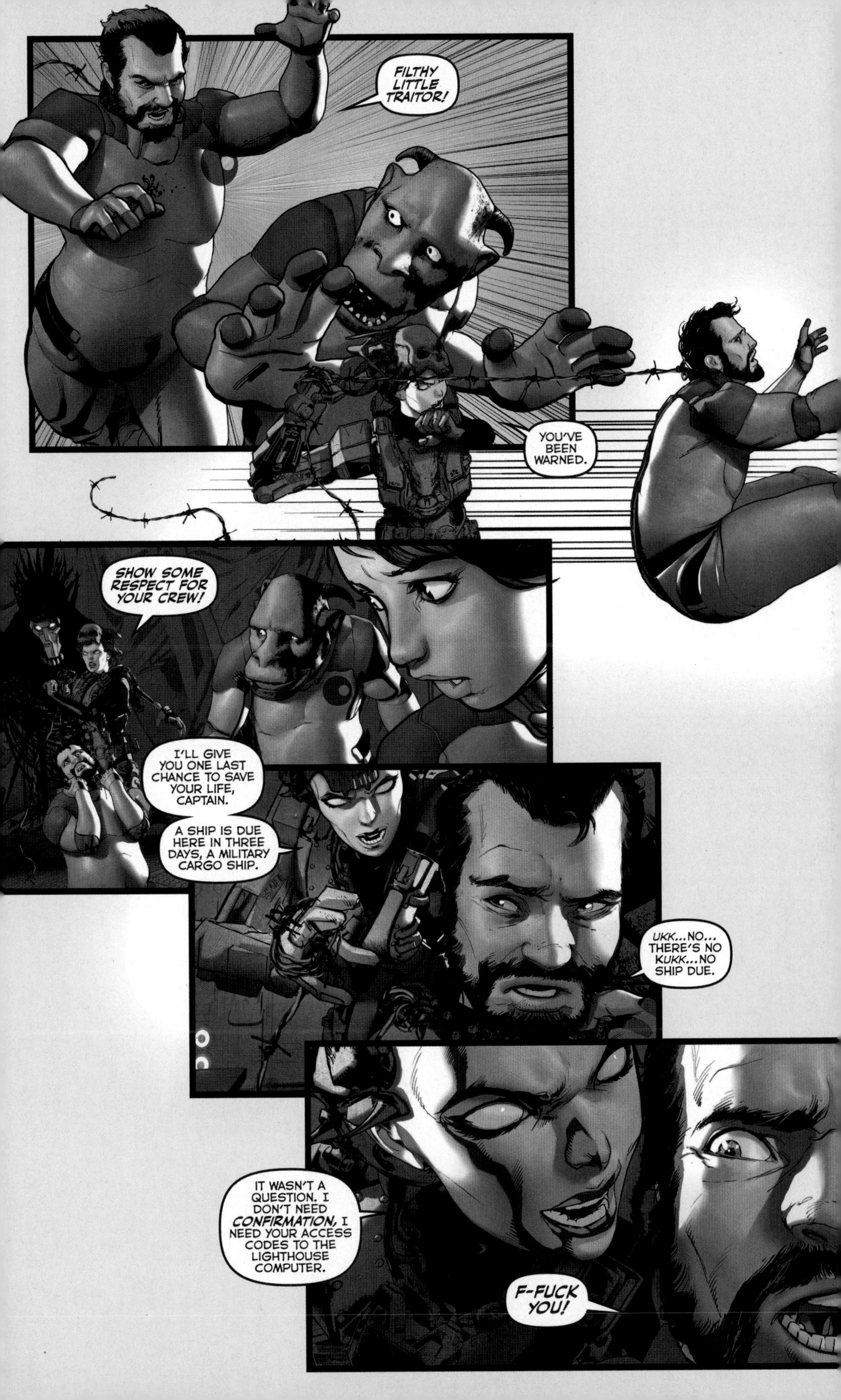
FILTHY LITTLE TRAITOR!
YOU'VE BEEN WARNED.
SHOW SOME RESPECT FOR YOUR CREW!
I'LL GIVE YOU ONE LAST CHANCE TO SAVE YOUR LIFE, CAPTAIN.
A SHIP IS DUE HERE IN THREE DAYS, A MILITARY CARGO SHIP.
UKK...NO... THERE'S NO KUKK...NO SHIP DUE.
IT WASN'T A QUESTION. I DON'T NEED CONFIRMATION, I NEED YOUR ACCESS CODES TO THE LIGHTHOUSE COMPUTER.
F-FUCK YOU!

LET ME FINISH.

YOU **WILL** GIVE ME THE CODES OR I WILL KILL THIS ONE...SLOWLY AND PAINFULLY, IN FRONT OF YOUR EYES.

SUCK MY BALLS, MOTHERF—

WRONG ANSWER.

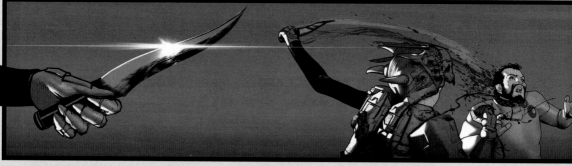

DAMMIT, CARCANTE!

I DIDN'T GIVE YOU PERMISSION TO KILL HIM.

HE WAS ABOUT TO INSULT MY MOTHER, CAPTAIN.

YOUR WORTHLESS MOTHER ABANDONED YOU WHEN YOU WERE THREE YEARS OLD!

WHACK

LOOK AT HIM. HE'S SMILING. HE THINKS HE'S SCREWED US.

SHALL WE TELL HIM BEFORE HE BLEEDS OUT?

M-URRRGH

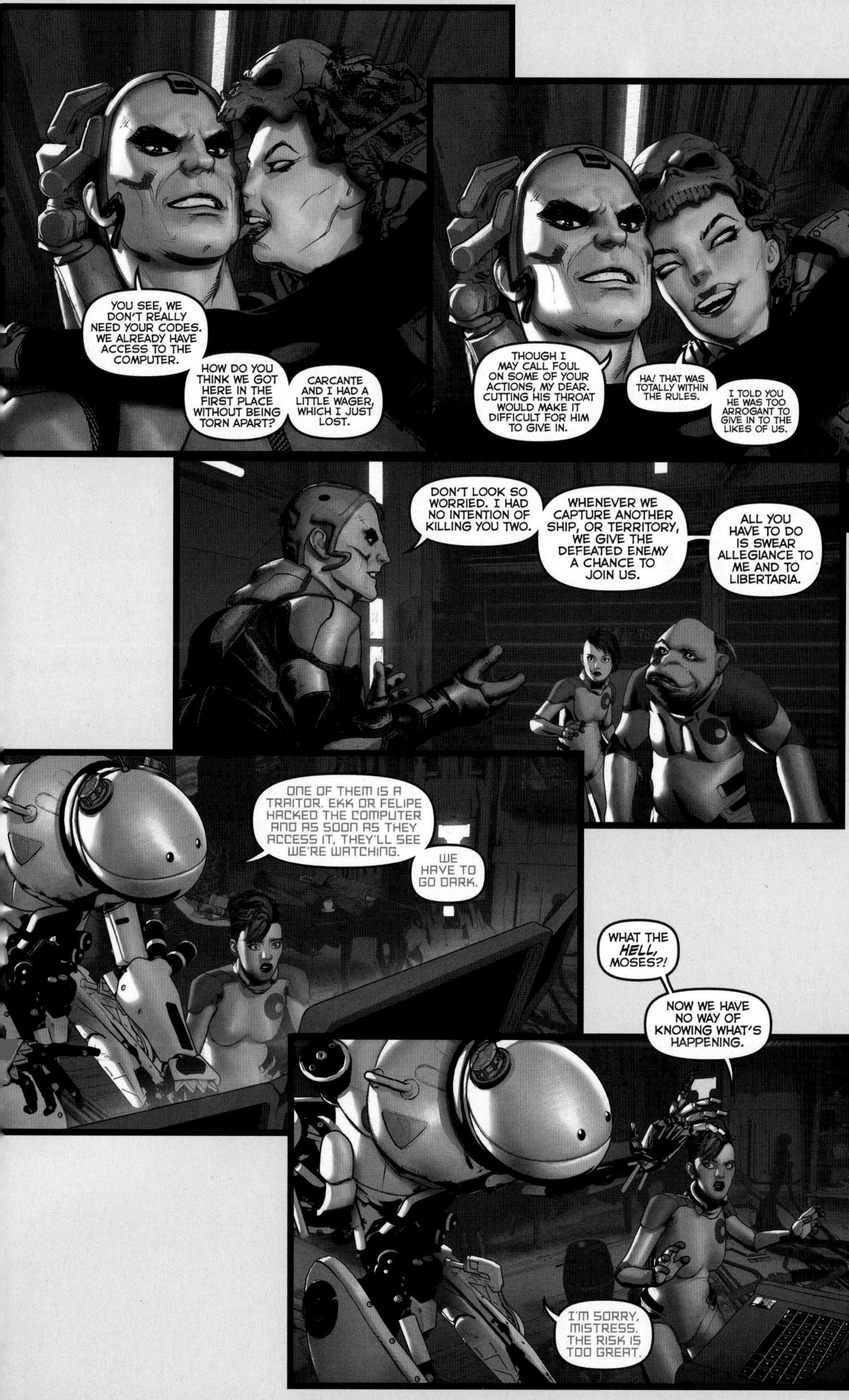
YOU SEE, WE DON'T REALLY NEED YOUR CODES. WE ALREADY HAVE ACCESS TO THE COMPUTER.
HOW DO YOU THINK WE GOT HERE IN THE FIRST PLACE WITHOUT BEING TORN APART?
CARCANTE AND I HAD A LITTLE WAGER, WHICH I JUST LOST.
THOUGH I MAY CALL FOUL ON SOME OF YOUR ACTIONS, MY DEAR. CUTTING HIS THROAT WOULD MAKE IT DIFFICULT FOR HIM TO GIVE IN.
HA! THAT WAS TOTALLY WITHIN THE RULES.
I TOLD YOU HE WAS TOO ARROGANT TO GIVE IN TO THE LIKES OF US.
DON'T LOOK SO WORRIED. I HAD NO INTENTION OF KILLING YOU TWO.
WHENEVER WE CAPTURE ANOTHER SHIP, OR TERRITORY, WE GIVE THE DEFEATED ENEMY A CHANCE TO JOIN US.
ALL YOU HAVE TO DO IS SWEAR ALLEGIANCE TO ME AND TO LIBERTARIA.
ONE OF THEM IS A TRAITOR. EKK OR FELIPE HACKED THE COMPUTER AND AS SOON AS THEY ACCESS IT, THEY'LL SEE WE'RE WATCHING.
WE HAVE TO GO DARK.
WHAT THE *HELL,* MOSES?!
NOW WE HAVE NO WAY OF KNOWING WHAT'S HAPPENING.
I'M SORRY, MISTRESS. THE RISK IS TOO GREAT.

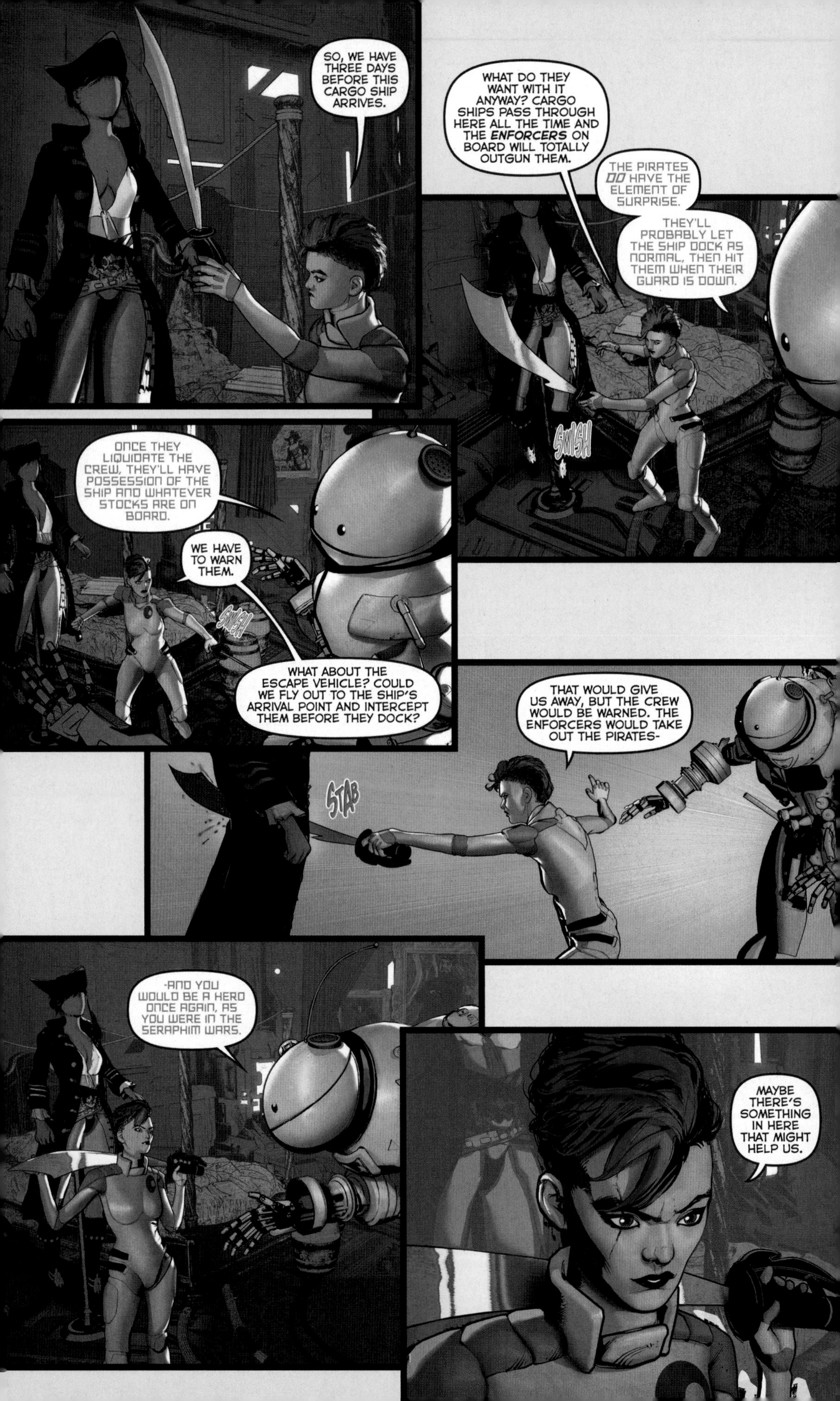

SO, WE HAVE THREE DAYS BEFORE THIS CARGO SHIP ARRIVES.
WHAT DO THEY WANT WITH IT ANYWAY? CARGO SHIPS PASS THROUGH HERE ALL THE TIME AND THE ENFORCERS ON BOARD WILL TOTALLY OUTGUN THEM.
THE PIRATES DO HAVE THE ELEMENT OF SURPRISE.
THEY'LL PROBABLY LET THE SHIP DOCK AS NORMAL, THEN HIT THEM WHEN THEIR GUARD IS DOWN.
SWISH
ONCE THEY LIQUIDATE THE CREW, THEY'LL HAVE POSSESSION OF THE SHIP AND WHATEVER STOCKS ARE ON BOARD.
WE HAVE TO WARN THEM.
SWISH
WHAT ABOUT THE ESCAPE VEHICLE? COULD WE FLY OUT TO THE SHIP'S ARRIVAL POINT AND INTERCEPT THEM BEFORE THEY DOCK?
THAT WOULD GIVE US AWAY, BUT THE CREW WOULD BE WARNED. THE ENFORCERS WOULD TAKE OUT THE PIRATES-
STAB
-AND YOU WOULD BE A HERO ONCE AGAIN, AS YOU WERE IN THE SERAPHIM WARS.
MAYBE THERE'S SOMETHING IN HERE THAT MIGHT HELP US.

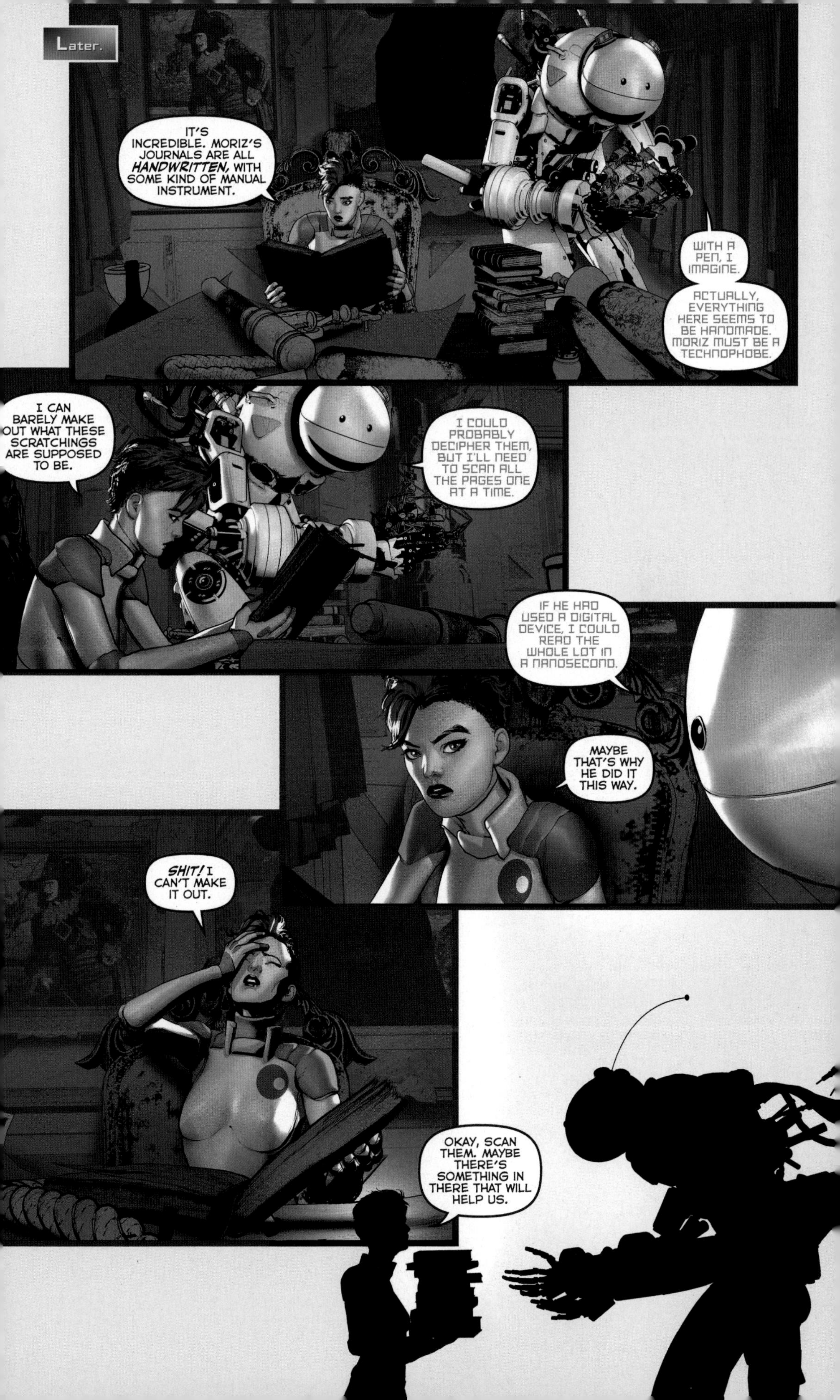
Later.
IT'S INCREDIBLE. MORIZ'S JOURNALS ARE ALL HANDWRITTEN, WITH SOME KIND OF MANUAL INSTRUMENT.
WITH A PEN, I IMAGINE.
ACTUALLY, EVERYTHING HERE SEEMS TO BE HANDMADE. MORIZ MUST BE A TECHNOPHOBE.
I CAN BARELY MAKE OUT WHAT THESE SCRATCHINGS ARE SUPPOSED TO BE.
I COULD PROBABLY DECIPHER THEM, BUT I'LL NEED TO SCAN ALL THE PAGES ONE AT A TIME.
IF HE HAD USED A DIGITAL DEVICE, I COULD READ THE WHOLE LOT IN A NANOSECOND.
MAYBE THAT'S WHY HE DID IT THIS WAY.
SHIT! I CAN'T MAKE IT OUT.
OKAY, SCAN THEM. MAYBE THERE'S SOMETHING IN THERE THAT WILL HELP US.

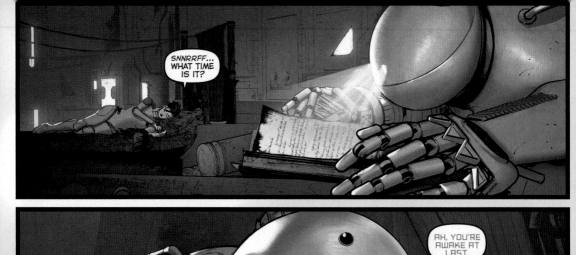

SNNRRFF...
WHAT TIME
IS IT?

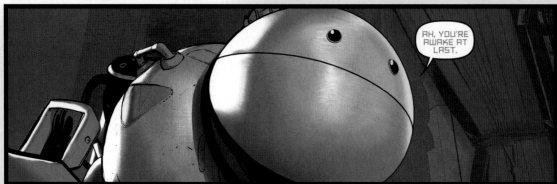

AH, YOU'RE
AWAKE AT
LAST.

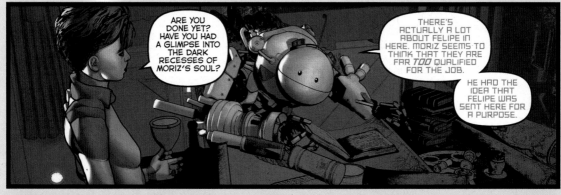

ARE YOU
DONE YET?
HAVE YOU HAD
A GLIMPSE INTO
THE DARK
RECESSES OF
MORIZ'S SOUL?

THERE'S
ACTUALLY A LOT
ABOUT FELIPE IN
HERE. MORIZ SEEMS TO
THINK THAT THEY ARE
FAR *TOO* QUALIFIED
FOR THE JOB.

HE HAD THE
IDEA THAT
FELIPE WAS
SENT HERE FOR
A PURPOSE.

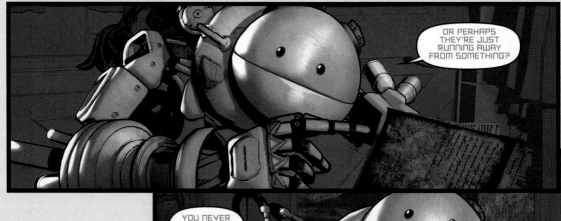

OR PERHAPS
THEY'RE JUST
RUNNING AWAY
FROM SOMETHING?

YOU NEVER
ACTUALLY
TOLD ME WHAT
HAPPENED ON
KOLAIRE.

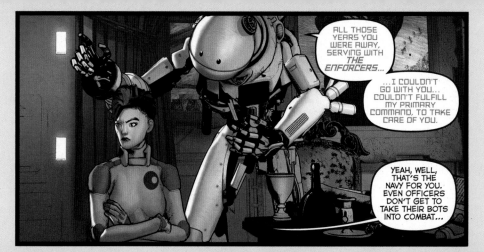

ALL THOSE YEARS YOU WERE AWAY, SERVING WITH *THE ENFORCERS*...

...I COULDN'T GO WITH YOU... COULDN'T FULFILL MY PRIMARY COMMAND, TO TAKE CARE OF YOU.

YEAH, WELL, THAT'S THE NAVY FOR YOU. EVEN OFFICERS DON'T GET TO TAKE THEIR BOTS INTO COMBAT...

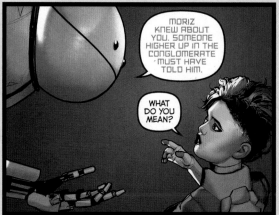

MORIZ KNEW ABOUT YOU. SOMEONE HIGHER UP IN THE CONGLOMERATE MUST HAVE TOLD HIM.

WHAT DO YOU MEAN?

IT'S ALL HERE IN THE JOURNAL...

I KNOW NOW. I KNOW WHAT YOU DID ON KOLAIRE.

MISTRESS, WE NEED TO TALK ABOUT THIS.

FUCK YOU, MOSES!

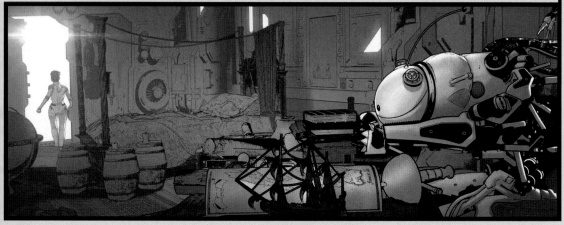

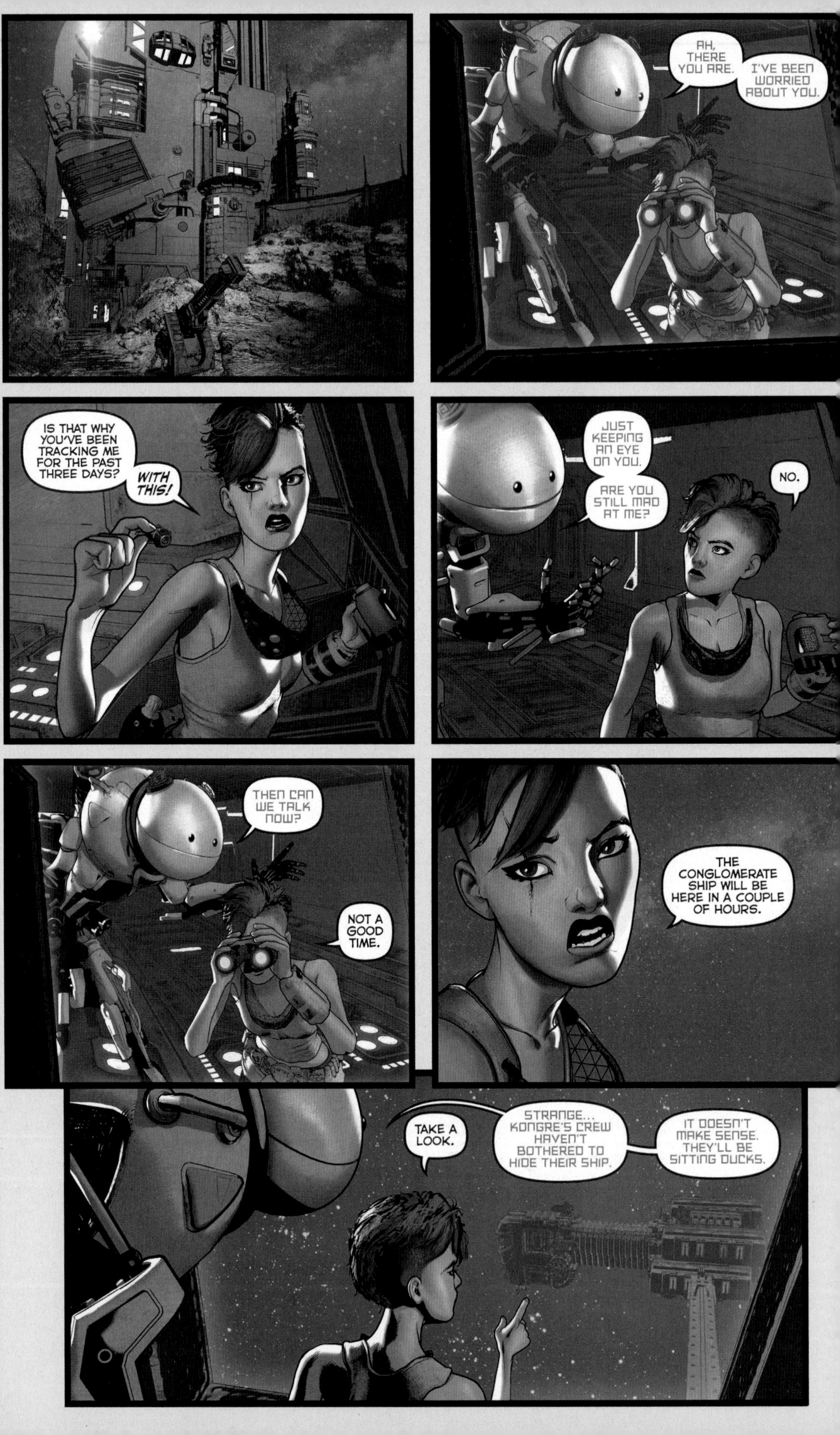
AH, THERE YOU ARE.
I'VE BEEN WORRIED ABOUT YOU.
IS THAT WHY YOU'VE BEEN TRACKING ME FOR THE PAST THREE DAYS?
WITH THIS!
JUST KEEPING AN EYE ON YOU.
ARE YOU STILL MAD AT ME?
NO.
THEN CAN WE TALK NOW?
NOT A GOOD TIME.
THE CONGLOMERATE SHIP WILL BE HERE IN A COUPLE OF HOURS.
TAKE A LOOK.
STRANGE... KONGRE'S CREW HAVEN'T BOTHERED TO HIDE THEIR SHIP.
IT DOESN'T MAKE SENSE. THEY'LL BE SITTING DUCKS.

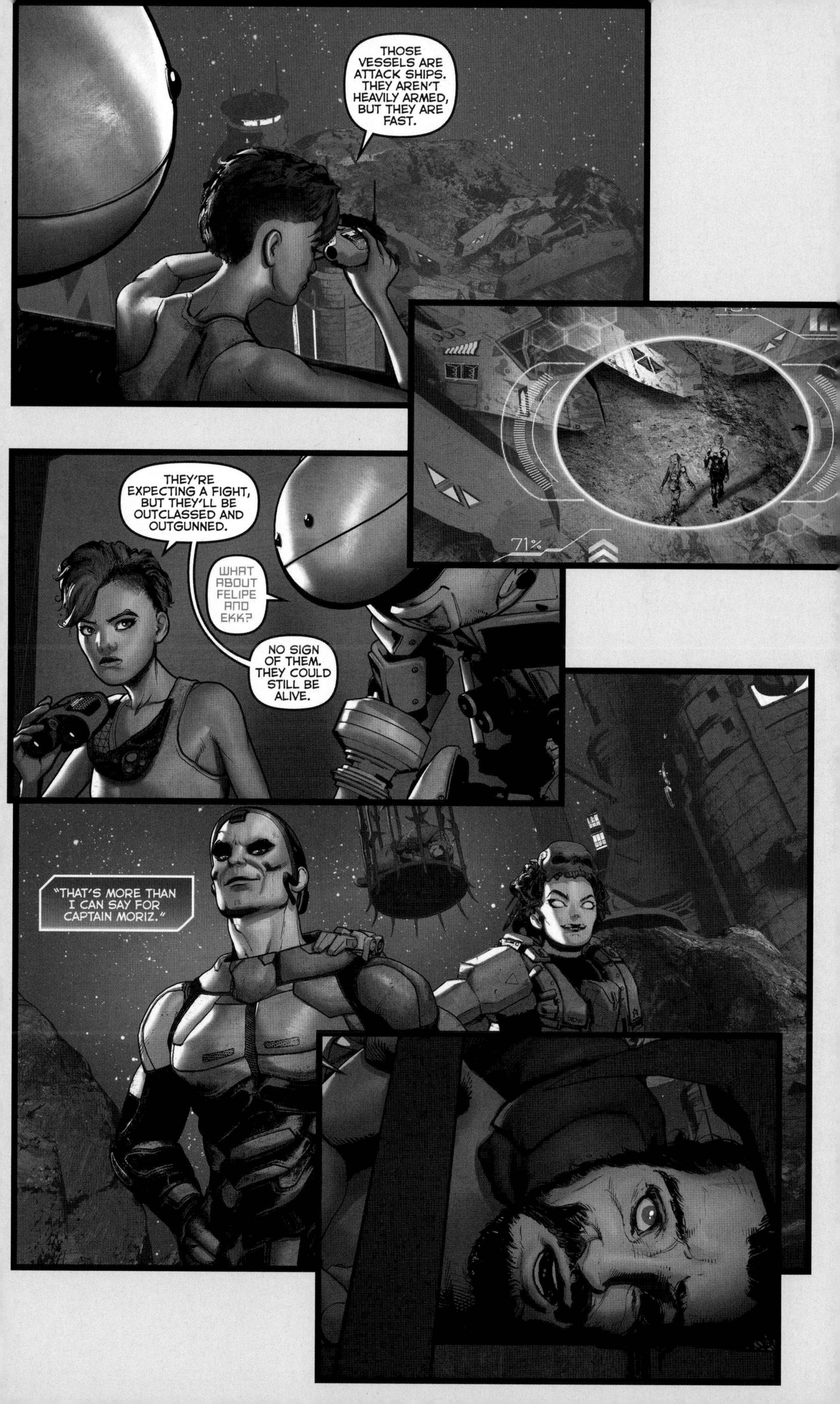
THOSE VESSELS ARE ATTACK SHIPS. THEY AREN'T HEAVILY ARMED, BUT THEY ARE FAST.
71%
THEY'RE EXPECTING A FIGHT, BUT THEY'LL BE OUTCLASSED AND OUTGUNNED.
WHAT ABOUT FELIPE AND EKK?
NO SIGN OF THEM. THEY COULD STILL BE ALIVE.
"THAT'S MORE THAN I CAN SAY FOR CAPTAIN MORIZ."

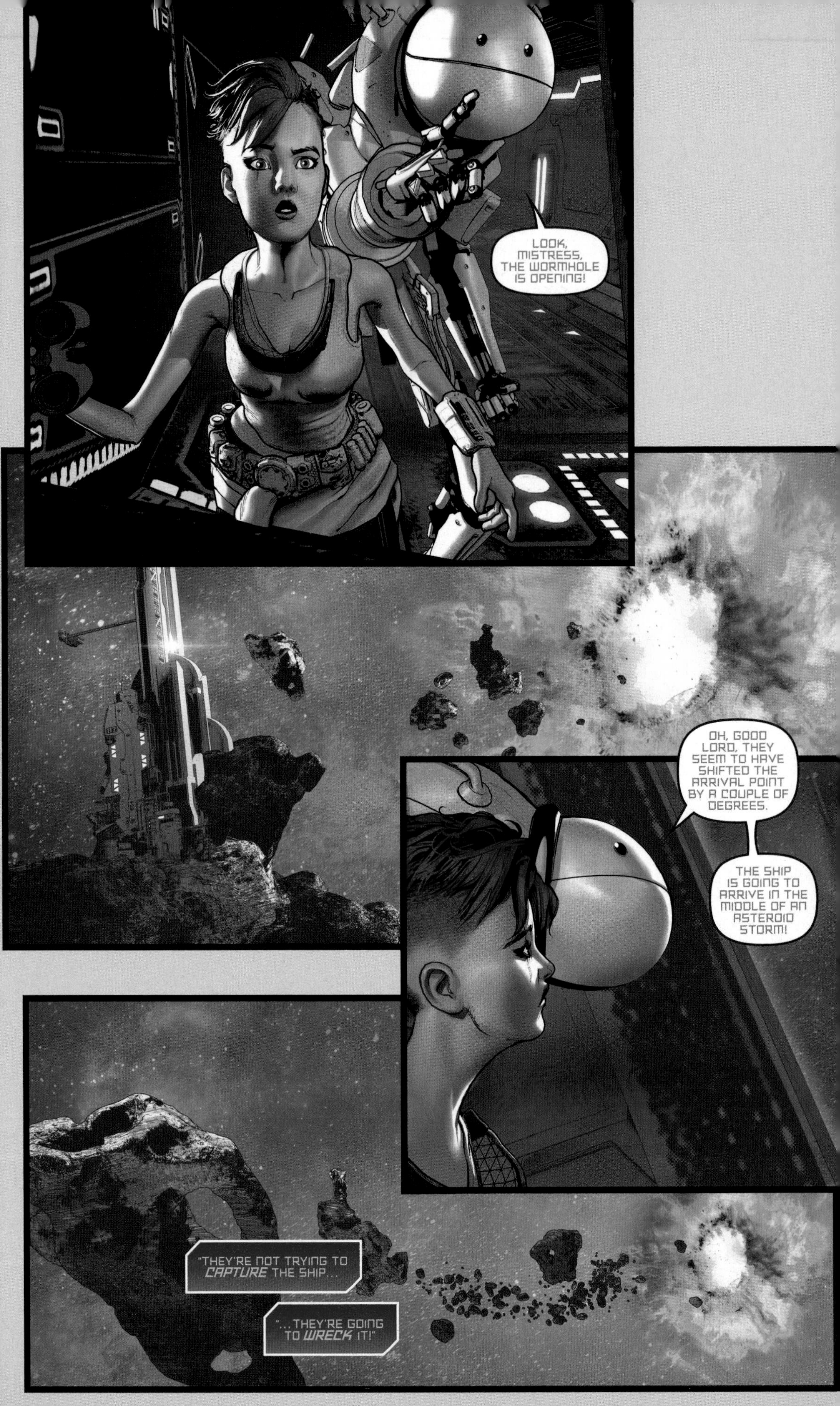
LOOK, MISTRESS, THE WORMHOLE IS OPENING!
OH, GOOD LORD, THEY SEEM TO HAVE SHIFTED THE ARRIVAL POINT BY A COUPLE OF DEGREES.
THE SHIP IS GOING TO ARRIVE IN THE MIDDLE OF AN ASTEROID STORM!
"THEY'RE NOT TRYING TO CAPTURE THE SHIP...
"...THEY'RE GOING TO WRECK IT!"

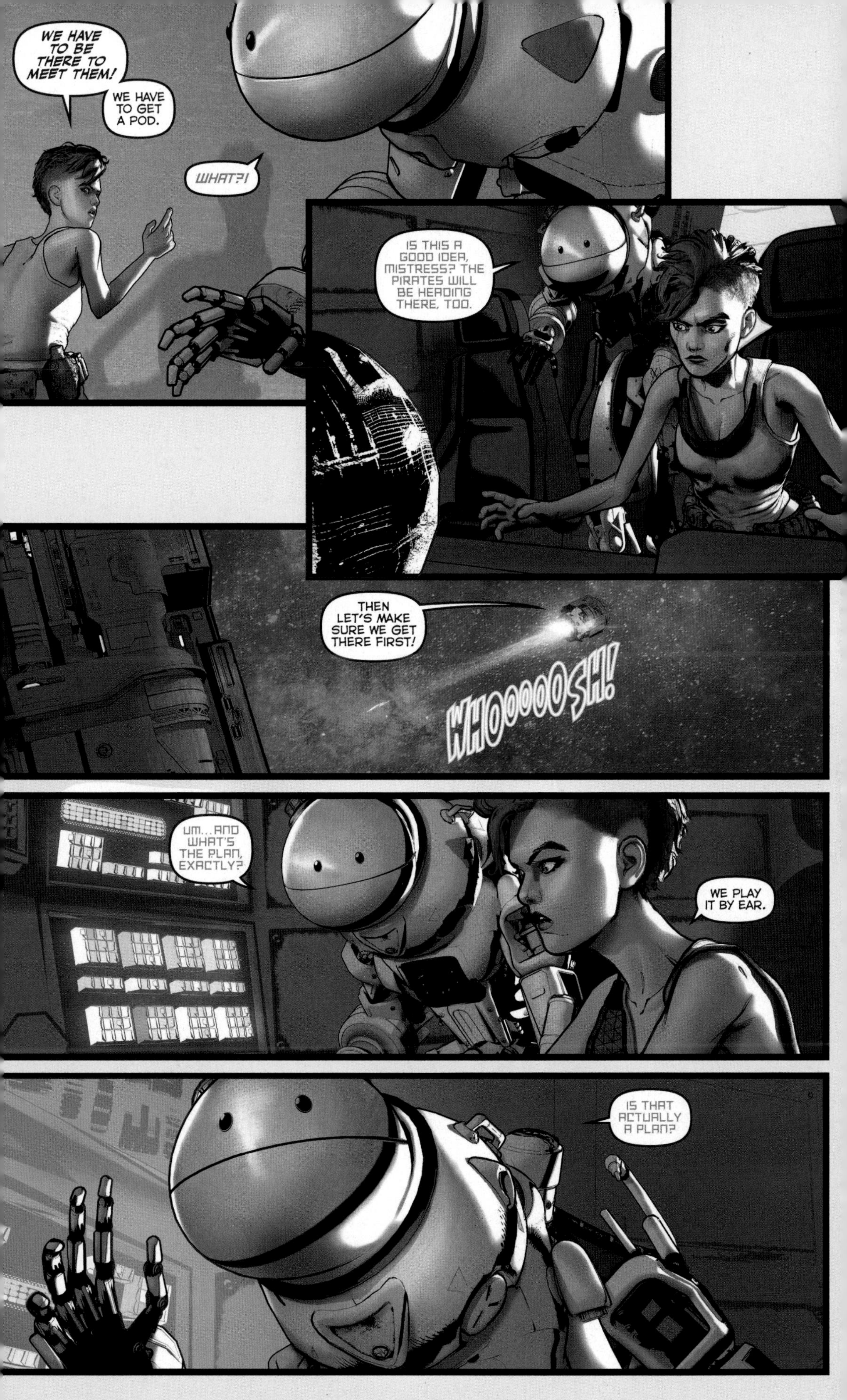

WE HAVE TO BE THERE TO MEET THEM!
WE HAVE TO GET A POD.
WHAT?!
IS THIS A GOOD IDEA, MISTRESS? THE PIRATES WILL BE HEADING THERE, TOO.
THEN LET'S MAKE SURE WE GET THERE FIRST!
WHOOOOOSH!
UM...AND WHAT'S THE PLAN, EXACTLY?
WE PLAY IT BY EAR.
IS THAT ACTUALLY A PLAN?

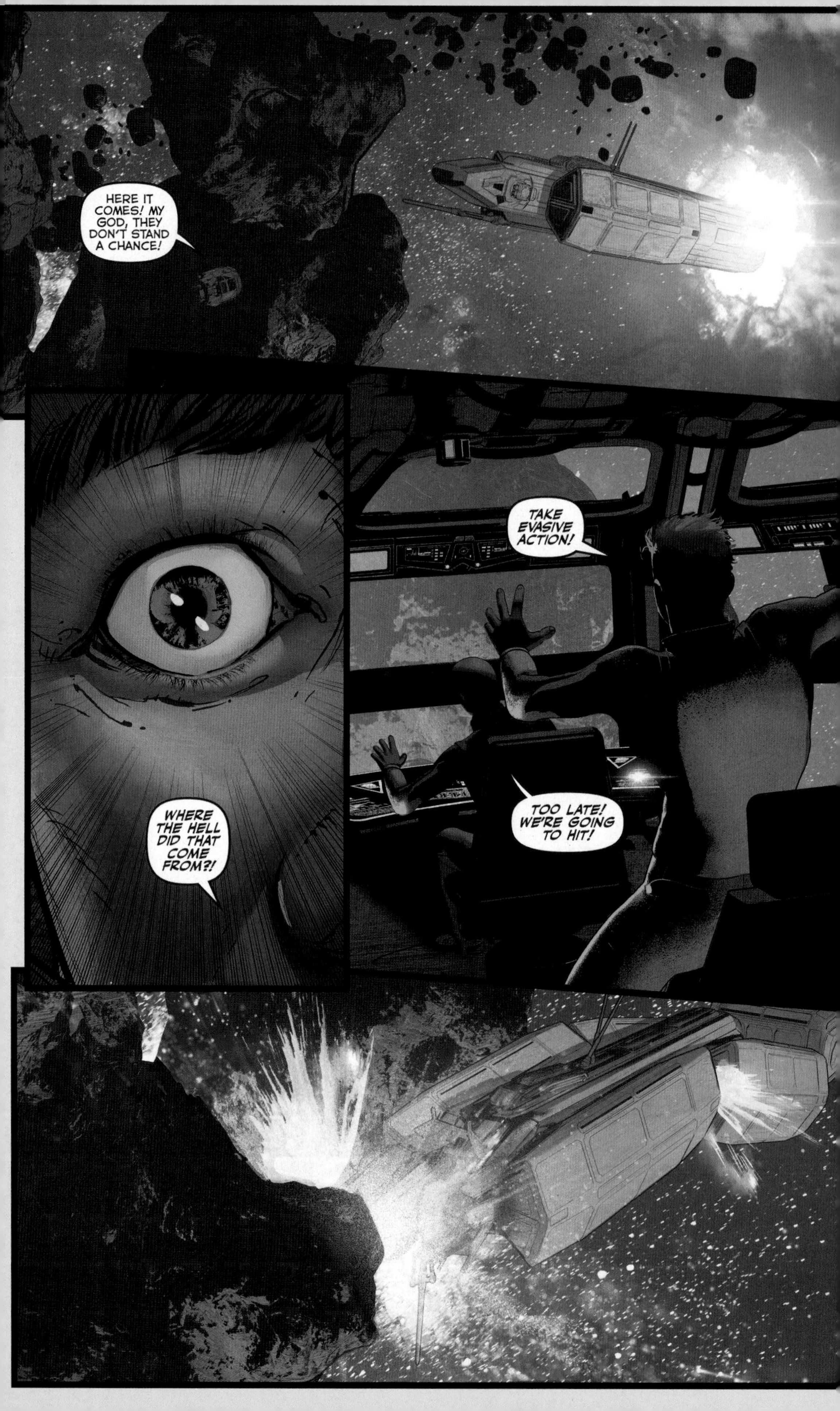
HERE IT COMES! MY GOD, THEY DON'T STAND A CHANCE!
WHERE THE HELL DID THAT COME FROM?!
TAKE EVASIVE ACTION!
TOO LATE! WE'RE GOING TO HIT!

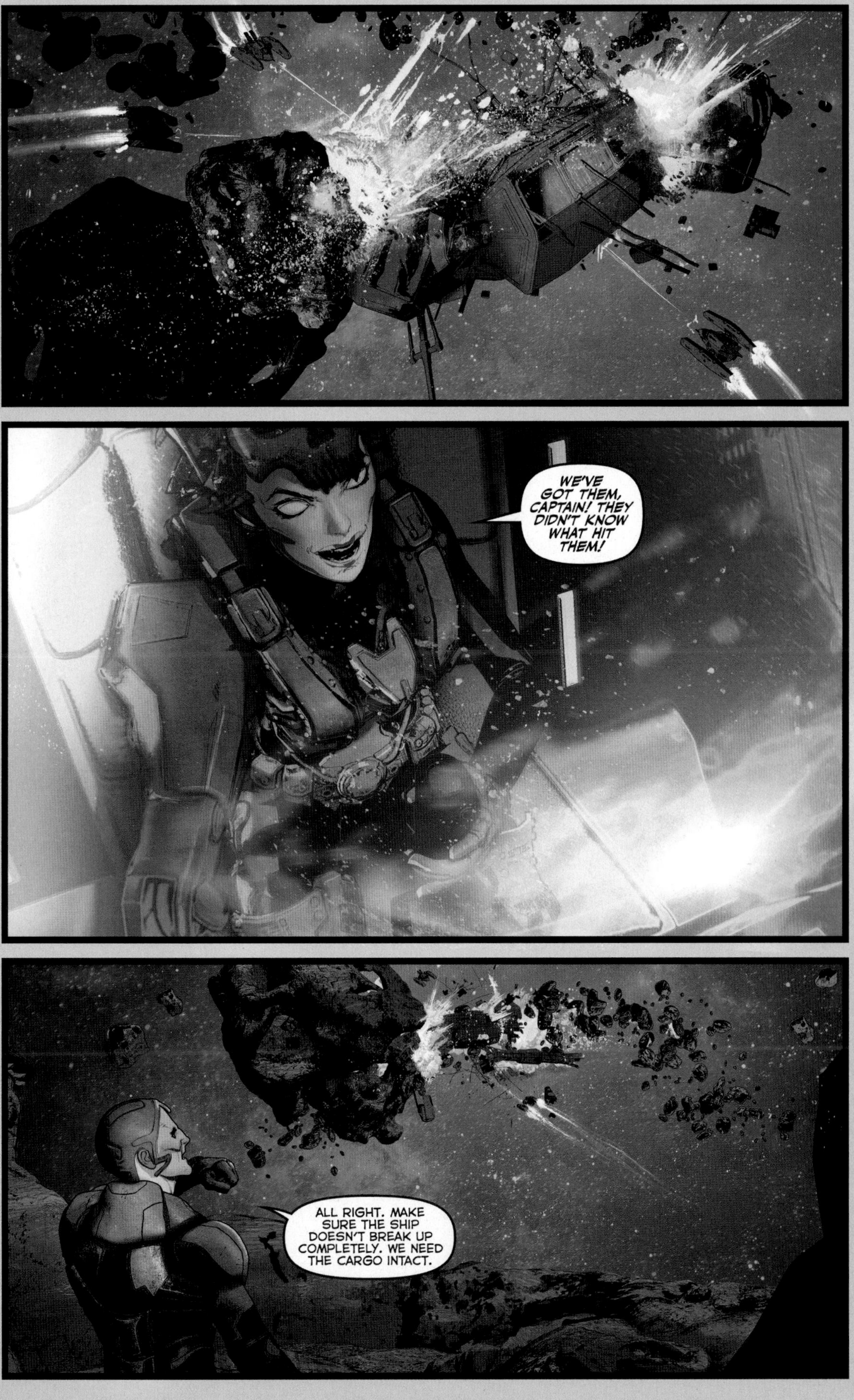
WE'VE GOT THEM, CAPTAIN! THEY DIDN'T KNOW WHAT HIT THEM!
ALL RIGHT. MAKE SURE THE SHIP DOESN'T BREAK UP COMPLETELY. WE NEED THE CARGO INTACT.

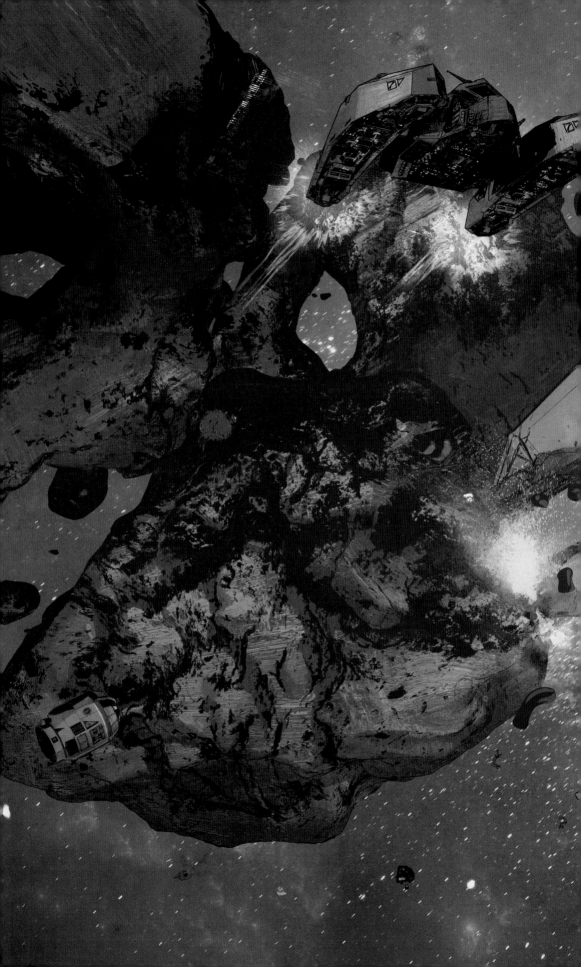

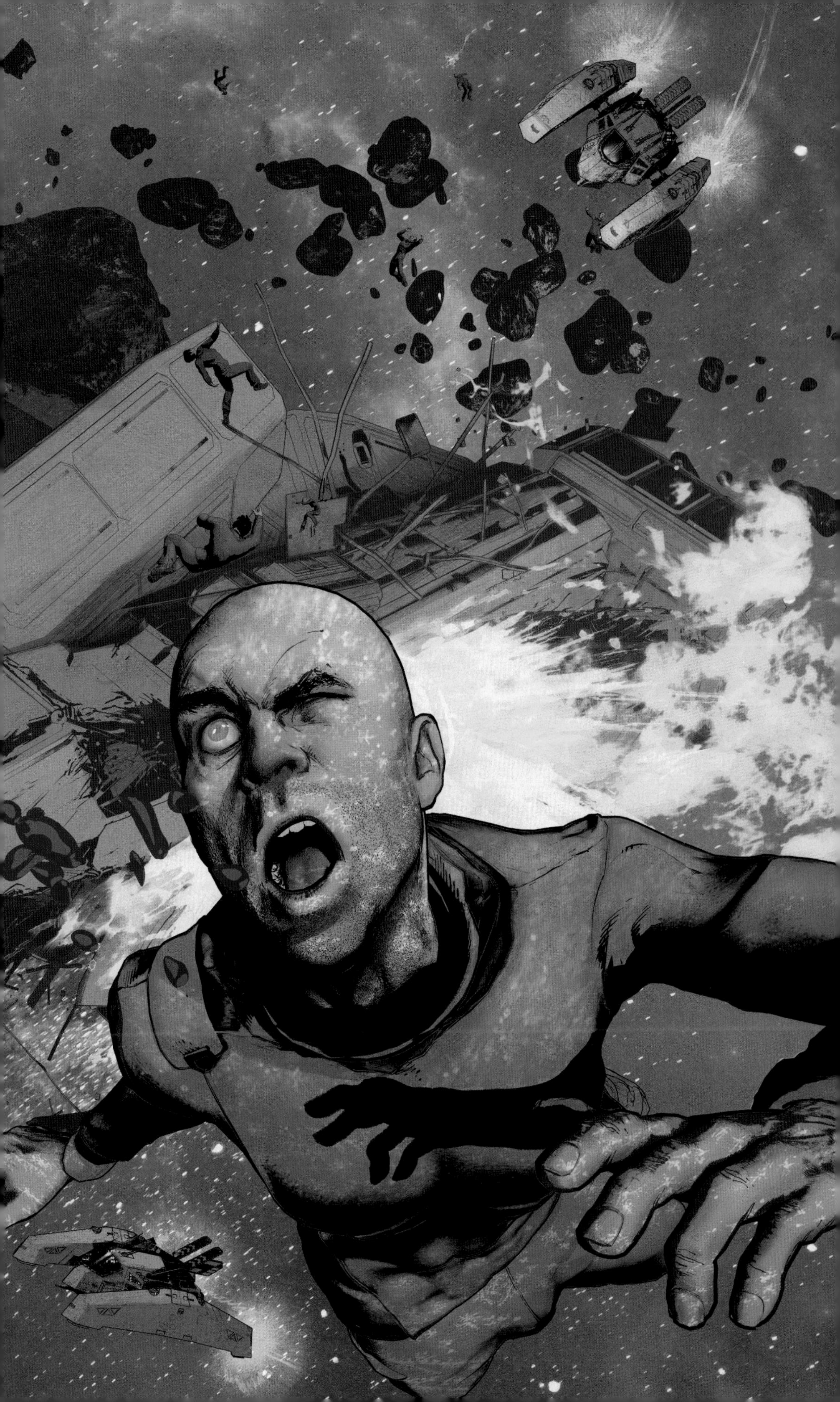

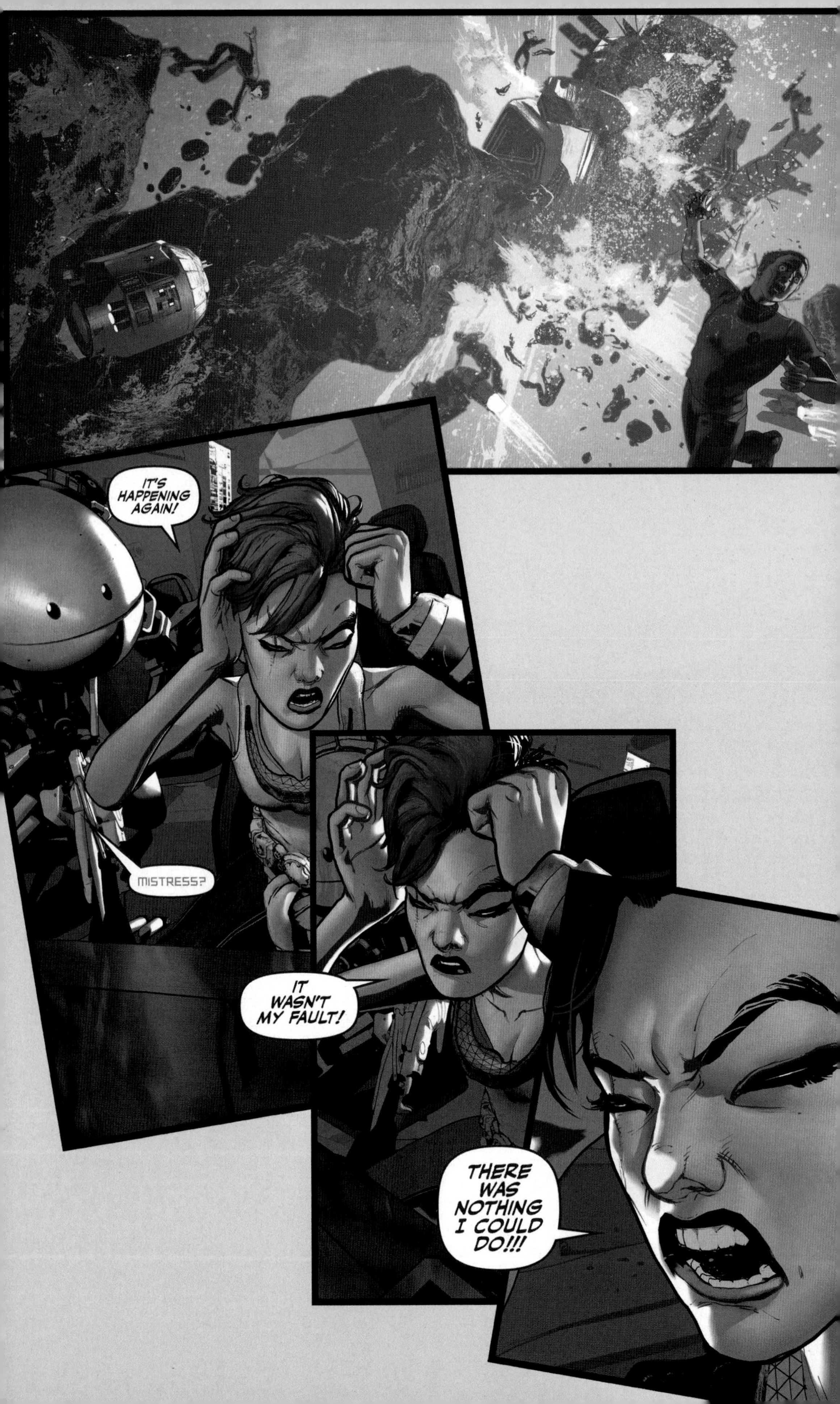
IT'S HAPPENING AGAIN!
MISTRESS?
IT WASN'T MY FAULT!
THERE WAS NOTHING I COULD DO!!!

Issue #2 Cover A

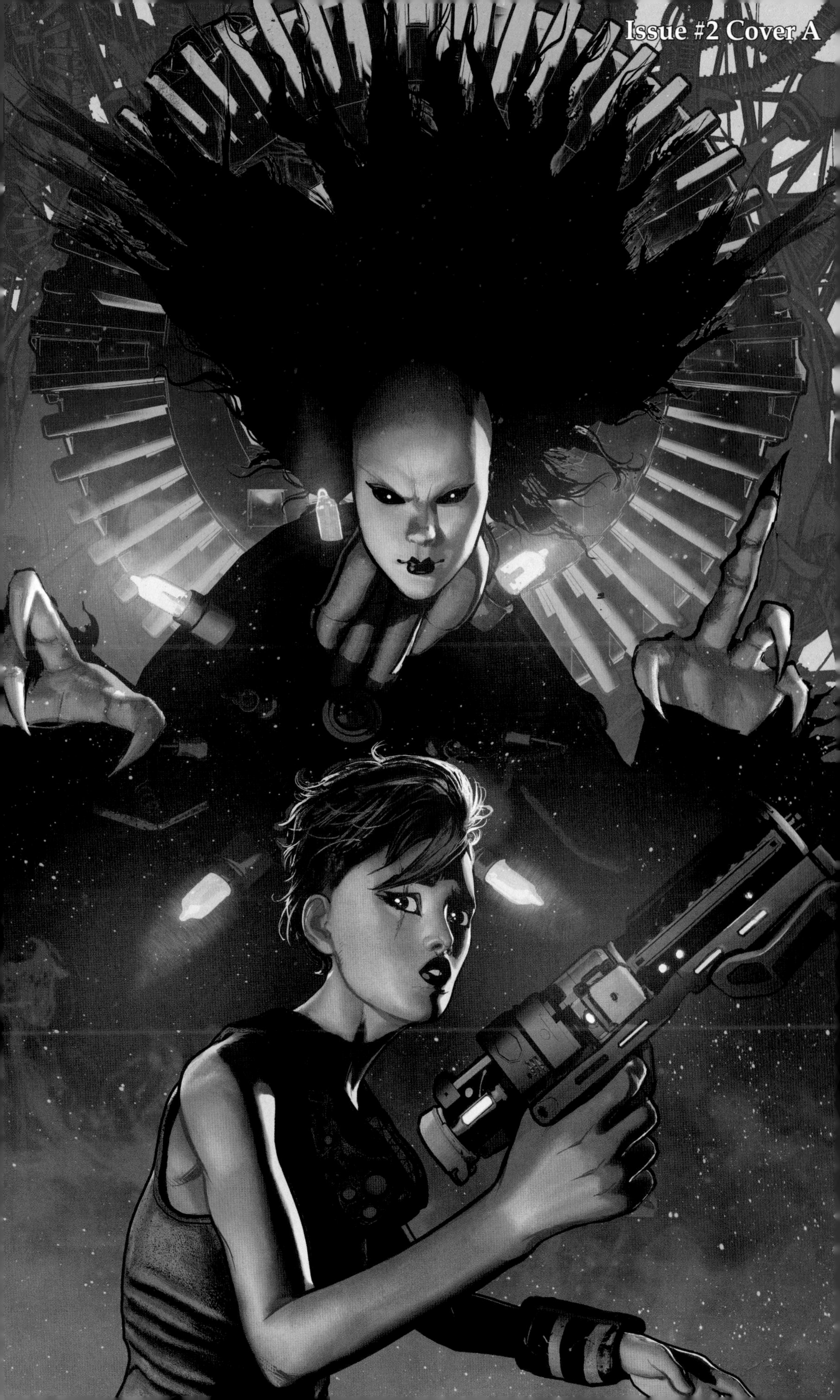

Issue #2 Cover B

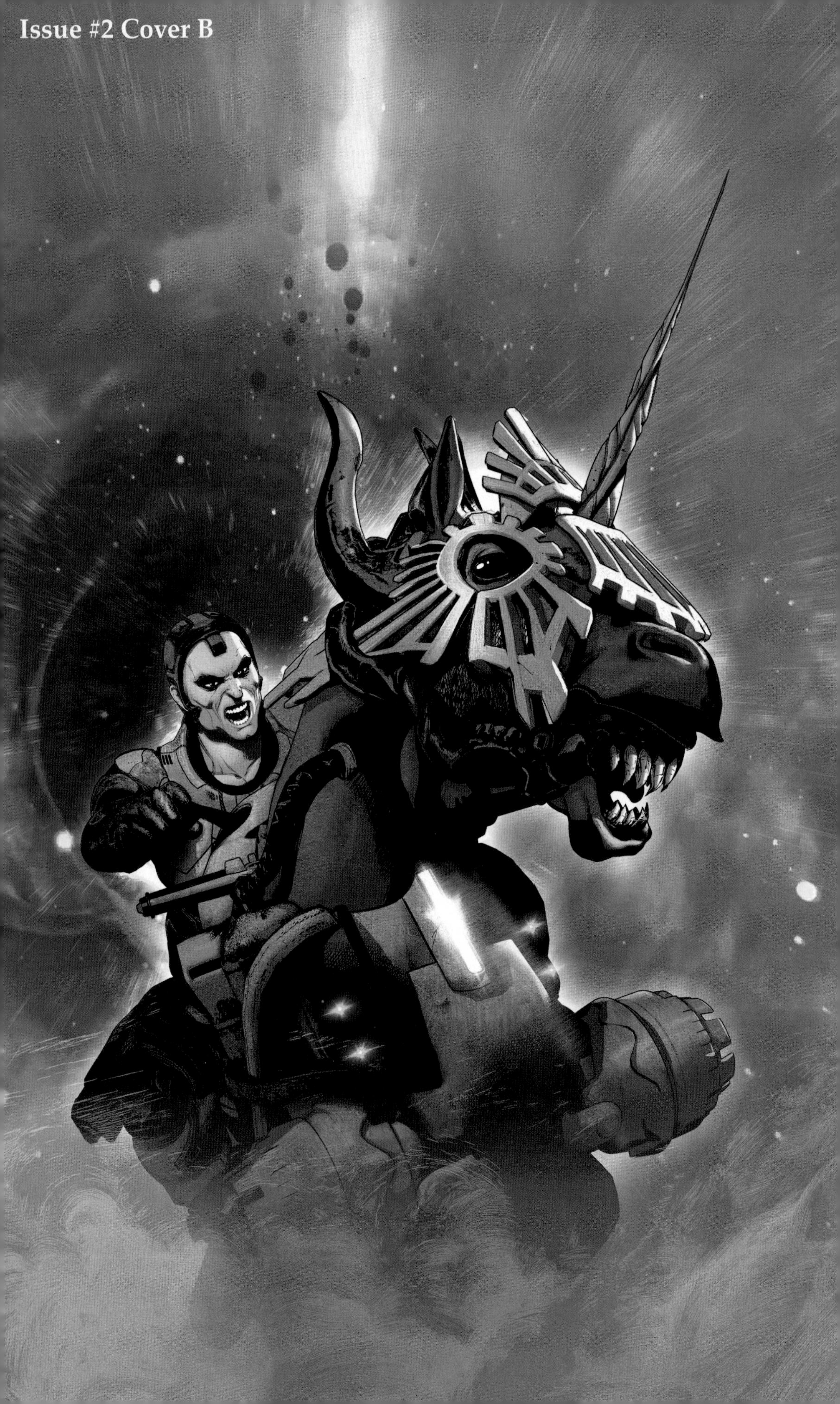

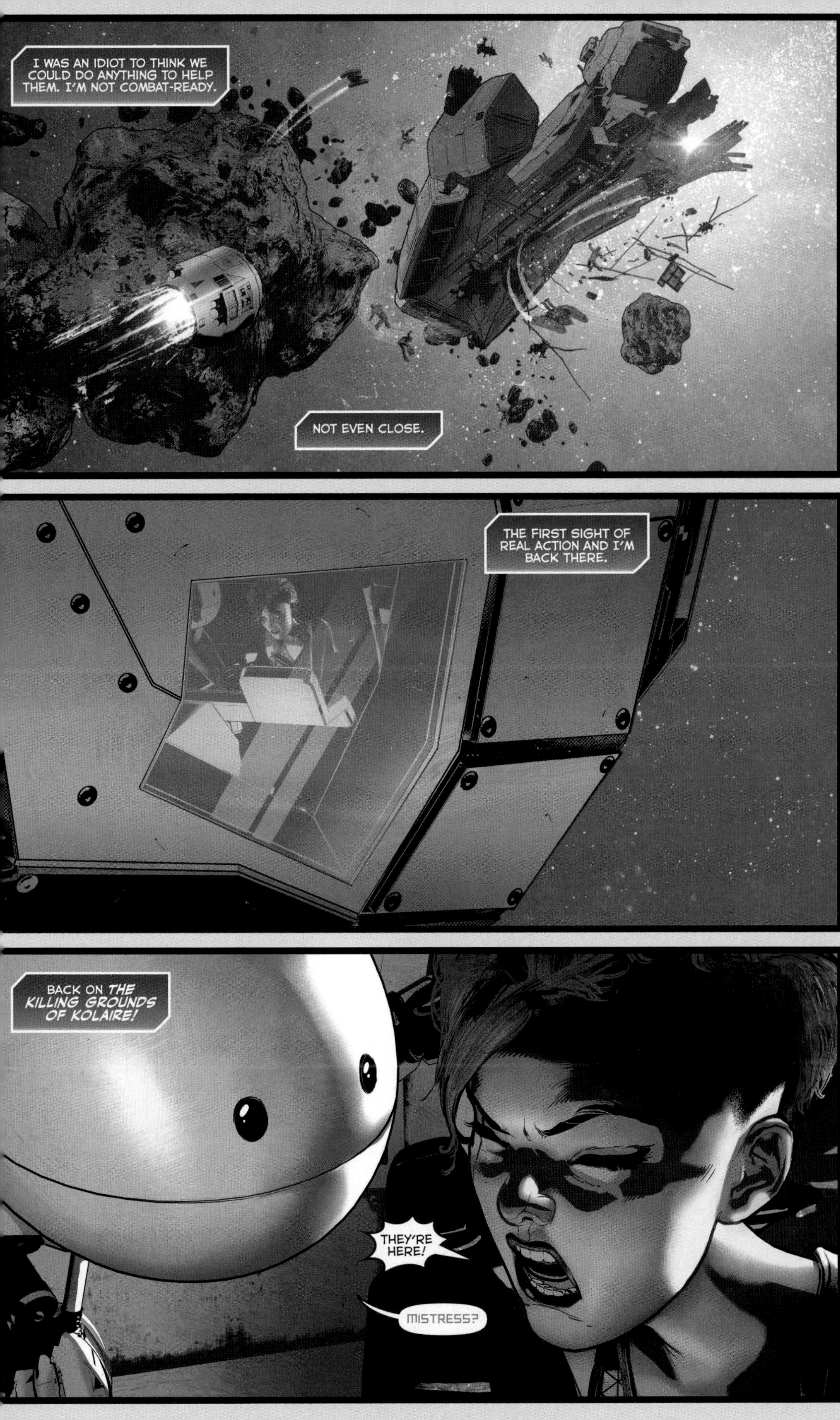
I WAS AN IDIOT TO THINK WE COULD DO ANYTHING TO HELP THEM. I'M NOT COMBAT-READY.
NOT EVEN CLOSE.
THE FIRST SIGHT OF REAL ACTION AND I'M BACK THERE.
BACK ON *THE KILLING GROUNDS OF KOLAIRE!*
THEY'RE HERE!
MISTRESS?

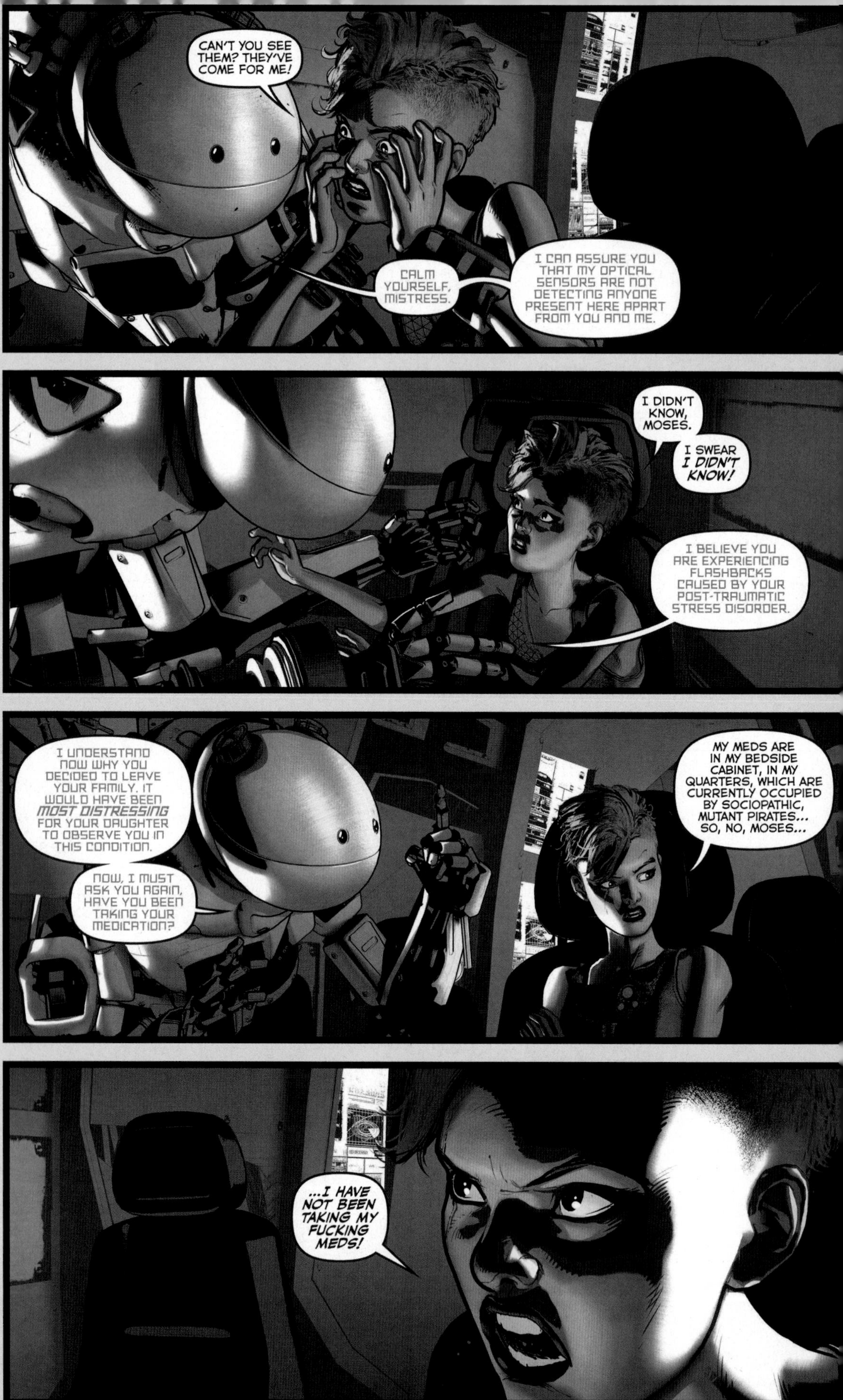
CAN'T YOU SEE THEM? THEY'VE COME FOR ME!
CALM YOURSELF, MISTRESS.
I CAN ASSURE YOU THAT MY OPTICAL SENSORS ARE NOT DETECTING ANYONE PRESENT HERE APART FROM YOU AND ME.
I DIDN'T KNOW, MOSES.
I SWEAR *I DIDN'T KNOW!*
I BELIEVE YOU ARE EXPERIENCING FLASHBACKS CAUSED BY YOUR POST-TRAUMATIC STRESS DISORDER.
I UNDERSTAND NOW WHY YOU DECIDED TO LEAVE YOUR FAMILY. IT WOULD HAVE BEEN *MOST DISTRESSING* FOR YOUR DAUGHTER TO OBSERVE YOU IN THIS CONDITION.
NOW, I MUST ASK YOU AGAIN, HAVE YOU BEEN TAKING YOUR MEDICATION?
MY MEDS ARE IN MY BEDSIDE CABINET, IN MY QUARTERS, WHICH ARE CURRENTLY OCCUPIED BY SOCIOPATHIC, MUTANT PIRATES... SO, NO, MOSES...
...I HAVE NOT BEEN TAKING MY FUCKING MEDS!

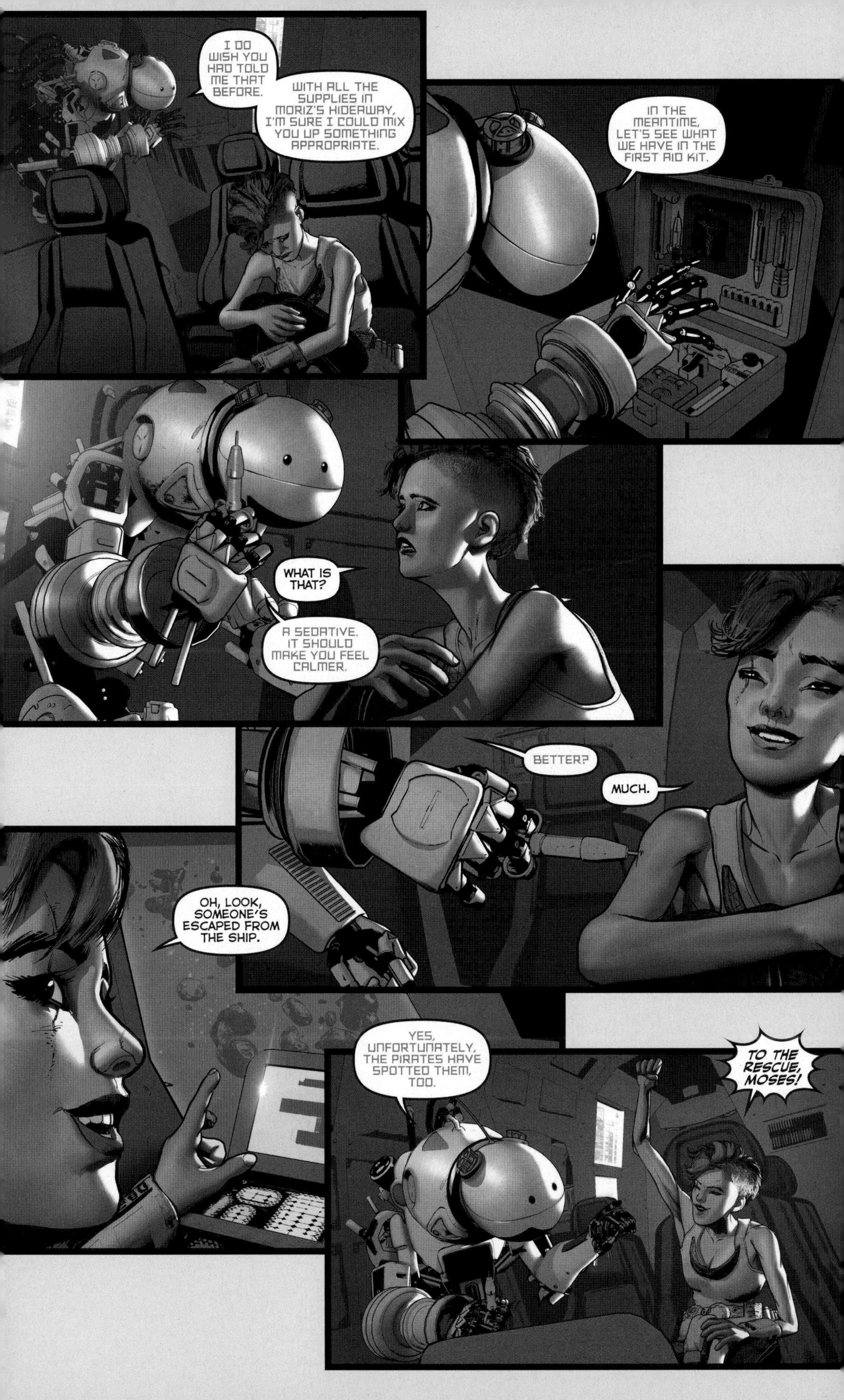
I DO WISH YOU HAD TOLD ME THAT BEFORE.
WITH ALL THE SUPPLIES IN MORIZ'S HIDEAWAY, I'M SURE I COULD MIX YOU UP SOMETHING APPROPRIATE.
IN THE MEANTIME, LET'S SEE WHAT WE HAVE IN THE FIRST AID KIT.
WHAT IS THAT?
A SEDATIVE. IT SHOULD MAKE YOU FEEL CALMER.
BETTER?
MUCH.
OH, LOOK, SOMEONE'S ESCAPED FROM THE SHIP.
YES, UNFORTUNATELY, THE PIRATES HAVE SPOTTED THEM, TOO.
TO THE RESCUE, MOSES!

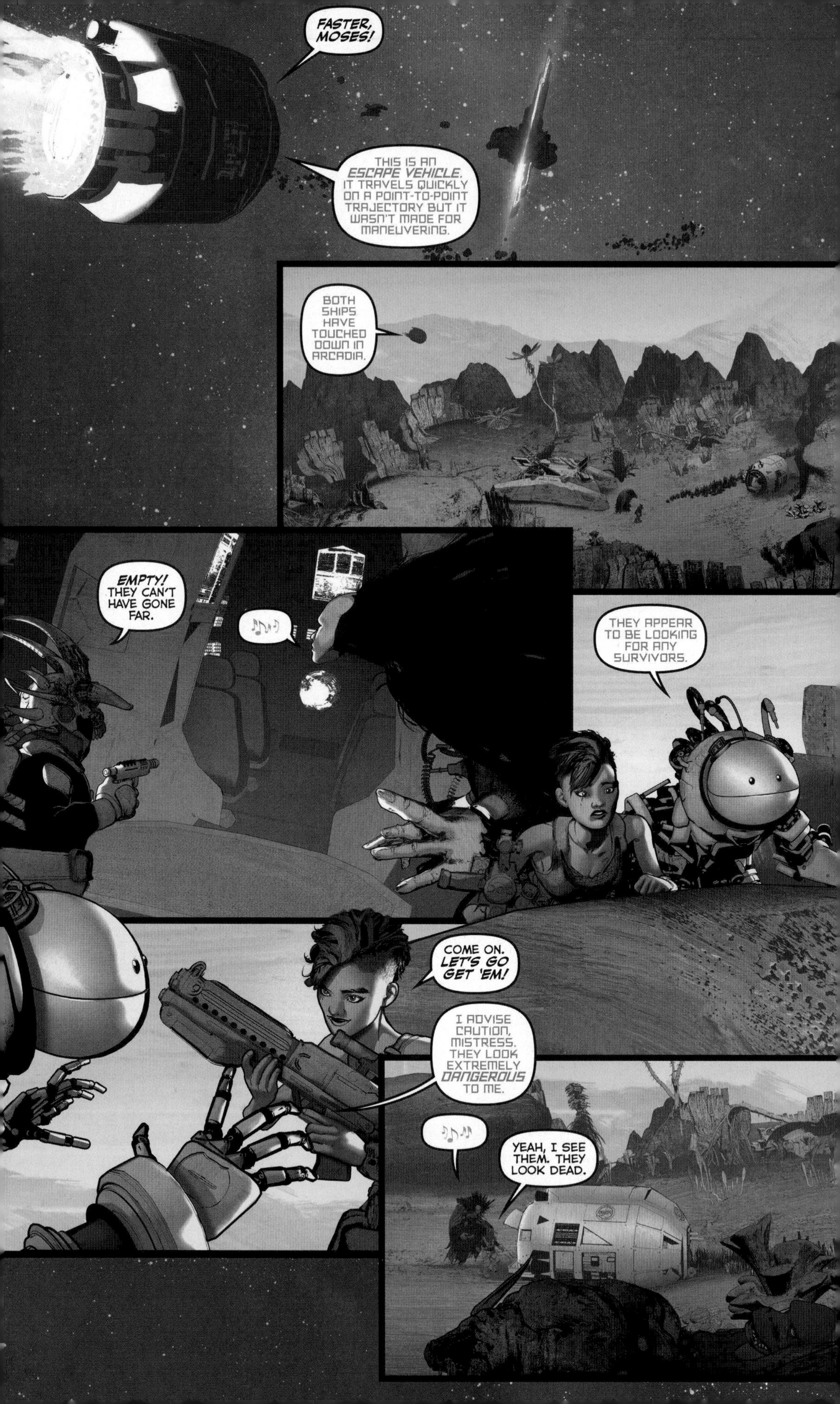
FASTER, MOSES!
THIS IS AN ESCAPE VEHICLE. IT TRAVELS QUICKLY ON A POINT-TO-POINT TRAJECTORY BUT IT WASN'T MADE FOR MANEUVERING.
BOTH SHIPS HAVE TOUCHED DOWN IN ARCADIA.
EMPTY! THEY CAN'T HAVE GONE FAR.
♪♫♪
THEY APPEAR TO BE LOOKING FOR ANY SURVIVORS.
COME ON. LET'S GO GET 'EM!
I ADVISE CAUTION, MISTRESS. THEY LOOK EXTREMELY DANGEROUS TO ME.
♪♫♪
YEAH, I SEE THEM. THEY LOOK DEAD.

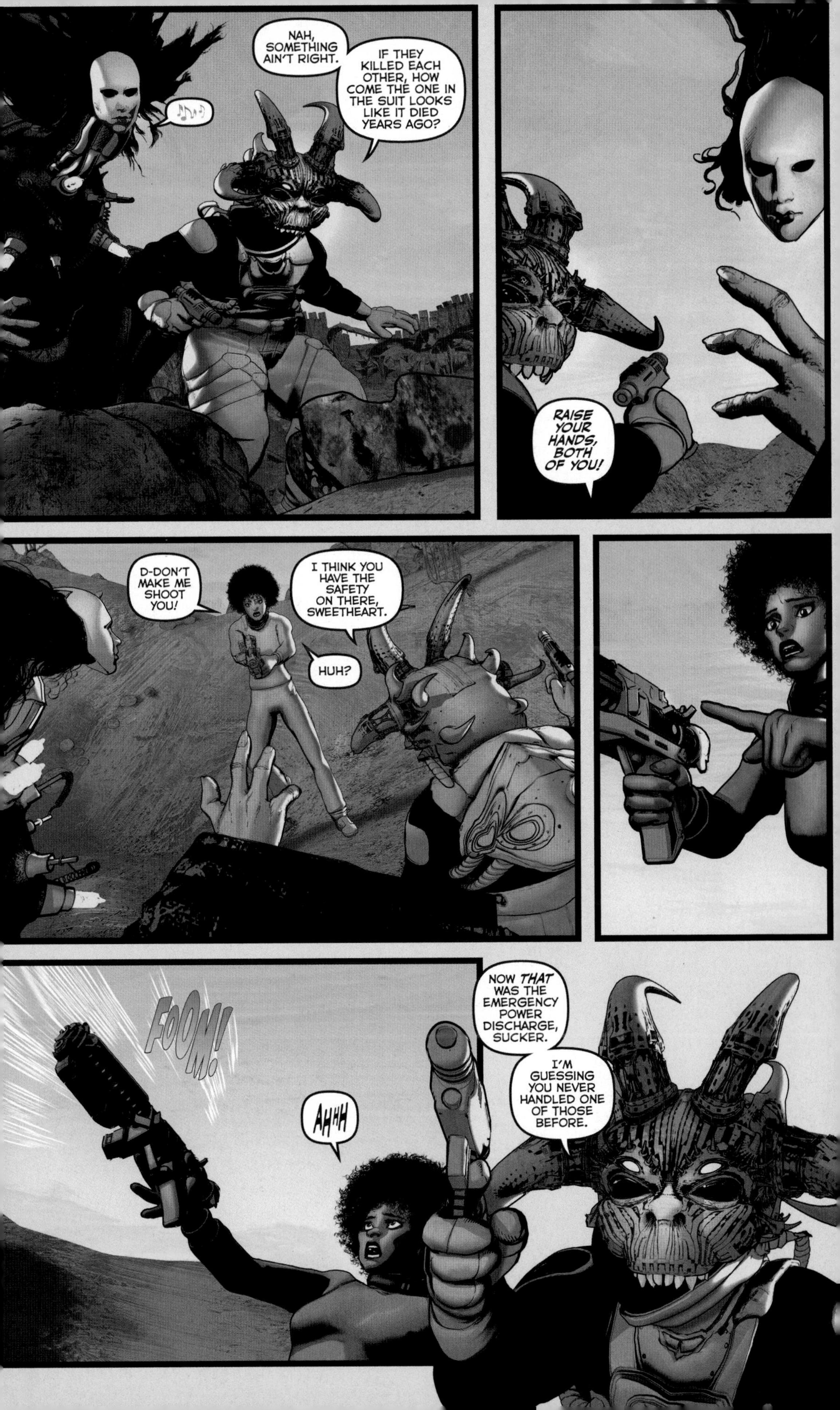
NAH, SOMETHING AIN'T RIGHT.
♫♪♪♫
IF THEY KILLED EACH OTHER, HOW COME THE ONE IN THE SUIT LOOKS LIKE IT DIED YEARS AGO?
RAISE YOUR HANDS, BOTH OF YOU!
D-DON'T MAKE ME SHOOT YOU!
I THINK YOU HAVE THE SAFETY ON THERE, SWEETHEART.
HUH?
FOOM!
AHHH
NOW *THAT* WAS THE EMERGENCY POWER DISCHARGE, SUCKER.
I'M GUESSING YOU NEVER HANDLED ONE OF THOSE BEFORE.

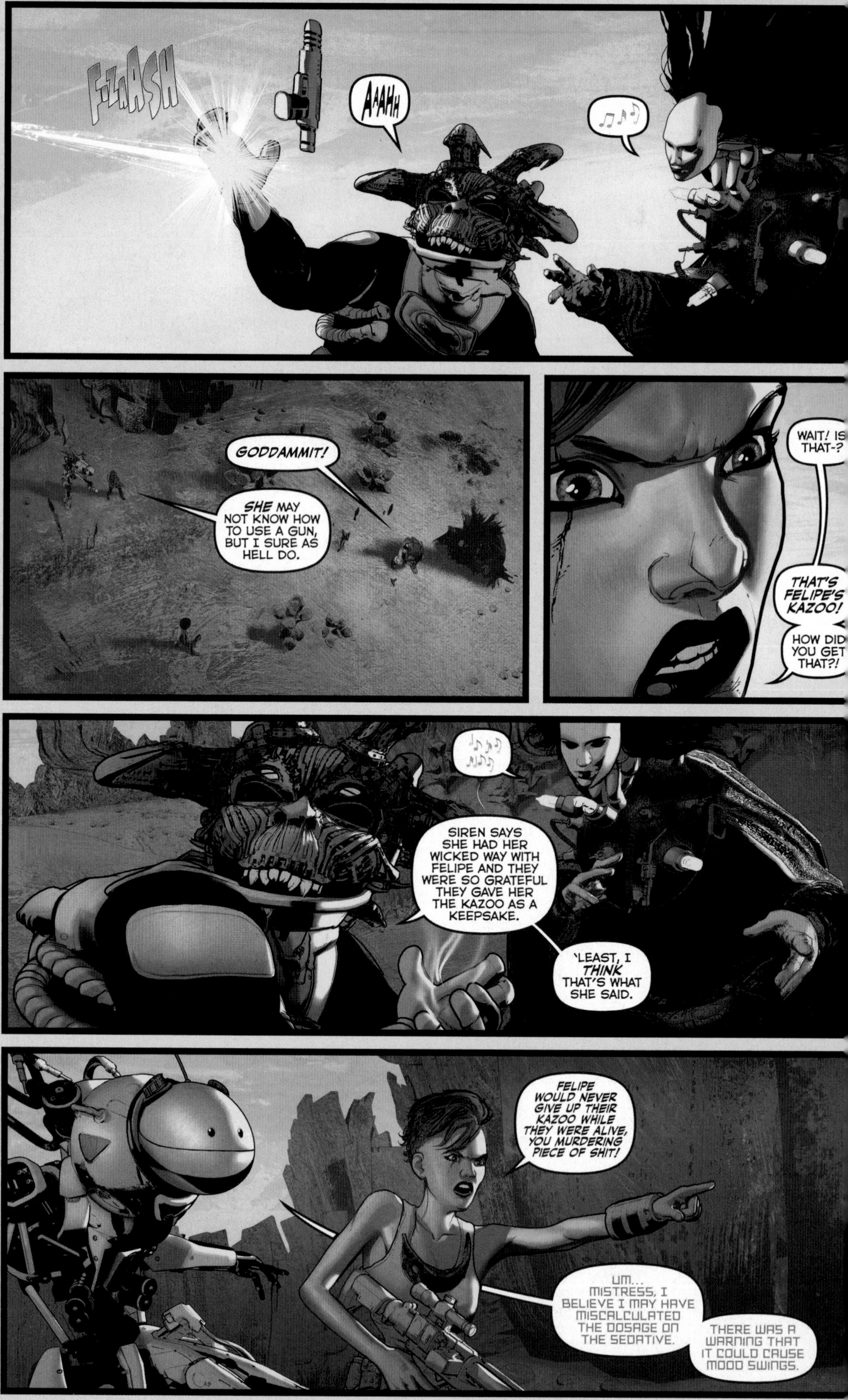
F-Z-Z-ASH
AAAHH
♫♪♪♫
GODDAMMIT!
SHE MAY NOT KNOW HOW TO USE A GUN, BUT I SURE AS HELL DO.
WAIT! IS THAT-?
THAT'S FELIPE'S KAZOO!
HOW DID YOU GET THAT?!
♪♪♪ ♪♪♪
SIREN SAYS SHE HAD HER WICKED WAY WITH FELIPE AND THEY WERE SO GRATEFUL THEY GAVE HER THE KAZOO AS A KEEPSAKE.
'LEAST, I THINK THAT'S WHAT SHE SAID.
FELIPE WOULD NEVER GIVE UP THEIR KAZOO WHILE THEY WERE ALIVE, YOU MURDERING PIECE OF SHIT!
UM... MISTRESS, I BELIEVE I MAY HAVE MISCALCULATED THE DOSAGE ON THE SEDATIVE.
THERE WAS A WARNING THAT IT COULD CAUSE MOOD SWINGS.

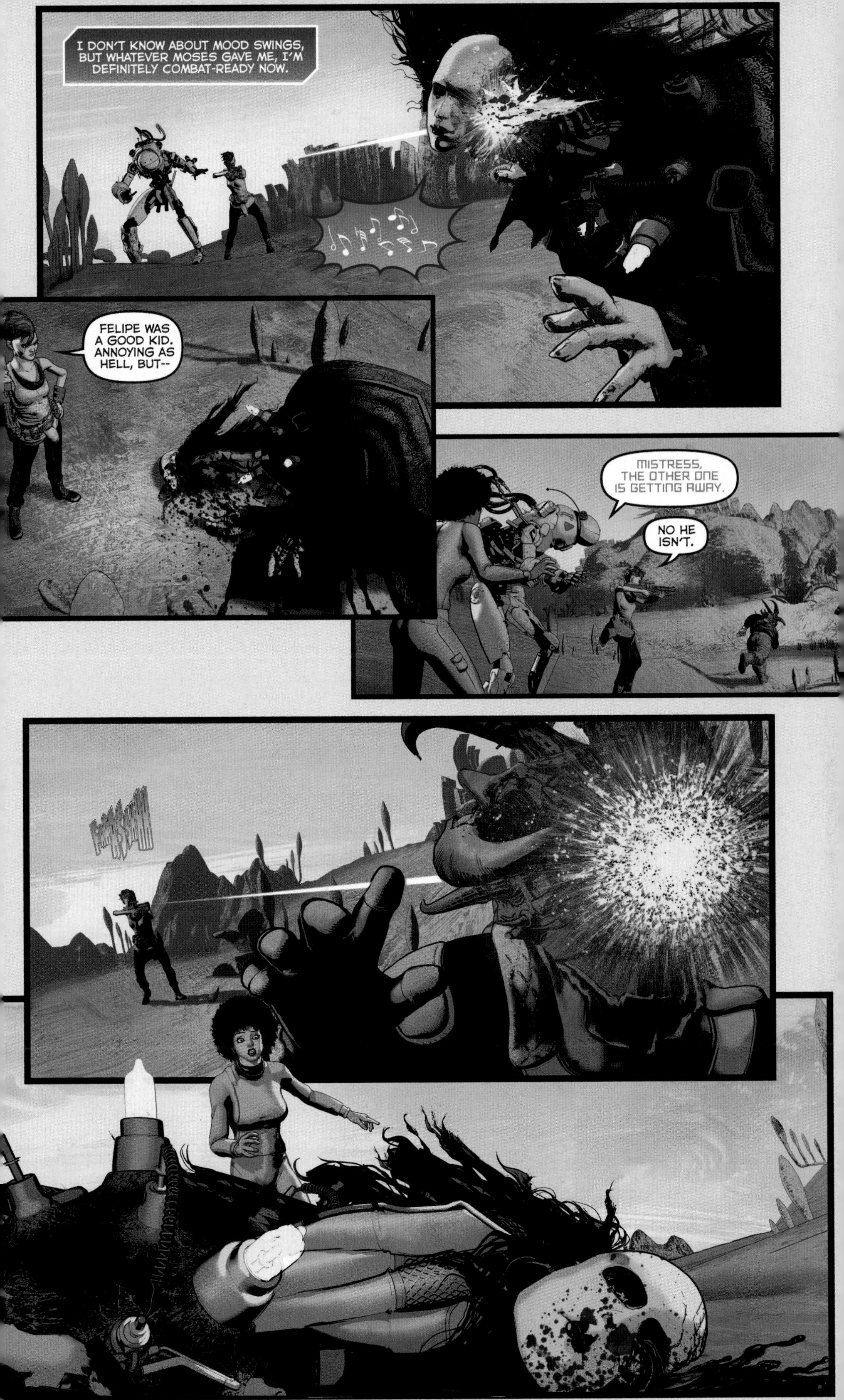
I DON'T KNOW ABOUT MOOD SWINGS, BUT WHATEVER MOSES GAVE ME, I'M DEFINITELY COMBAT-READY NOW.
FELIPE WAS A GOOD KID. ANNOYING AS HELL, BUT--
MISTRESS, THE OTHER ONE IS GETTING AWAY.
NO HE ISN'T.

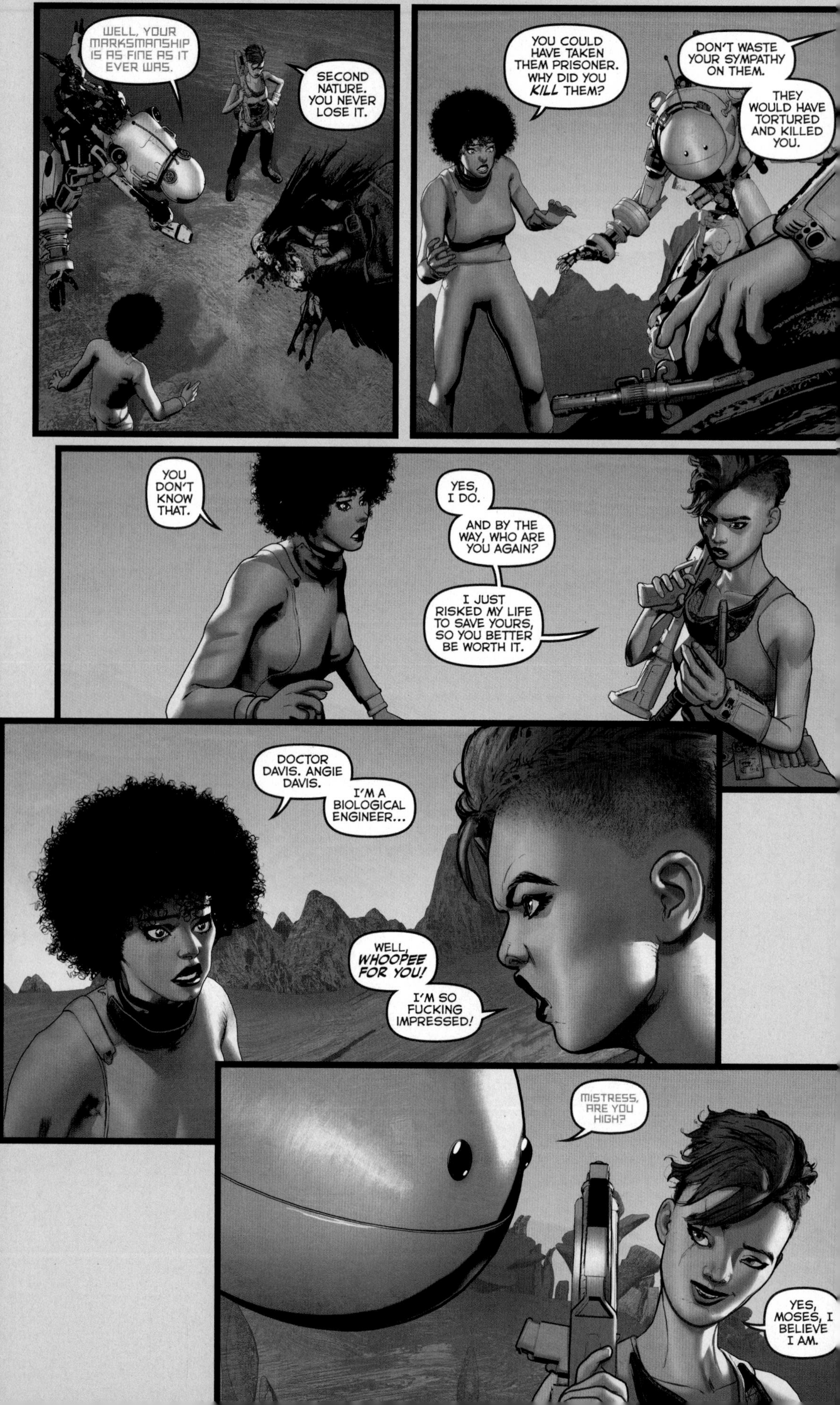
WELL, YOUR MARKSMANSHIP IS AS FINE AS IT EVER WAS.
SECOND NATURE. YOU NEVER LOSE IT.
YOU COULD HAVE TAKEN THEM PRISONER. WHY DID YOU KILL THEM?
DON'T WASTE YOUR SYMPATHY ON THEM.
THEY WOULD HAVE TORTURED AND KILLED YOU.
YOU DON'T KNOW THAT.
YES, I DO.
AND BY THE WAY, WHO ARE YOU AGAIN?
I JUST RISKED MY LIFE TO SAVE YOURS, SO YOU BETTER BE WORTH IT.
DOCTOR DAVIS. ANGIE DAVIS.
I'M A BIOLOGICAL ENGINEER...
WELL, WHOOPEE FOR YOU!
I'M SO FUCKING IMPRESSED!
MISTRESS, ARE YOU HIGH?
YES, MOSES, I BELIEVE I AM.

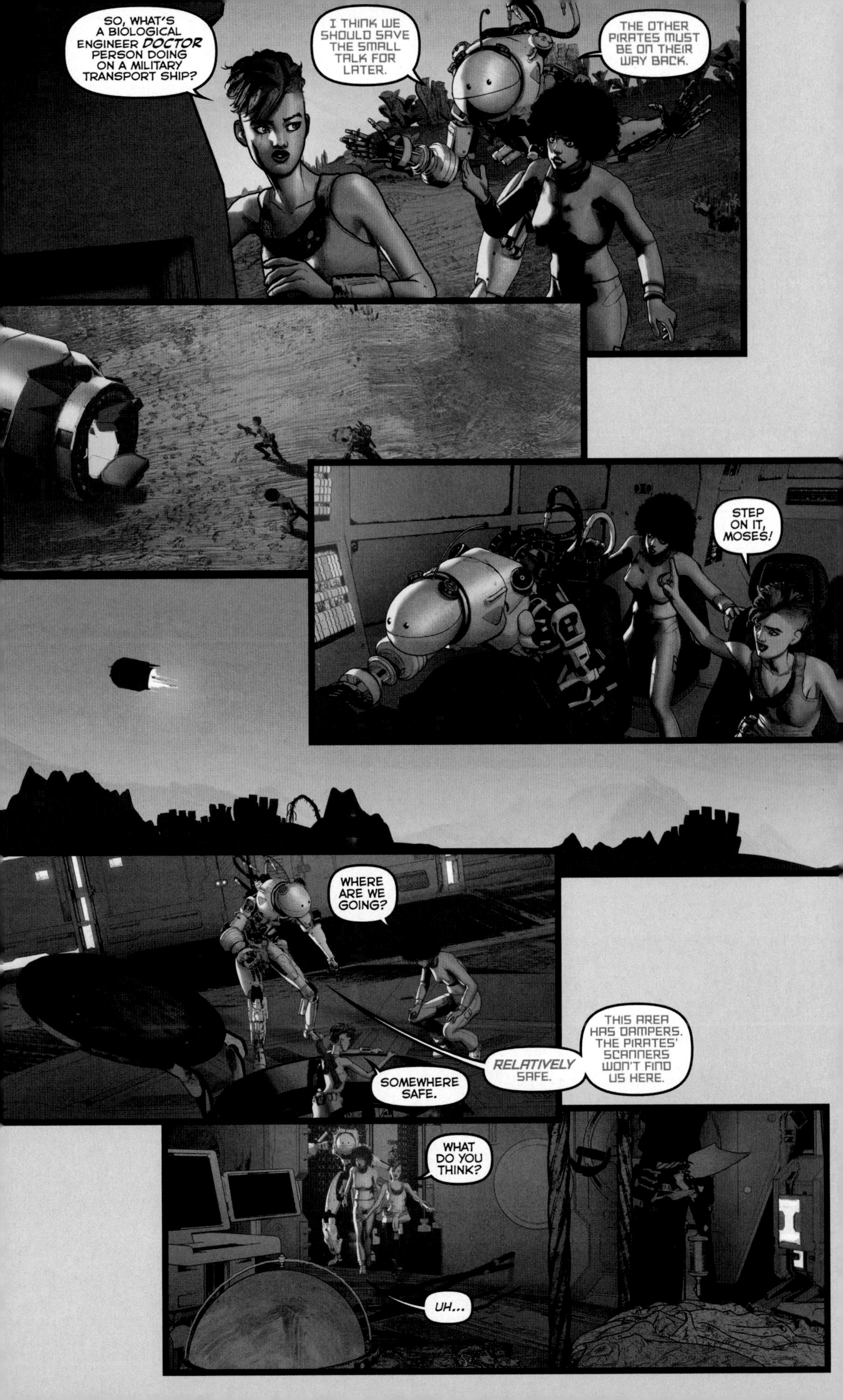
SO, WHAT'S A BIOLOGICAL ENGINEER DOCTOR PERSON DOING ON A MILITARY TRANSPORT SHIP?
I THINK WE SHOULD SAVE THE SMALL TALK FOR LATER.
THE OTHER PIRATES MUST BE ON THEIR WAY BACK.
STEP ON IT, MOSES!
WHERE ARE WE GOING?
SOMEWHERE SAFE.
RELATIVELY SAFE.
THIS AREA HAS DAMPERS. THE PIRATES' SCANNERS WON'T FIND US HERE.
WHAT DO YOU THINK?
UH...

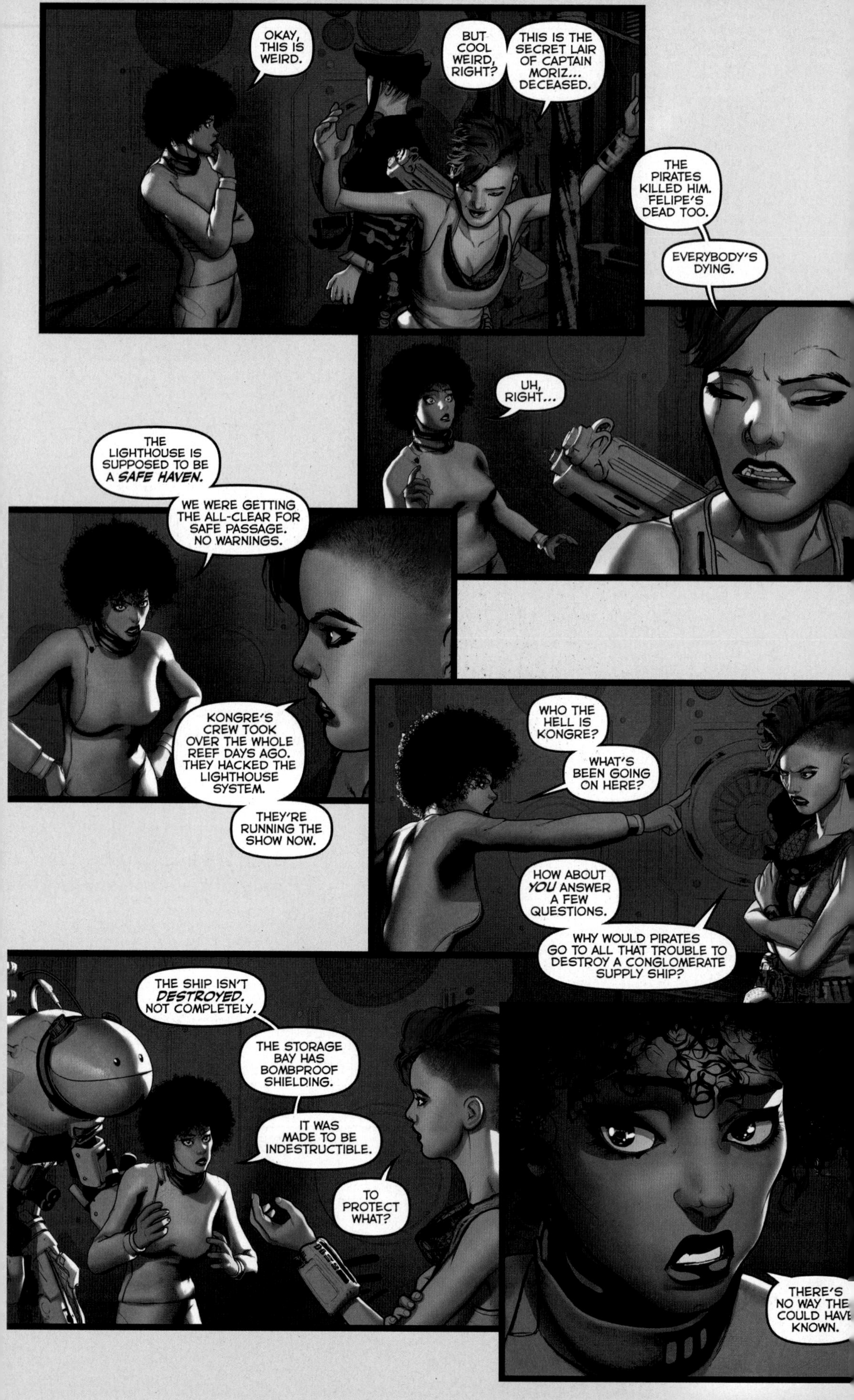
OKAY, THIS IS WEIRD.
BUT COOL WEIRD, RIGHT?
THIS IS THE SECRET LAIR OF CAPTAIN MORIZ... DECEASED.
THE PIRATES KILLED HIM. FELIPE'S DEAD TOO.
EVERYBODY'S DYING.
UH, RIGHT...
THE LIGHTHOUSE IS SUPPOSED TO BE A *SAFE HAVEN.*
WE WERE GETTING THE ALL-CLEAR FOR SAFE PASSAGE. NO WARNINGS.
KONGRE'S CREW TOOK OVER THE WHOLE REEF DAYS AGO. THEY HACKED THE LIGHTHOUSE SYSTEM.
THEY'RE RUNNING THE SHOW NOW.
WHO THE HELL IS KONGRE?
WHAT'S BEEN GOING ON HERE?
HOW ABOUT *YOU* ANSWER A FEW QUESTIONS.
WHY WOULD PIRATES GO TO ALL THAT TROUBLE TO DESTROY A CONGLOMERATE SUPPLY SHIP?
THE SHIP ISN'T *DESTROYED.* NOT COMPLETELY.
THE STORAGE BAY HAS BOMBPROOF SHIELDING.
IT WAS MADE TO BE INDESTRUCTIBLE.
TO PROTECT WHAT?
THERE'S NO WAY THE COULD HAVE KNOWN.

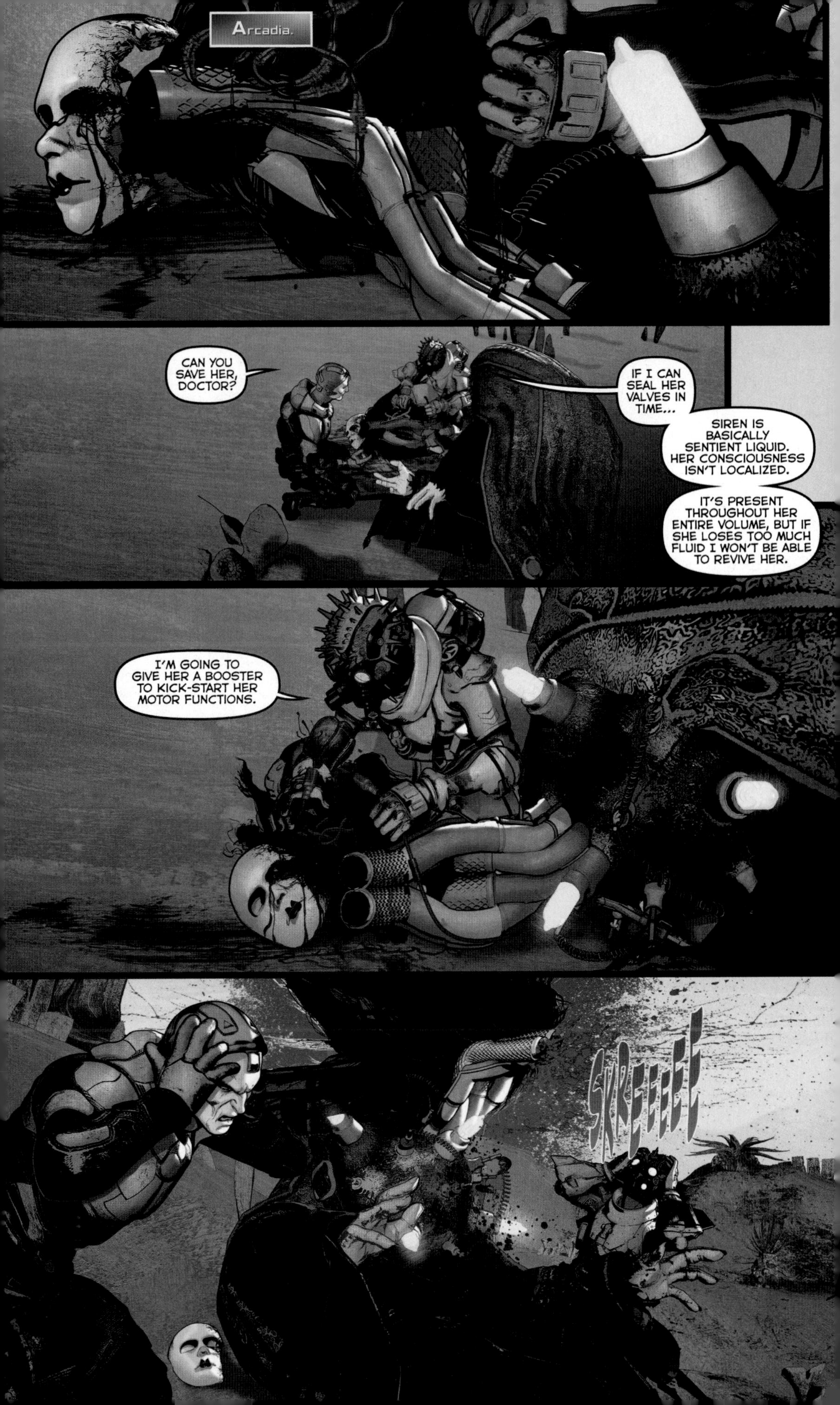
Arcadia.
CAN YOU SAVE HER, DOCTOR?
IF I CAN SEAL HER VALVES IN TIME...
SIREN IS BASICALLY SENTIENT LIQUID. HER CONSCIOUSNESS ISN'T LOCALIZED.
IT'S PRESENT THROUGHOUT HER ENTIRE VOLUME, BUT IF SHE LOSES TOO MUCH FLUID I WON'T BE ABLE TO REVIVE HER.
I'M GOING TO GIVE HER A BOOSTER TO KICK-START HER MOTOR FUNCTIONS.
SKREEEEE

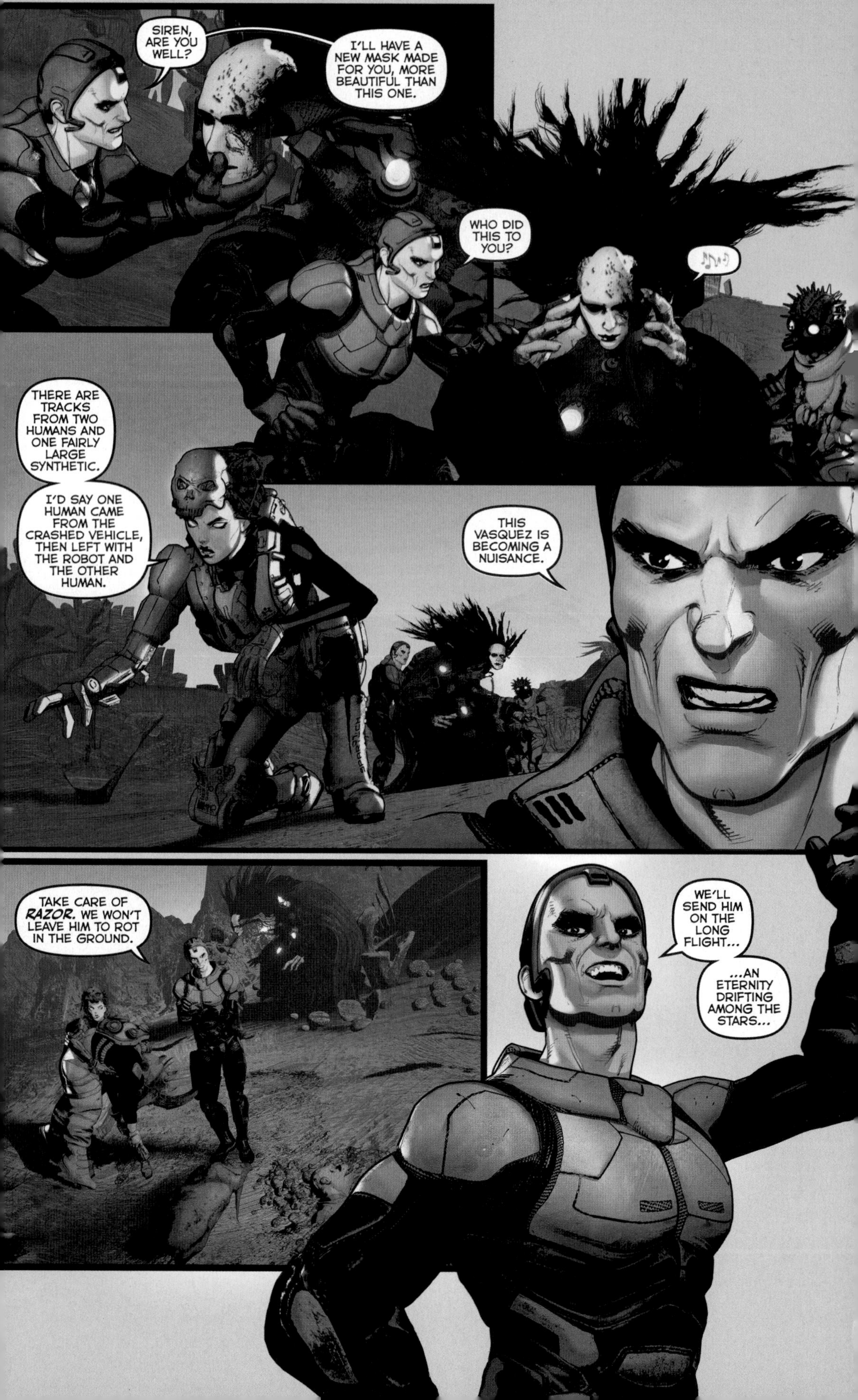

SIREN, ARE YOU WELL?
I'LL HAVE A NEW MASK MADE FOR YOU, MORE BEAUTIFUL THAN THIS ONE.
WHO DID THIS TO YOU?
THERE ARE TRACKS FROM TWO HUMANS AND ONE FAIRLY LARGE SYNTHETIC.
I'D SAY ONE HUMAN CAME FROM THE CRASHED VEHICLE, THEN LEFT WITH THE ROBOT AND THE OTHER HUMAN.
THIS VASQUEZ IS BECOMING A NUISANCE.
TAKE CARE OF ***RAZOR.*** WE WON'T LEAVE HIM TO ROT IN THE GROUND.
WE'LL SEND HIM ON THE LONG FLIGHT...
...AN ETERNITY DRIFTING AMONG THE STARS...

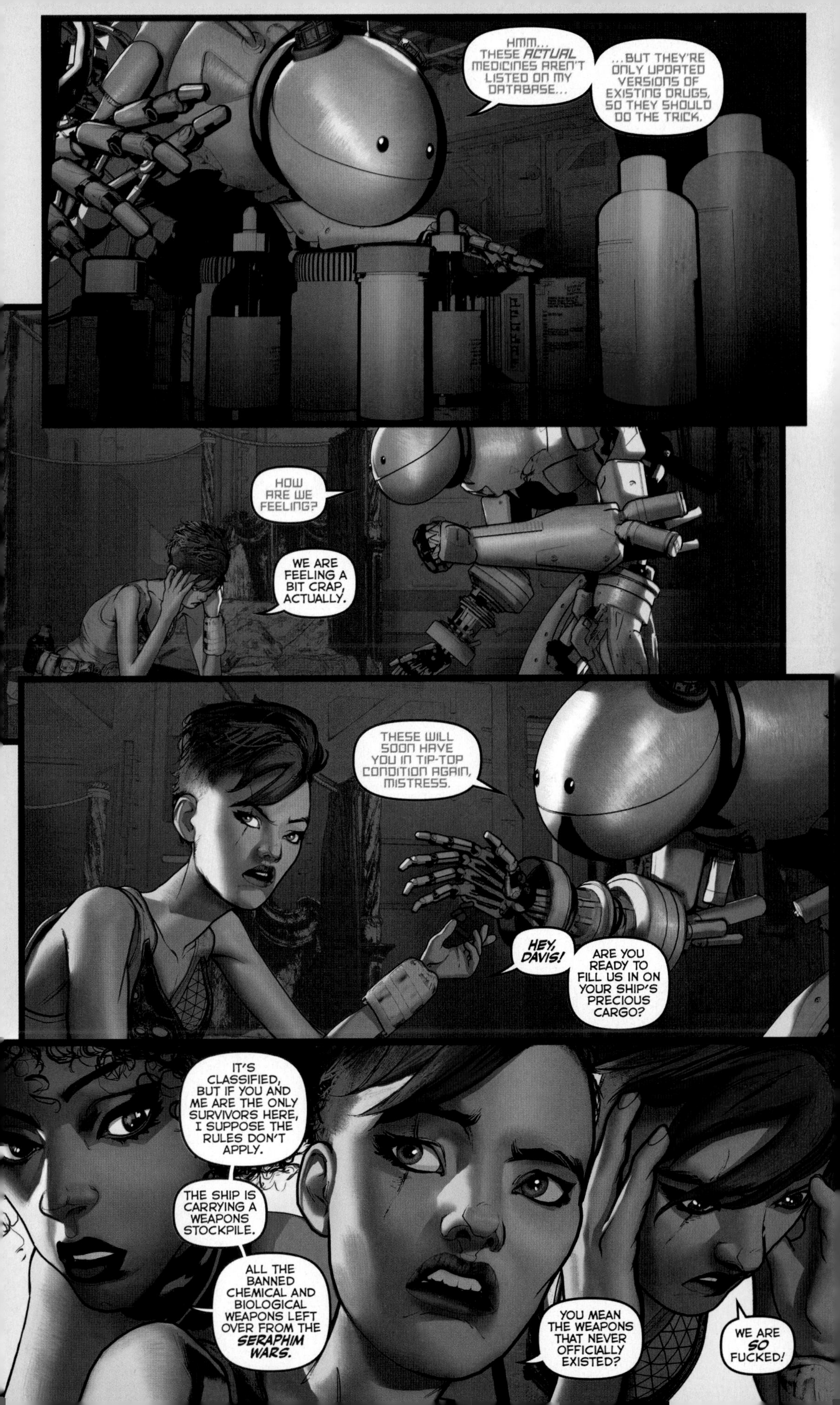
HMM... THESE ACTUAL MEDICINES AREN'T LISTED ON MY DATABASE...
...BUT THEY'RE ONLY UPDATED VERSIONS OF EXISTING DRUGS, SO THEY SHOULD DO THE TRICK.
HOW ARE WE FEELING?
WE ARE FEELING A BIT CRAP, ACTUALLY.
THESE WILL SOON HAVE YOU IN TIP-TOP CONDITION AGAIN, MISTRESS.
HEY, DAVIS!
ARE YOU READY TO FILL US IN ON YOUR SHIP'S PRECIOUS CARGO?
IT'S CLASSIFIED, BUT IF YOU AND ME ARE THE ONLY SURVIVORS HERE, I SUPPOSE THE RULES DON'T APPLY.
THE SHIP IS CARRYING A WEAPONS STOCKPILE.
ALL THE BANNED CHEMICAL AND BIOLOGICAL WEAPONS LEFT OVER FROM THE SERAPHIM WARS.
YOU MEAN THE WEAPONS THAT NEVER OFFICIALLY EXISTED?
WE ARE SO FUCKED!

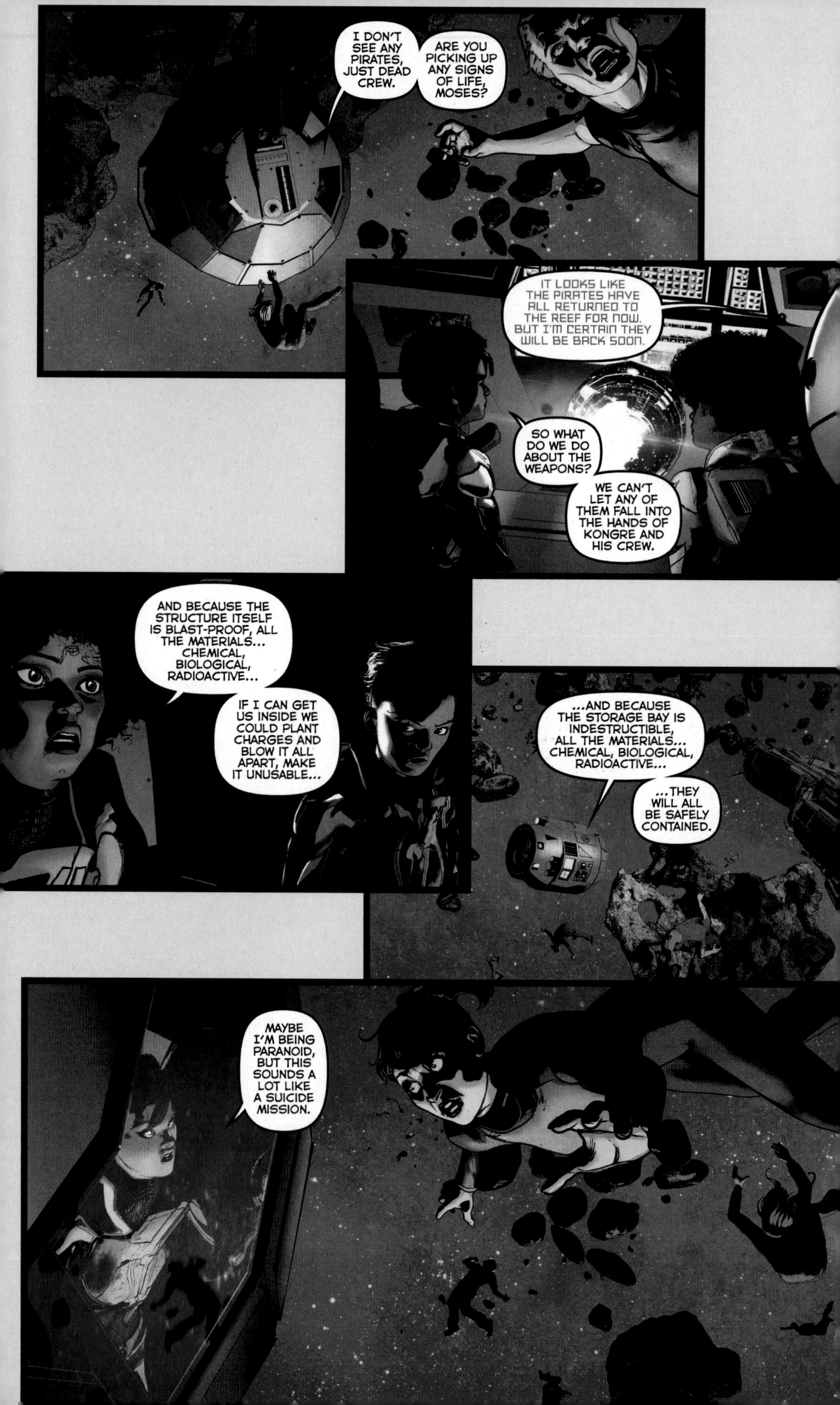

I DON'T SEE ANY PIRATES, JUST DEAD CREW.
ARE YOU PICKING UP ANY SIGNS OF LIFE, MOSES?
IT LOOKS LIKE THE PIRATES HAVE ALL RETURNED TO THE REEF FOR NOW. BUT I'M CERTAIN THEY WILL BE BACK SOON.
SO WHAT DO WE DO ABOUT THE WEAPONS?
WE CAN'T LET ANY OF THEM FALL INTO THE HANDS OF KONGRE AND HIS CREW.
AND BECAUSE THE STRUCTURE ITSELF IS BLAST-PROOF, ALL THE MATERIALS... CHEMICAL, BIOLOGICAL, RADIOACTIVE...
IF I CAN GET US INSIDE WE COULD PLANT CHARGES AND BLOW IT ALL APART, MAKE IT UNUSABLE...
...AND BECAUSE THE STORAGE BAY IS INDESTRUCTIBLE, ALL THE MATERIALS... CHEMICAL, BIOLOGICAL, RADIOACTIVE...
...THEY WILL ALL BE SAFELY CONTAINED.
MAYBE I'M BEING PARANOID, BUT THIS SOUNDS A LOT LIKE A SUICIDE MISSION.

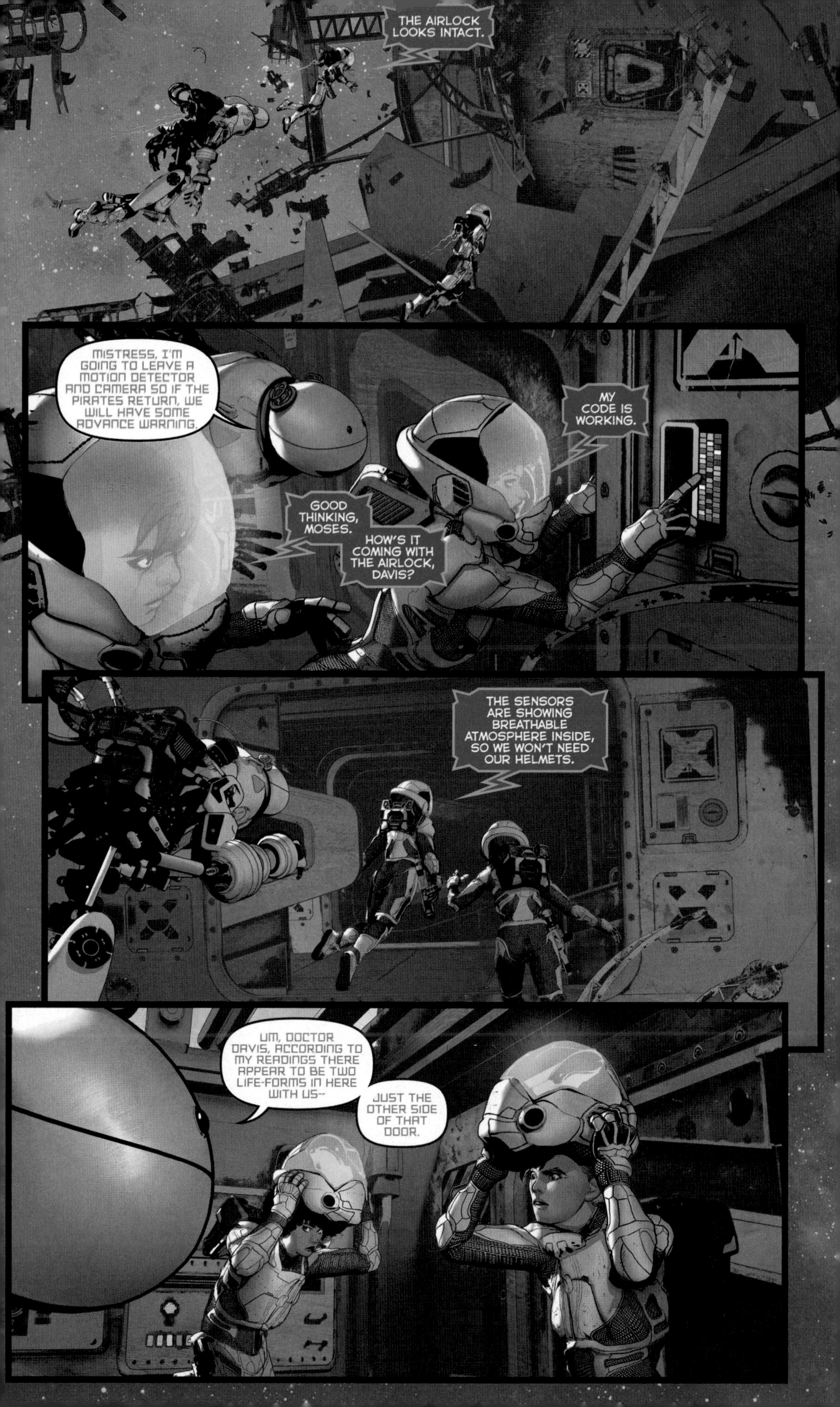
THE AIRLOCK LOOKS INTACT.
MISTRESS, I'M GOING TO LEAVE A MOTION DETECTOR AND CAMERA SO IF THE PIRATES RETURN, WE WILL HAVE SOME ADVANCE WARNING.
MY CODE IS WORKING.
GOOD THINKING, MOSES.
HOW'S IT COMING WITH THE AIRLOCK, DAVIS?
THE SENSORS ARE SHOWING BREATHABLE ATMOSPHERE INSIDE, SO WE WON'T NEED OUR HELMETS.
UM, DOCTOR DAVIS, ACCORDING TO MY READINGS THERE APPEAR TO BE TWO LIFE-FORMS IN HERE WITH US--
JUST THE OTHER SIDE OF THAT DOOR.

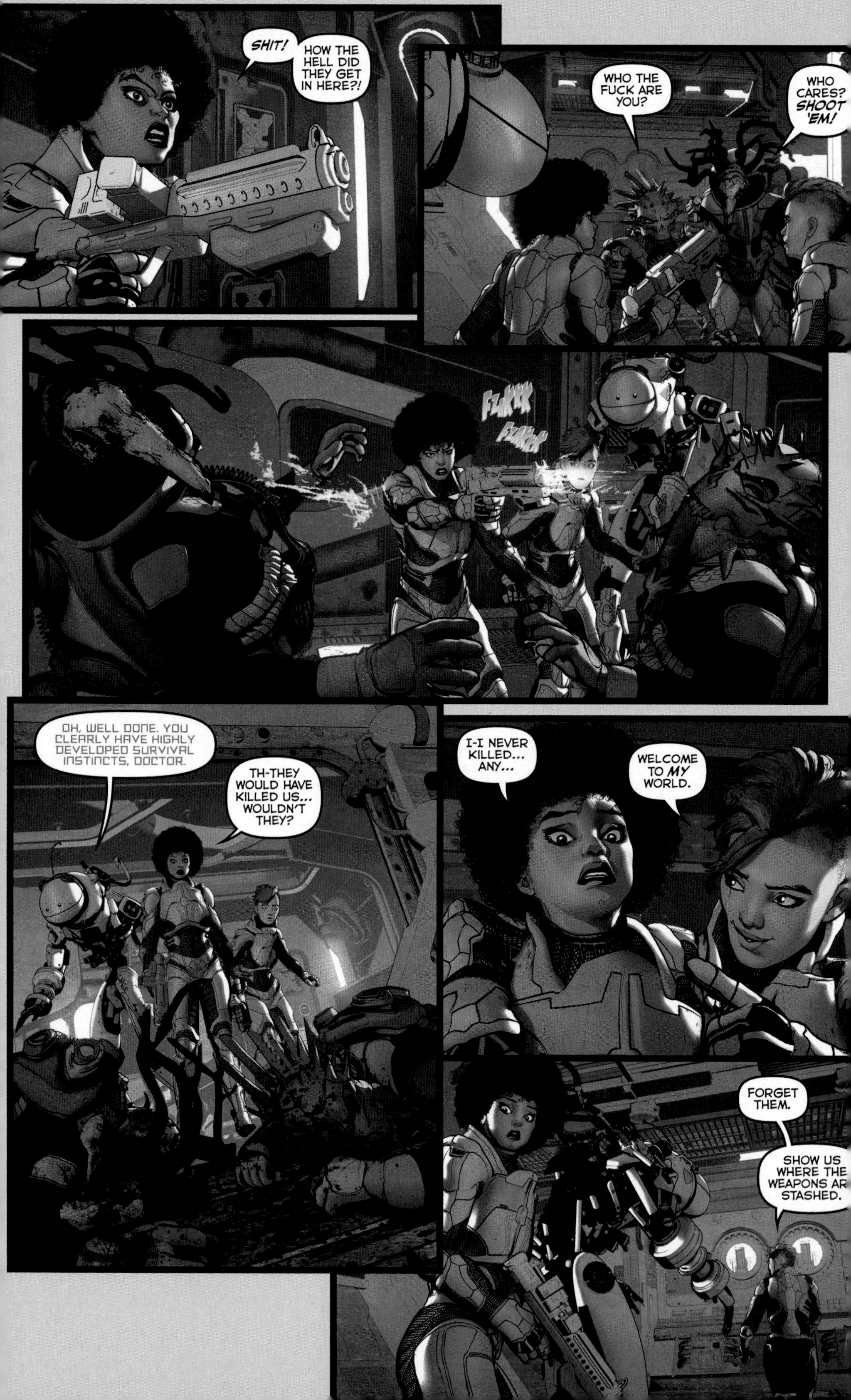
SHIT!
HOW THE HELL DID THEY GET IN HERE?!
WHO THE FUCK ARE YOU?
WHO CARES? SHOOT 'EM!
FZAKKK
FZAKKK
OH, WELL DONE. YOU CLEARLY HAVE HIGHLY DEVELOPED SURVIVAL INSTINCTS, DOCTOR.
TH-THEY WOULD HAVE KILLED US... WOULDN'T THEY?
I-I NEVER KILLED... ANY...
WELCOME TO MY WORLD.
FORGET THEM.
SHOW US WHERE THE WEAPONS AR STASHED.

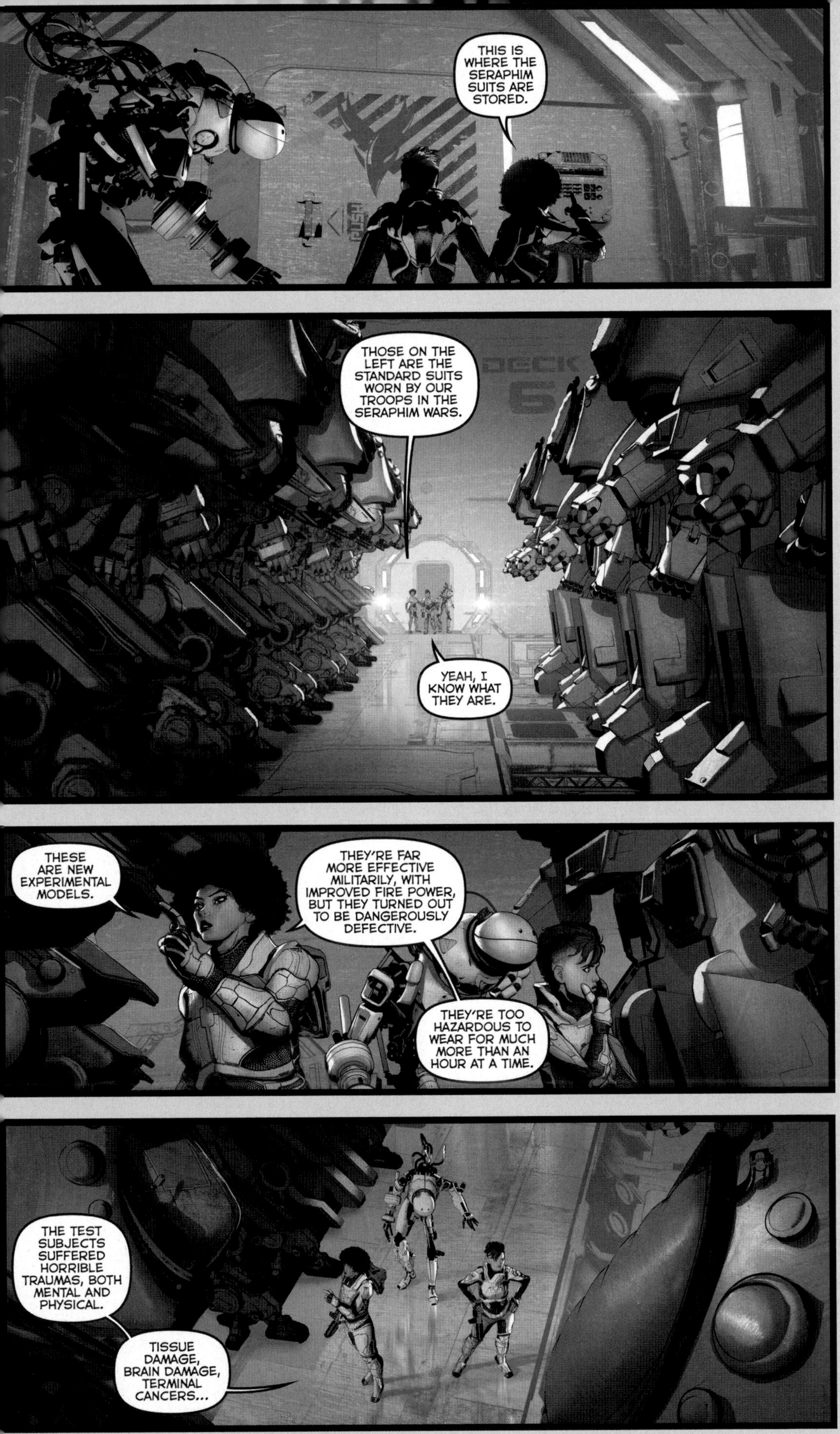
THIS IS WHERE THE SERAPHIM SUITS ARE STORED.
THOSE ON THE LEFT ARE THE STANDARD SUITS WORN BY OUR TROOPS IN THE SERAPHIM WARS.
DECK 6
YEAH, I KNOW WHAT THEY ARE.
THESE ARE NEW EXPERIMENTAL MODELS.
THEY'RE FAR MORE EFFECTIVE MILITARILY, WITH IMPROVED FIRE POWER, BUT THEY TURNED OUT TO BE DANGEROUSLY DEFECTIVE.
THEY'RE TOO HAZARDOUS TO WEAR FOR MUCH MORE THAN AN HOUR AT A TIME.
THE TEST SUBJECTS SUFFERED HORRIBLE TRAUMAS, BOTH MENTAL AND PHYSICAL.
TISSUE DAMAGE, BRAIN DAMAGE, TERMINAL CANCERS...

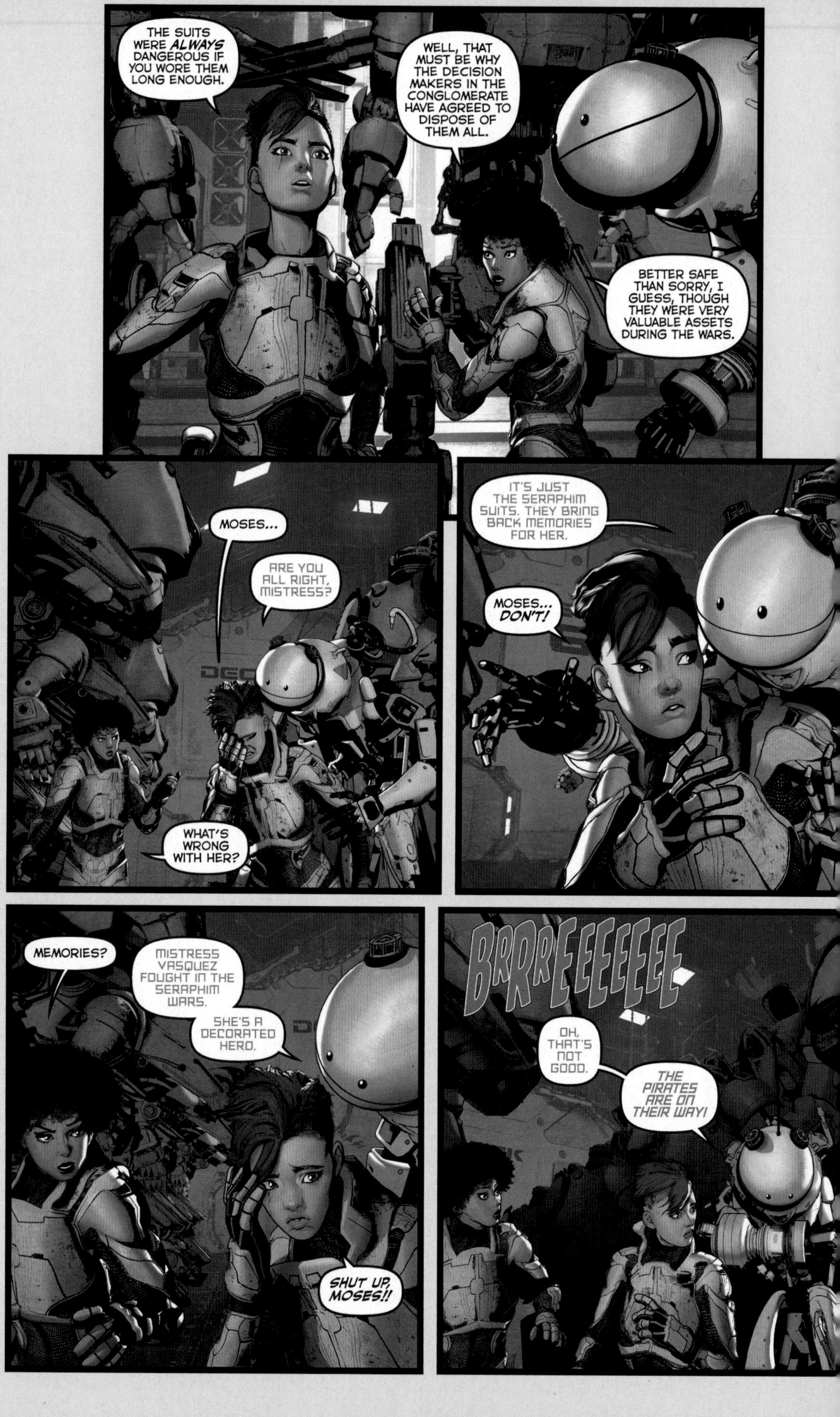

THE SUITS WERE ALWAYS DANGEROUS IF YOU WORE THEM LONG ENOUGH.
WELL, THAT MUST BE WHY THE DECISION MAKERS IN THE CONGLOMERATE HAVE AGREED TO DISPOSE OF THEM ALL.
BETTER SAFE THAN SORRY, I GUESS, THOUGH THEY WERE VERY VALUABLE ASSETS DURING THE WARS.
MOSES...
ARE YOU ALL RIGHT, MISTRESS?
WHAT'S WRONG WITH HER?
IT'S JUST THE SERAPHIM SUITS. THEY BRING BACK MEMORIES FOR HER.
MOSES... DON'T!
MEMORIES?
MISTRESS VASQUEZ FOUGHT IN THE SERAPHIM WARS.
SHE'S A DECORATED HERO.
SHUT UP, MOSES!!
BRRREEEEEEE
OH, THAT'S NOT GOOD.
THE PIRATES ARE ON THEIR WAY!

AIRLOCK 3
HOW CLOSE ARE THEY?
TOO CLOSE. WE WON'T MAKE IT TO OUR VESSEL IN TIME.
THERE'S NOWHERE TO HIDE IN HERE. THEY'LL PICK UP OUR LIFE SIGNS, JUST LIKE WE DID THE TWO PIRATES. WE'RE SCREWED.
OKAY, I HAVE AN IDEA. THE ESCAPE POD IS OUT OF SIGHT, SO THE PIRATES WON'T SPOT IT.
"HOW GOOD ARE YOU AT PLAYING DEAD?"

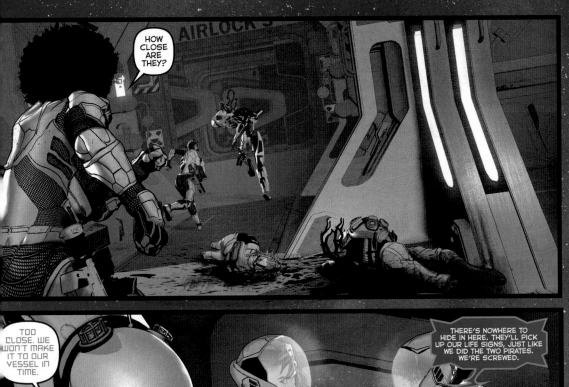

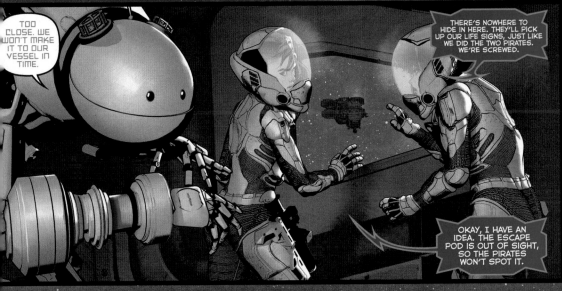

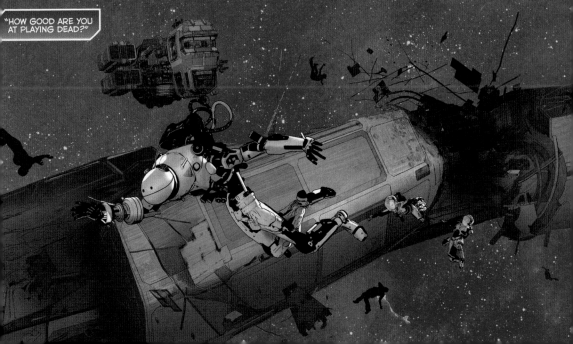

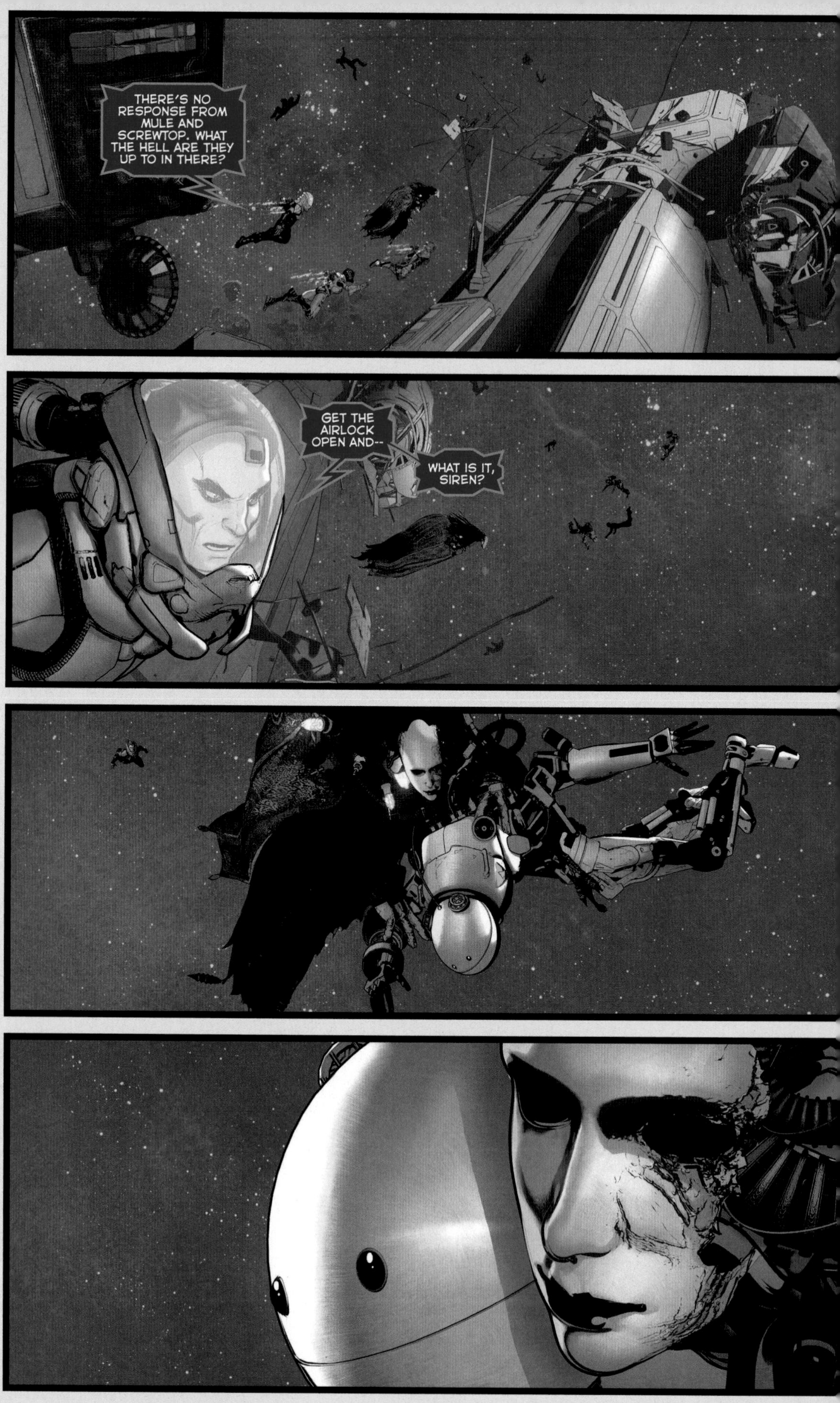
THERE'S NO RESPONSE FROM MULE AND SCREWTOP. WHAT THE HELL ARE THEY UP TO IN THERE?
GET THE AIRLOCK OPEN AND--
WHAT IS IT, SIREN?

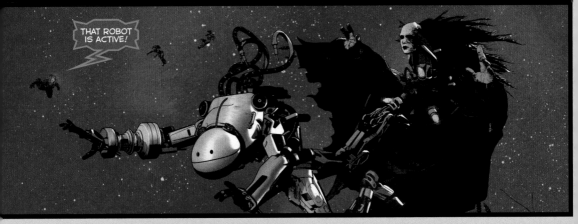

THAT ROBOT IS ACTIVE!

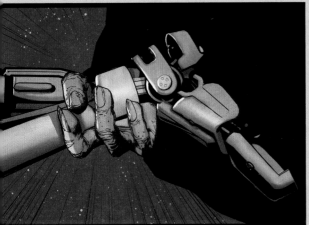

ALL RIGHT, SIREN, I'VE GOT THIS.

GET THAT HEAP OF JUNK INSIDE.

IF THAT'S THE ROBOT FROM THE LIGHTHOUSE, THERE MUST BE OTHERS.

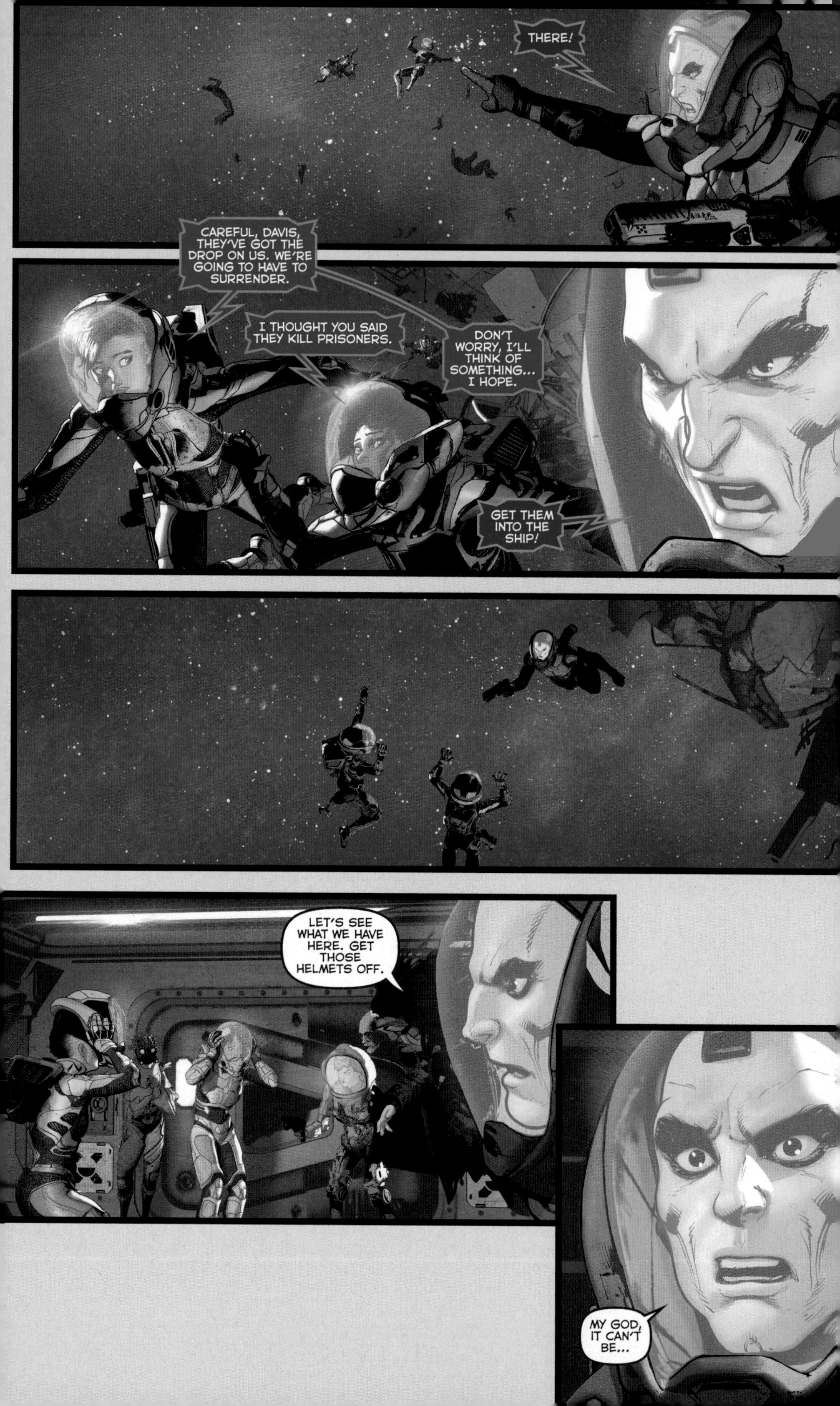
THERE!
CAREFUL, DAVIS, THEY'VE GOT THE DROP ON US. WE'RE GOING TO HAVE TO SURRENDER.
I THOUGHT YOU SAID THEY KILL PRISONERS.
DON'T WORRY, I'LL THINK OF SOMETHING... I HOPE.
GET THEM INTO THE SHIP!
LET'S SEE WHAT WE HAVE HERE. GET THOSE HELMETS OFF.
MY GOD, IT CAN'T BE...

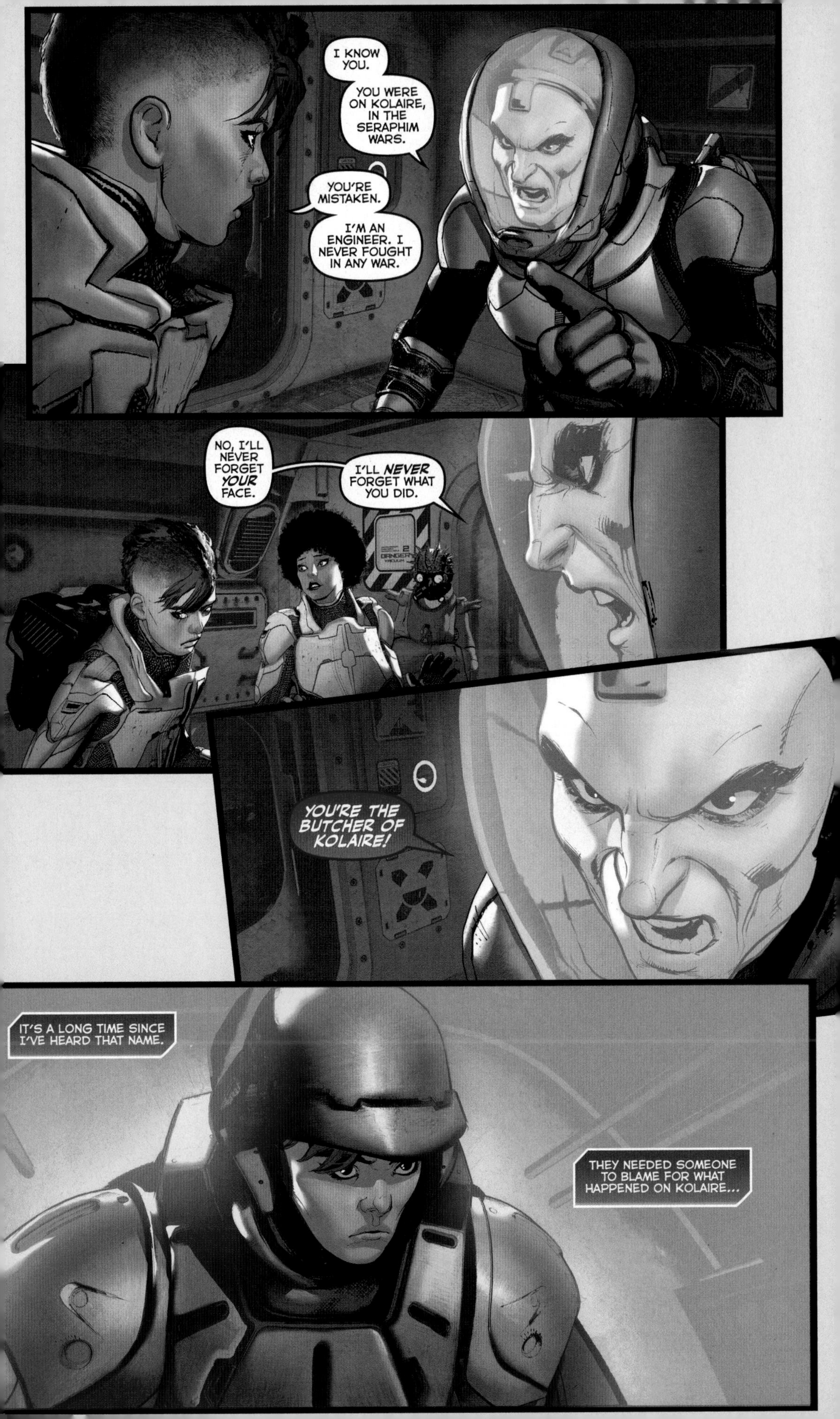
I KNOW YOU.
YOU WERE ON KOLAIRE, IN THE SERAPHIM WARS.
YOU'RE MISTAKEN.
I'M AN ENGINEER. I NEVER FOUGHT IN ANY WAR.
NO, I'LL NEVER FORGET YOUR FACE.
I'LL NEVER FORGET WHAT YOU DID.
DANGER
VACUUM
YOU'RE THE BUTCHER OF KOLAIRE!
IT'S A LONG TIME SINCE I'VE HEARD THAT NAME.
THEY NEEDED SOMEONE TO BLAME FOR WHAT HAPPENED ON KOLAIRE...

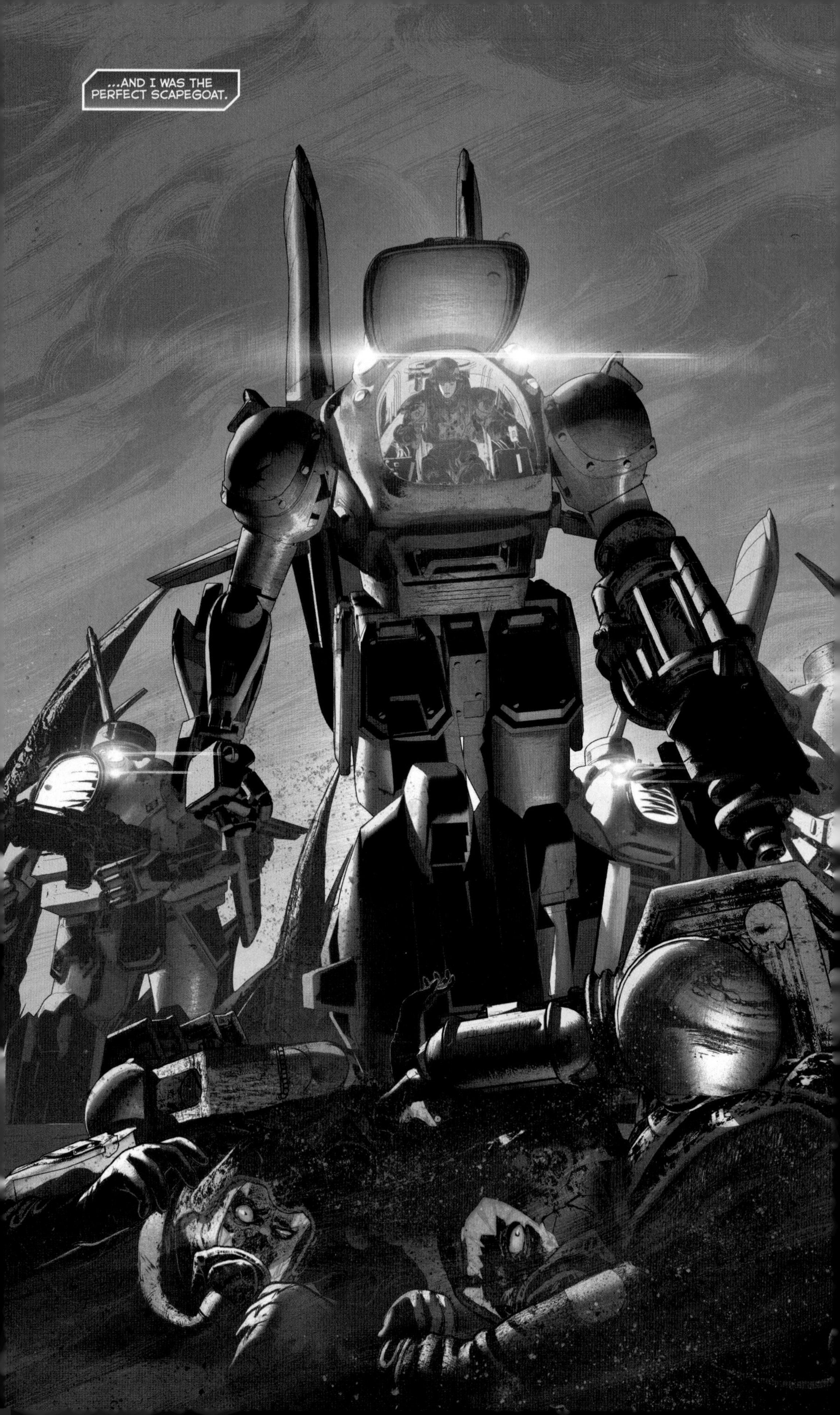
...AND I WAS THE PERFECT SCAPEGOAT.

Issue #3 Cover A

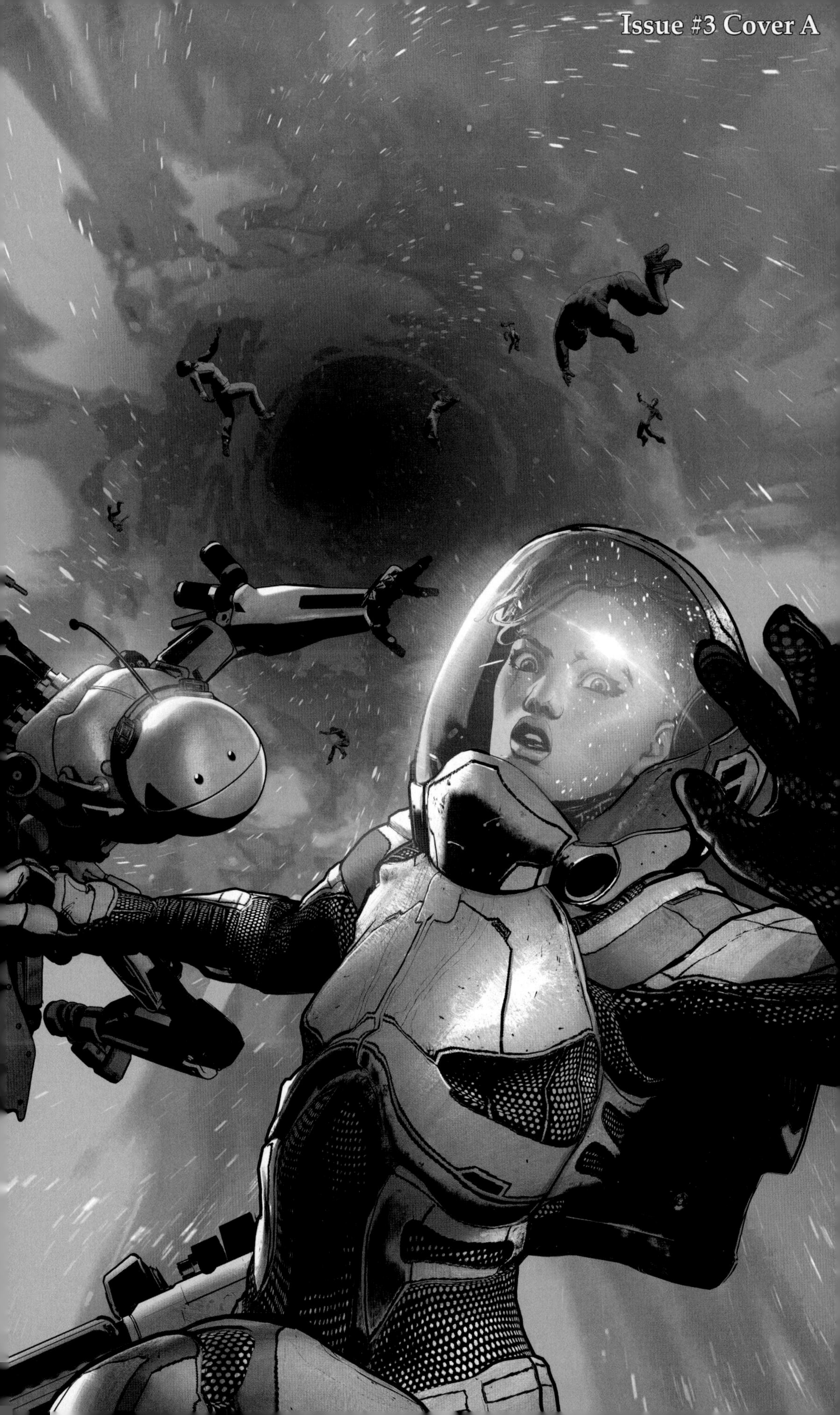

Issue #3 Cover B

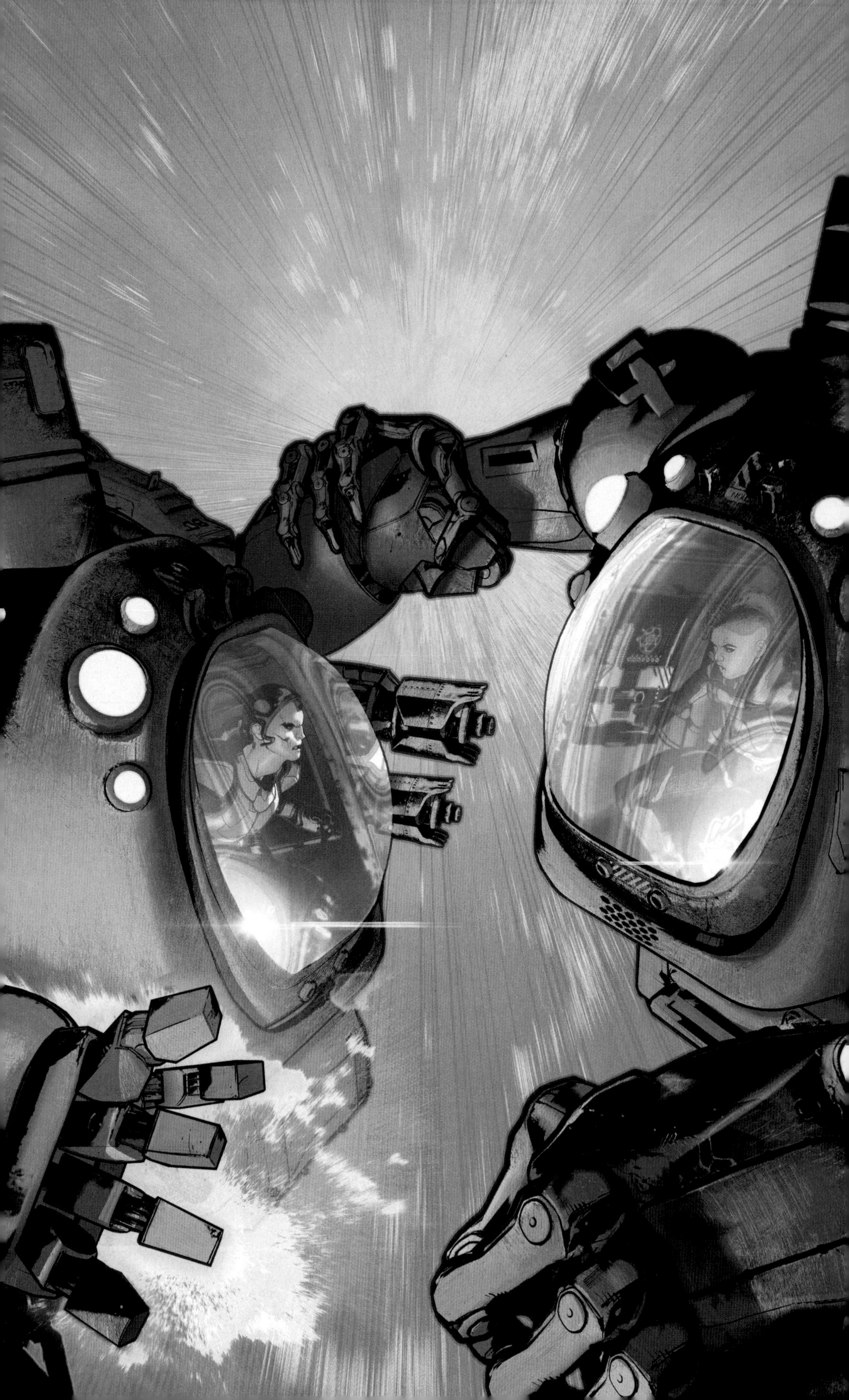

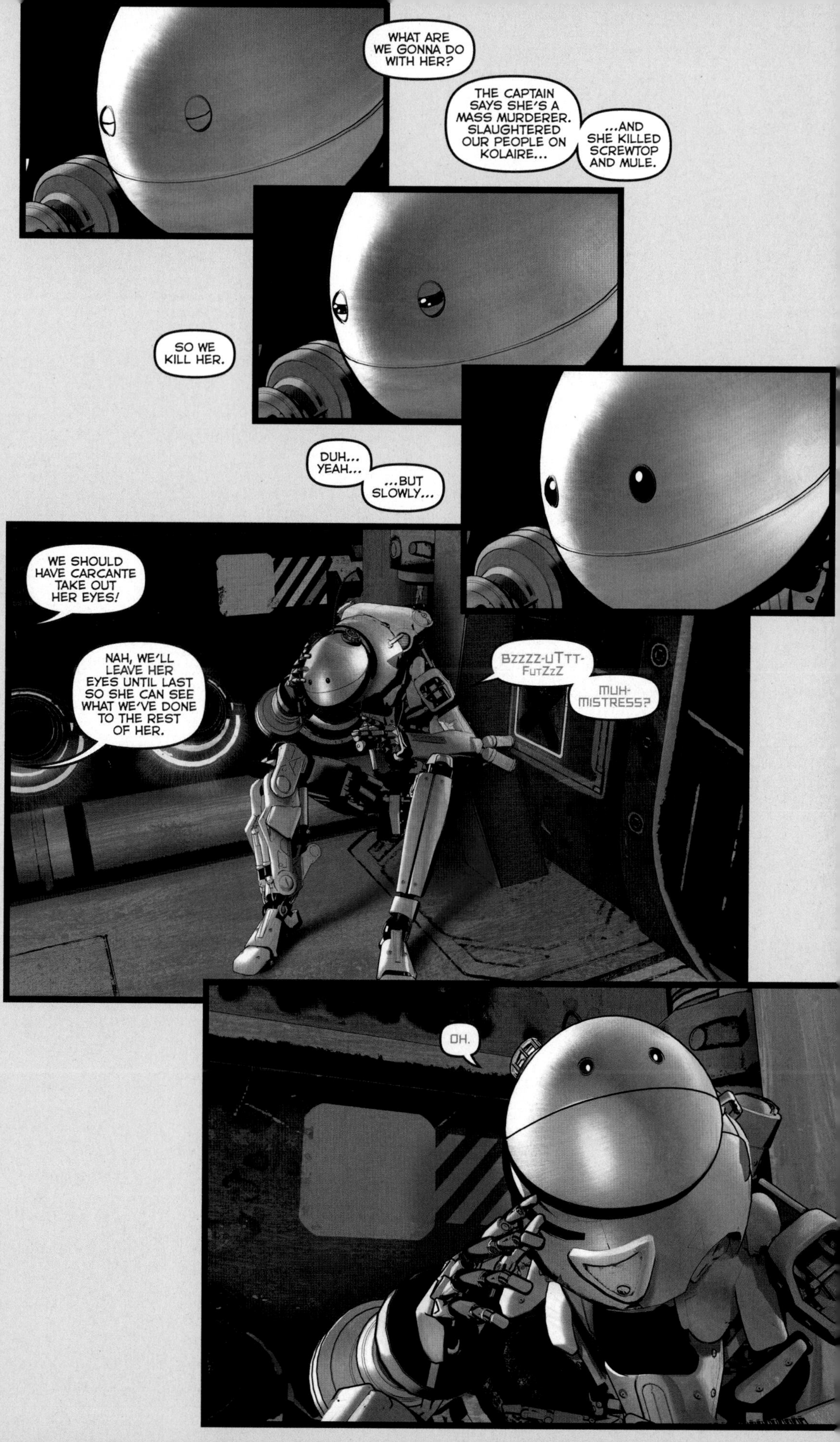
WHAT ARE WE GONNA DO WITH HER?
THE CAPTAIN SAYS SHE'S A MASS MURDERER. SLAUGHTERED OUR PEOPLE ON KOLAIRE...
...AND SHE KILLED SCREWTOP AND MULE.
SO WE KILL HER.
DUH... YEAH...
...BUT SLOWLY...
WE SHOULD HAVE CARCANTE TAKE OUT HER EYES!
NAH, WE'LL LEAVE HER EYES UNTIL LAST SO SHE CAN SEE WHAT WE'VE DONE TO THE REST OF HER.
BZZZZ-UTTT-FUTZZZ
MUH-MISTRESS?
OH.

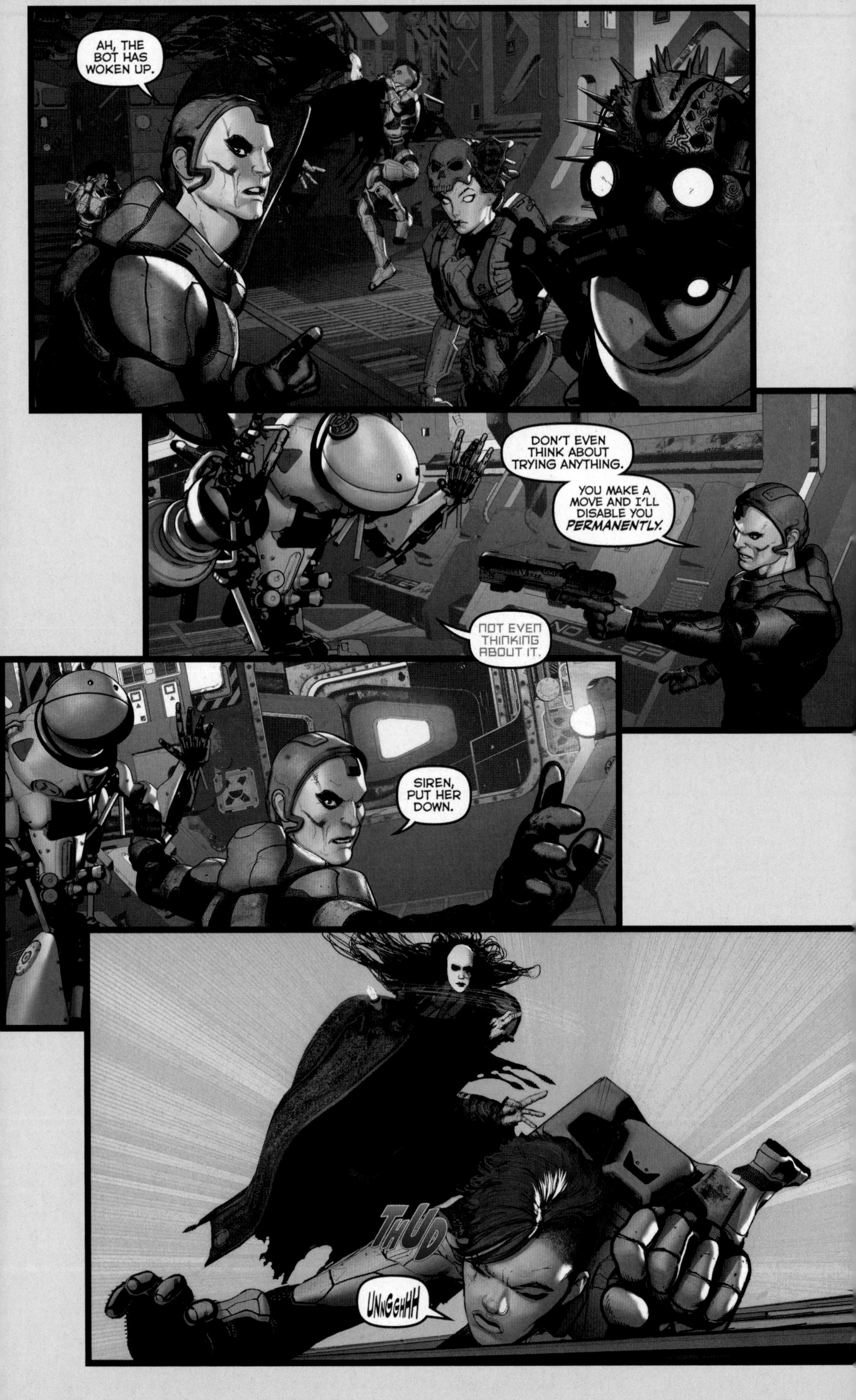
AH, THE BOT HAS WOKEN UP.
DON'T EVEN THINK ABOUT TRYING ANYTHING.
YOU MAKE A MOVE AND I'LL DISABLE YOU *PERMANENTLY.*
NOT EVEN THINKING ABOUT IT.
SIREN, PUT HER DOWN.
THUD
UNNGGHHH

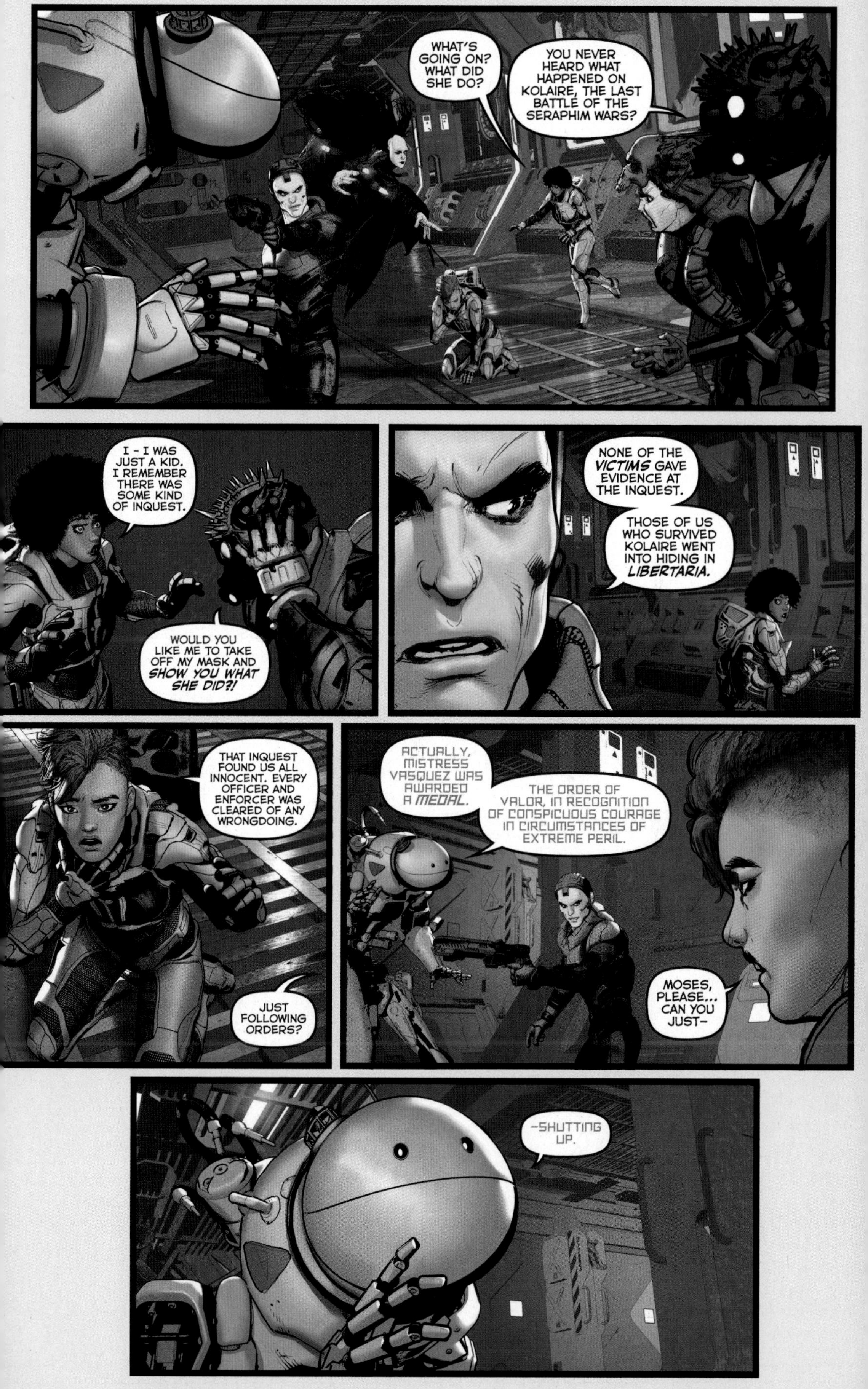
WHAT'S GOING ON? WHAT DID SHE DO?
YOU NEVER HEARD WHAT HAPPENED ON KOLAIRE, THE LAST BATTLE OF THE SERAPHIM WARS?
I - I WAS JUST A KID. I REMEMBER THERE WAS SOME KIND OF INQUEST.
WOULD YOU LIKE ME TO TAKE OFF MY MASK AND SHOW YOU WHAT SHE DID?!
NONE OF THE VICTIMS GAVE EVIDENCE AT THE INQUEST.
THOSE OF US WHO SURVIVED KOLAIRE WENT INTO HIDING IN LIBERTARIA.
THAT INQUEST FOUND US ALL INNOCENT. EVERY OFFICER AND ENFORCER WAS CLEARED OF ANY WRONGDOING.
JUST FOLLOWING ORDERS?
ACTUALLY, MISTRESS VASQUEZ WAS AWARDED A MEDAL.
THE ORDER OF VALOR, IN RECOGNITION OF CONSPICUOUS COURAGE IN CIRCUMSTANCES OF EXTREME PERIL.
MOSES, PLEASE... CAN YOU JUST-
-SHUTTING UP.

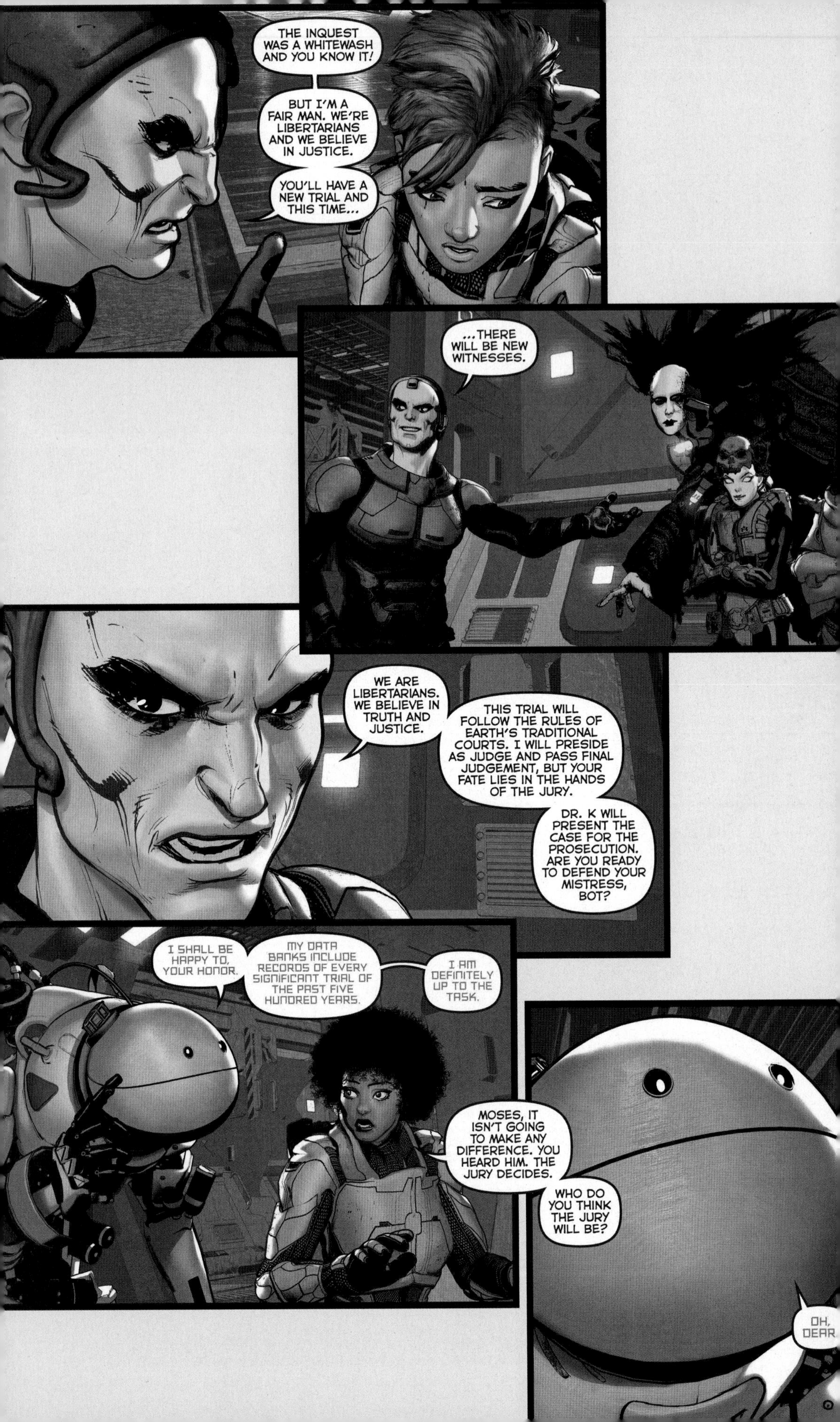
THE INQUEST WAS A WHITEWASH AND YOU KNOW IT!
BUT I'M A FAIR MAN. WE'RE LIBERTARIANS AND WE BELIEVE IN JUSTICE.
YOU'LL HAVE A NEW TRIAL AND THIS TIME...
...THERE WILL BE NEW WITNESSES.
WE ARE LIBERTARIANS. WE BELIEVE IN TRUTH AND JUSTICE.
THIS TRIAL WILL FOLLOW THE RULES OF EARTH'S TRADITIONAL COURTS. I WILL PRESIDE AS JUDGE AND PASS FINAL JUDGEMENT, BUT YOUR FATE LIES IN THE HANDS OF THE JURY.
DR. K WILL PRESENT THE CASE FOR THE PROSECUTION. ARE YOU READY TO DEFEND YOUR MISTRESS, BOT?
I SHALL BE HAPPY TO, YOUR HONOR.
MY DATA BANKS INCLUDE RECORDS OF EVERY SIGNIFICANT TRIAL OF THE PAST FIVE HUNDRED YEARS.
I AM DEFINITELY UP TO THE TASK.
MOSES, IT ISN'T GOING TO MAKE ANY DIFFERENCE. YOU HEARD HIM. THE JURY DECIDES.
WHO DO YOU THINK THE JURY WILL BE?
OH, DEAR

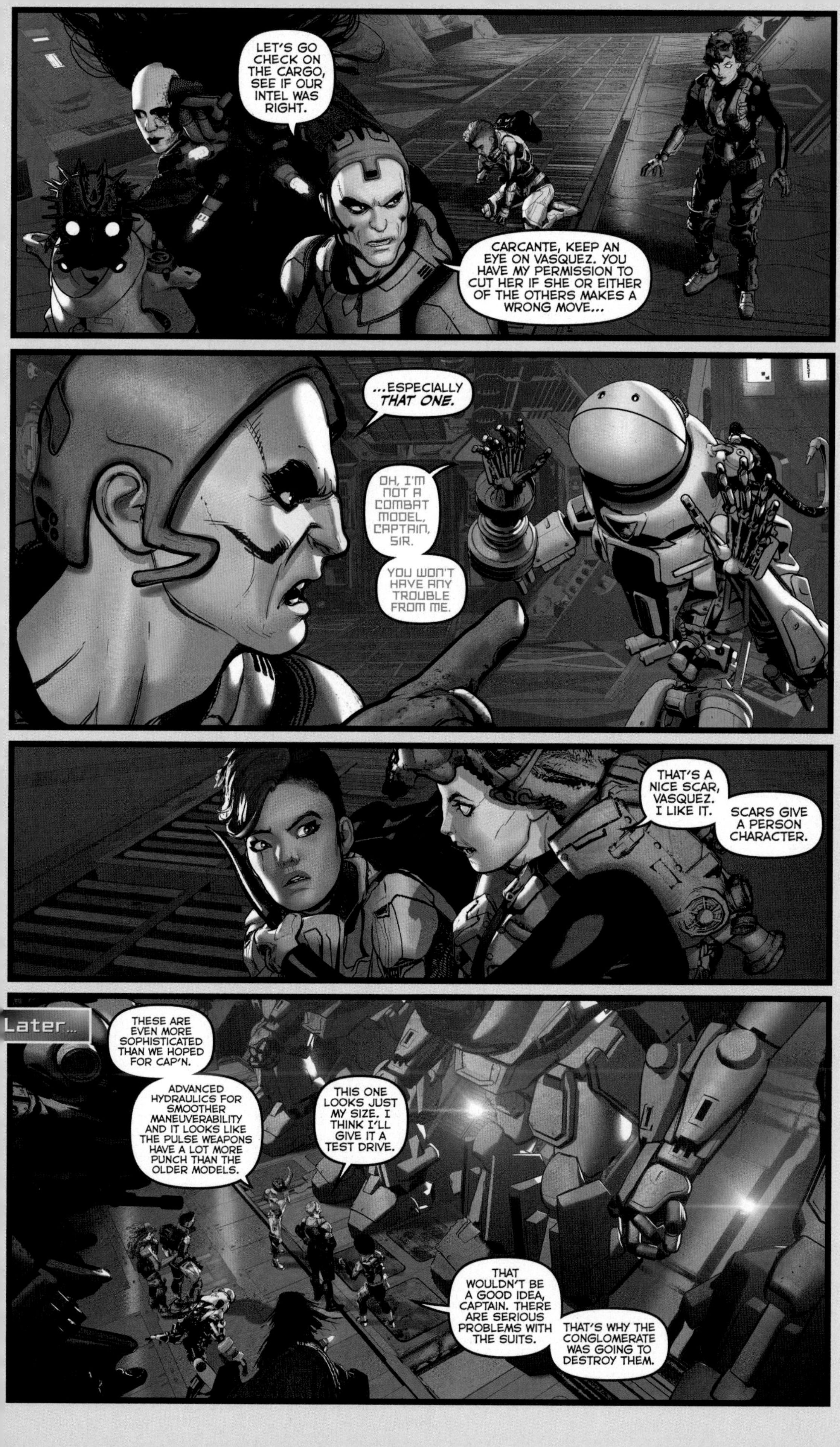
LET'S GO CHECK ON THE CARGO, SEE IF OUR INTEL WAS RIGHT.
CARCANTE, KEEP AN EYE ON VASQUEZ. YOU HAVE MY PERMISSION TO CUT HER IF SHE OR EITHER OF THE OTHERS MAKES A WRONG MOVE...
...ESPECIALLY *THAT ONE.*
OH, I'M NOT A COMBAT MODEL, CAPTAIN, SIR.
YOU WON'T HAVE ANY TROUBLE FROM ME.
THAT'S A NICE SCAR, VASQUEZ. I LIKE IT.
SCARS GIVE A PERSON CHARACTER.
Later...
THESE ARE EVEN MORE SOPHISTICATED THAN WE HOPED FOR CAP'N.
ADVANCED HYDRAULICS FOR SMOOTHER MANEUVERABILITY AND IT LOOKS LIKE THE PULSE WEAPONS HAVE A LOT MORE PUNCH THAN THE OLDER MODELS.
THIS ONE LOOKS JUST MY SIZE. I THINK I'LL GIVE IT A TEST DRIVE.
THAT WOULDN'T BE A GOOD IDEA, CAPTAIN. THERE ARE SERIOUS PROBLEMS WITH THE SUITS.
THAT'S WHY THE CONGLOMERATE WAS GOING TO DESTROY THEM.

DESTROY THEM!?

DO YOU REALLY EXPECT US TO BELIEVE THAT THE CONGLOMERATE IS SENDING THESE WEAPONS HALFWAY ACROSS THE GALAXY TO GET RID OF THEM WHEN THEY COULD HAVE JUST DUMPED THE LOT IN THE HEART OF THE NEAREST SUN?

EVEN SO, THEY MAY BE UNSTABLE.

IT WOULD BE IRRESPONSIBLE TO RISK YOUR LIFE.

I'LL GIVE IT A SPIN, CAP'N.

"IRRESPONSIBLE" IS MY MIDDLE NAME.

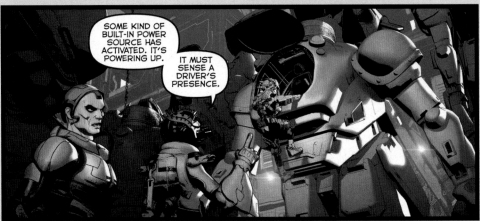

SOME KIND OF BUILT-IN POWER SOURCE HAS ACTIVATED. IT'S POWERING UP.

IT MUST SENSE A DRIVER'S PRESENCE.

THE SUIT IS RESPONDING AUTOMATICALLY TO M--

WAIT... WHAT THE FUCK?!

AARRGEHHH

WHAT'S IT DOING TO HER?

THE SUIT IS EXCHANGING DATA...AND, UH... AND FLUIDS. IT INJECTS CHEMICAL STIMULANTS INTO THE BLOOD AND SENDS NANITES TO CONNECT DIRECTLY WITH THE NEURONES' INFORMATION STREAM.

YOUR FRIEND IS ESTABLISHING A SYMBIOTIC RELATIONSHIP WITH THE SUIT.

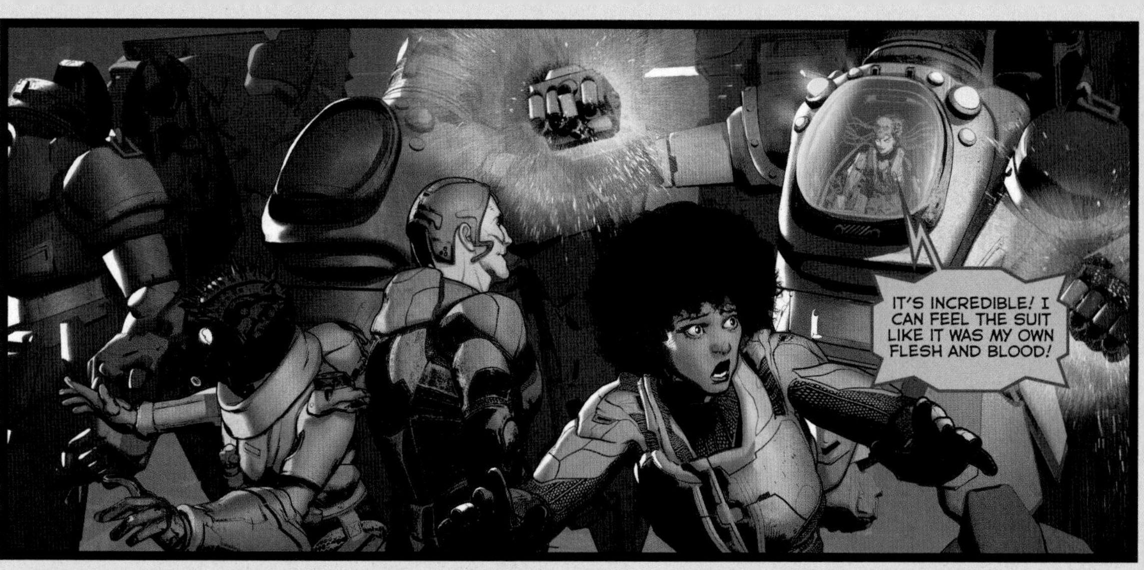
IT'S INCREDIBLE! I CAN FEEL THE SUIT LIKE IT WAS MY OWN FLESH AND BLOOD!

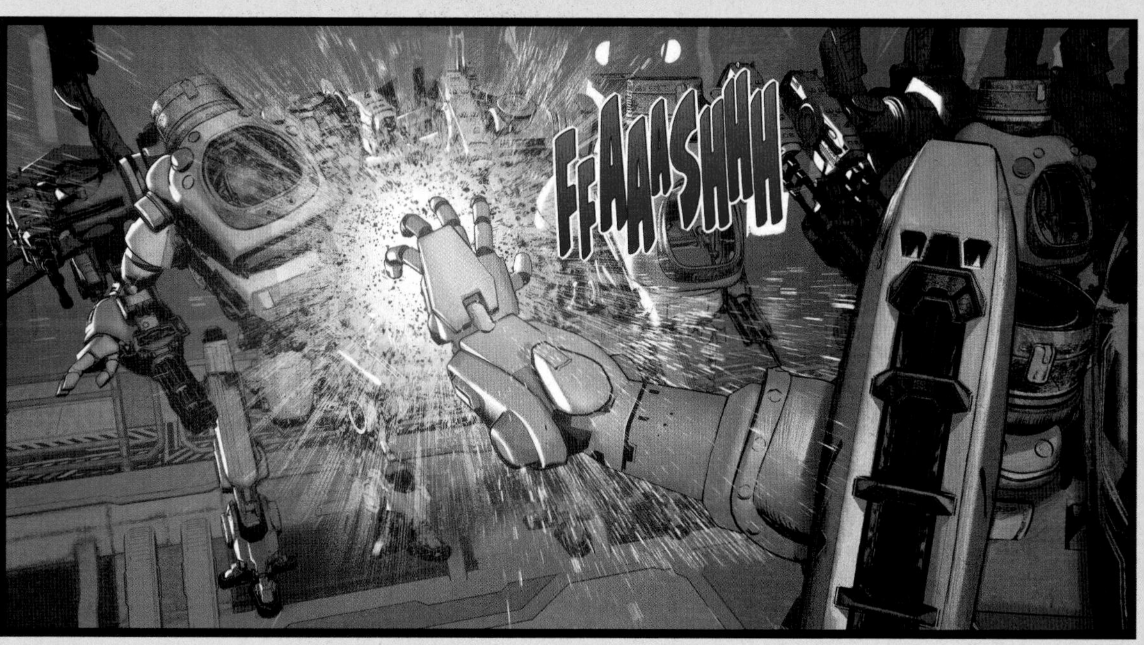
FFAAASHHH

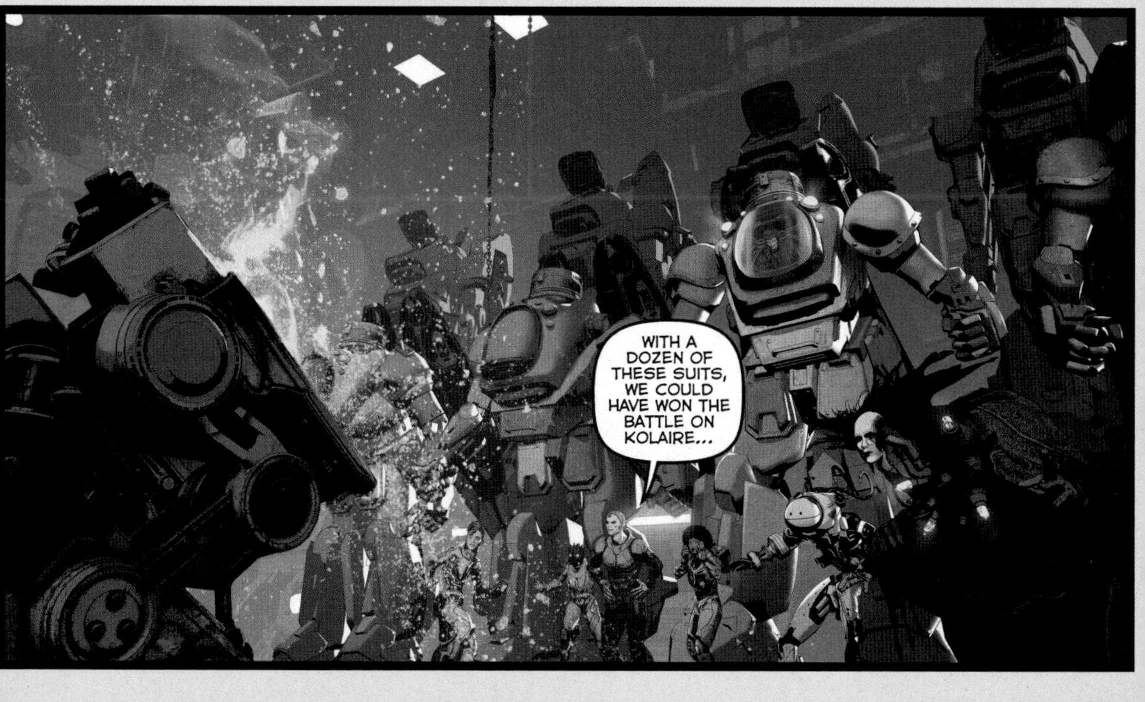
WITH A DOZEN OF THESE SUITS, WE COULD HAVE WON THE BATTLE ON KOLAIRE...

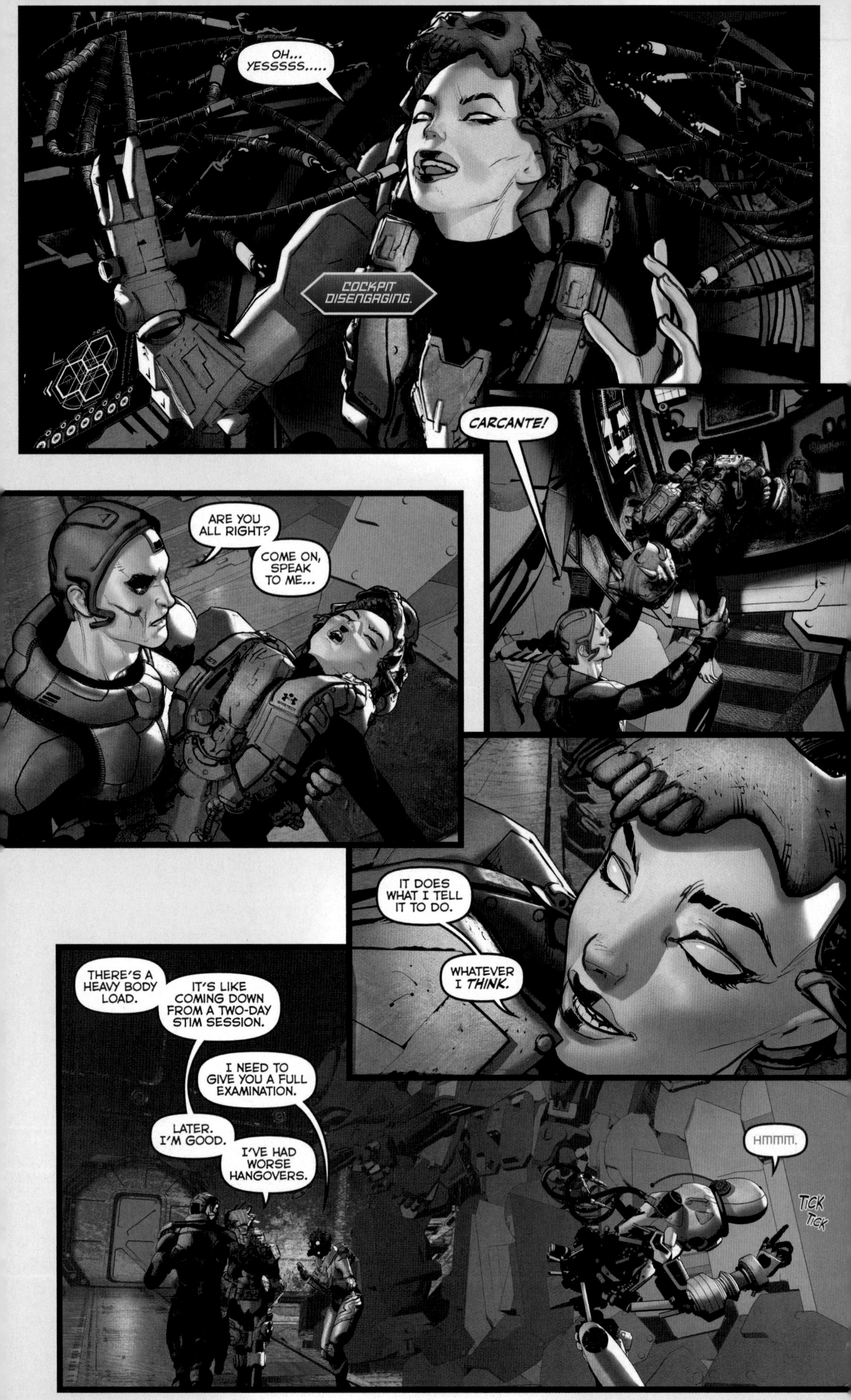

OH... YESSSSS.....
COCKPIT DISENGAGING.
CARCANTE!
ARE YOU ALL RIGHT?
COME ON, SPEAK TO ME...
IT DOES WHAT I TELL IT TO DO.
WHATEVER I *THINK*.
THERE'S A HEAVY BODY LOAD.
IT'S LIKE COMING DOWN FROM A TWO-DAY STIM SESSION.
I NEED TO GIVE YOU A FULL EXAMINATION.
LATER. I'M GOOD.
I'VE HAD WORSE HANGOVERS.
HMMM.
TICK TICK

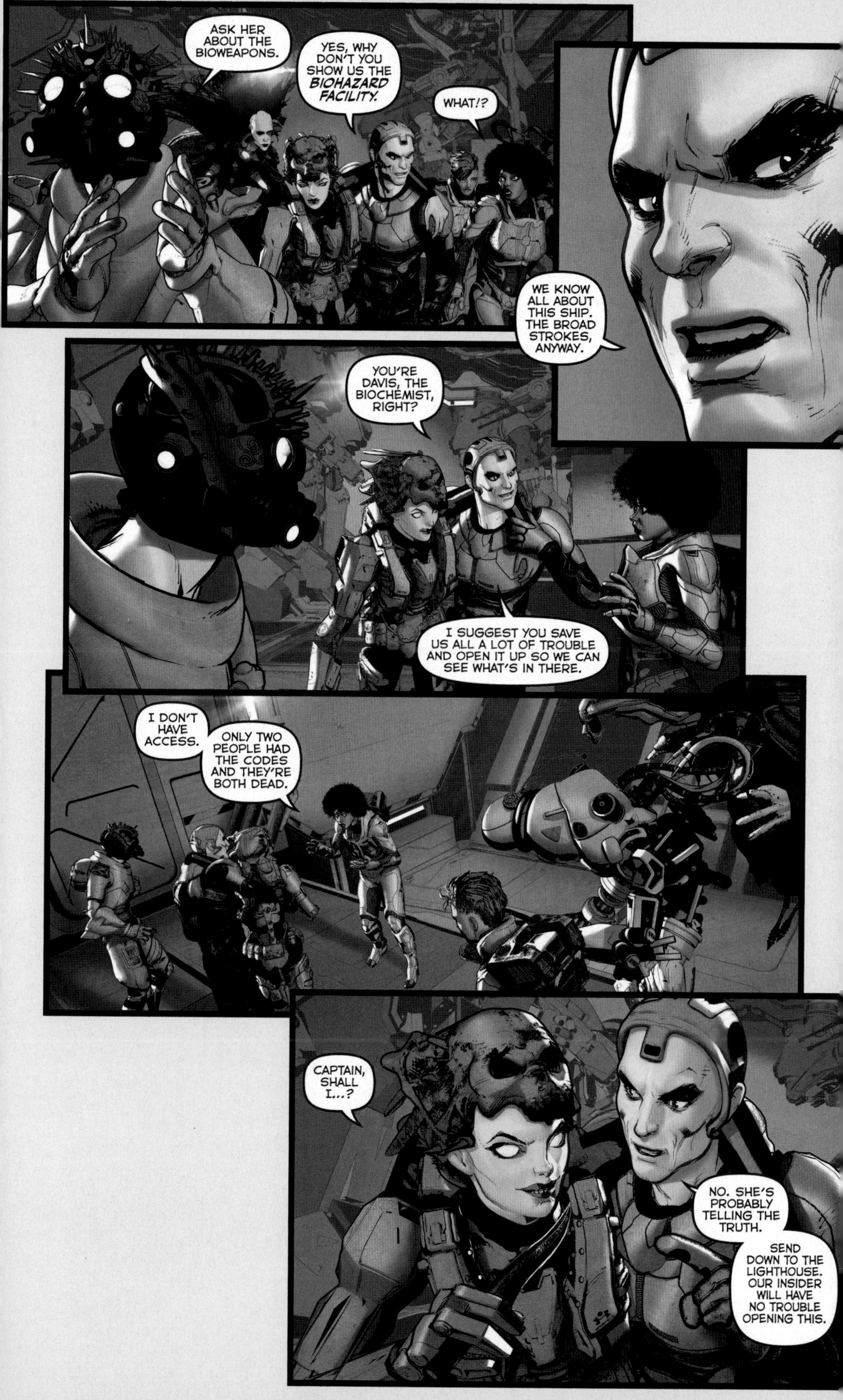
ASK HER ABOUT THE BIOWEAPONS.
YES, WHY DON'T YOU SHOW US THE *BIOHAZARD FACILITY.*
WHAT!?
WE KNOW ALL ABOUT THIS SHIP. THE BROAD STROKES, ANYWAY.
YOU'RE DAVIS, THE BIOCHEMIST, RIGHT?
I SUGGEST YOU SAVE US ALL A LOT OF TROUBLE AND OPEN IT UP SO WE CAN SEE WHAT'S IN THERE.
I DON'T HAVE ACCESS.
ONLY TWO PEOPLE HAD THE CODES AND THEY'RE BOTH DEAD.
CAPTAIN, SHALL I...?
NO. SHE'S PROBABLY TELLING THE TRUTH.
SEND DOWN TO THE LIGHTHOUSE. OUR INSIDER WILL HAVE NO TROUBLE OPENING THIS.

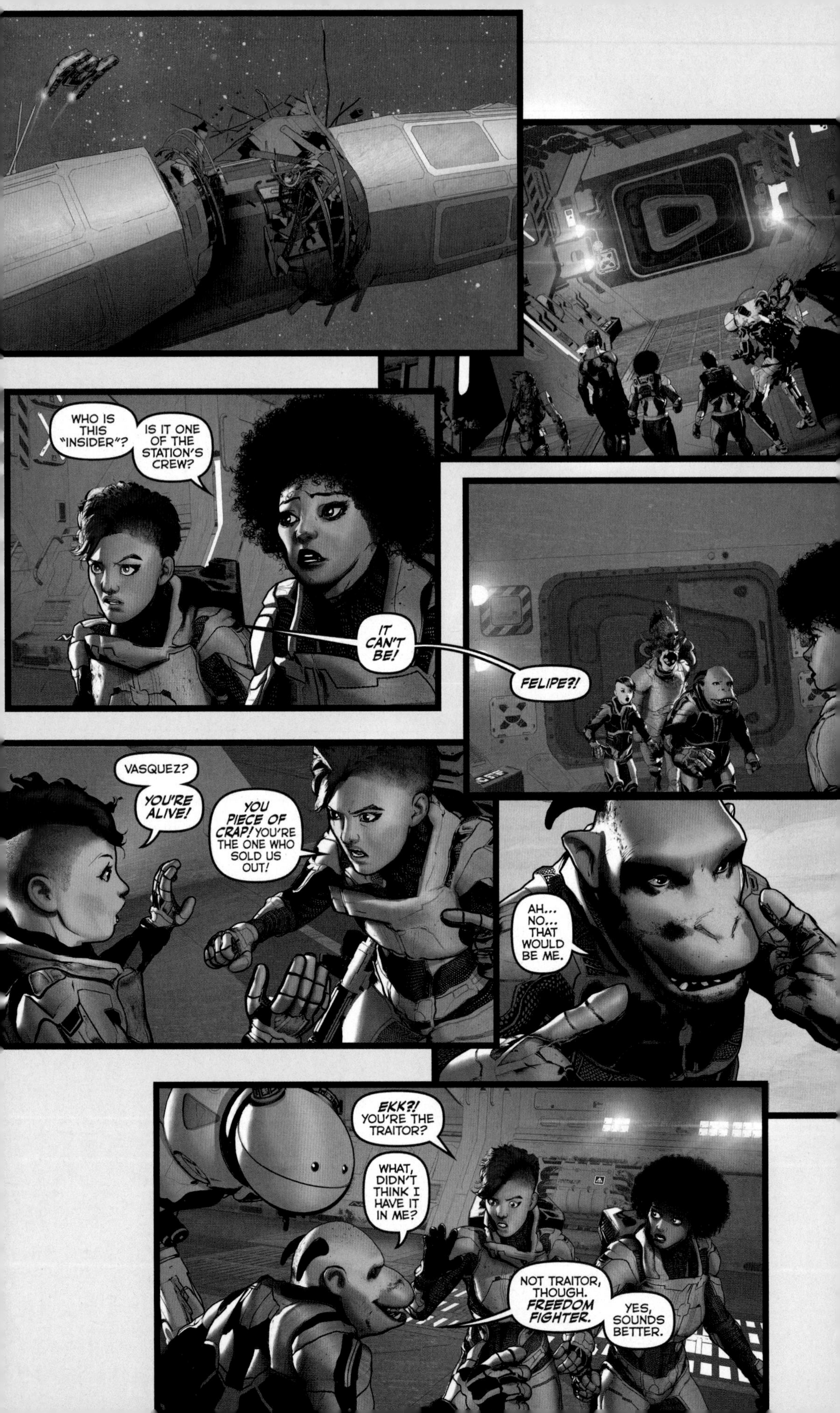
WHO IS THIS "INSIDER"?
IS IT ONE OF THE STATION'S CREW?
IT CAN'T BE!
FELIPE?!
VASQUEZ?
YOU'RE ALIVE!
YOU PIECE OF CRAP! YOU'RE THE ONE WHO SOLD US OUT!
AH... NO... THAT WOULD BE ME.
EKK?! YOU'RE THE TRAITOR?
WHAT, DIDN'T THINK I HAVE IT IN ME?
NOT TRAITOR, THOUGH. FREEDOM FIGHTER.
YES, SOUNDS BETTER.

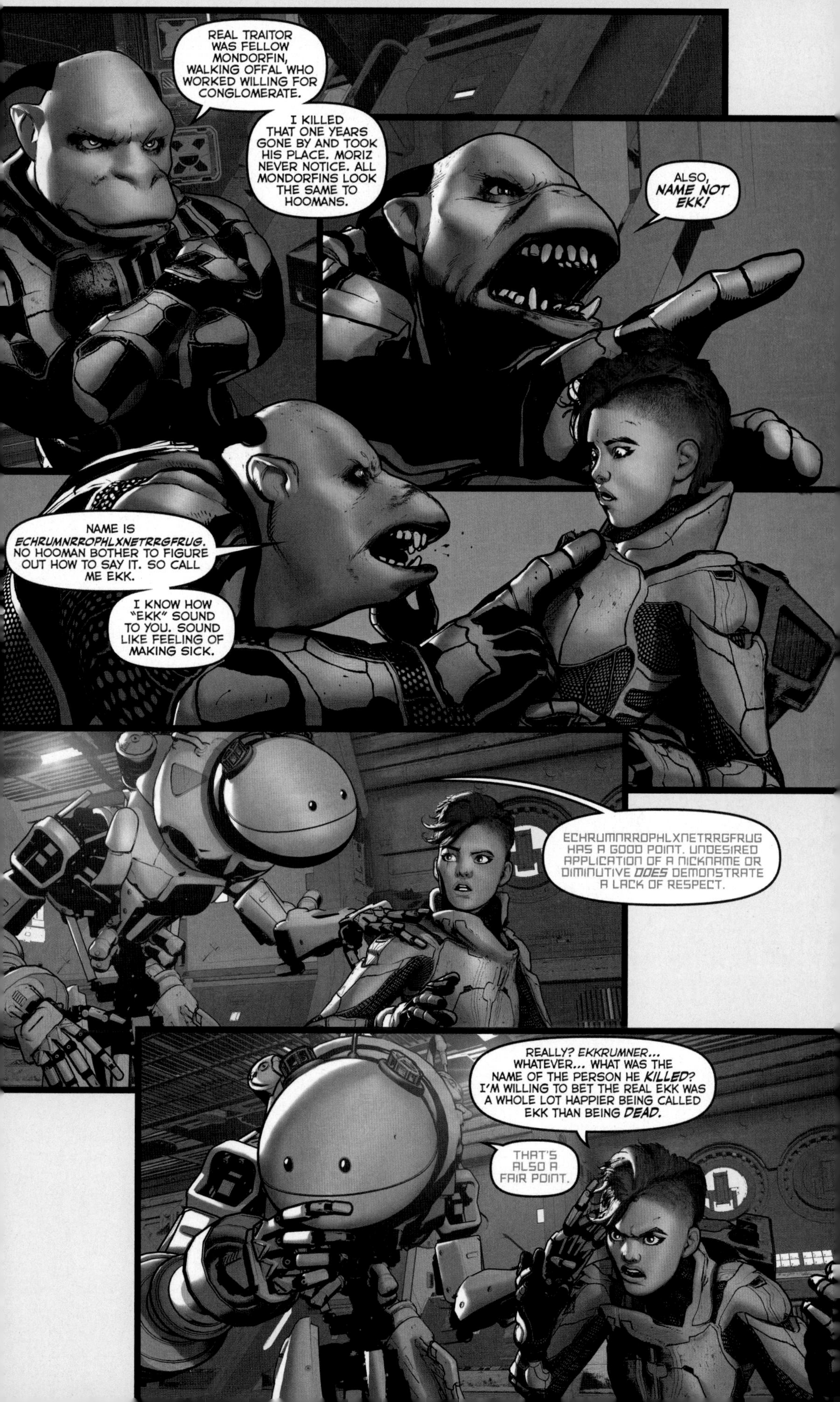
REAL TRAITOR WAS FELLOW MONDORFIN, WALKING OFFAL WHO WORKED WILLING FOR CONGLOMERATE.
I KILLED THAT ONE YEARS GONE BY AND TOOK HIS PLACE. MORIZ NEVER NOTICE. ALL MONDORFINS LOOK THE SAME TO HOOMANS.
ALSO, NAME NOT EKK!
NAME IS ECHRUMNRROPHLXNETRRGFRUG. NO HOOMAN BOTHER TO FIGURE OUT HOW TO SAY IT. SO CALL ME EKK.
I KNOW HOW "EKK" SOUND TO YOU. SOUND LIKE FEELING OF MAKING SICK.
ECHRUMNRROPHLXNETRRGFRUG HAS A GOOD POINT. UNDESIRED APPLICATION OF A NICKNAME OR DIMINUTIVE DOES DEMONSTRATE A LACK OF RESPECT.
REALLY? EKKRUMNER... WHATEVER... WHAT WAS THE NAME OF THE PERSON HE KILLED? I'M WILLING TO BET THE REAL EKK WAS A WHOLE LOT HAPPIER BEING CALLED EKK THAN BEING DEAD.
THAT'S ALSO A FAIR POINT.

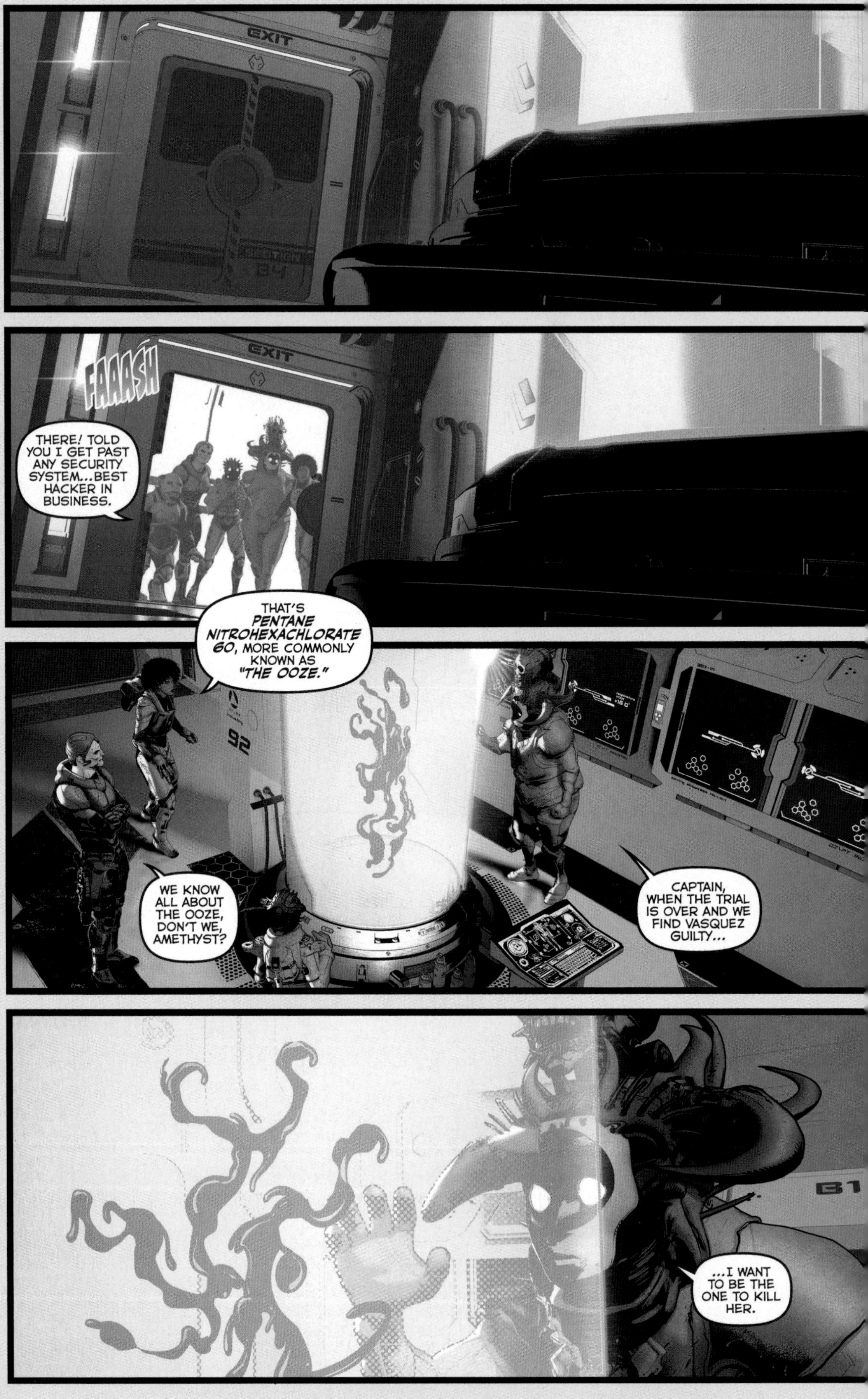
EXIT
FAAASH
THERE! TOLD YOU I GET PAST ANY SECURITY SYSTEM...BEST HACKER IN BUSINESS.
THAT'S *PENTANE NITROHEXACHLORATE 60*, MORE COMMONLY KNOWN AS *"THE OOZE."*
92
WE KNOW ALL ABOUT THE OOZE, DON'T WE, AMETHYST?
CAPTAIN, WHEN THE TRIAL IS OVER AND WE FIND VASQUEZ GUILTY...
B1
...I WANT TO BE THE ONE TO KILL HER.

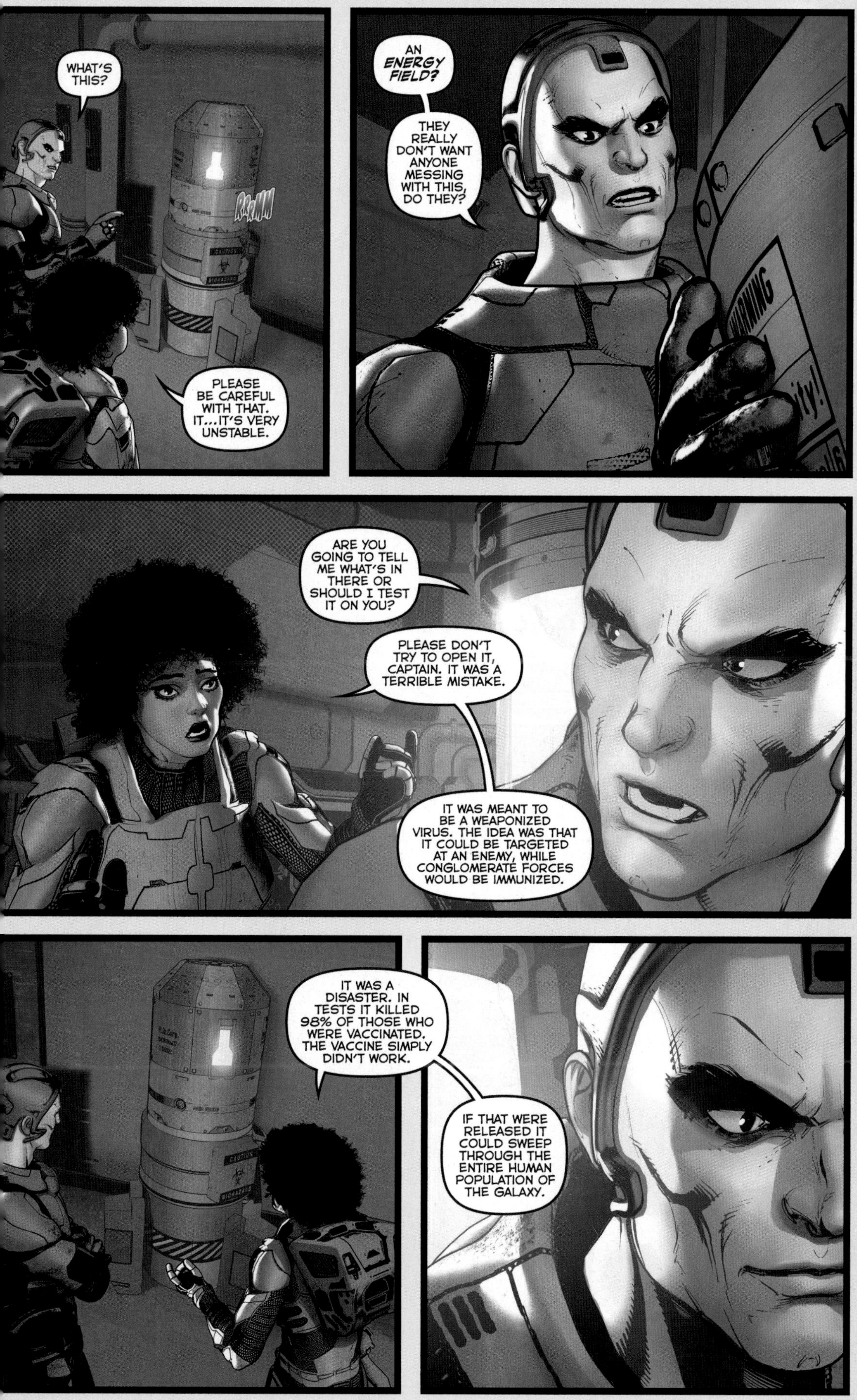

WHAT'S THIS?
RRRMM
PLEASE BE CAREFUL WITH THAT. IT...IT'S VERY UNSTABLE.
AN *ENERGY FIELD?*
THEY REALLY DON'T WANT ANYONE MESSING WITH THIS, DO THEY?
WARNING
ARE YOU GOING TO TELL ME WHAT'S IN THERE OR SHOULD I TEST IT ON YOU?
PLEASE DON'T TRY TO OPEN IT, CAPTAIN. IT WAS A TERRIBLE MISTAKE.
IT WAS MEANT TO BE A WEAPONIZED VIRUS. THE IDEA WAS THAT IT COULD BE TARGETED AT AN ENEMY, WHILE CONGLOMERATE FORCES WOULD BE IMMUNIZED.
IT WAS A DISASTER. IN TESTS IT KILLED 98% OF THOSE WHO WERE VACCINATED. THE VACCINE SIMPLY DIDN'T WORK.
IF THAT WERE RELEASED IT COULD SWEEP THROUGH THE ENTIRE HUMAN POPULATION OF THE GALAXY.

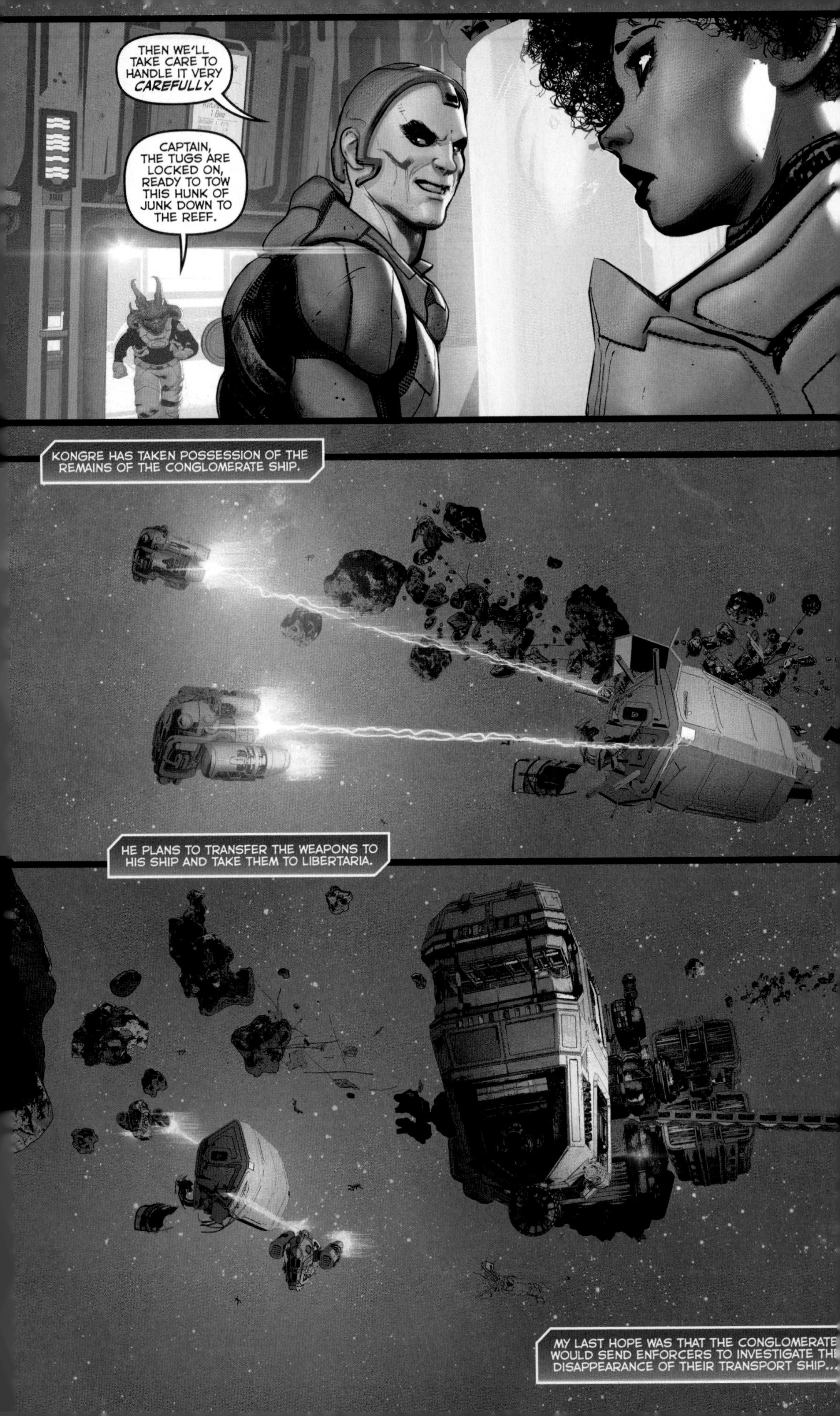
THEN WE'LL TAKE CARE TO HANDLE IT VERY *CAREFULLY.*
CAPTAIN, THE TUGS ARE LOCKED ON, READY TO TOW THIS HUNK OF JUNK DOWN TO THE REEF.
KONGRE HAS TAKEN POSSESSION OF THE REMAINS OF THE CONGLOMERATE SHIP.
HE PLANS TO TRANSFER THE WEAPONS TO HIS SHIP AND TAKE THEM TO LIBERTARIA.
MY LAST HOPE WAS THAT THE CONGLOMERATE WOULD SEND ENFORCERS TO INVESTIGATE TH DISAPPEARANCE OF THEIR TRANSPORT SHIP...

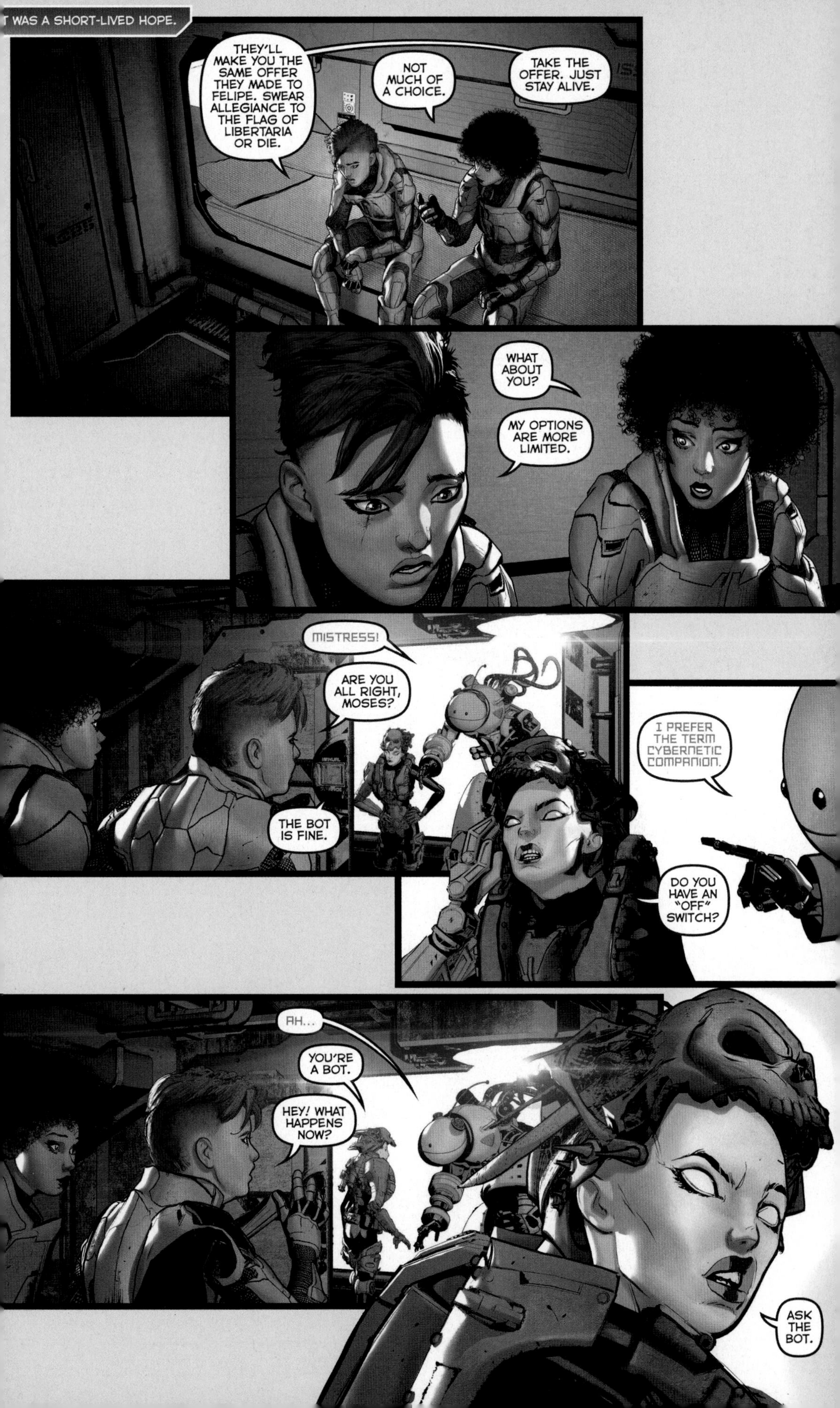
T WAS A SHORT-LIVED HOPE.
THEY'LL MAKE YOU THE SAME OFFER THEY MADE TO FELIPE. SWEAR ALLEGIANCE TO THE FLAG OF LIBERTARIA OR DIE.
NOT MUCH OF A CHOICE.
TAKE THE OFFER. JUST STAY ALIVE.
WHAT ABOUT YOU?
MY OPTIONS ARE MORE LIMITED.
MISTRESS!
ARE YOU ALL RIGHT, MOSES?
THE BOT IS FINE.
I PREFER THE TERM CYBERNETIC COMPANION.
DO YOU HAVE AN "OFF" SWITCH?
AH...
YOU'RE A BOT.
HEY! WHAT HAPPENS NOW?
ASK THE BOT.

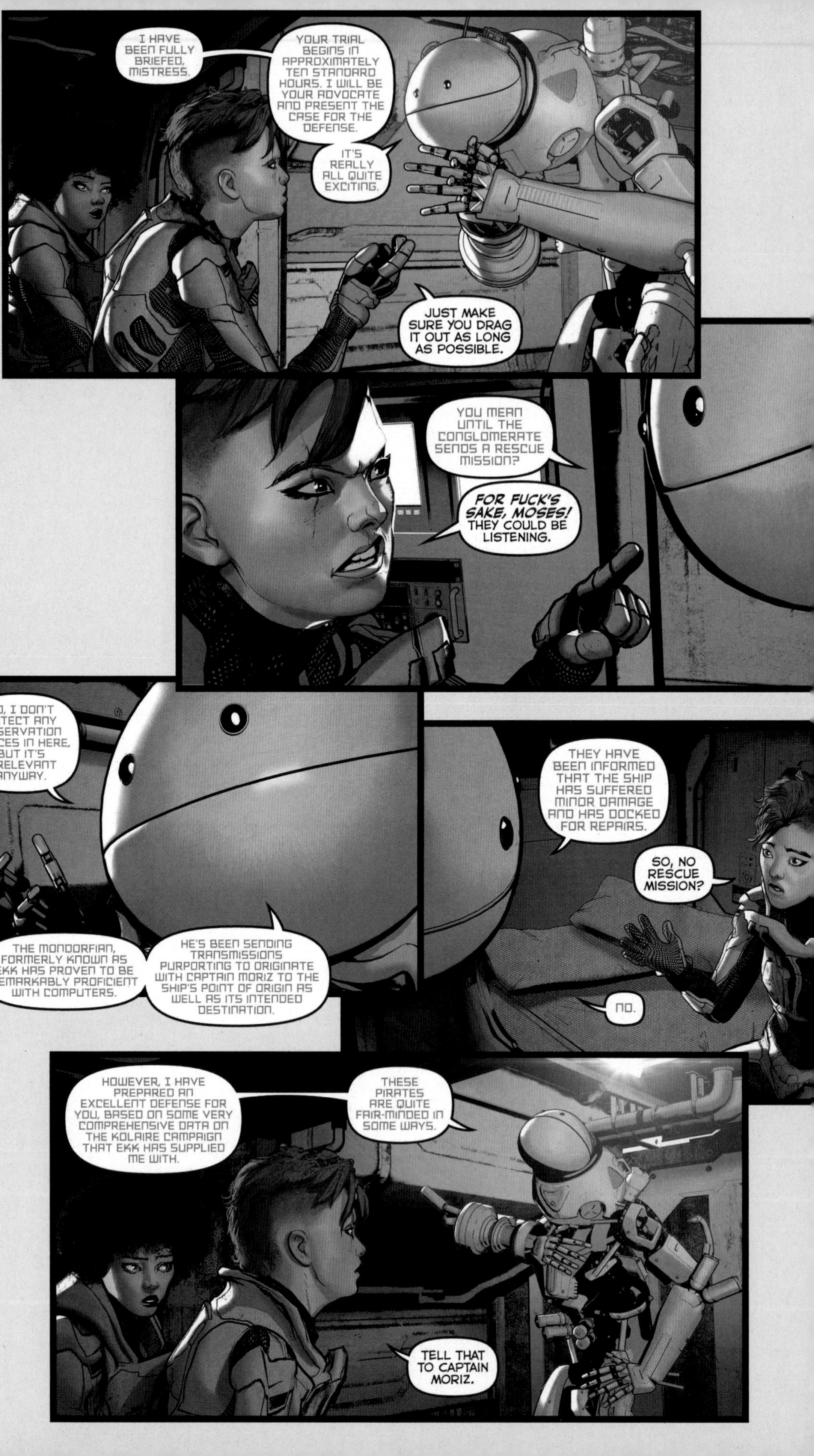

I HAVE BEEN FULLY BRIEFED, MISTRESS.
YOUR TRIAL BEGINS IN APPROXIMATELY TEN STANDARD HOURS. I WILL BE YOUR ADVOCATE AND PRESENT THE CASE FOR THE DEFENSE.
IT'S REALLY ALL QUITE EXCITING.
JUST MAKE SURE YOU DRAG IT OUT AS LONG AS POSSIBLE.
YOU MEAN UNTIL THE CONGLOMERATE SENDS A RESCUE MISSION?
FOR FUCK'S SAKE, MOSES! THEY COULD BE LISTENING.
NO, I DON'T DETECT ANY OBSERVATION DEVICES IN HERE, BUT IT'S IRRELEVANT ANYWAY.
THE MONDORFIAN, FORMERLY KNOWN AS EKK HAS PROVEN TO BE REMARKABLY PROFICIENT WITH COMPUTERS.
HE'S BEEN SENDING TRANSMISSIONS PURPORTING TO ORIGINATE WITH CAPTAIN MORIZ TO THE SHIP'S POINT OF ORIGIN AS WELL AS ITS INTENDED DESTINATION.
THEY HAVE BEEN INFORMED THAT THE SHIP HAS SUFFERED MINOR DAMAGE AND HAS DOCKED FOR REPAIRS.
SO, NO RESCUE MISSION?
NO.
HOWEVER, I HAVE PREPARED AN EXCELLENT DEFENSE FOR YOU, BASED ON SOME VERY COMPREHENSIVE DATA ON THE KOLAIRE CAMPAIGN THAT EKK HAS SUPPLIED ME WITH.
THESE PIRATES ARE QUITE FAIR-MINDED IN SOME WAYS.
TELL THAT TO CAPTAIN MORIZ.

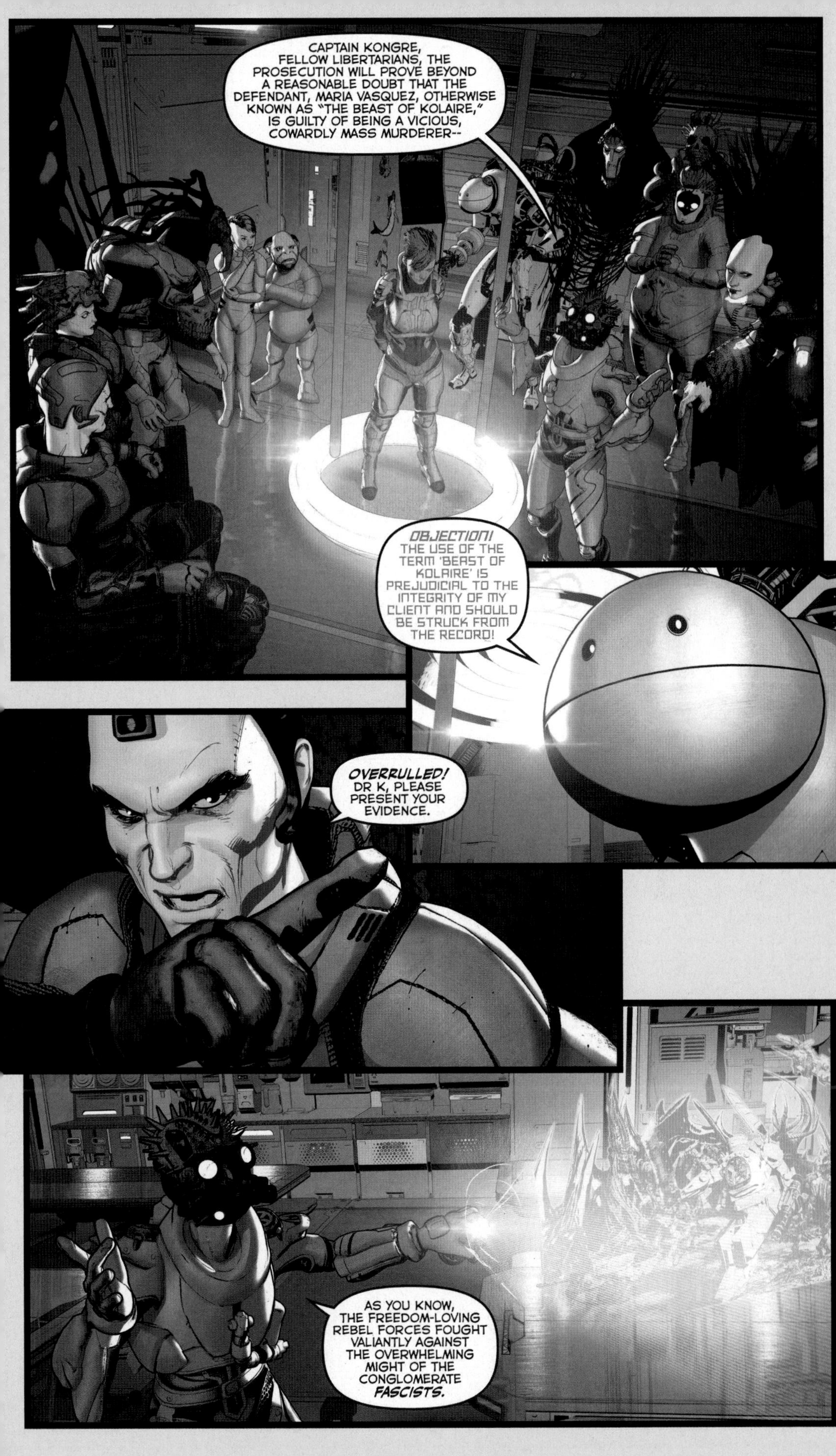
CAPTAIN KONGRE, FELLOW LIBERTARIANS, THE PROSECUTION WILL PROVE BEYOND A REASONABLE DOUBT THAT THE DEFENDANT, MARIA VASQUEZ, OTHERWISE KNOWN AS "THE BEAST OF KOLAIRE," IS GUILTY OF BEING A VICIOUS, COWARDLY MASS MURDERER--
OBJECTION! THE USE OF THE TERM 'BEAST OF KOLAIRE' IS PREJUDICIAL TO THE INTEGRITY OF MY CLIENT AND SHOULD BE STRUCK FROM THE RECORD!
OVERRULLED! DR K, PLEASE PRESENT YOUR EVIDENCE.
AS YOU KNOW, THE FREEDOM-LOVING REBEL FORCES FOUGHT VALIANTLY AGAINST THE OVERWHELMING MIGHT OF THE CONGLOMERATE FASCISTS.

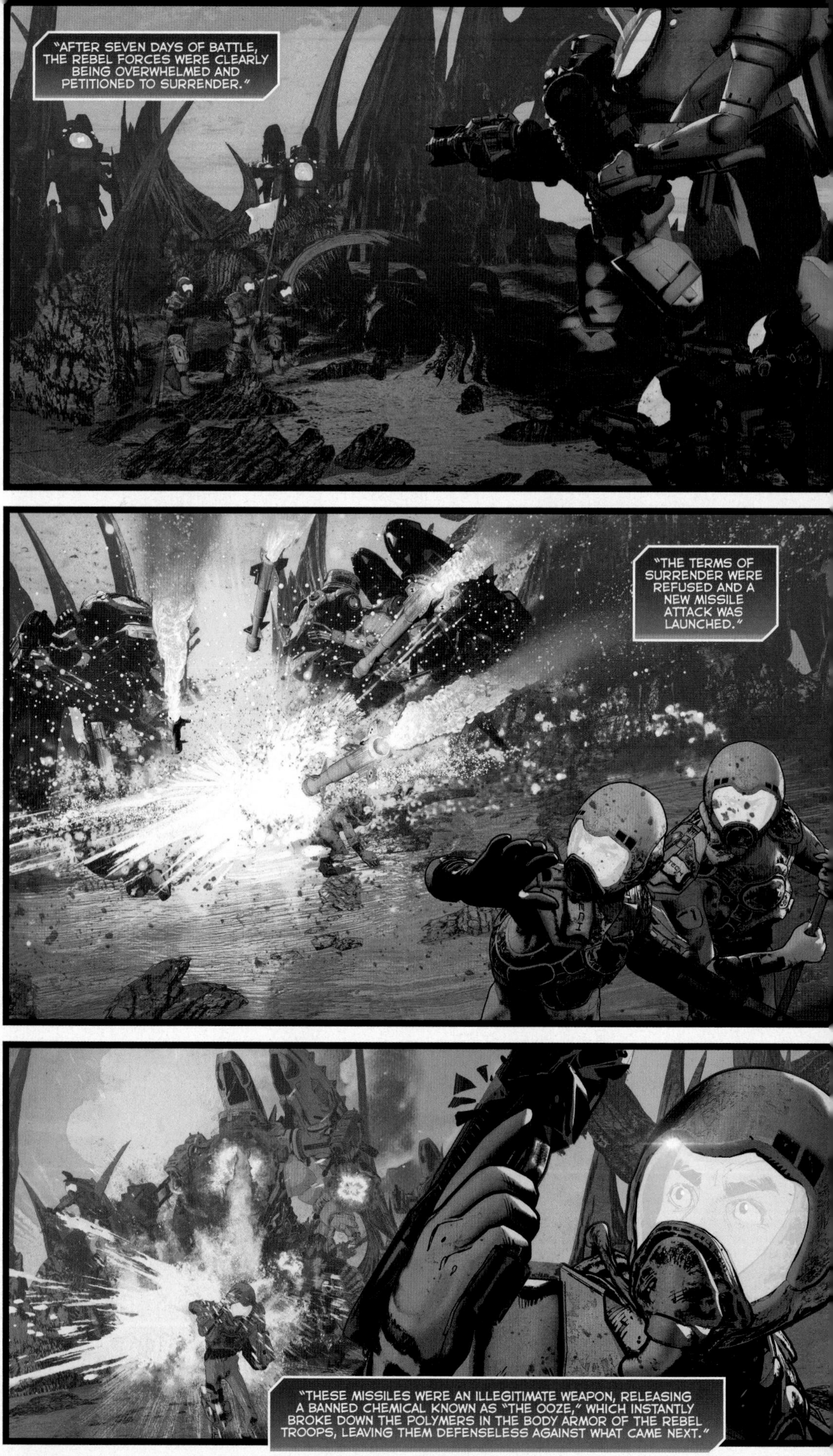
"AFTER SEVEN DAYS OF BATTLE, THE REBEL FORCES WERE CLEARLY BEING OVERWHELMED AND PETITIONED TO SURRENDER."
"THE TERMS OF SURRENDER WERE REFUSED AND A NEW MISSILE ATTACK WAS LAUNCHED."
"THESE MISSILES WERE AN ILLEGITIMATE WEAPON, RELEASING A BANNED CHEMICAL KNOWN AS "THE OOZE," WHICH INSTANTLY BROKE DOWN THE POLYMERS IN THE BODY ARMOR OF THE REBEL TROOPS, LEAVING THEM DEFENSELESS AGAINST WHAT CAME NEXT."

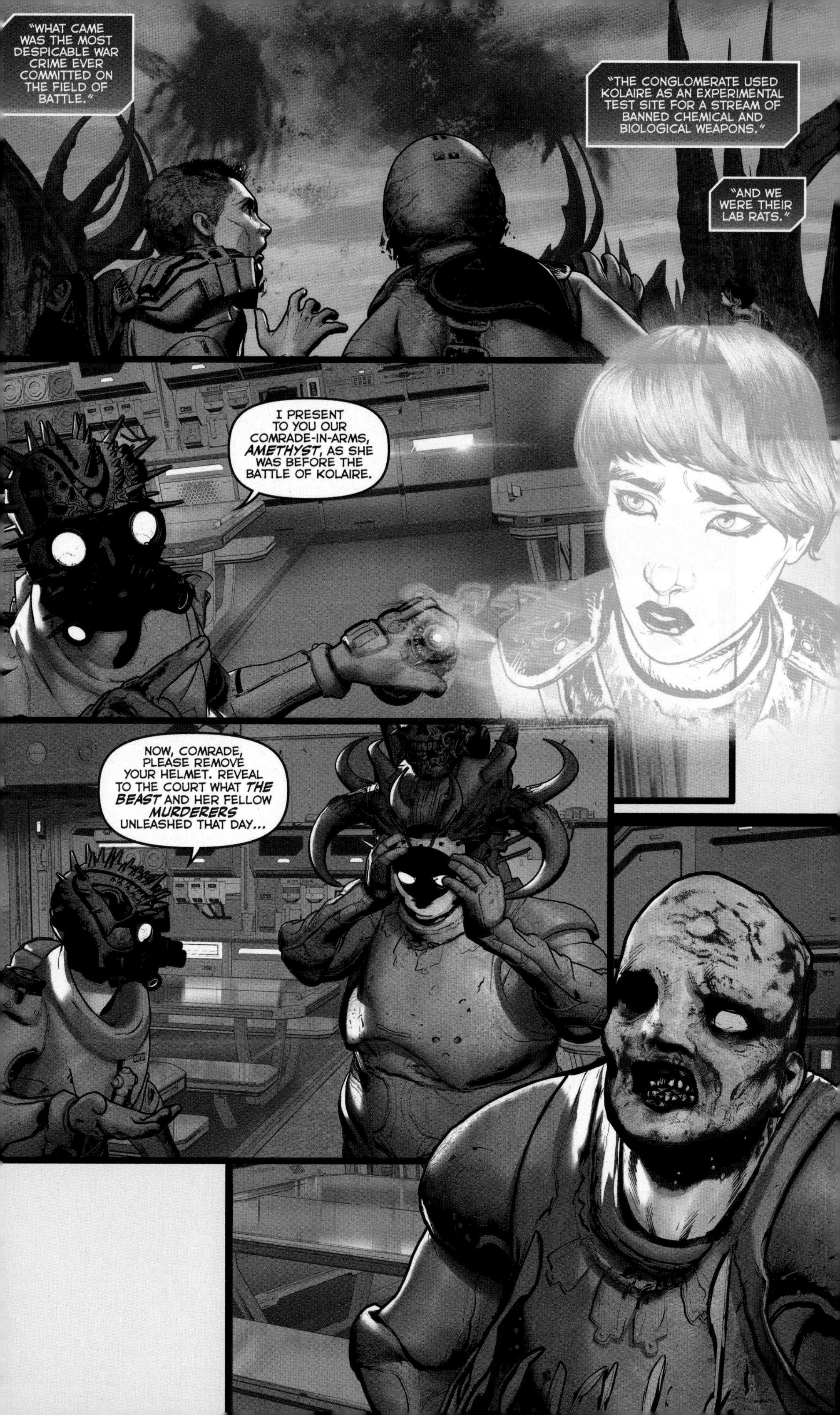
"WHAT CAME WAS THE MOST DESPICABLE WAR CRIME EVER COMMITTED ON THE FIELD OF BATTLE."
"THE CONGLOMERATE USED KOLAIRE AS AN EXPERIMENTAL TEST SITE FOR A STREAM OF BANNED CHEMICAL AND BIOLOGICAL WEAPONS."
"AND WE WERE THEIR LAB RATS."
I PRESENT TO YOU OUR COMRADE-IN-ARMS, *AMETHYST*, AS SHE WAS BEFORE THE BATTLE OF KOLAIRE.
NOW, COMRADE, PLEASE REMOVE YOUR HELMET. REVEAL TO THE COURT WHAT *THE BEAST* AND HER FELLOW *MURDERERS* UNLEASHED THAT DAY...

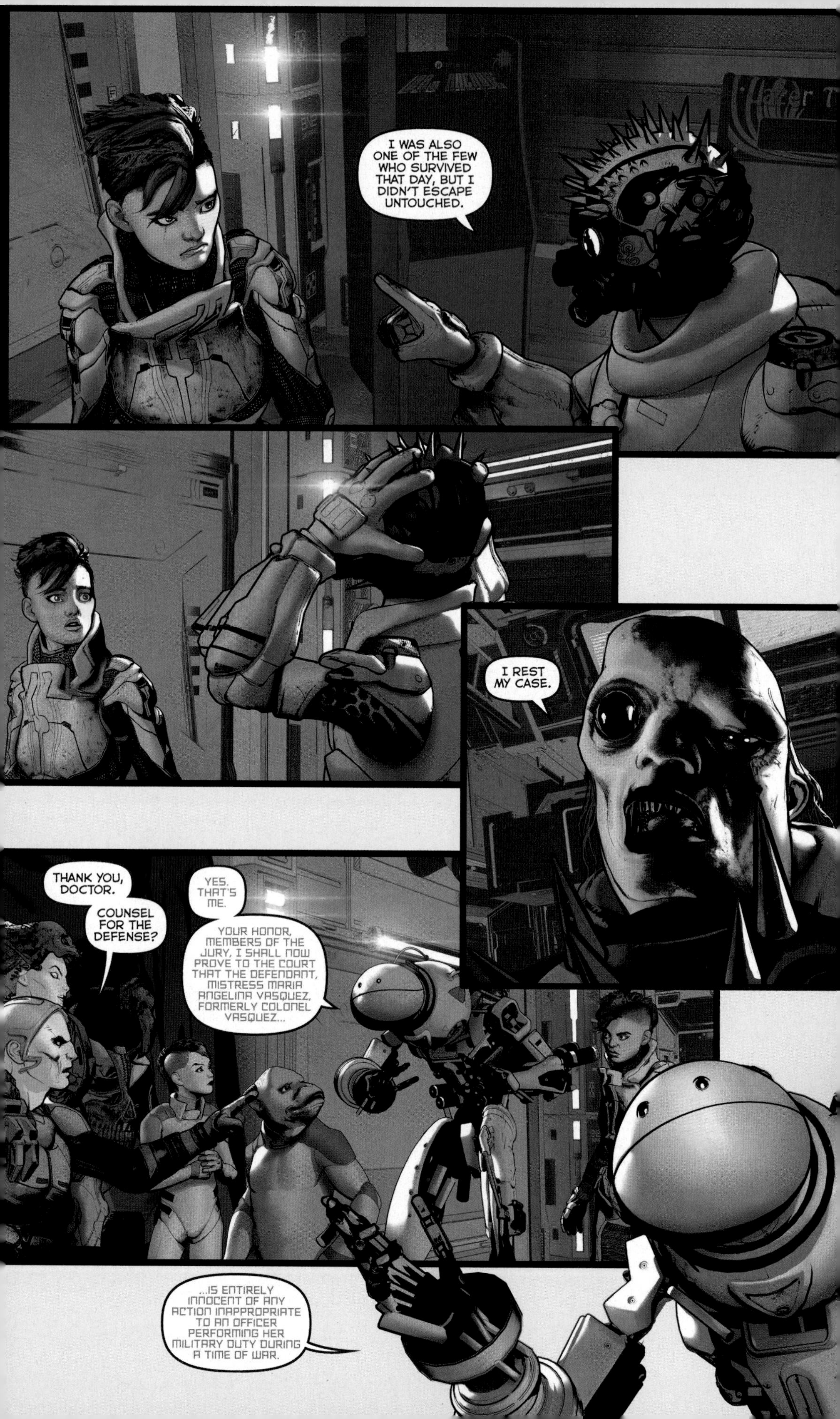
I WAS ALSO ONE OF THE FEW WHO SURVIVED THAT DAY, BUT I DIDN'T ESCAPE UNTOUCHED.
I REST MY CASE.
THANK YOU, DOCTOR.
COUNSEL FOR THE DEFENSE?
YES. THAT'S ME.
YOUR HONOR, MEMBERS OF THE JURY, I SHALL NOW PROVE TO THE COURT THAT THE DEFENDANT, MISTRESS MARIA ANGELINA VASQUEZ, FORMERLY COLONEL VASQUEZ...
...IS ENTIRELY INNOCENT OF ANY ACTION INAPPROPRIATE TO AN OFFICER PERFORMING HER MILITARY DUTY DURING A TIME OF WAR.

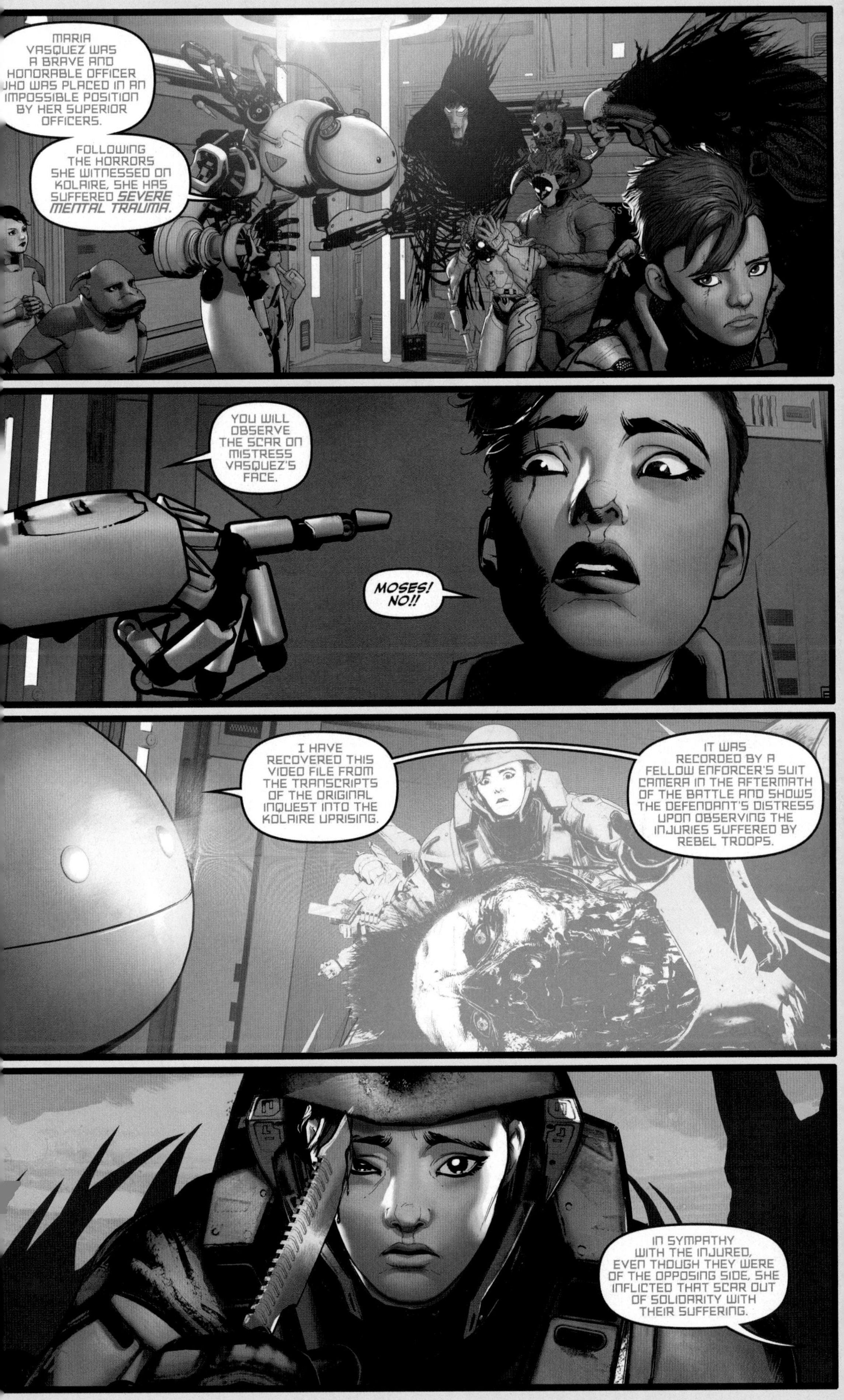
MARIA VASQUEZ WAS A BRAVE AND HONORABLE OFFICER WHO WAS PLACED IN AN IMPOSSIBLE POSITION BY HER SUPERIOR OFFICERS.
FOLLOWING THE HORRORS SHE WITNESSED ON KOLAIRE, SHE HAS SUFFERED *SEVERE MENTAL TRAUMA*.
YOU WILL OBSERVE THE SCAR ON MISTRESS VASQUEZ'S FACE.
MOSES! NO!!
I HAVE RECOVERED THIS VIDEO FILE FROM THE TRANSCRIPTS OF THE ORIGINAL INQUEST INTO THE KOLAIRE UPRISING.
IT WAS RECORDED BY A FELLOW ENFORCER'S SUIT CAMERA IN THE AFTERMATH OF THE BATTLE AND SHOWS THE DEFENDANT'S DISTRESS UPON OBSERVING THE INJURIES SUFFERED BY REBEL TROOPS.
IN SYMPATHY WITH THE INJURED, EVEN THOUGH THEY WERE OF THE OPPOSING SIDE, SHE INFLICTED THAT SCAR OUT OF SOLIDARITY WITH THEIR SUFFERING.

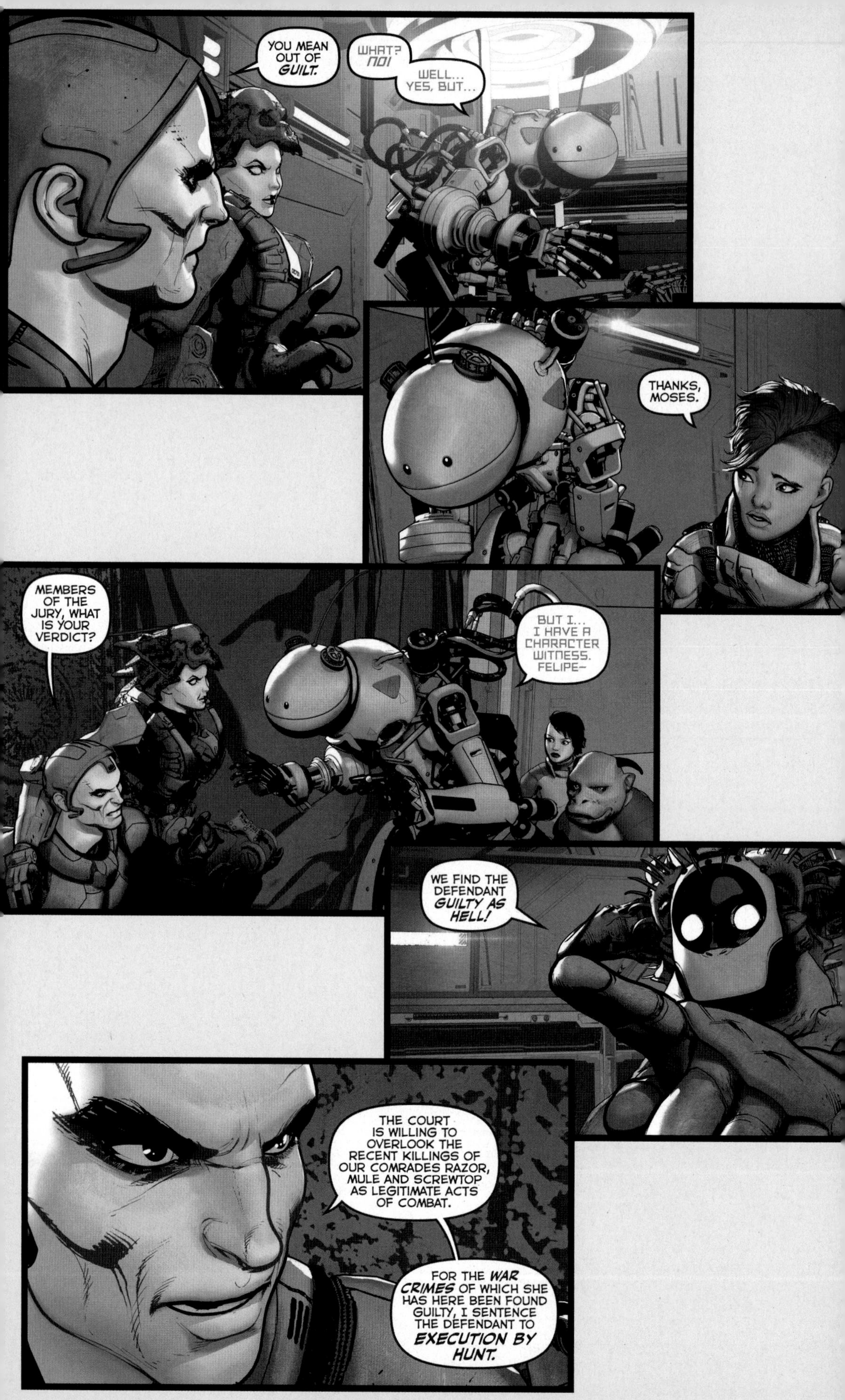

YOU MEAN OUT OF *GUILT.*
WHAT? *NO!*
WELL... YES, BUT...
THANKS, MOSES.
MEMBERS OF THE JURY, WHAT IS YOUR VERDICT?
BUT I... I HAVE A CHARACTER WITNESS. FELIPE–
WE FIND THE DEFENDANT *GUILTY AS HELL!*
THE COURT IS WILLING TO OVERLOOK THE RECENT KILLINGS OF OUR COMRADES RAZOR, MULE AND SCREWTOP AS LEGITIMATE ACTS OF COMBAT.
FOR THE *WAR CRIMES* OF WHICH SHE HAS HERE BEEN FOUND GUILTY, I SENTENCE THE DEFENDANT TO *EXECUTION BY HUNT.*

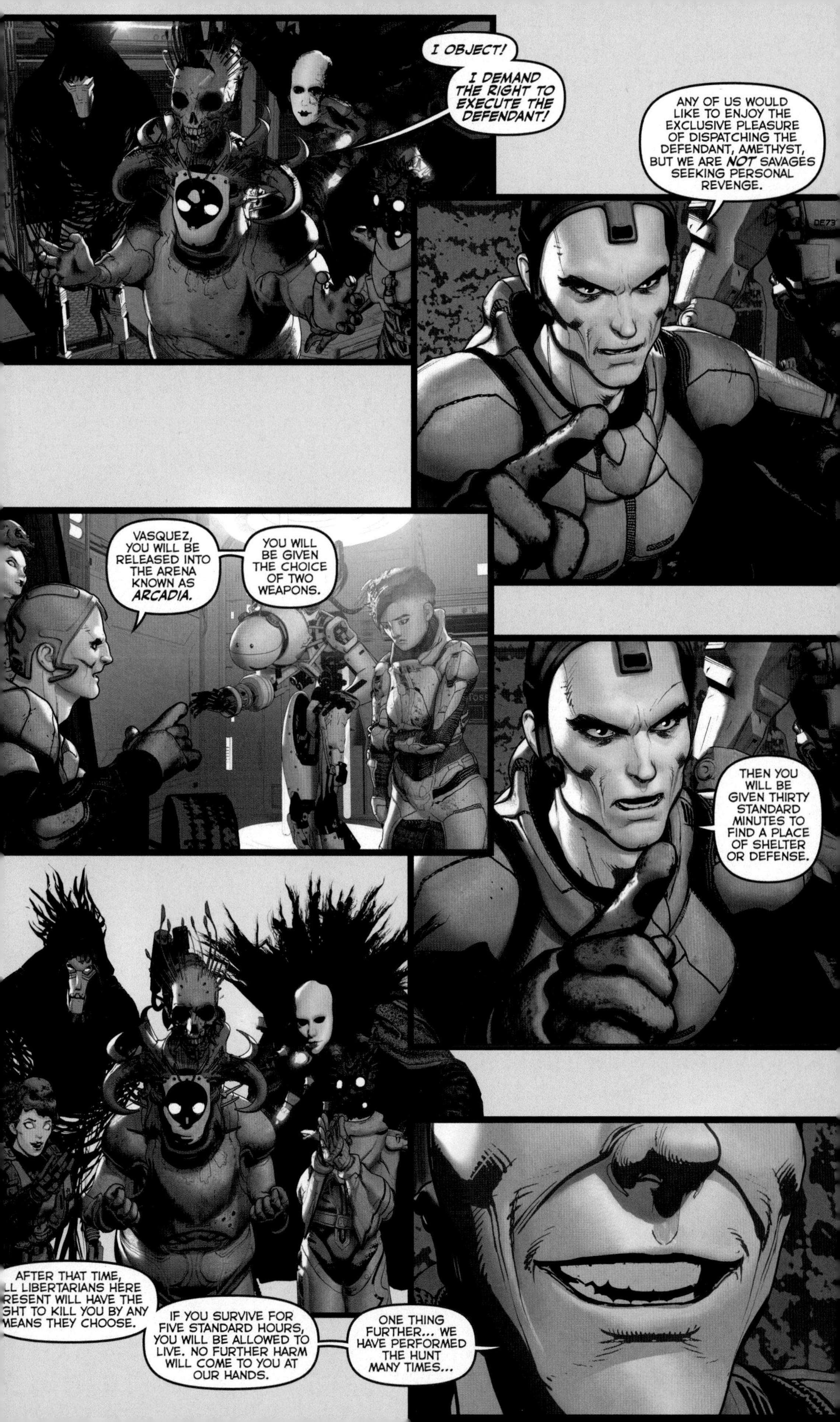

I OBJECT!
I DEMAND THE RIGHT TO EXECUTE THE DEFENDANT!
ANY OF US WOULD LIKE TO ENJOY THE EXCLUSIVE PLEASURE OF DISPATCHING THE DEFENDANT, AMETHYST, BUT WE ARE NOT SAVAGES SEEKING PERSONAL REVENGE.
DE73
VASQUEZ, YOU WILL BE RELEASED INTO THE ARENA KNOWN AS ARCADIA.
YOU WILL BE GIVEN THE CHOICE OF TWO WEAPONS.
THEN YOU WILL BE GIVEN THIRTY STANDARD MINUTES TO FIND A PLACE OF SHELTER OR DEFENSE.
AFTER THAT TIME, LL LIBERTARIANS HERE RESENT WILL HAVE THE GHT TO KILL YOU BY ANY MEANS THEY CHOOSE.
IF YOU SURVIVE FOR FIVE STANDARD HOURS, YOU WILL BE ALLOWED TO LIVE. NO FURTHER HARM WILL COME TO YOU AT OUR HANDS.
ONE THING FURTHER... WE HAVE PERFORMED THE HUNT MANY TIMES...

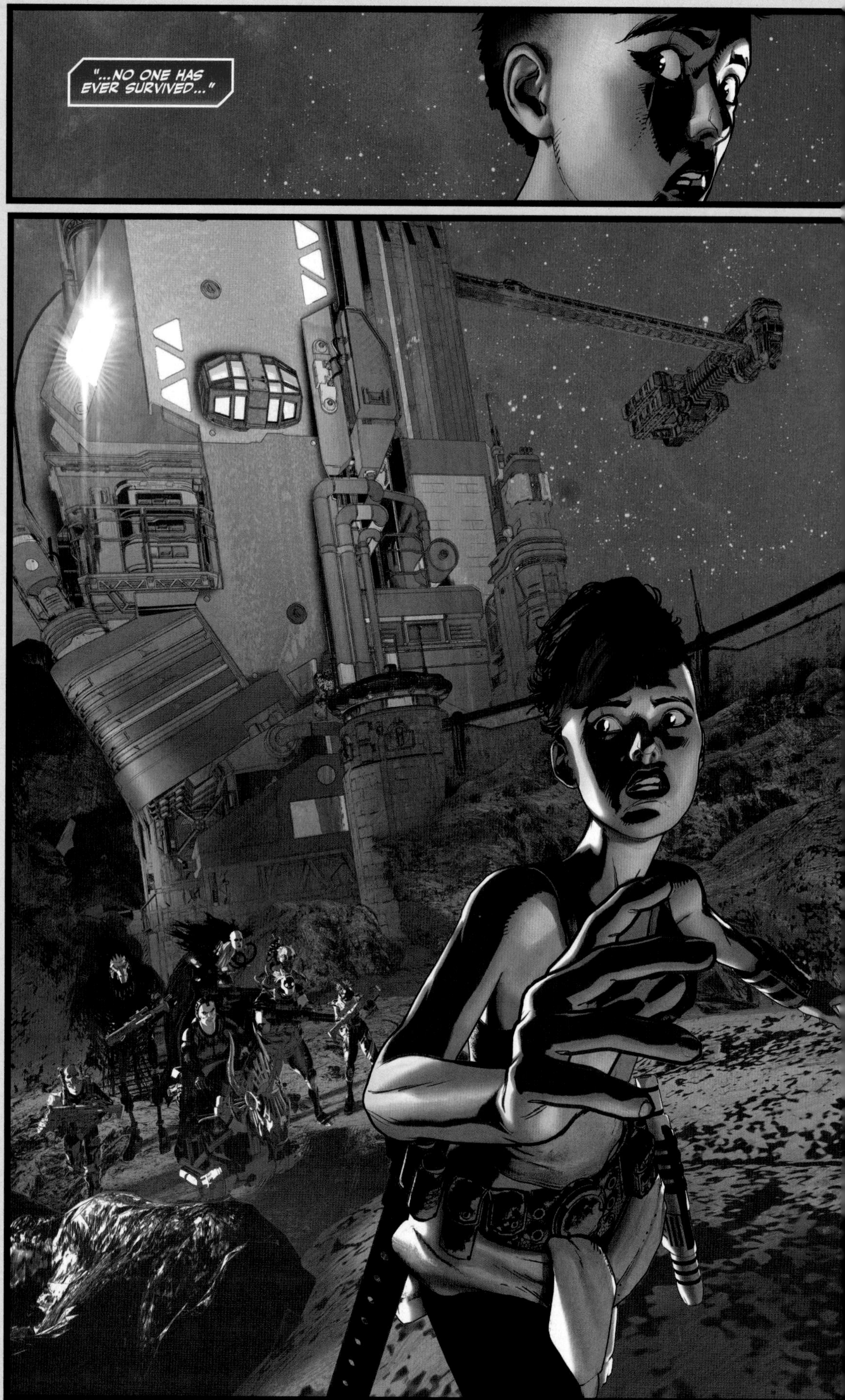
"...NO ONE HAS EVER SURVIVED..."

Issue #4 Cover A

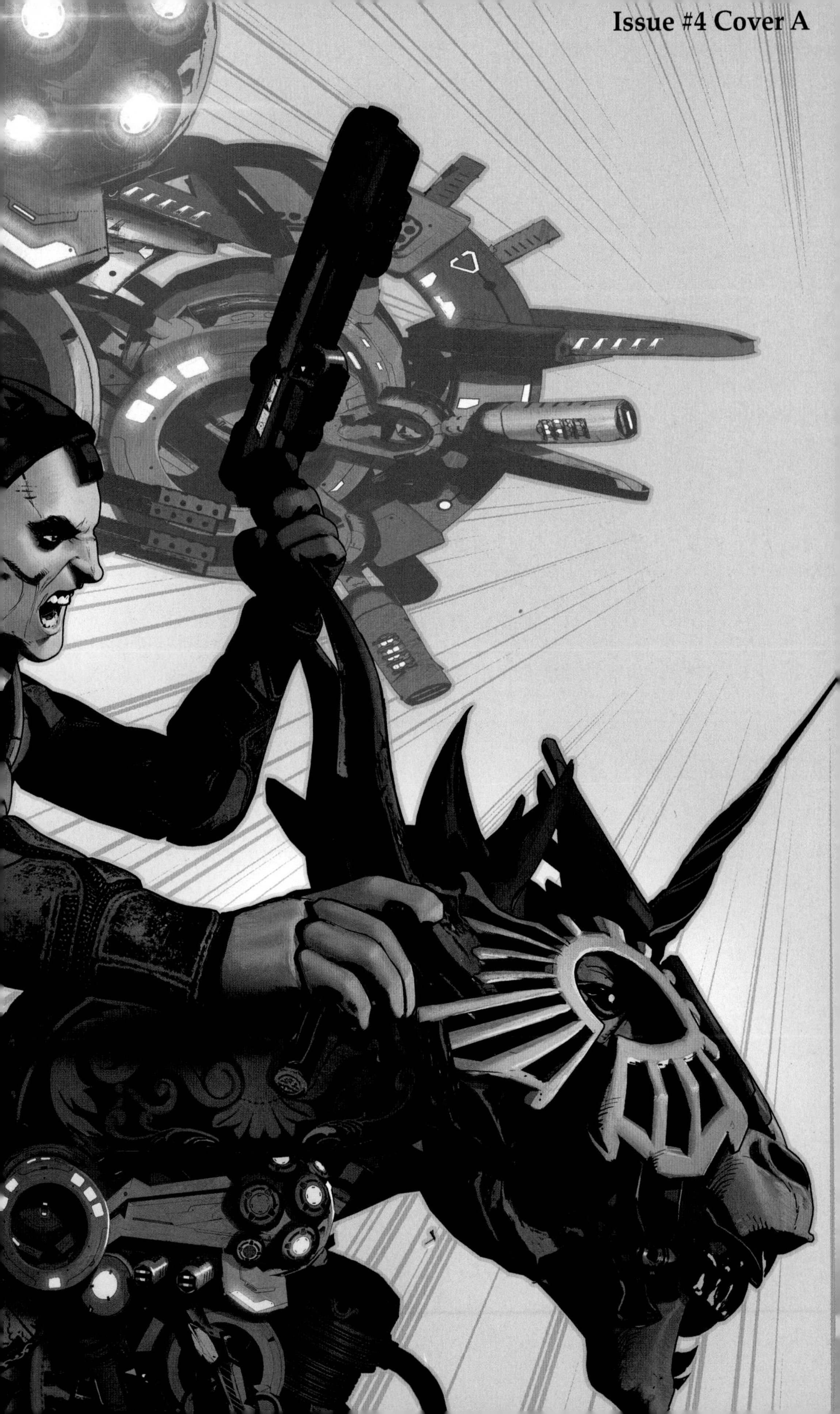

Issue #4 Cover B

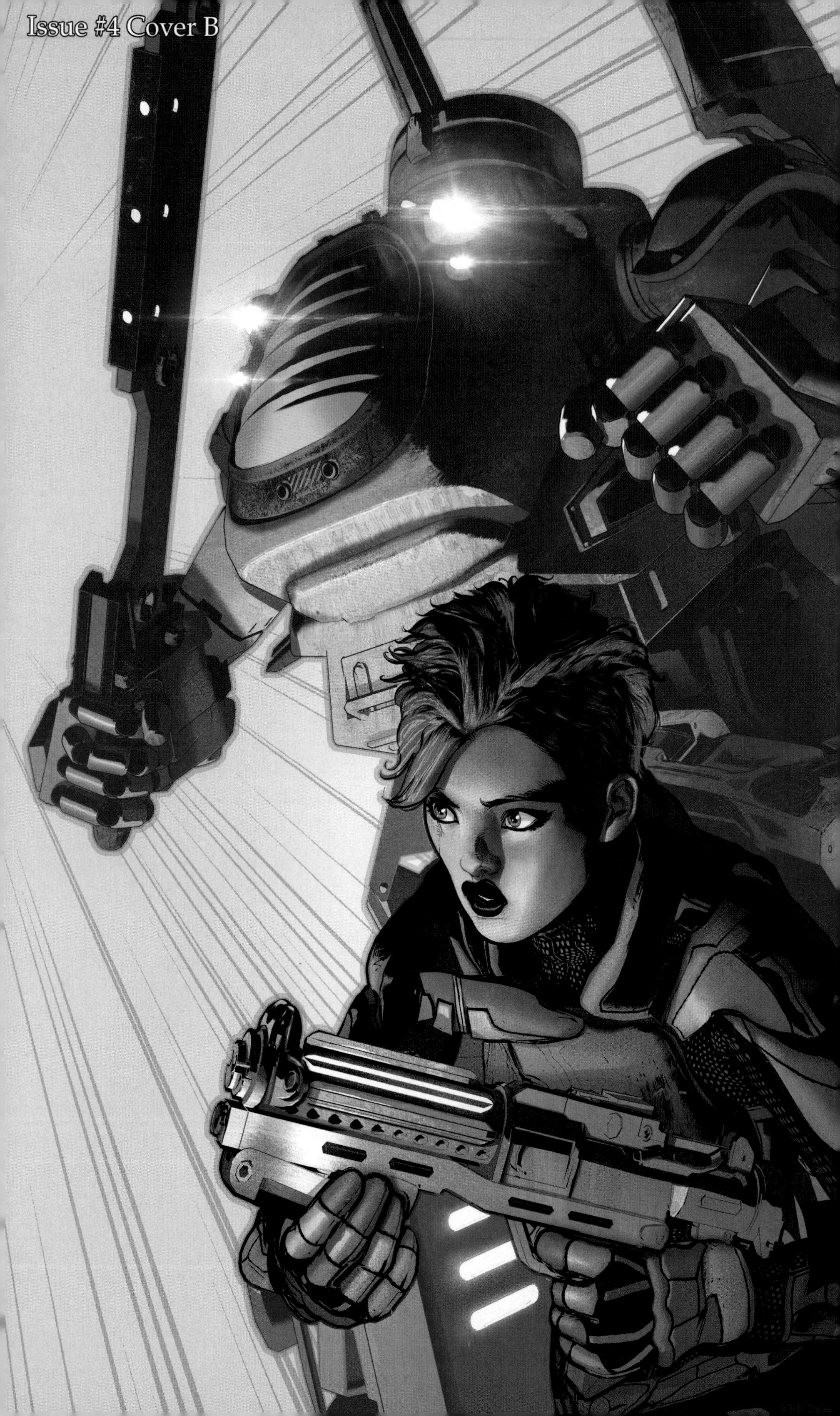

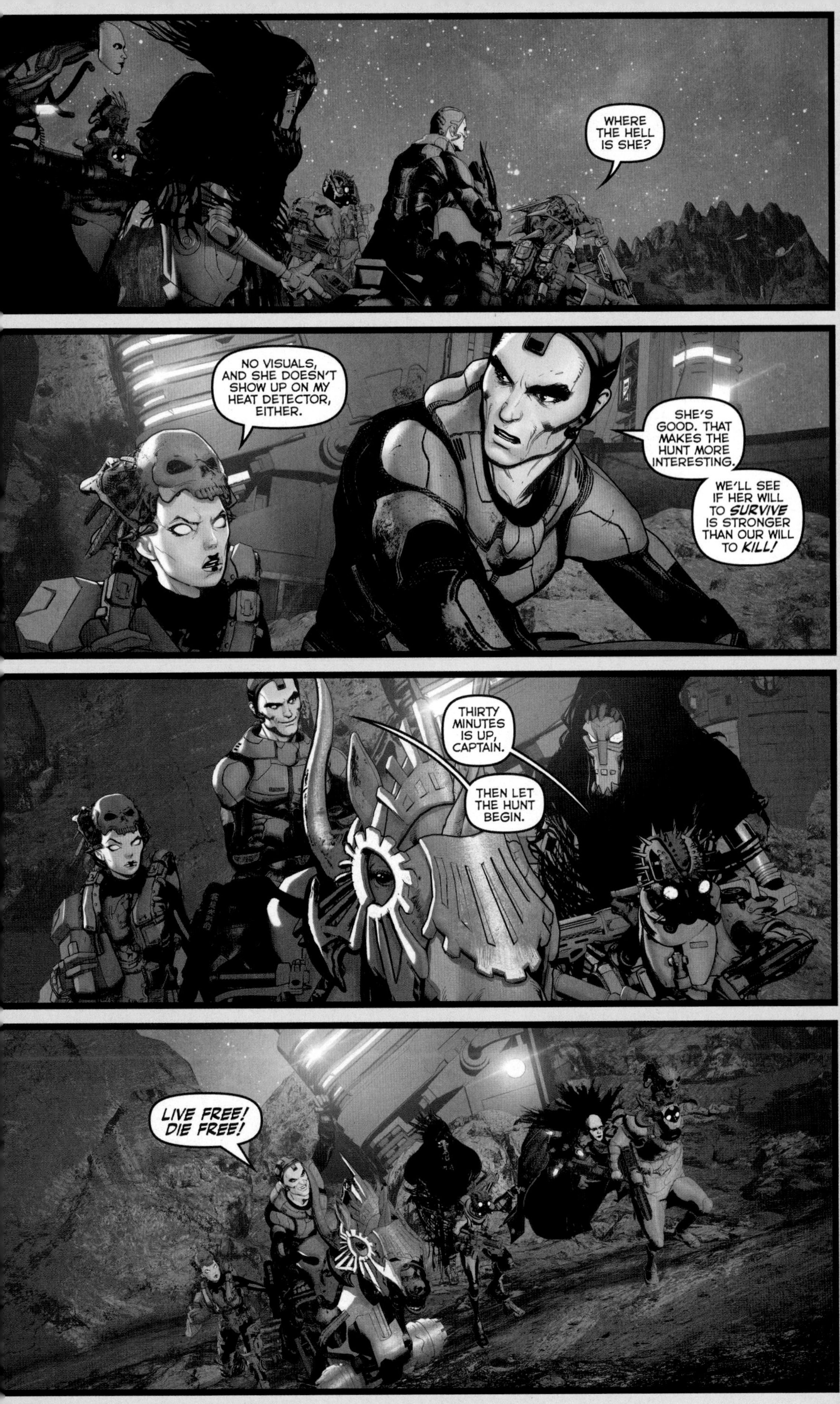
WHERE THE HELL IS SHE?
NO VISUALS, AND SHE DOESN'T SHOW UP ON MY HEAT DETECTOR, EITHER.
SHE'S GOOD. THAT MAKES THE HUNT MORE INTERESTING.
WE'LL SEE IF HER WILL TO ***SURVIVE*** IS STRONGER THAN OUR WILL TO ***KILL!***
THIRTY MINUTES IS UP, CAPTAIN.
THEN LET THE HUNT BEGIN.
LIVE FREE! DIE FREE!

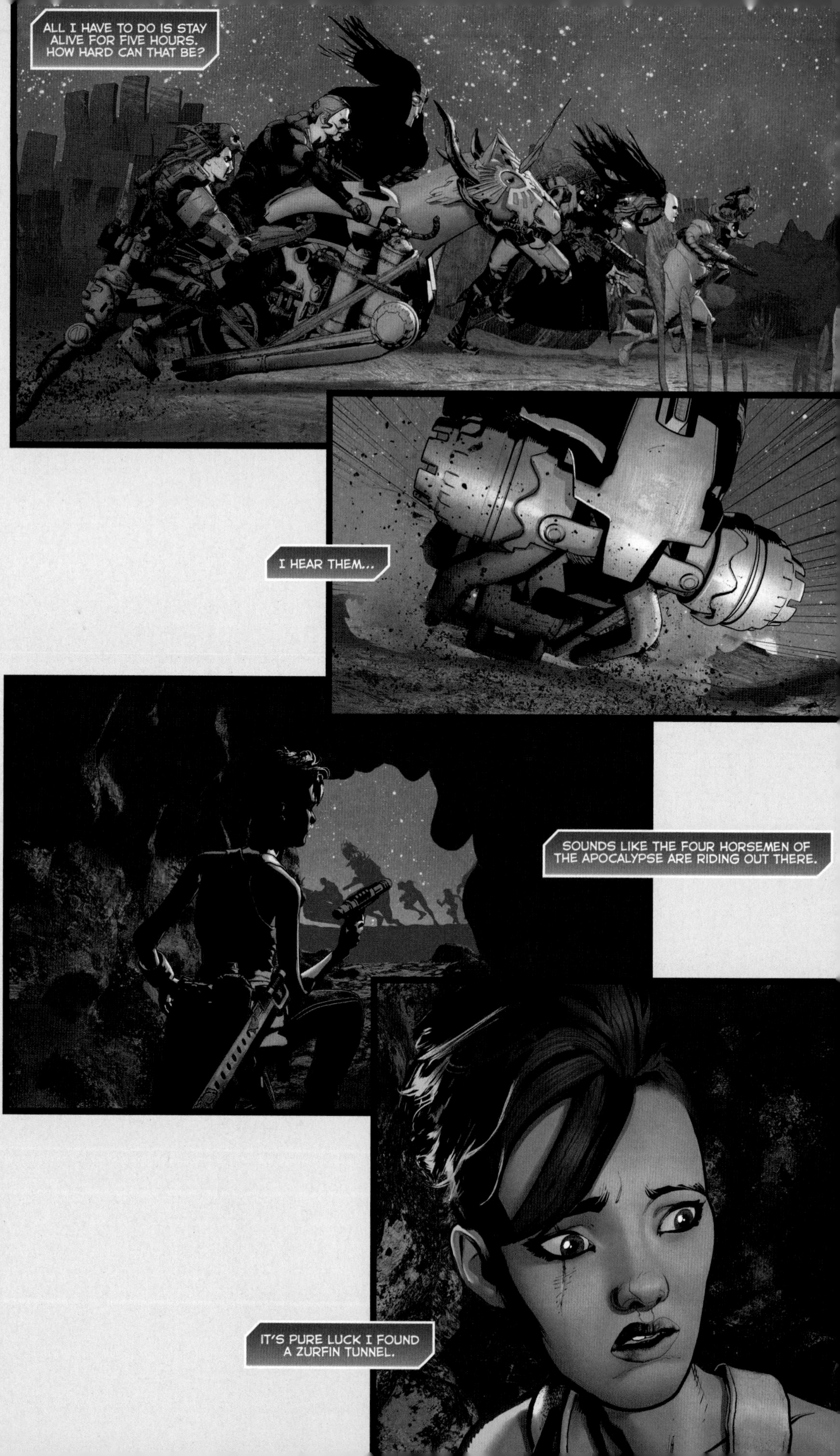
ALL I HAVE TO DO IS STAY ALIVE FOR FIVE HOURS. HOW HARD CAN THAT BE?
I HEAR THEM...
SOUNDS LIKE THE FOUR HORSEMEN OF THE APOCALYPSE ARE RIDING OUT THERE.
IT'S PURE LUCK I FOUND A ZURFIN TUNNEL.

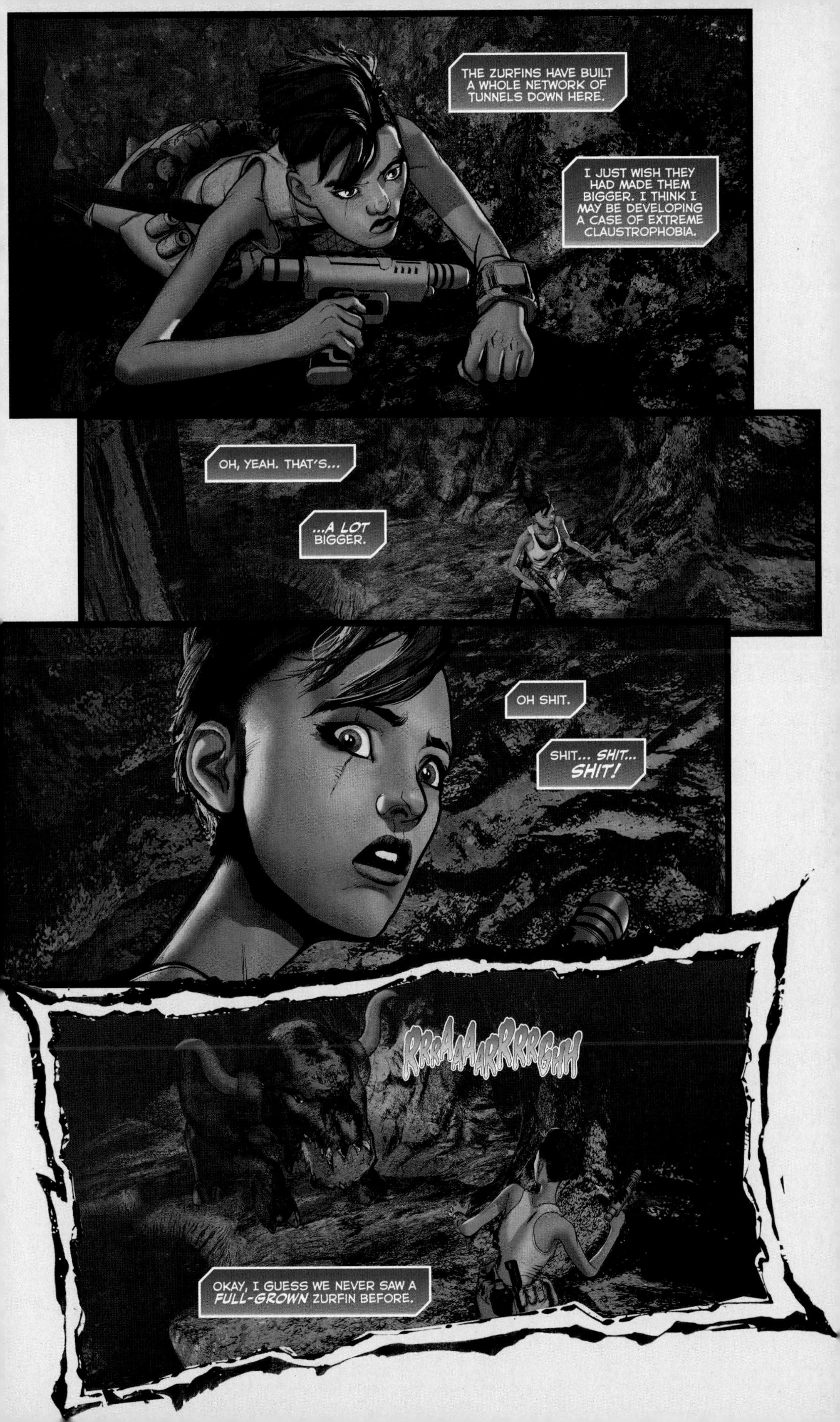
THE ZURFINS HAVE BUILT A WHOLE NETWORK OF TUNNELS DOWN HERE.
I JUST WISH THEY HAD MADE THEM BIGGER. I THINK I MAY BE DEVELOPING A CASE OF EXTREME CLAUSTROPHOBIA.
OH, YEAH. THAT'S...
...A LOT BIGGER.
OH SHIT.
SHIT... SHIT... SHIT!
RRRAAAARRRRGHH
OKAY, I GUESS WE NEVER SAW A FULL-GROWN ZURFIN BEFORE.

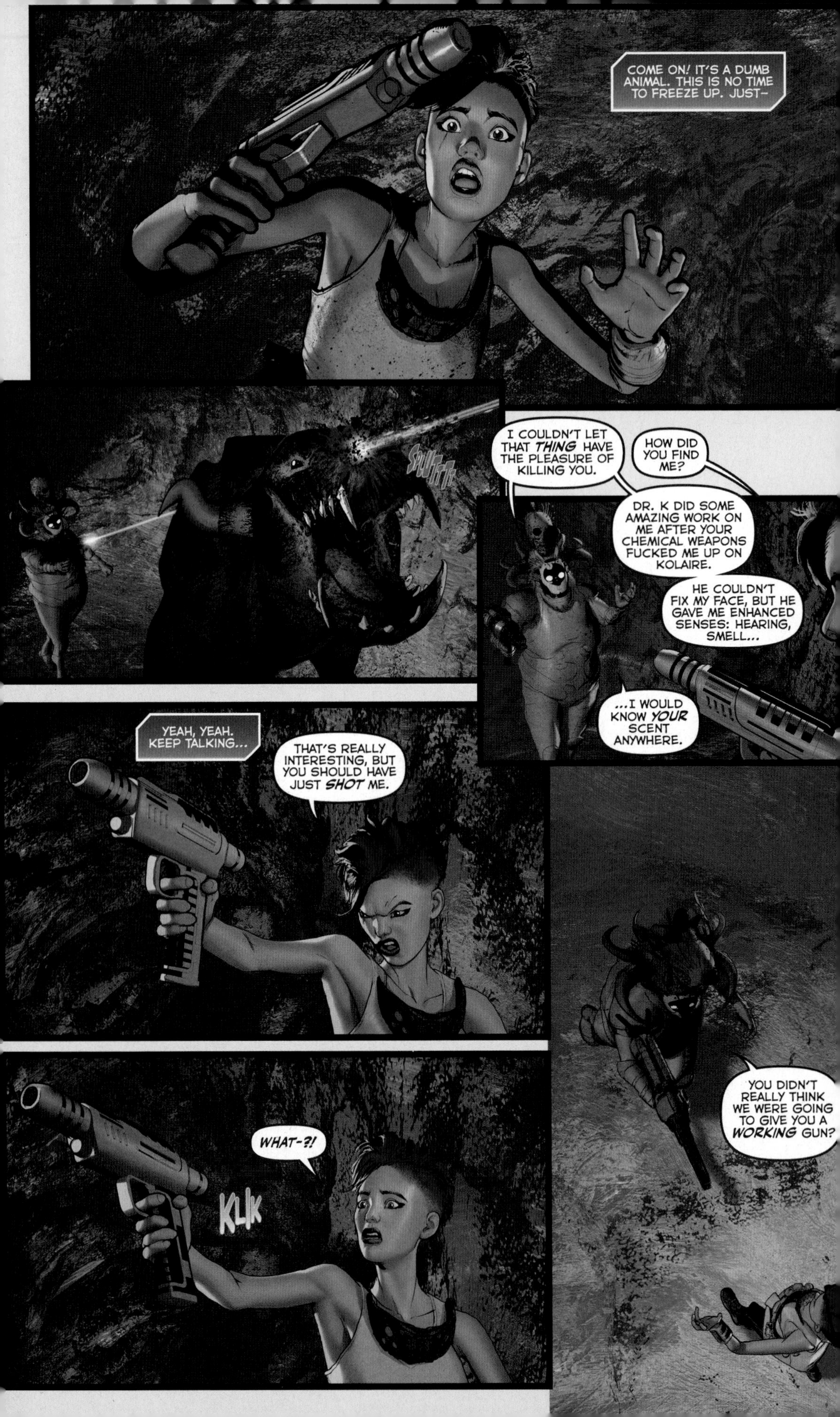
COME ON! IT'S A DUMB ANIMAL. THIS IS NO TIME TO FREEZE UP. JUST–
SPLUTT
I COULDN'T LET THAT *THING* HAVE THE PLEASURE OF KILLING YOU.
HOW DID YOU FIND ME?
DR. K DID SOME AMAZING WORK ON ME AFTER YOUR CHEMICAL WEAPONS FUCKED ME UP ON KOLAIRE.
HE COULDN'T FIX MY FACE, BUT HE GAVE ME ENHANCED SENSES: HEARING, SMELL...
...I WOULD KNOW *YOUR* SCENT ANYWHERE.
YEAH, YEAH. KEEP TALKING...
THAT'S REALLY INTERESTING, BUT YOU SHOULD HAVE JUST *SHOT* ME.
WHAT-?!
KLIK
YOU DIDN'T REALLY THINK WE WERE GOING TO GIVE YOU A *WORKING* GUN?

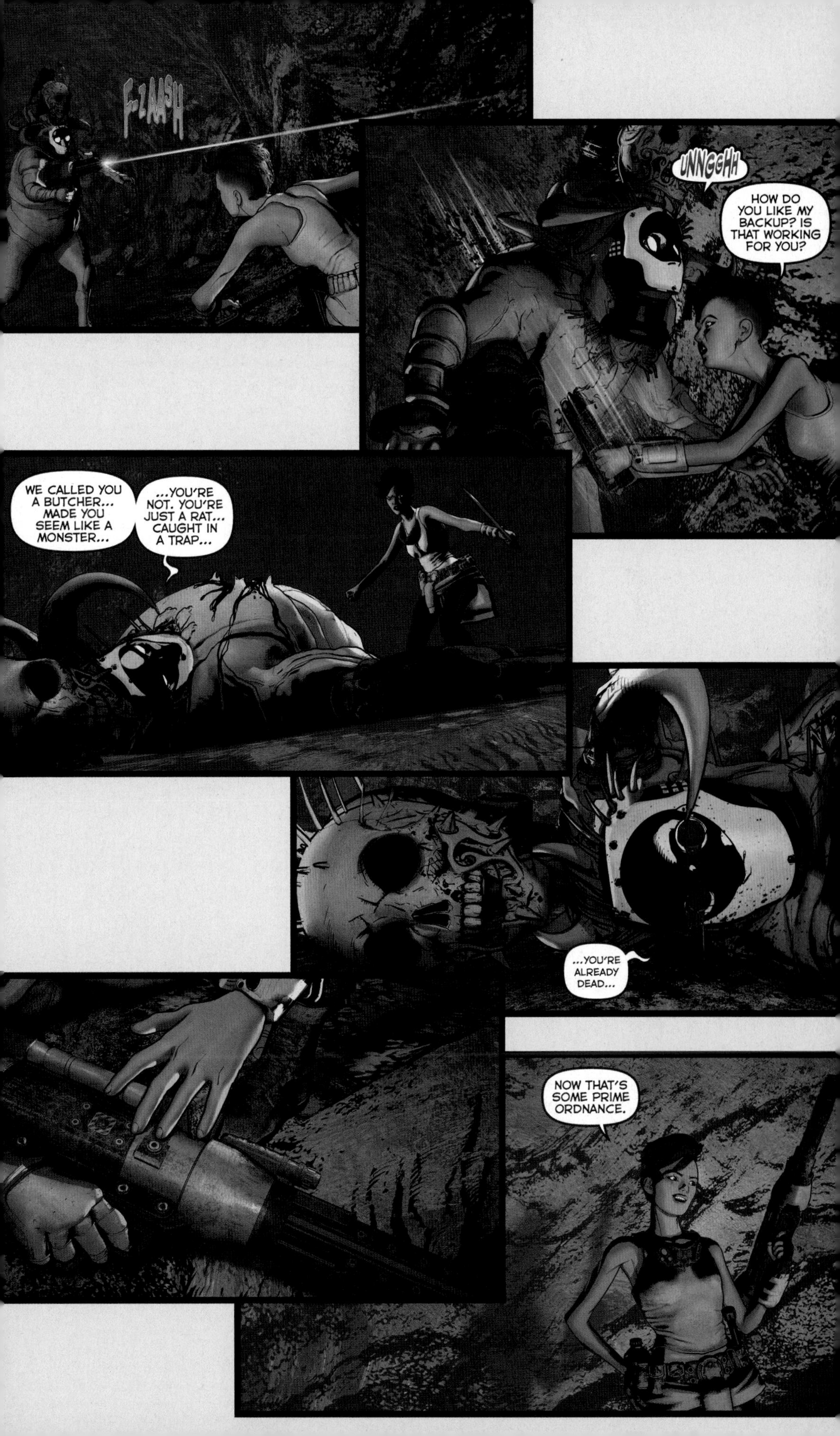
F-ZAASH
UNNGGHH
HOW DO YOU LIKE MY BACKUP? IS THAT WORKING FOR YOU?
WE CALLED YOU A BUTCHER... MADE YOU SEEM LIKE A MONSTER...
...YOU'RE NOT. YOU'RE JUST A RAT... CAUGHT IN A TRAP...
...YOU'RE ALREADY DEAD...
NOW THAT'S SOME PRIME ORDNANCE.

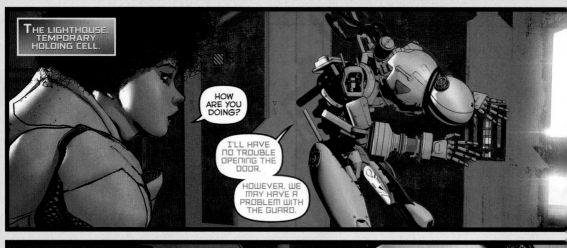

THE LIGHTHOUSE. TEMPORARY HOLDING CELL.
HOW ARE YOU DOING?
I'LL HAVE NO TROUBLE OPENING THE DOOR.
HOWEVER, WE MAY HAVE A PROBLEM WITH THE GUARD.
REALLY? I WOULD THINK YOU COULD TAKE THEM OUT WITHOUT TOO MUCH TROUBLE.
AH, WELL, YOU SEE, THERE'S THE *ROBOTIC CODE.*
MY IMPERATIVE IS TO DO WHATEVER IT TAKES TO PROTECT MISTRESS VASQUEZ, EXCEPT...
...I'M NOT ALLOWED TO KILL SENTIENT BEINGS ABOVE CATEGORY 3 INTELLIGENCE.
IT'S A *FAIL-SAFE* THAT WAS BUILT INTO DOMESTIC ARTIFICIAL INTELLIGENCE IN THE OLD DAYS.
SO WHAT CAN WE DO ABOUT THAT?
WELL, YOU, AS A LEVEL *FIVE* SENTIENT, CAN OVERRIDE THAT FAIL-SAFE...
...PROVIDED I ALLOW YOU TO INTERFERE WITH MY HARD DRIVE.
UH... RIGHT.

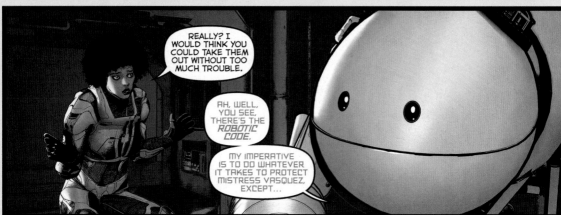

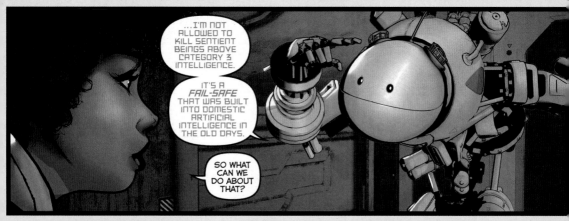

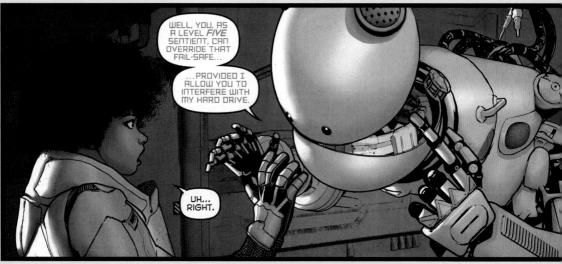

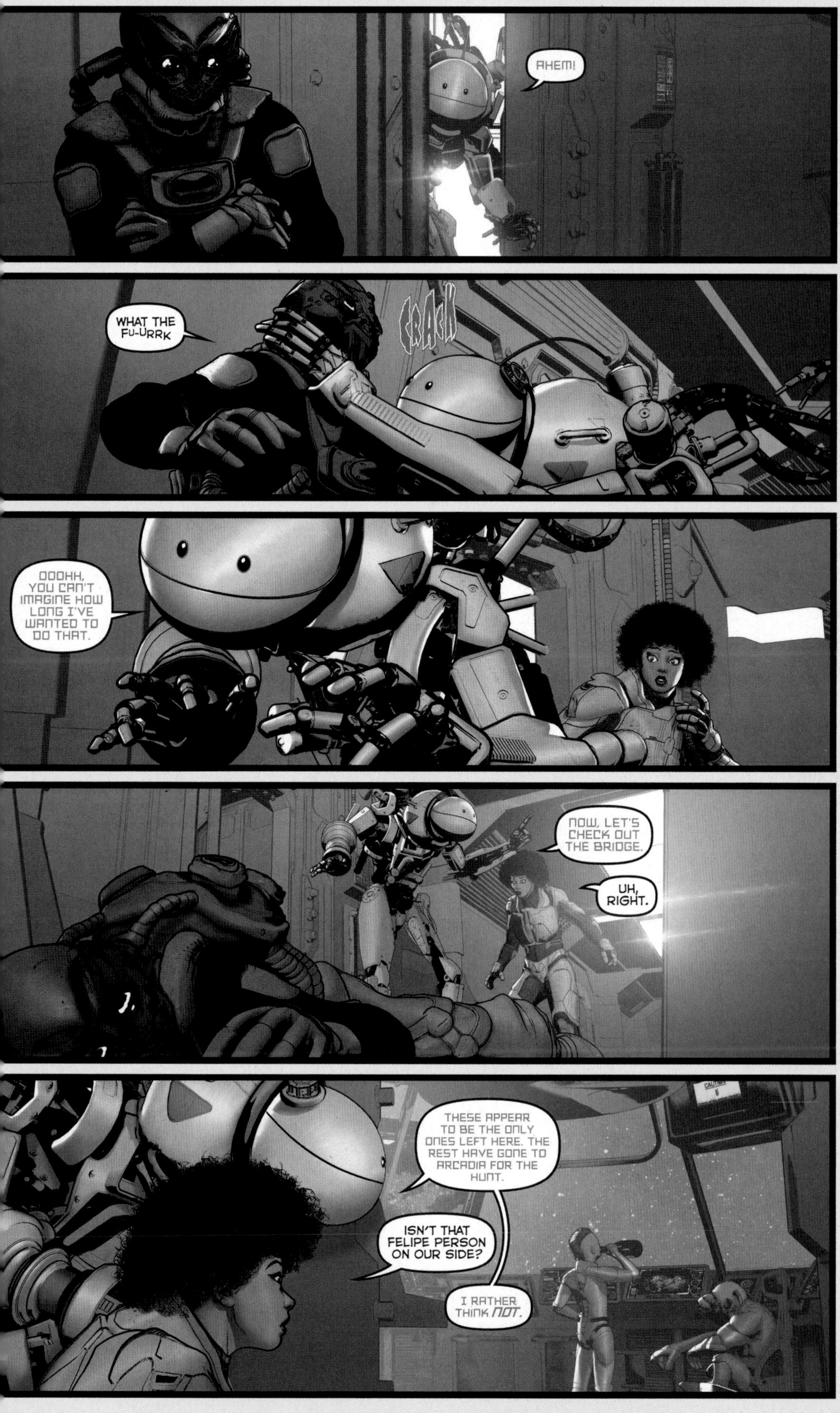
AHEM!
WHAT THE FU-URRK
CRACK
OOOHH, YOU CAN'T IMAGINE HOW LONG I'VE WANTED TO DO THAT.
NOW, LET'S CHECK OUT THE BRIDGE.
UH, RIGHT.
THESE APPEAR TO BE THE ONLY ONES LEFT HERE. THE REST HAVE GONE TO ARCADIA FOR THE HUNT.
ISN'T THAT FELIPE PERSON ON OUR SIDE?
I RATHER THINK NOT.

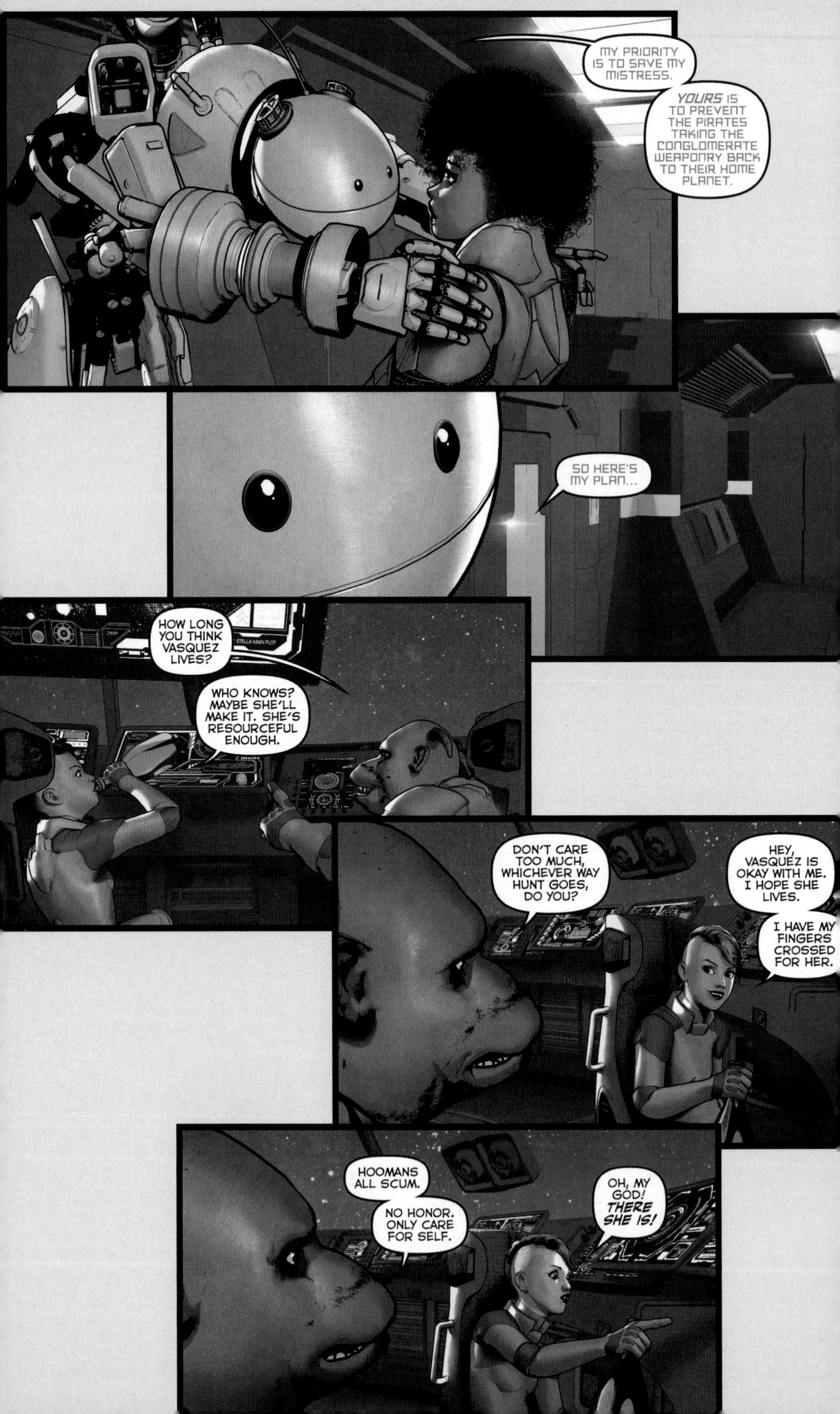
MY PRIORITY IS TO SAVE MY MISTRESS.
YOURS IS TO PREVENT THE PIRATES TAKING THE CONGLOMERATE WEAPONRY BACK TO THEIR HOME PLANET.
SO HERE'S MY PLAN...
HOW LONG YOU THINK VASQUEZ LIVES?
WHO KNOWS? MAYBE SHE'LL MAKE IT. SHE'S RESOURCEFUL ENOUGH.
DON'T CARE TOO MUCH, WHICHEVER WAY HUNT GOES, DO YOU?
HEY, VASQUEZ IS OKAY WITH ME. I HOPE SHE LIVES.
I HAVE MY FINGERS CROSSED FOR HER.
HOOMANS ALL SCUM.
NO HONOR. ONLY CARE FOR SELF.
OH, MY GOD! THERE SHE IS!

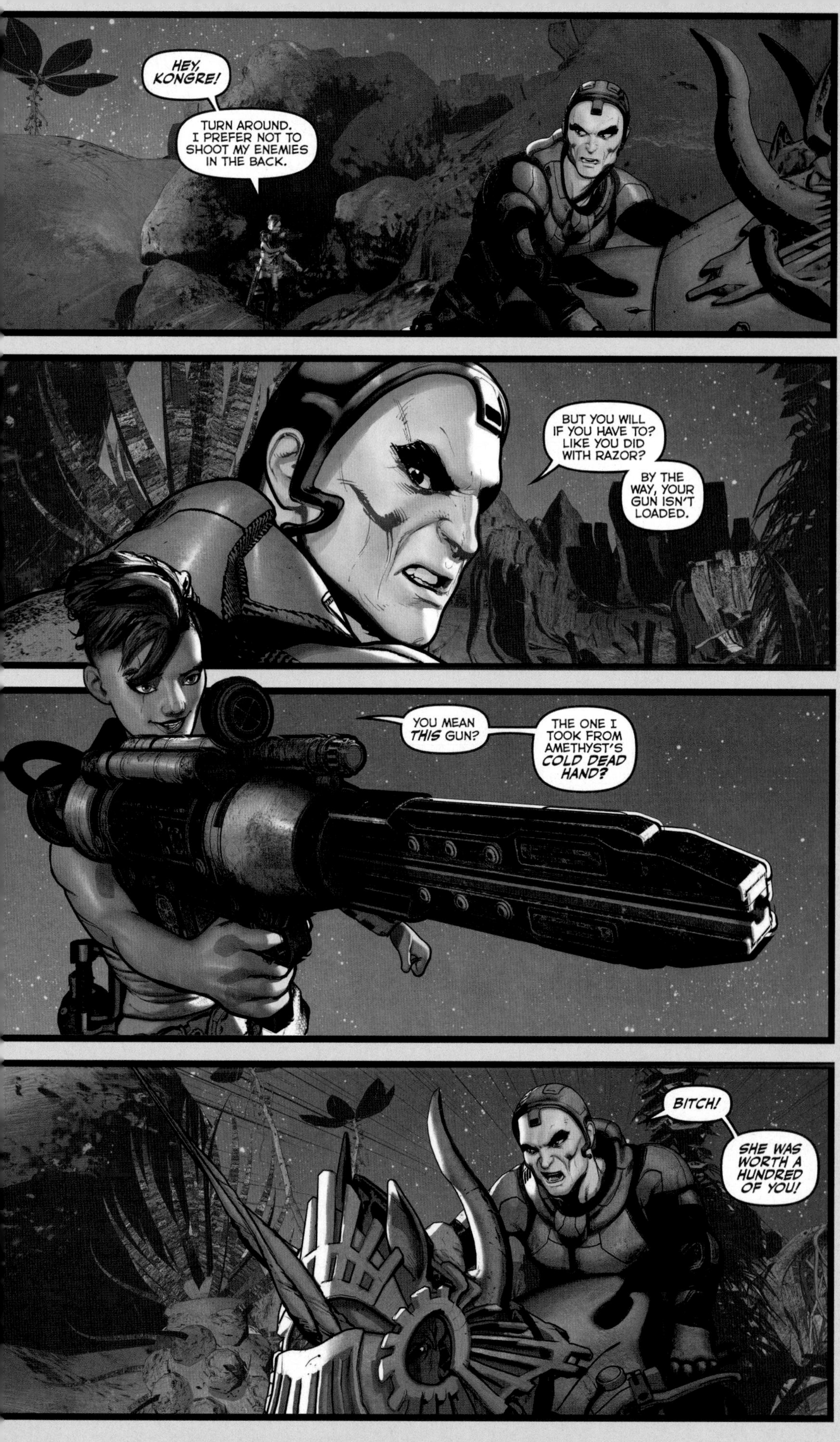
HEY, KONGRE!
TURN AROUND. I PREFER NOT TO SHOOT MY ENEMIES IN THE BACK.
BUT YOU WILL IF YOU HAVE TO? LIKE YOU DID WITH RAZOR?
BY THE WAY, YOUR GUN ISN'T LOADED.
YOU MEAN *THIS* GUN?
THE ONE I TOOK FROM AMETHYST'S *COLD DEAD HAND?*
BITCH!
SHE WAS WORTH A HUNDRED OF YOU!

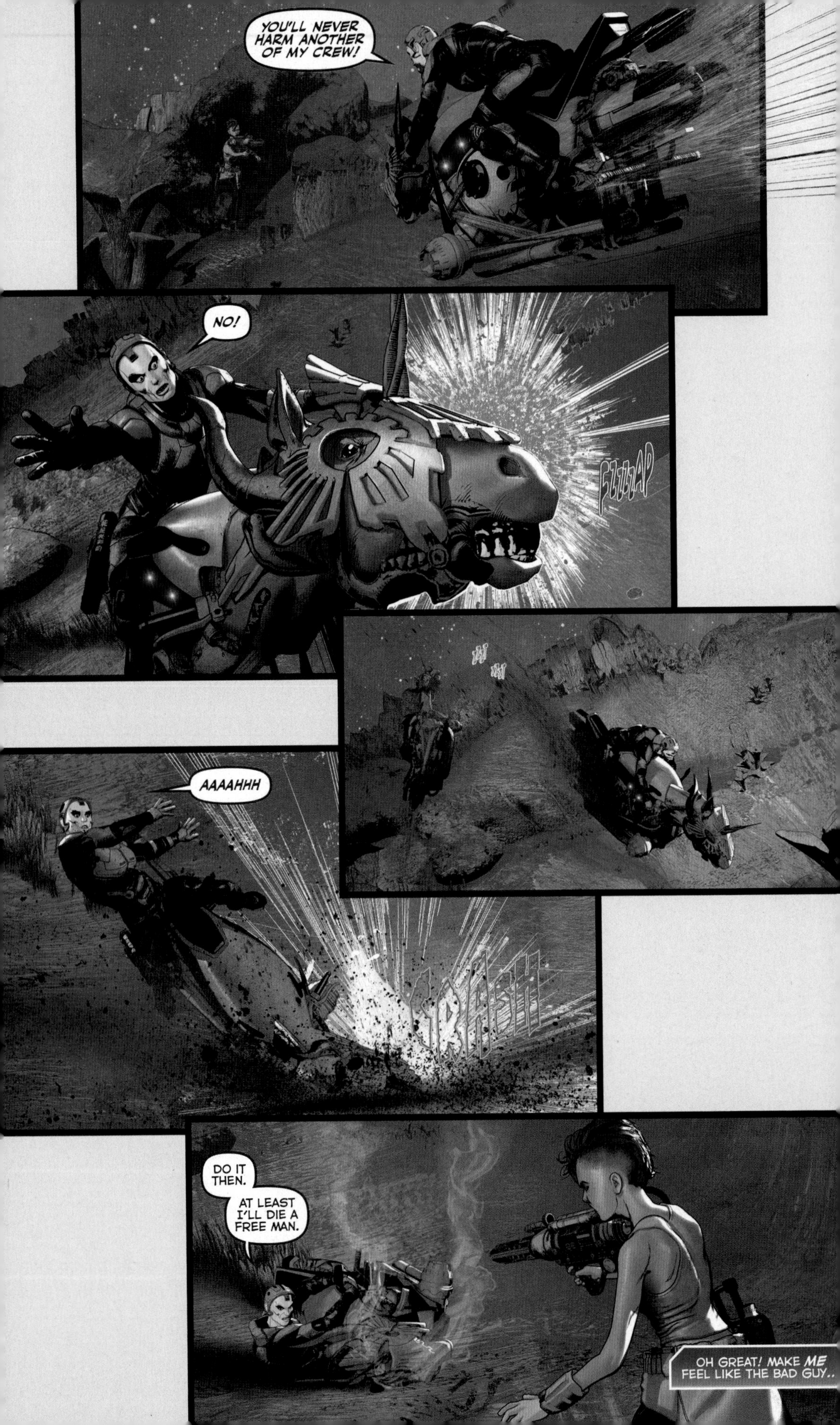
YOU'LL NEVER HARM ANOTHER OF MY CREW!
NO!
FZZZAP
AAAAHHH
CRASH
DO IT THEN.
AT LEAST I'LL DIE A FREE MAN.
OH GREAT! MAKE *ME* FEEL LIKE THE BAD GUY..

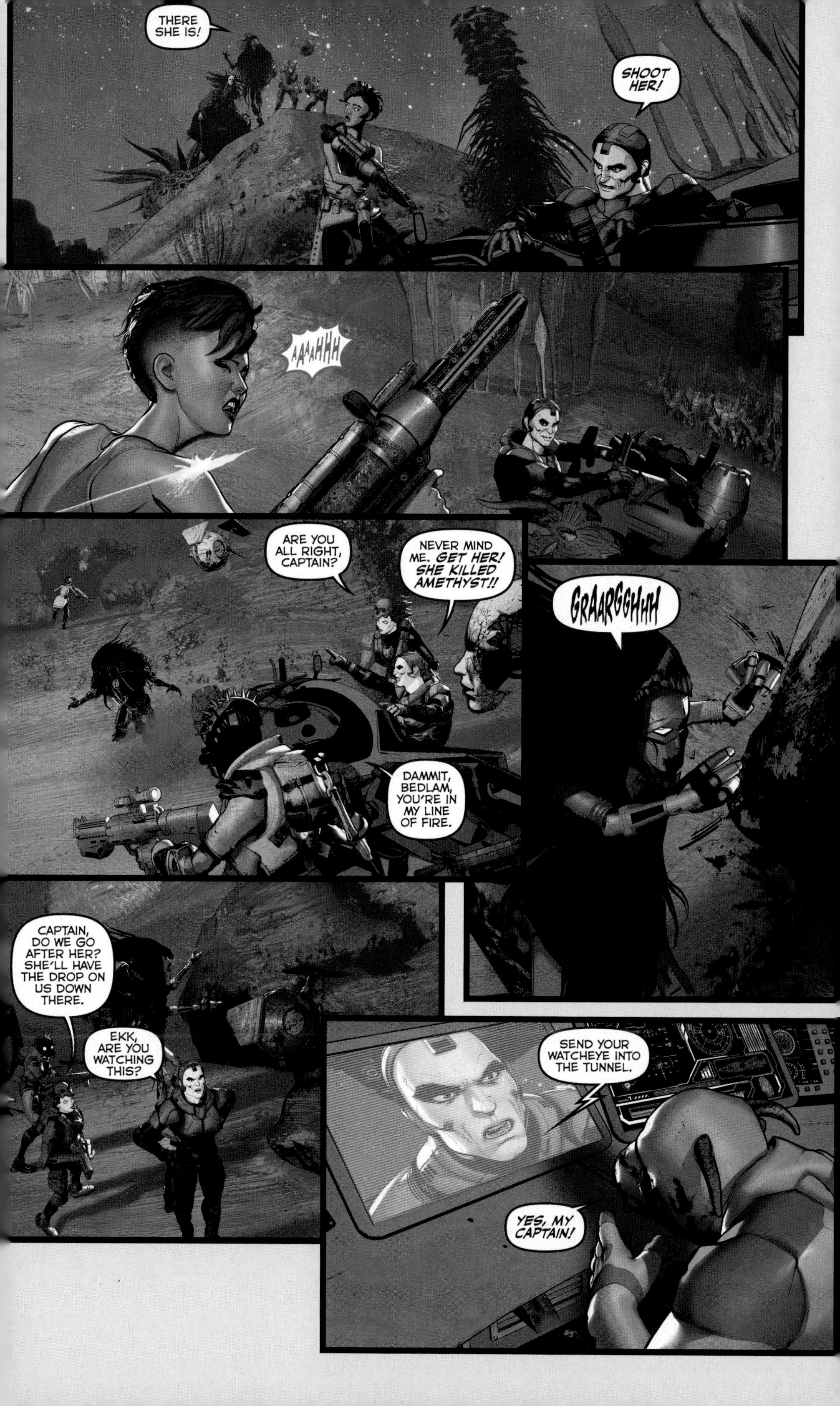

THERE SHE IS!
SHOOT HER!
AAAAHHH
ARE YOU ALL RIGHT, CAPTAIN?
NEVER MIND ME. GET HER! SHE KILLED AMETHYST!!
DAMMIT, BEDLAM, YOU'RE IN MY LINE OF FIRE.
GRAARGGHHH
CAPTAIN, DO WE GO AFTER HER? SHE'LL HAVE THE DROP ON US DOWN THERE.
EKK, ARE YOU WATCHING THIS?
SEND YOUR WATCHEYE INTO THE TUNNEL.
YES, MY CAPTAIN!

TRACKING TARGET.
WHAT DID I TELL YOU? VASQUEZ HAS THE CHOPS FOR THIS.
DOCTOR DAVIS, ARE YOU IN POSITION?
OKAY, MOSES, I THINK I HAVE THIS FIGURED OUT.
I'M REALIGNING THE CANNON NOW.
FIRE AT WILL, DAVIS.
MISTRESS VASQUEZ NEEDS A DISTRACTION AND SHE NEEDS IT NOW!
DISTRACTION COMING UP!!

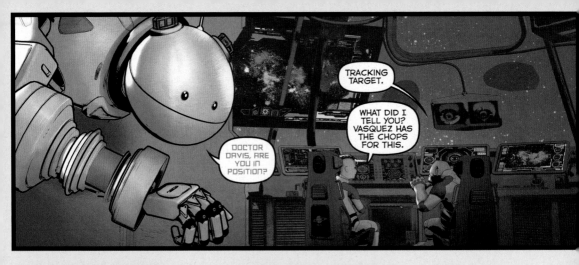

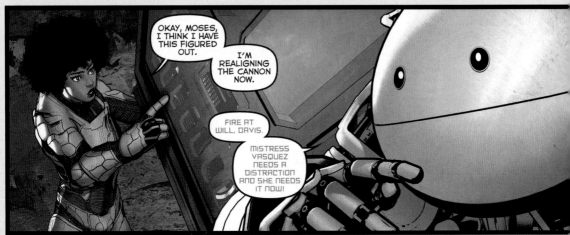

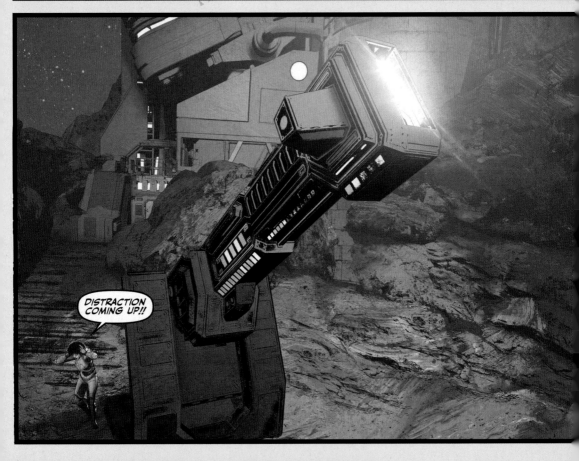

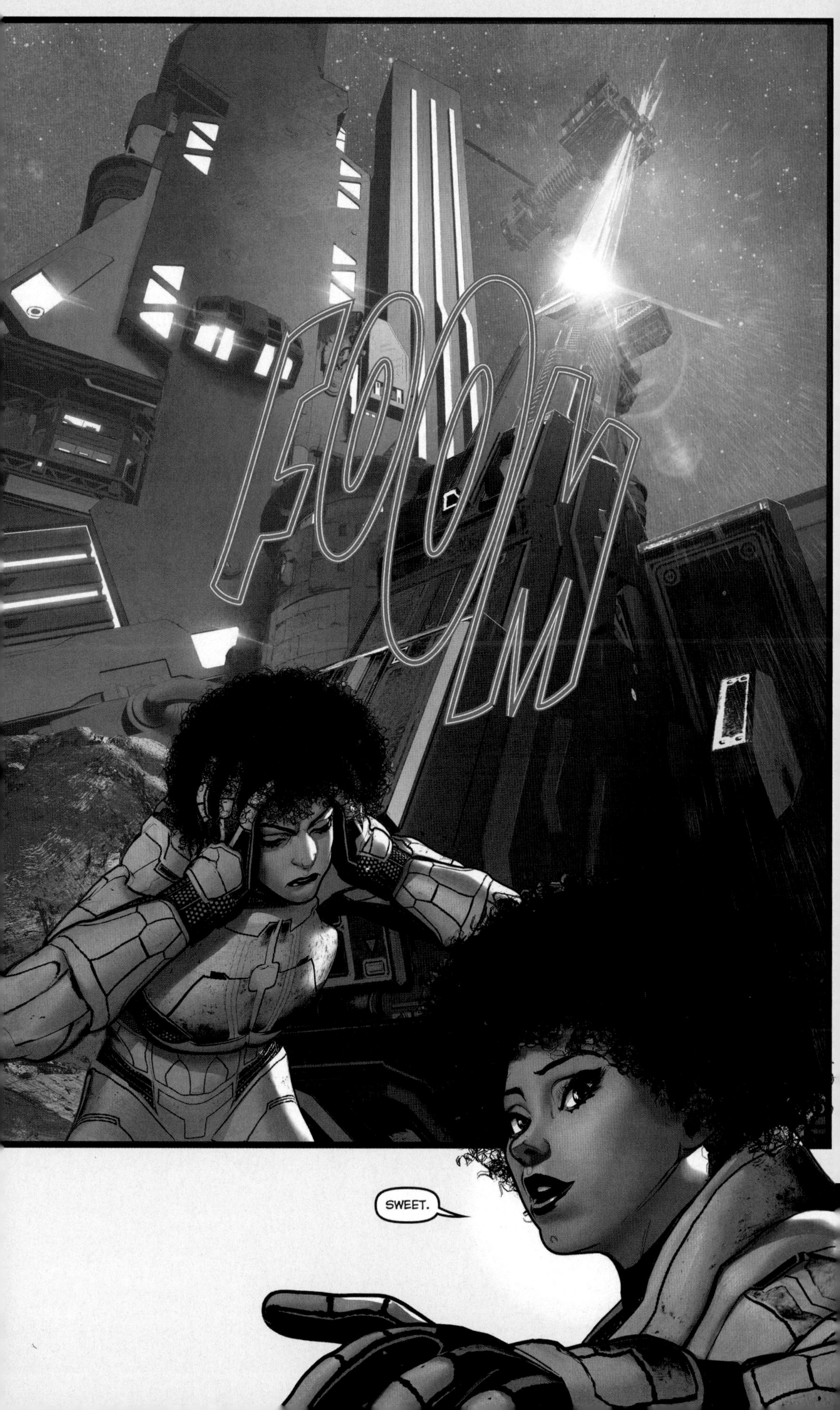
FOOOM
SWEET.

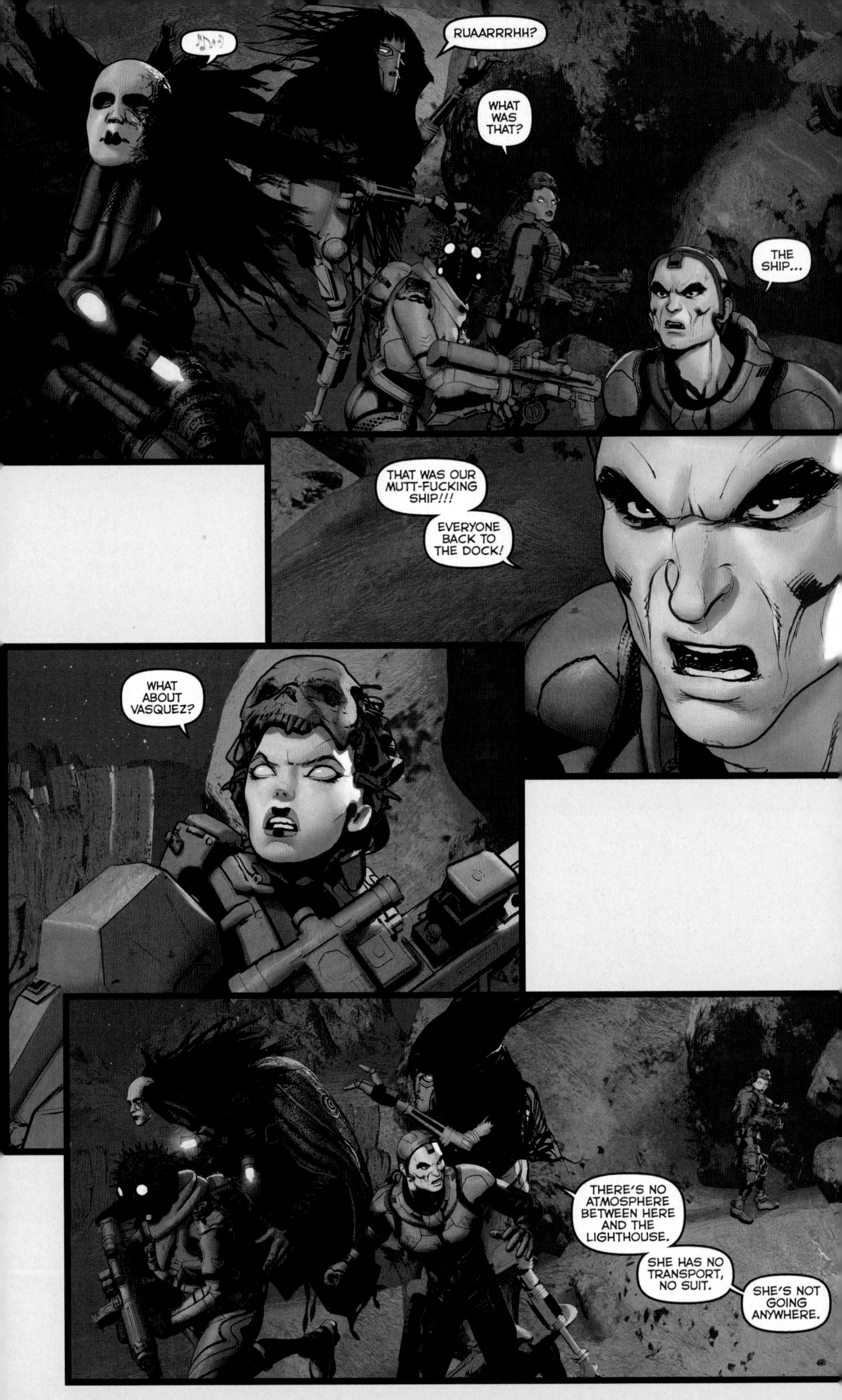
♫♪♪
RUAARRRHH?
WHAT WAS THAT?
THE SHIP...
THAT WAS OUR MUTT-FUCKING SHIP!!!
EVERYONE BACK TO THE DOCK!
WHAT ABOUT VASQUEZ?
THERE'S NO ATMOSPHERE BETWEEN HERE AND THE LIGHTHOUSE.
SHE HAS NO TRANSPORT, NO SUIT.
SHE'S NOT GOING ANYWHERE.

WHAT'S THE DAMAGE?

ONE ENGINE NEEDS A MAJOR OVERHAUL.

WE CAN JERRY-RIG IT SO WE CAN LIMP HOME IN A FEW DAYS.

GET IT DONE.

I'M HEADING UP TO THE BRIDGE.

WHERE IS SHE?

THESE ARE THE LAST MOMENTS WE RECORDED.

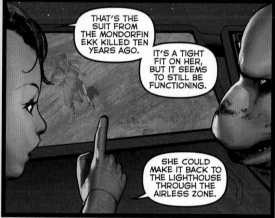

THAT'S THE SUIT FROM THE MONDORFIN EKK KILLED TEN YEARS AGO.

IT'S A TIGHT FIT ON HER, BUT IT SEEMS TO STILL BE FUNCTIONING.

SHE COULD MAKE IT BACK TO THE LIGHTHOUSE THROUGH THE AIRLESS ZONE.

UH... THIS WHERE SHE SEES CAMERA...

KRRRSSSSSS

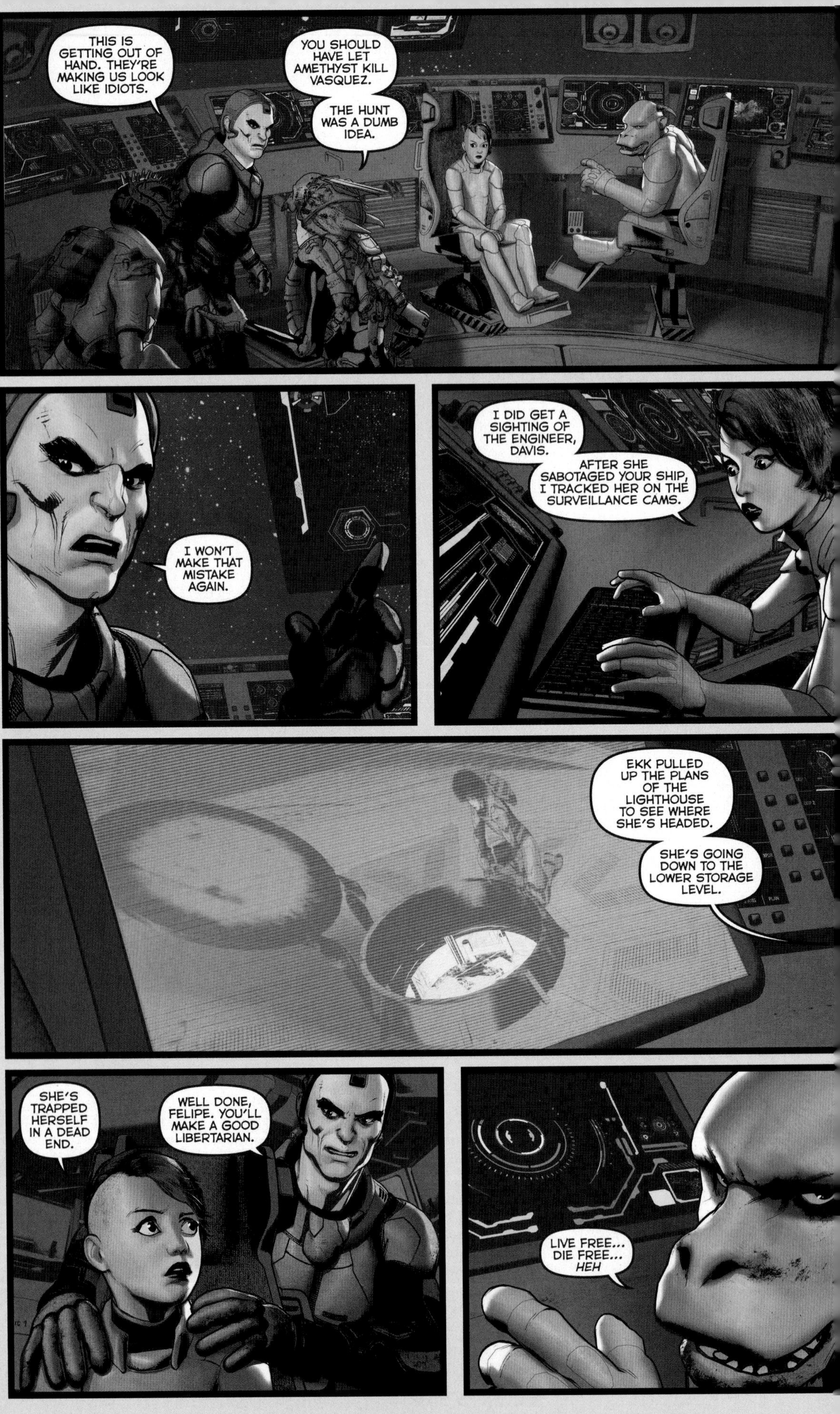
THIS IS GETTING OUT OF HAND. THEY'RE MAKING US LOOK LIKE IDIOTS.
YOU SHOULD HAVE LET AMETHYST KILL VASQUEZ.
THE HUNT WAS A DUMB IDEA.
I WON'T MAKE THAT MISTAKE AGAIN.
I DID GET A SIGHTING OF THE ENGINEER, DAVIS.
AFTER SHE SABOTAGED YOUR SHIP, I TRACKED HER ON THE SURVEILLANCE CAMS.
EKK PULLED UP THE PLANS OF THE LIGHTHOUSE TO SEE WHERE SHE'S HEADED.
SHE'S GOING DOWN TO THE LOWER STORAGE LEVEL.
SHE'S TRAPPED HERSELF IN A DEAD END.
WELL DONE, FELIPE. YOU'LL MAKE A GOOD LIBERTARIAN.
LIVE FREE... DIE FREE... *HEH*

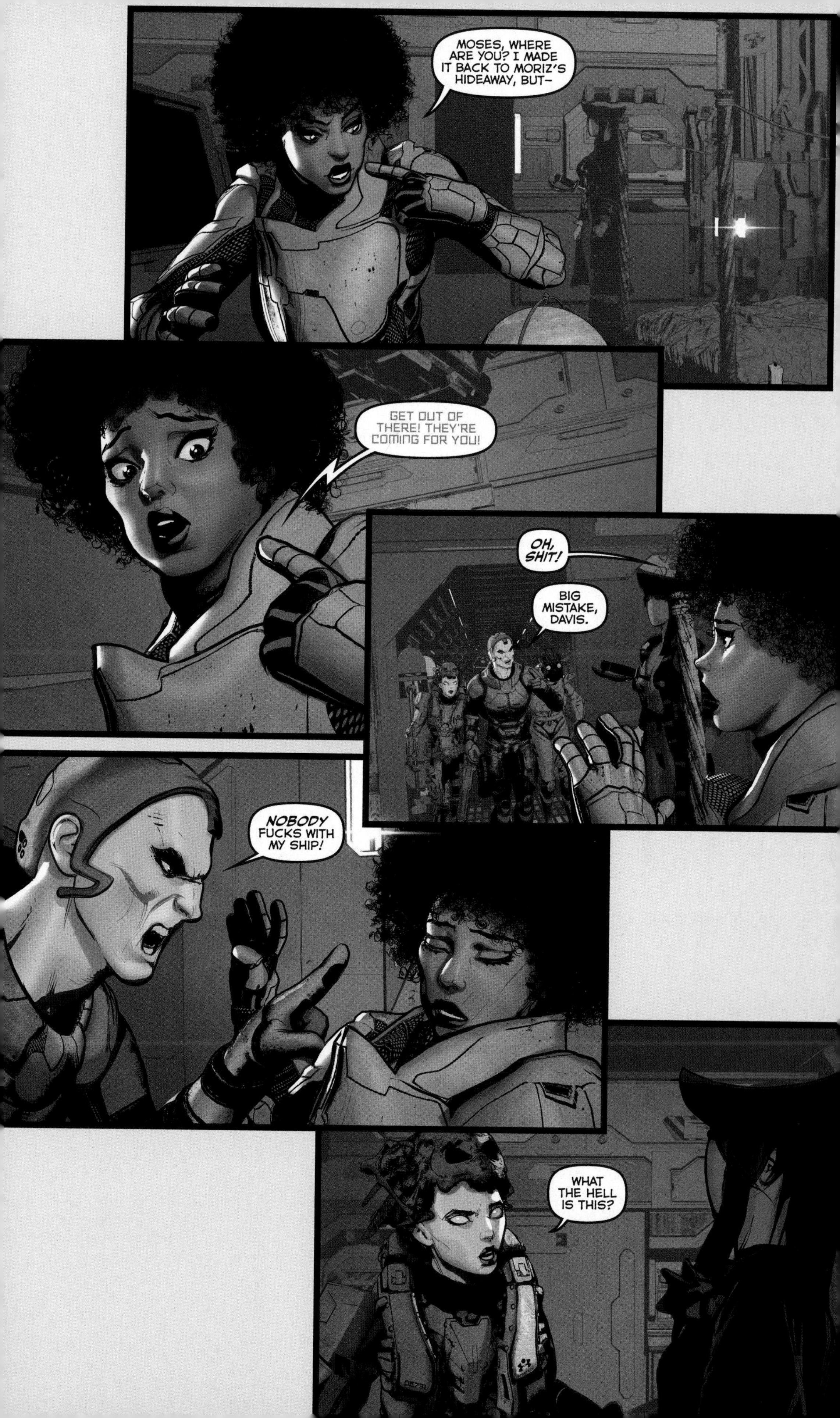
MOSES, WHERE ARE YOU? I MADE IT BACK TO MORIZ'S HIDEAWAY, BUT–
GET OUT OF THERE! THEY'RE COMING FOR YOU!
OH, SHIT!
BIG MISTAKE, DAVIS.
NOBODY FUCKS WITH MY SHIP!
WHAT THE HELL IS THIS?

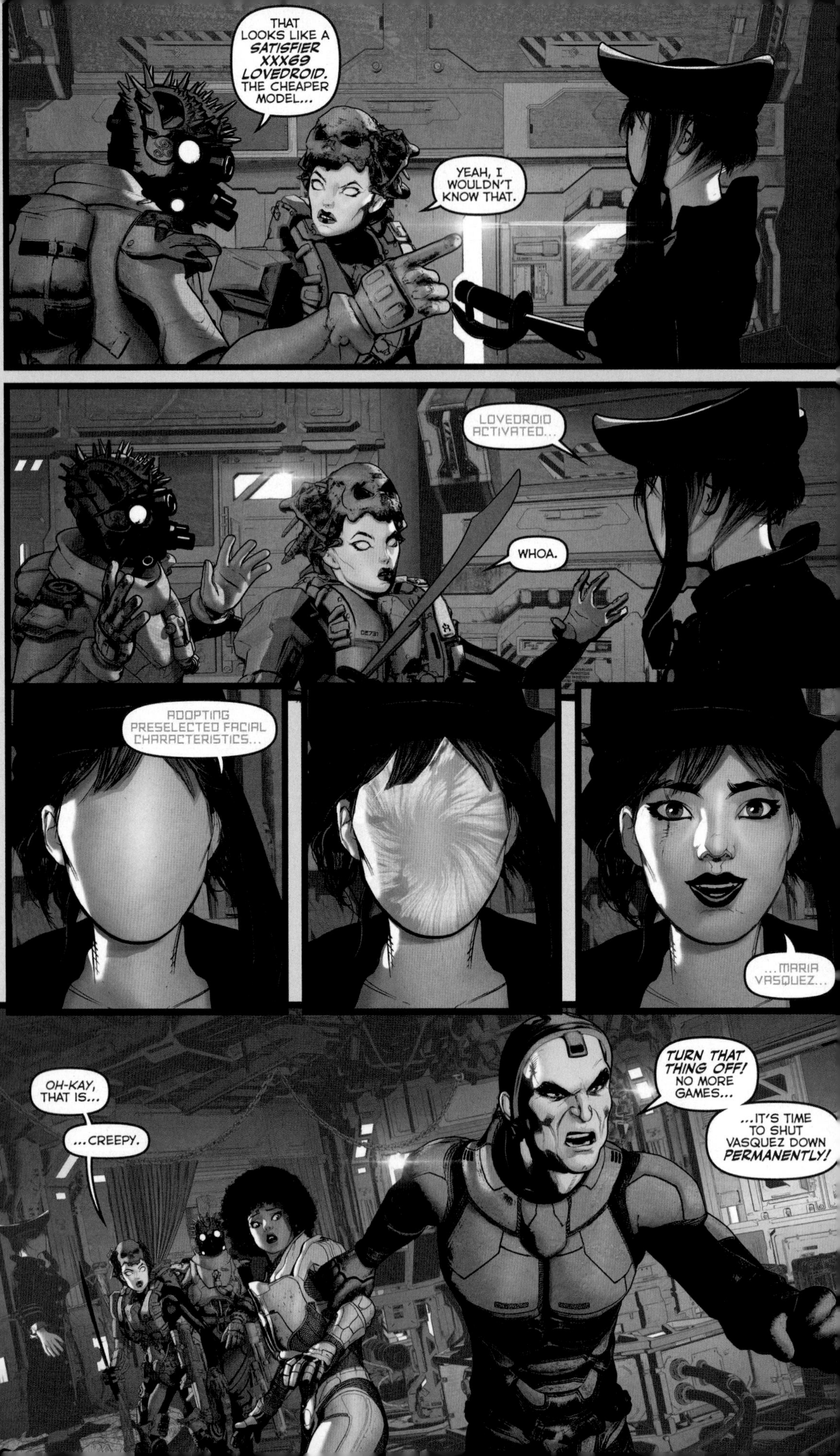

THAT LOOKS LIKE A *SATISFIER XXX69 LOVEDROID.* THE CHEAPER MODEL...
YEAH, I WOULDN'T KNOW THAT.
LOVEDROID ACTIVATED...
WHOA.
ADOPTING PRESELECTED FACIAL CHARACTERISTICS...
...MARIA VASQUEZ...
OH-KAY, THAT IS...
...CREEPY.
TURN THAT THING OFF! NO MORE GAMES...
...IT'S TIME TO SHUT VASQUEZ DOWN *PERMANENTLY!*

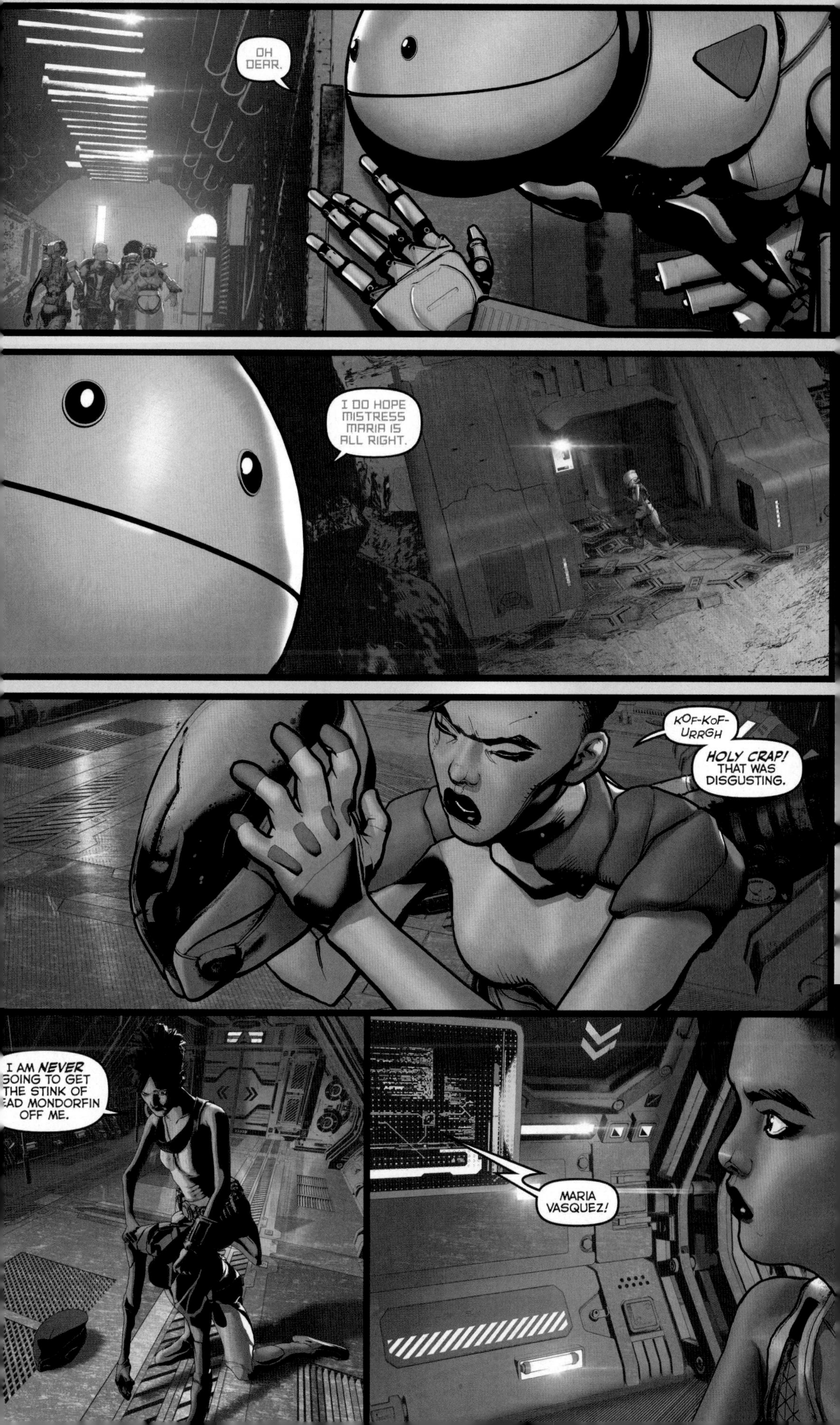
OH DEAR.
I DO HOPE MISTRESS MARIA IS ALL RIGHT.
KOF-KOF-URRGH
HOLY CRAP! THAT WAS DISGUSTING.
I AM NEVER GOING TO GET THE STINK OF EAD MONDORFIN OFF ME.
MARIA VASQUEZ!

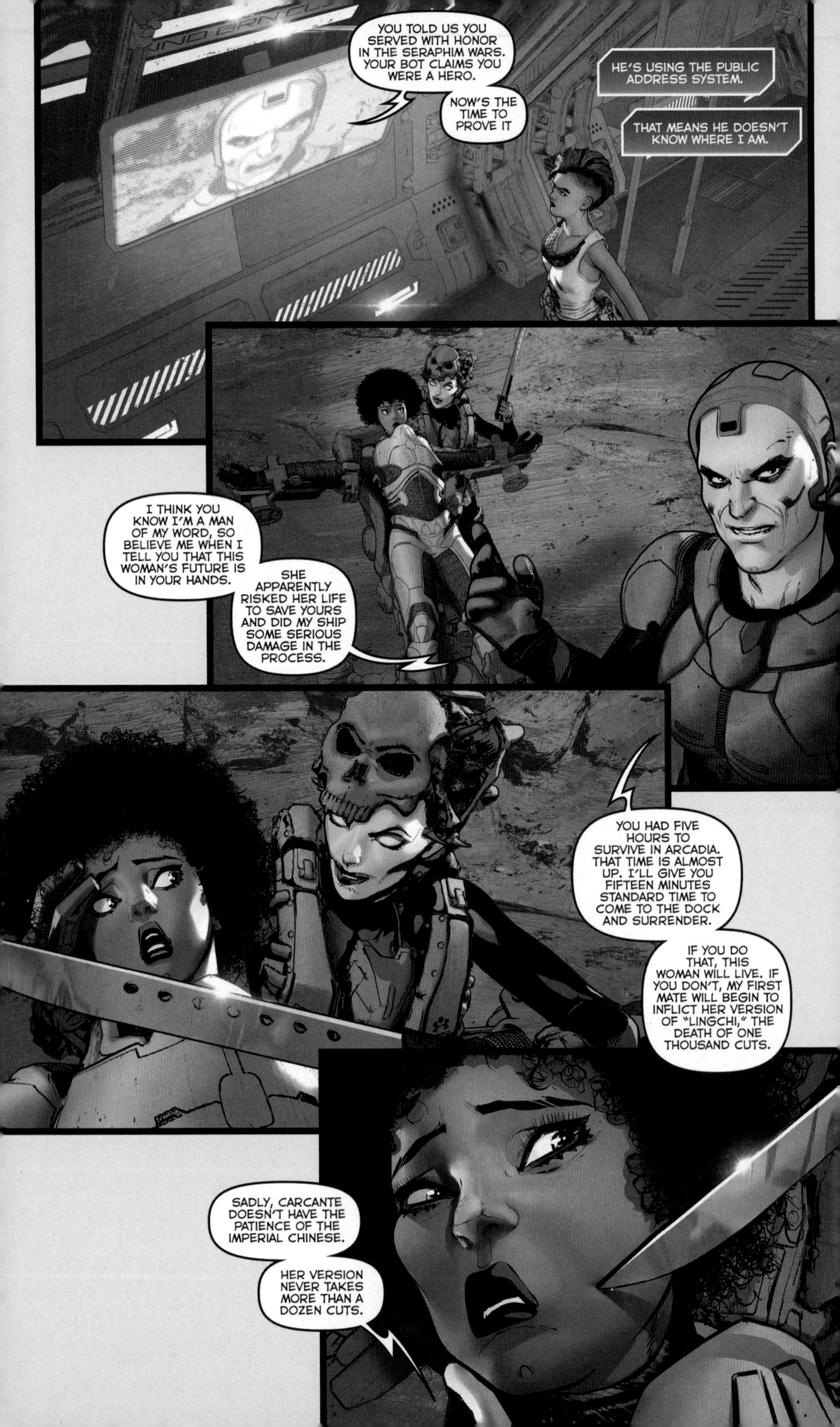
YOU TOLD US YOU SERVED WITH HONOR IN THE SERAPHIM WARS. YOUR BOT CLAIMS YOU WERE A HERO.
NOW'S THE TIME TO PROVE IT
HE'S USING THE PUBLIC ADDRESS SYSTEM.
THAT MEANS HE DOESN'T KNOW WHERE I AM.
I THINK YOU KNOW I'M A MAN OF MY WORD, SO BELIEVE ME WHEN I TELL YOU THAT THIS WOMAN'S FUTURE IS IN YOUR HANDS.
SHE APPARENTLY RISKED HER LIFE TO SAVE YOURS AND DID MY SHIP SOME SERIOUS DAMAGE IN THE PROCESS.
YOU HAD FIVE HOURS TO SURVIVE IN ARCADIA. THAT TIME IS ALMOST UP. I'LL GIVE YOU FIFTEEN MINUTES STANDARD TIME TO COME TO THE DOCK AND SURRENDER.
IF YOU DO THAT, THIS WOMAN WILL LIVE. IF YOU DON'T, MY FIRST MATE WILL BEGIN TO INFLICT HER VERSION OF "LINGCHI," THE DEATH OF ONE THOUSAND CUTS.
SADLY, CARCANTE DOESN'T HAVE THE PATIENCE OF THE IMPERIAL CHINESE.
HER VERSION NEVER TAKES MORE THAN A DOZEN CUTS.

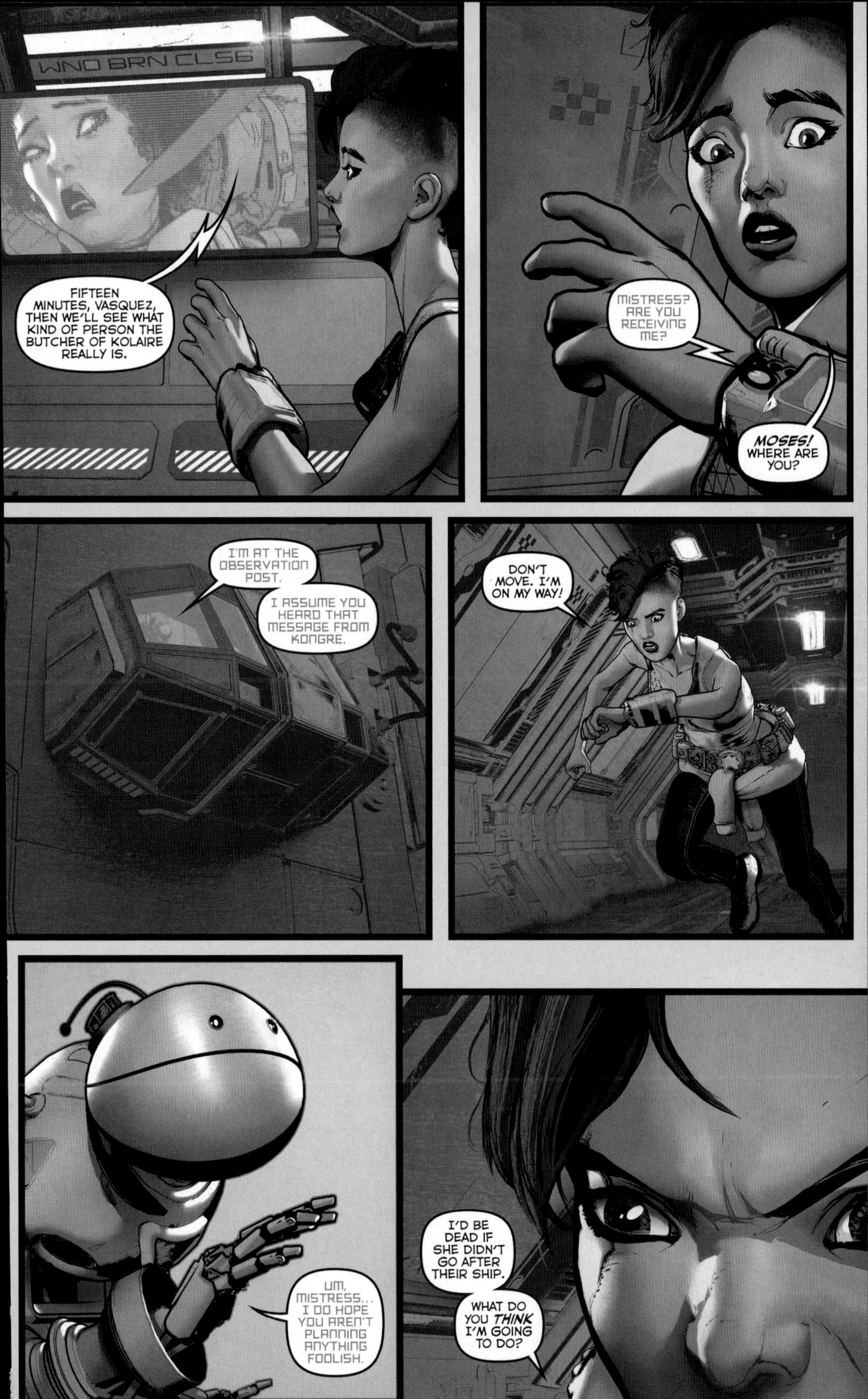

WND BRN CLS6
FIFTEEN MINUTES, VASQUEZ, THEN WE'LL SEE WHAT KIND OF PERSON THE BUTCHER OF KOLAIRE REALLY IS.
MISTRESS? ARE YOU RECEIVING ME?
MOSES! WHERE ARE YOU?
I'M AT THE OBSERVATION POST.
I ASSUME YOU HEARD THAT MESSAGE FROM KONGRE.
DON'T MOVE. I'M ON MY WAY!
UM, MISTRESS... I DO HOPE YOU AREN'T PLANNING ANYTHING FOOLISH.
I'D BE DEAD IF SHE DIDN'T GO AFTER THEIR SHIP.
WHAT DO YOU *THINK* I'M GOING TO DO?

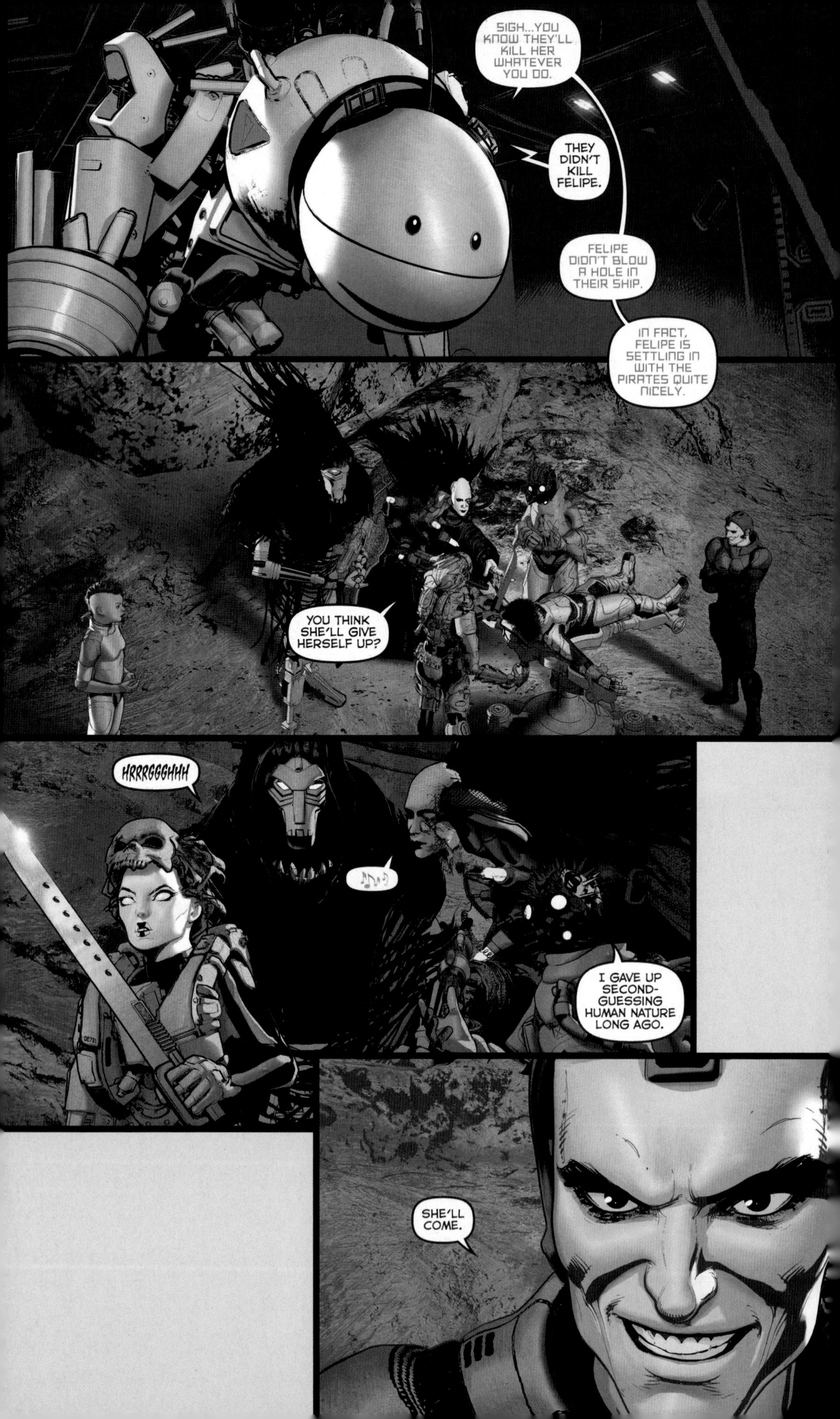
SIGH...YOU KNOW THEY'LL KILL HER WHATEVER YOU DO.
THEY DIDN'T KILL FELIPE.
FELIPE DIDN'T BLOW A HOLE IN THEIR SHIP.
IN FACT, FELIPE IS SETTLING IN WITH THE PIRATES QUITE NICELY.
YOU THINK SHE'LL GIVE HERSELF UP?
HRRRGGGHHH
♪♫♪
I GAVE UP SECOND-GUESSING HUMAN NATURE LONG AGO.
SHE'LL COME.

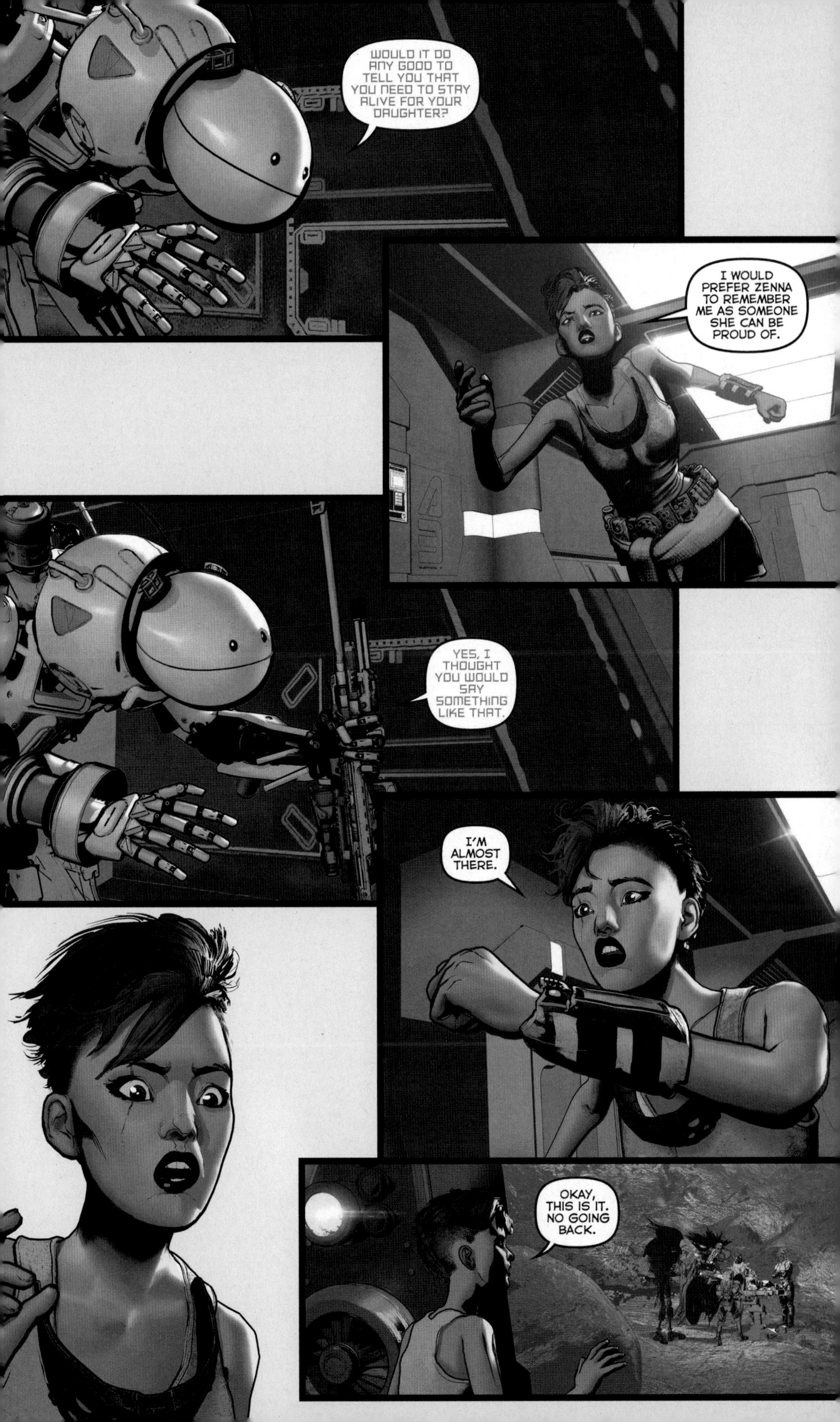
WOULD IT DO ANY GOOD TO TELL YOU THAT YOU NEED TO STAY ALIVE FOR YOUR DAUGHTER?
I WOULD PREFER ZENNA TO REMEMBER ME AS SOMEONE SHE CAN BE PROUD OF.
YES, I THOUGHT YOU WOULD SAY SOMETHING LIKE THAT.
I'M ALMOST THERE.
OKAY, THIS IS IT. NO GOING BACK.

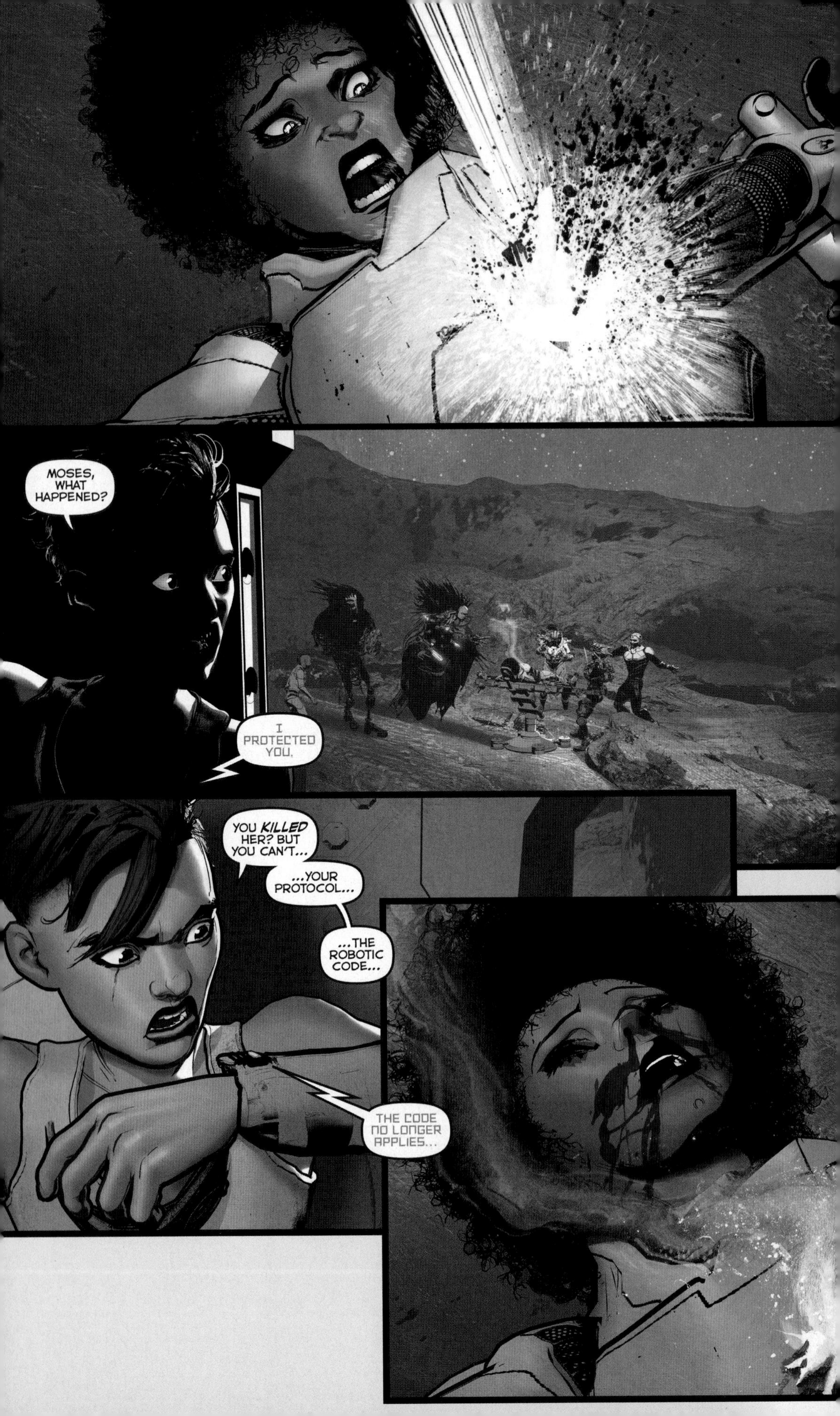
MOSES, WHAT HAPPENED?
I PROTECTED YOU.
YOU *KILLED* HER? BUT YOU CAN'T...
...YOUR PROTOCOL...
...THE ROBOTIC CODE...
THE CODE NO LONGER APPLIES...

Issue #5 Cover A

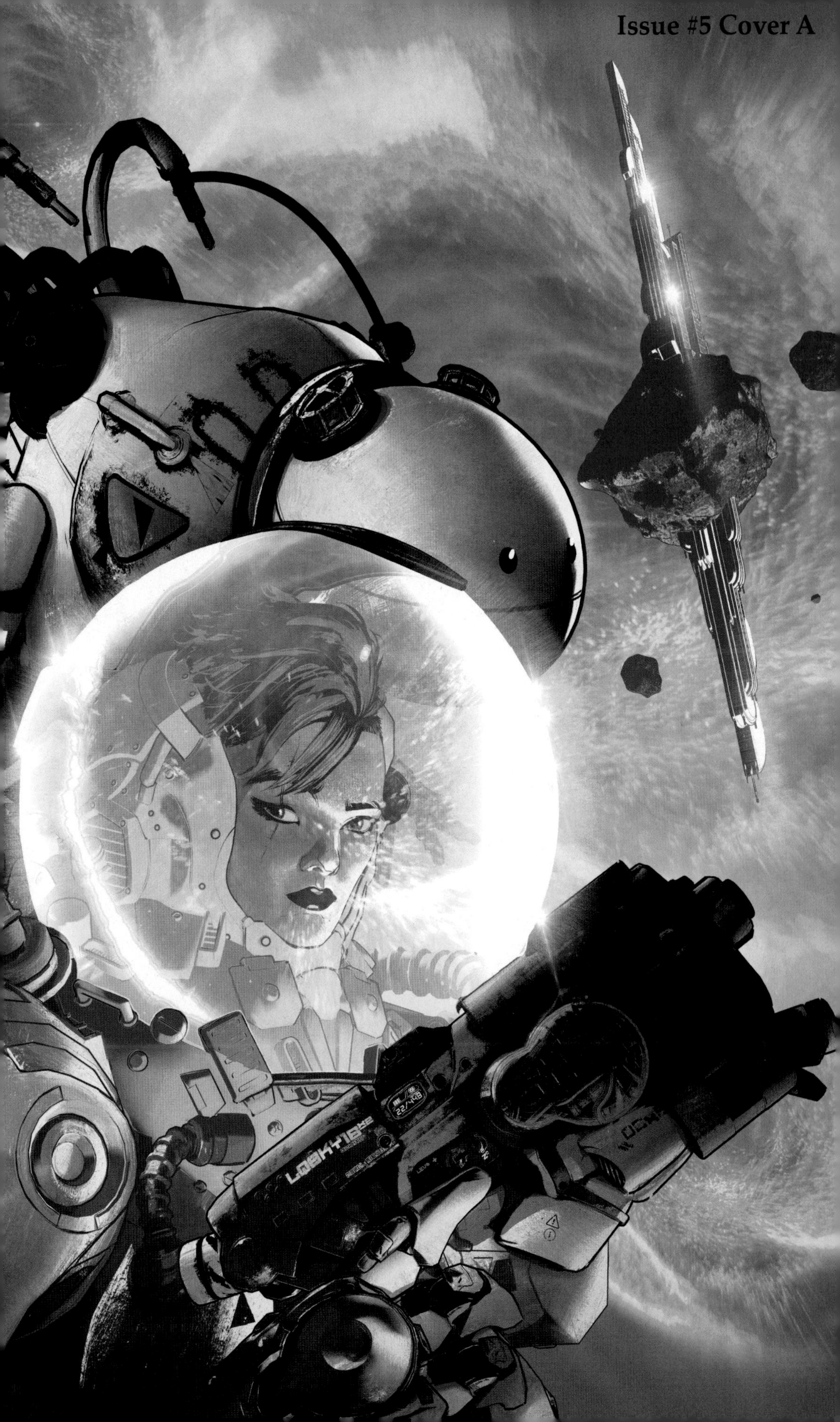

Issue #5 Cover B

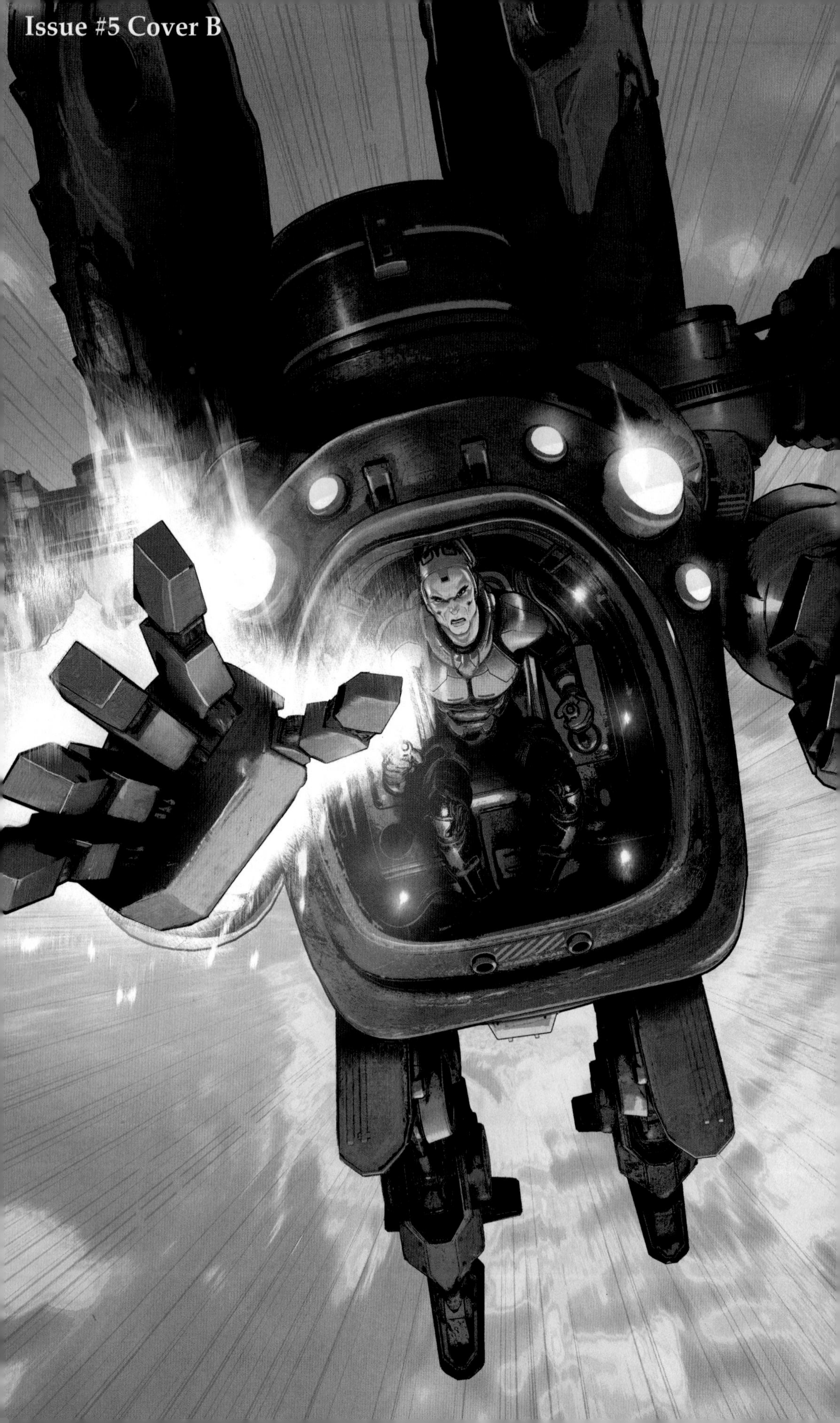

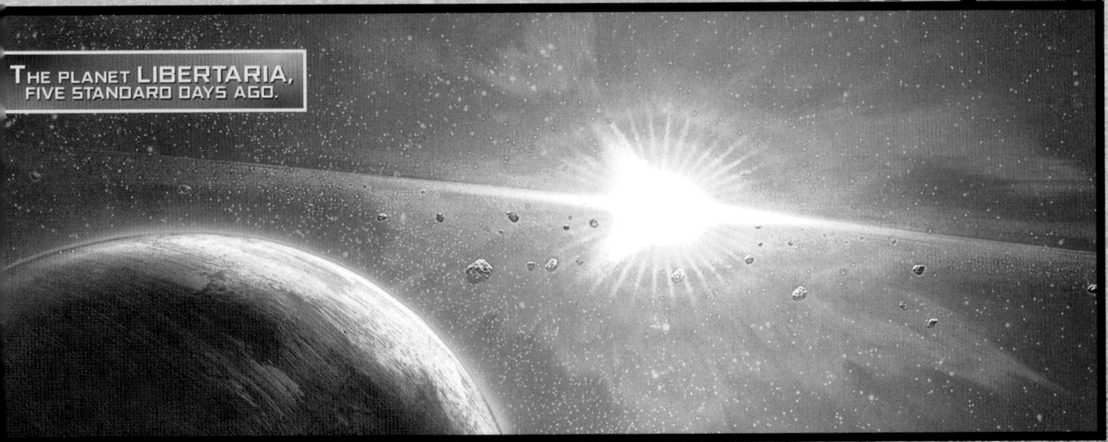
THE PLANET LIBERTARIA, FIVE STANDARD DAYS AGO.

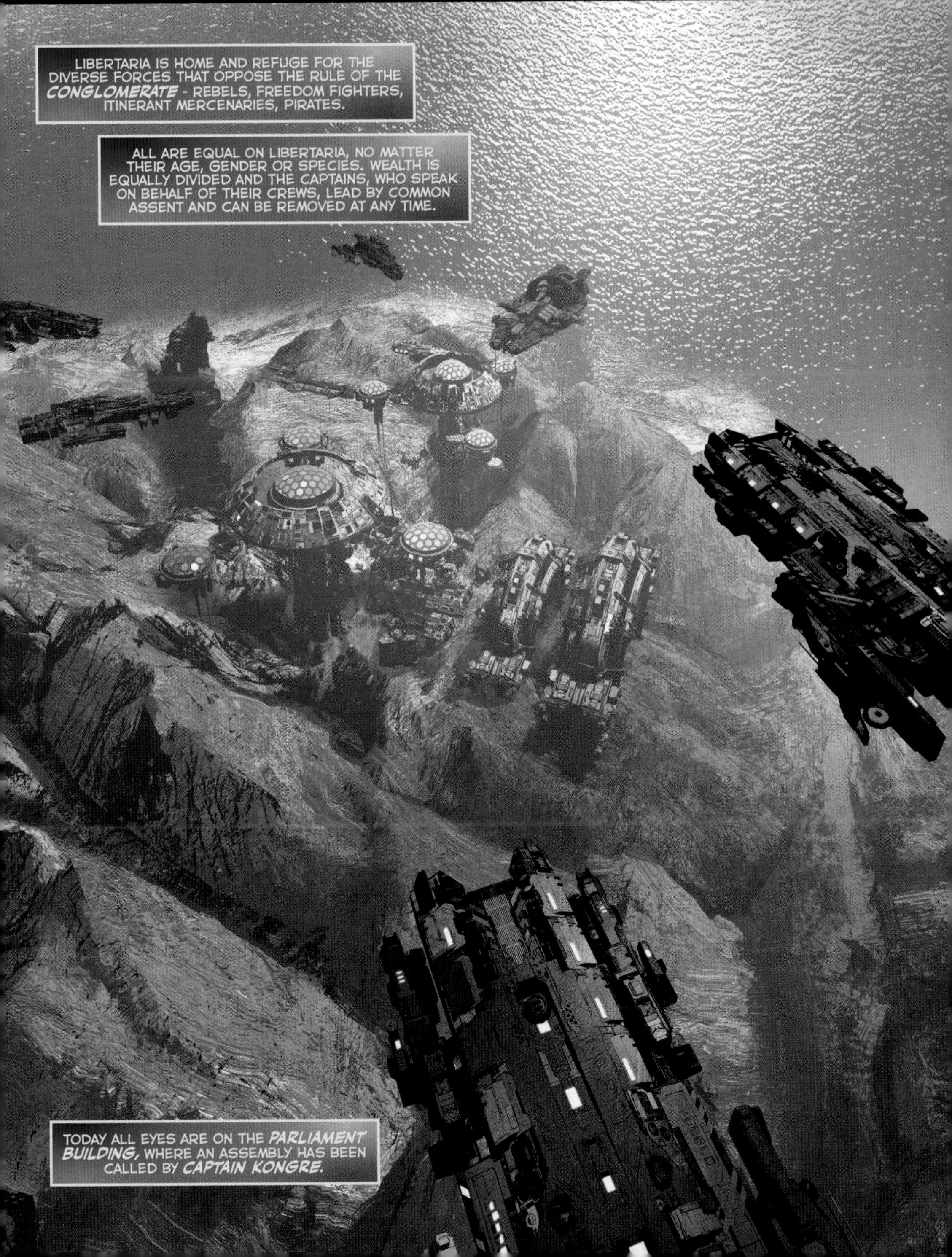
LIBERTARIA IS HOME AND REFUGE FOR THE DIVERSE FORCES THAT OPPOSE THE RULE OF THE *CONGLOMERATE* - REBELS, FREEDOM FIGHTERS, ITINERANT MERCENARIES, PIRATES.
ALL ARE EQUAL ON LIBERTARIA, NO MATTER THEIR AGE, GENDER OR SPECIES. WEALTH IS EQUALLY DIVIDED AND THE CAPTAINS, WHO SPEAK ON BEHALF OF THEIR CREWS, LEAD BY COMMON ASSENT AND CAN BE REMOVED AT ANY TIME.
TODAY ALL EYES ARE ON THE *PARLIAMENT BUILDING,* WHERE AN ASSEMBLY HAS BEEN CALLED BY *CAPTAIN KONGRE.*

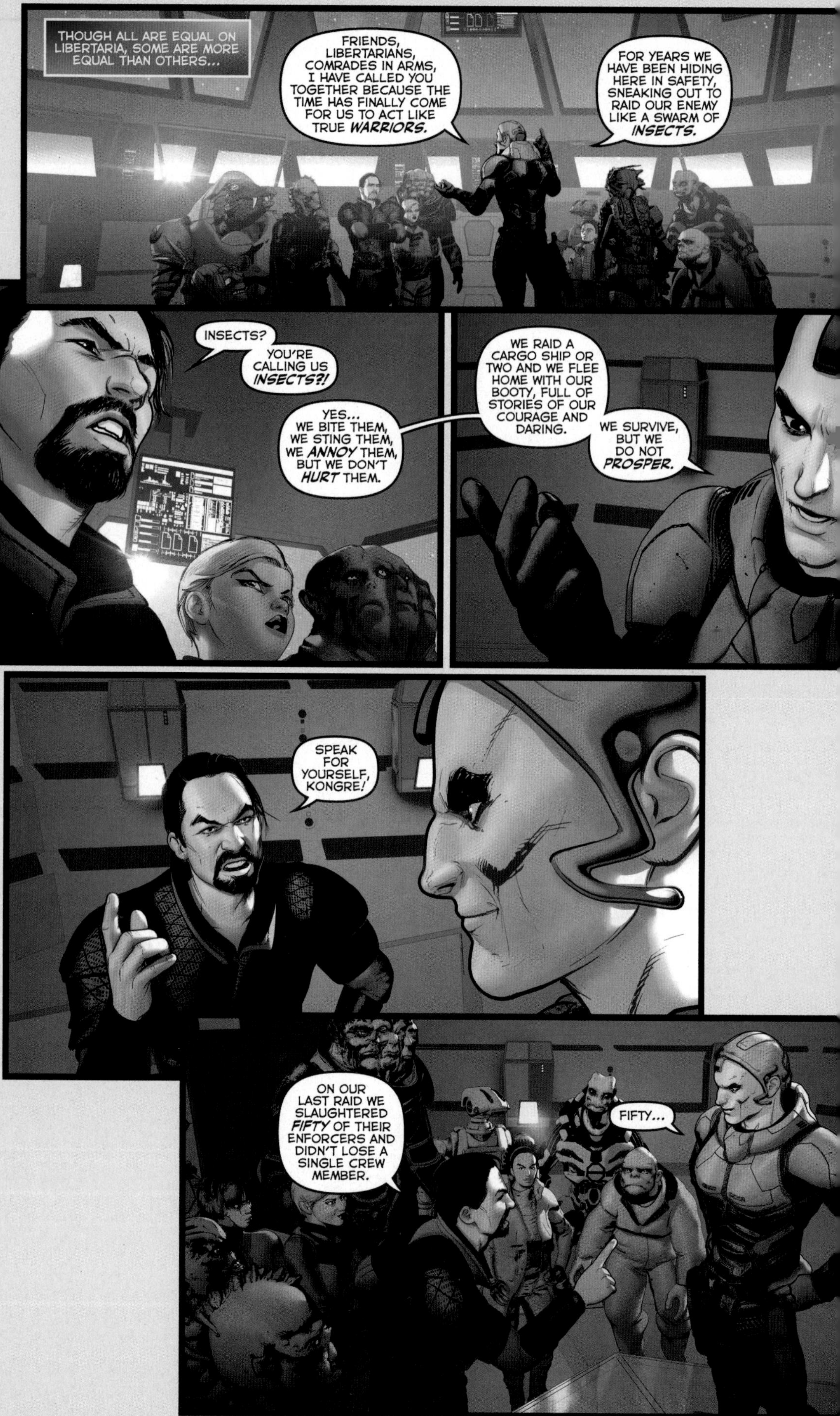
THOUGH ALL ARE EQUAL ON LIBERTARIA, SOME ARE MORE EQUAL THAN OTHERS...
FRIENDS, LIBERTARIANS, COMRADES IN ARMS, I HAVE CALLED YOU TOGETHER BECAUSE THE TIME HAS FINALLY COME FOR US TO ACT LIKE TRUE *WARRIORS.*
FOR YEARS WE HAVE BEEN HIDING HERE IN SAFETY, SNEAKING OUT TO RAID OUR ENEMY LIKE A SWARM OF *INSECTS.*
INSECTS?
YOU'RE CALLING US *INSECTS?!*
YES... WE BITE THEM, WE STING THEM, WE *ANNOY* THEM, BUT WE DON'T *HURT* THEM.
WE RAID A CARGO SHIP OR TWO AND WE FLEE HOME WITH OUR BOOTY, FULL OF STORIES OF OUR COURAGE AND DARING.
WE SURVIVE, BUT WE DO NOT *PROSPER.*
SPEAK FOR YOURSELF, KONGRE!
ON OUR LAST RAID WE SLAUGHTERED *FIFTY* OF THEIR ENFORCERS AND DIDN'T LOSE A SINGLE CREW MEMBER.
FIFTY...

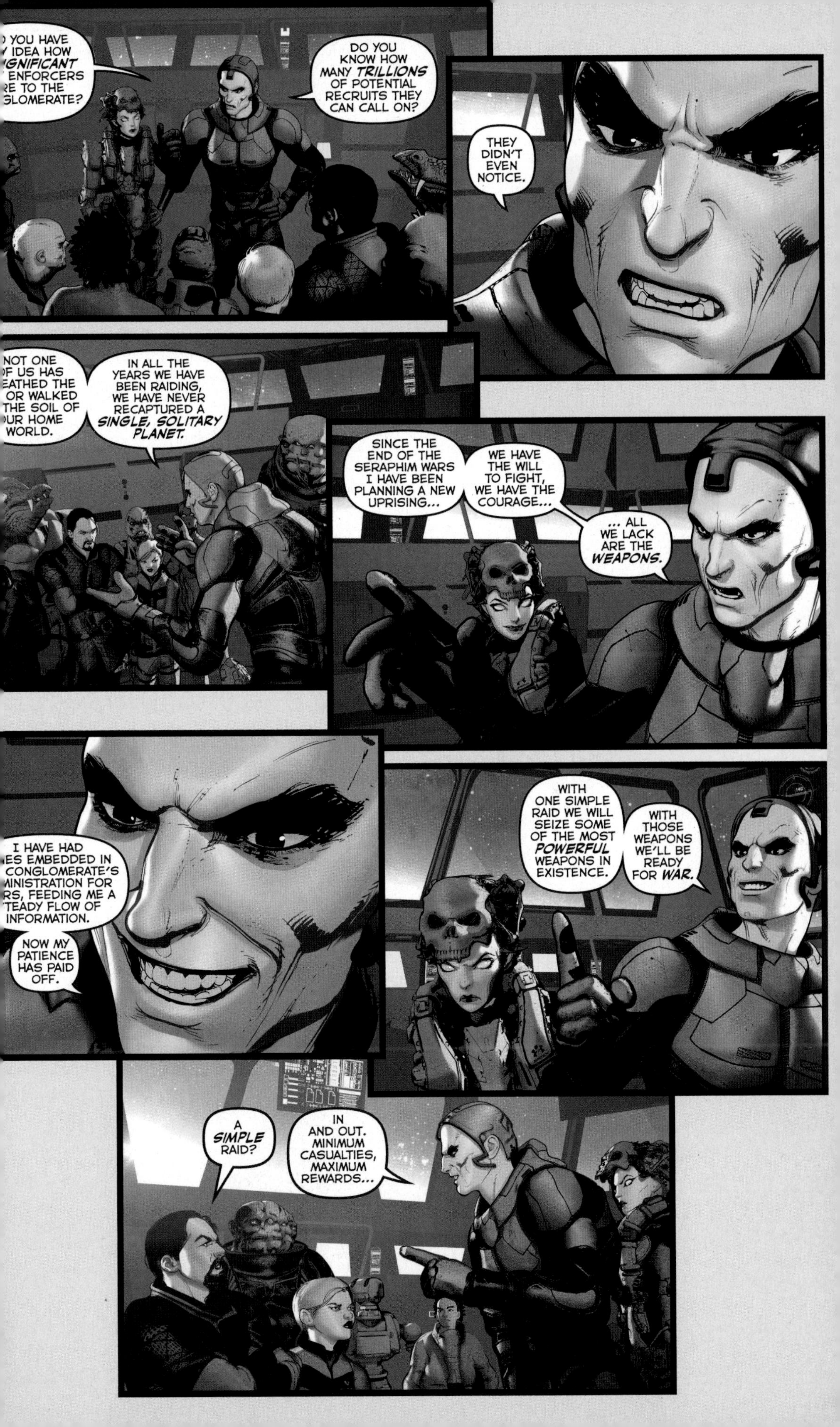
O YOU HAVE
Y IDEA HOW
IGNIFICANT
ENFORCERS
RE TO THE
GLOMERATE?
DO YOU KNOW HOW MANY TRILLIONS OF POTENTIAL RECRUITS THEY CAN CALL ON?
THEY DIDN'T EVEN NOTICE.
NOT ONE
F US HAS
EATHED THE
OR WALKED
THE SOIL OF
UR HOME
WORLD.
IN ALL THE YEARS WE HAVE BEEN RAIDING, WE HAVE NEVER RECAPTURED A SINGLE, SOLITARY PLANET.
SINCE THE END OF THE SERAPHIM WARS I HAVE BEEN PLANNING A NEW UPRISING...
WE HAVE THE WILL TO FIGHT, WE HAVE THE COURAGE...
... ALL WE LACK ARE THE WEAPONS.
I HAVE HAD
ES EMBEDDED IN
CONGLOMERATE'S
MINISTRATION FOR
RS, FEEDING ME A
TEADY FLOW OF
INFORMATION.
NOW MY PATIENCE HAS PAID OFF.
WITH ONE SIMPLE RAID WE WILL SEIZE SOME OF THE MOST POWERFUL WEAPONS IN EXISTENCE.
WITH THOSE WEAPONS WE'LL BE READY FOR WAR.
A SIMPLE RAID?
IN AND OUT. MINIMUM CASUALTIES, MAXIMUM REWARDS...

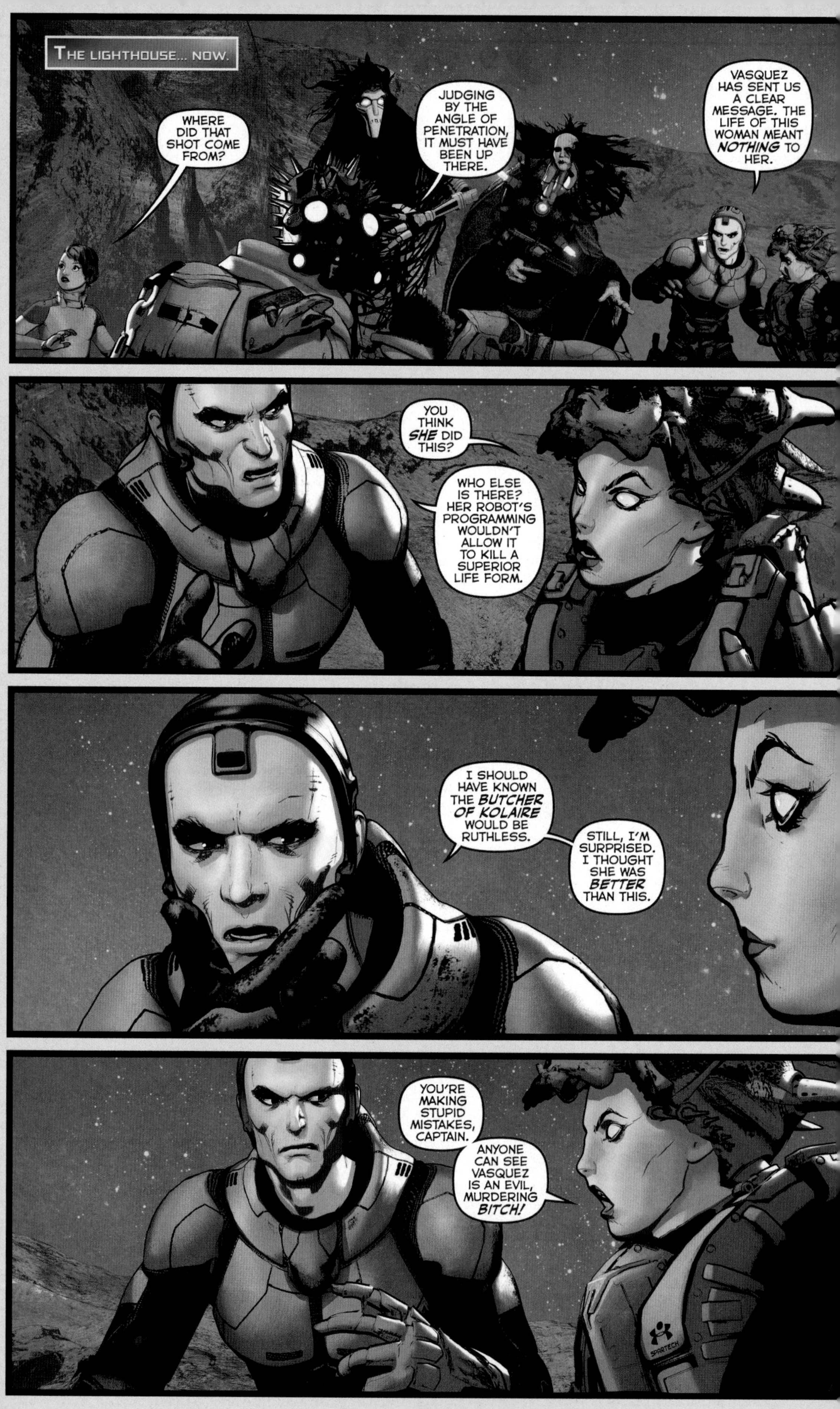
THE LIGHTHOUSE... NOW.
WHERE DID THAT SHOT COME FROM?
JUDGING BY THE ANGLE OF PENETRATION, IT MUST HAVE BEEN UP THERE.
VASQUEZ HAS SENT US A CLEAR MESSAGE. THE LIFE OF THIS WOMAN MEANT NOTHING TO HER.
YOU THINK SHE DID THIS?
WHO ELSE IS THERE? HER ROBOT'S PROGRAMMING WOULDN'T ALLOW IT TO KILL A SUPERIOR LIFE FORM.
I SHOULD HAVE KNOWN THE BUTCHER OF KOLAIRE WOULD BE RUTHLESS.
STILL, I'M SURPRISED. I THOUGHT SHE WAS BETTER THAN THIS.
YOU'RE MAKING STUPID MISTAKES, CAPTAIN.
ANYONE CAN SEE VASQUEZ IS AN EVIL, MURDERING BITCH!
SPARTECH

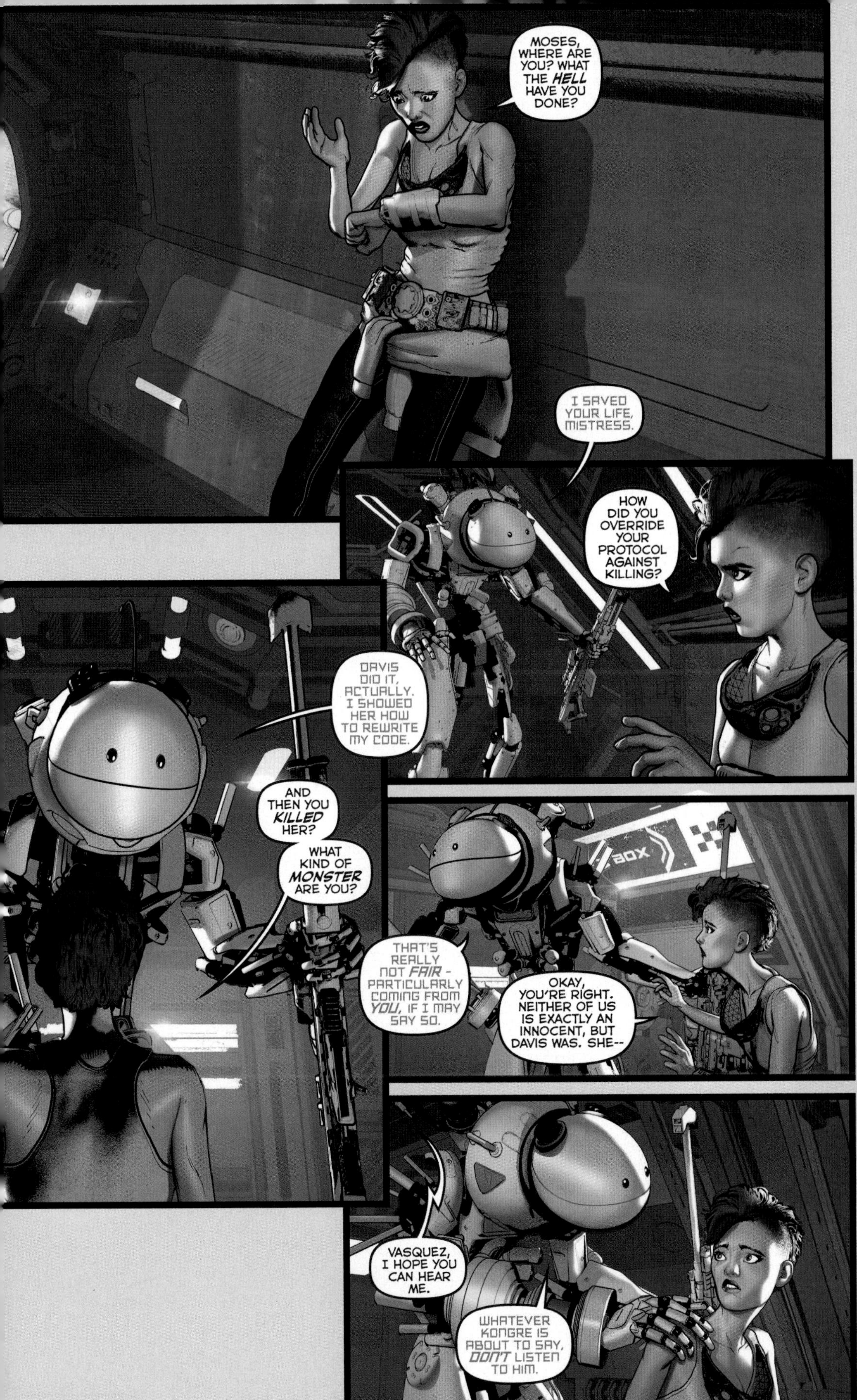
MOSES, WHERE ARE YOU? WHAT THE *HELL* HAVE YOU DONE?
I SAVED YOUR LIFE, MISTRESS.
HOW DID YOU OVERRIDE YOUR PROTOCOL AGAINST KILLING?
DAVIS DID IT, ACTUALLY. I SHOWED HER HOW TO REWRITE MY CODE.
AND THEN YOU *KILLED* HER?
WHAT KIND OF *MONSTER* ARE YOU?
THAT'S REALLY NOT *FAIR* - PARTICULARLY COMING FROM *YOU*, IF I MAY SAY SO.
OKAY, YOU'RE RIGHT. NEITHER OF US IS EXACTLY AN INNOCENT, BUT DAVIS WAS. SHE--
BOX
VASQUEZ, I HOPE YOU CAN HEAR ME.
WHATEVER KONGRE IS ABOUT TO SAY, *DON'T* LISTEN TO HIM.

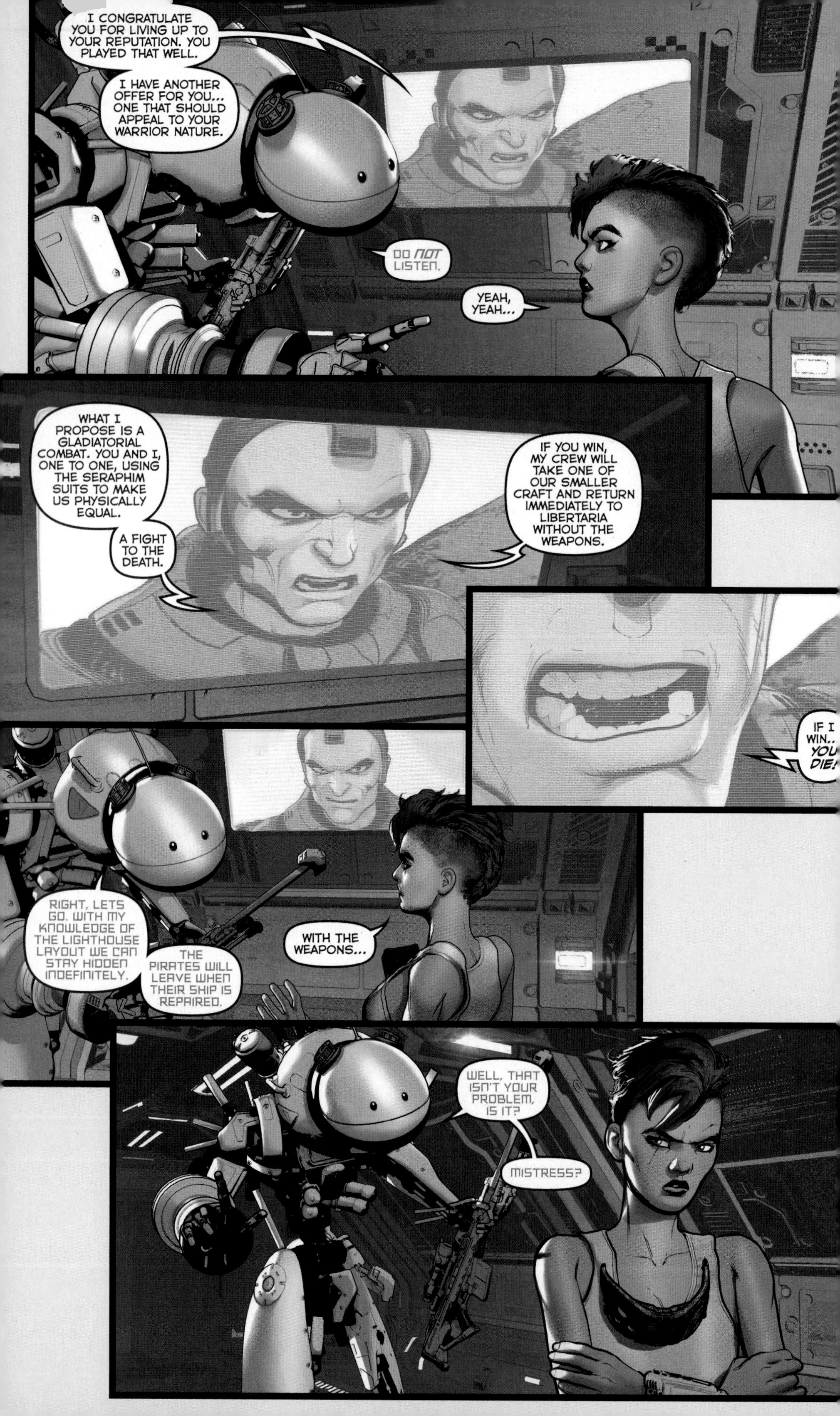
I CONGRATULATE YOU FOR LIVING UP TO YOUR REPUTATION. YOU PLAYED THAT WELL.
I HAVE ANOTHER OFFER FOR YOU... ONE THAT SHOULD APPEAL TO YOUR WARRIOR NATURE.
DO NOT LISTEN.
YEAH, YEAH...
WHAT I PROPOSE IS A GLADIATORIAL COMBAT. YOU AND I, ONE TO ONE, USING THE SERAPHIM SUITS TO MAKE US PHYSICALLY EQUAL.
A FIGHT TO THE DEATH.
IF YOU WIN, MY CREW WILL TAKE ONE OF OUR SMALLER CRAFT AND RETURN IMMEDIATELY TO LIBERTARIA WITHOUT THE WEAPONS.
IF I WIN... YOU DIE!
RIGHT, LETS GO. WITH MY KNOWLEDGE OF THE LIGHTHOUSE LAYOUT WE CAN STAY HIDDEN INDEFINITELY.
THE PIRATES WILL LEAVE WHEN THEIR SHIP IS REPAIRED.
WITH THE WEAPONS...
WELL, THAT ISN'T YOUR PROBLEM, IS IT?
MISTRESS?

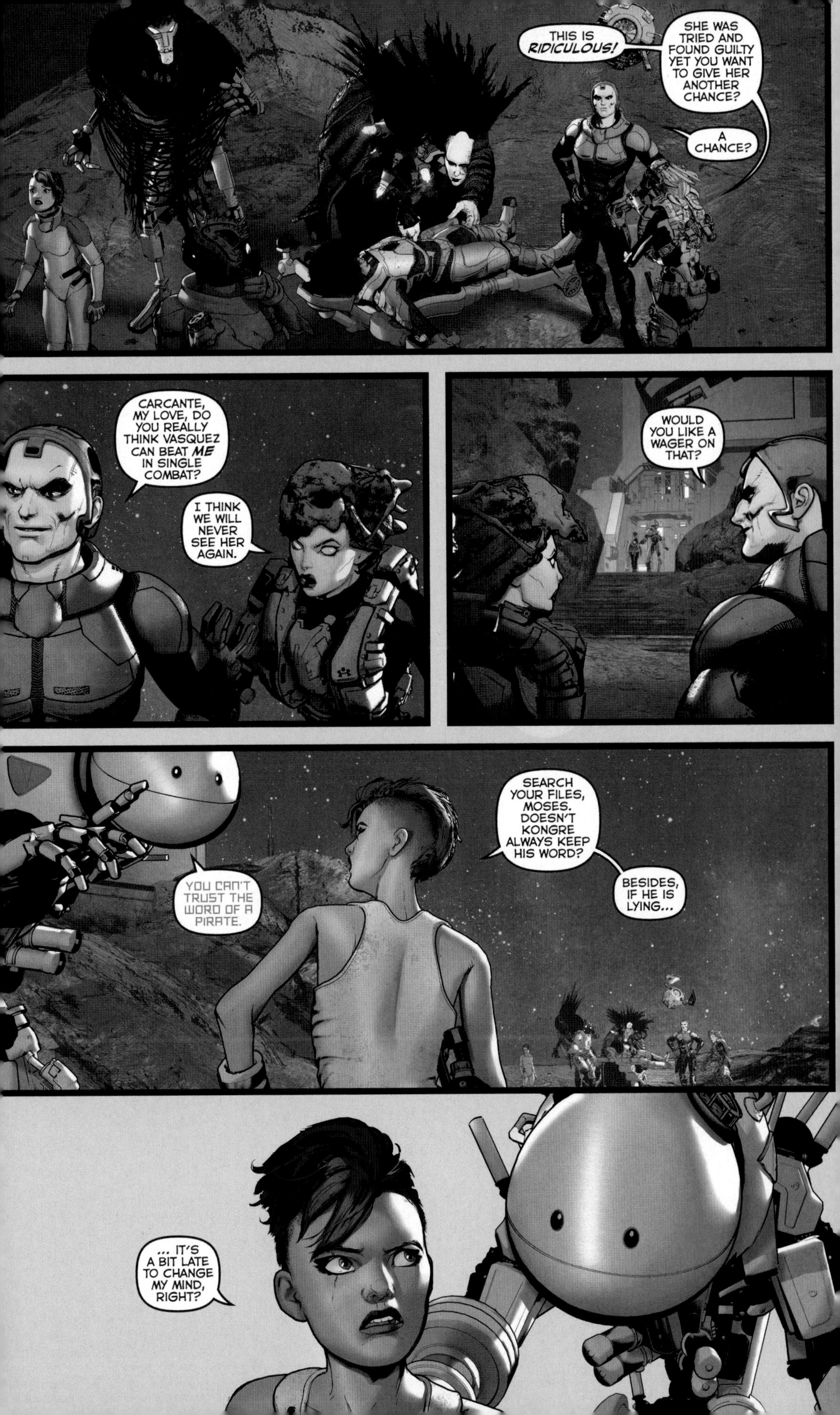
THIS IS *RIDICULOUS!*
SHE WAS TRIED AND FOUND GUILTY YET YOU WANT TO GIVE HER ANOTHER CHANCE?
A CHANCE?
CARCANTE, MY LOVE, DO YOU REALLY THINK VASQUEZ CAN BEAT *ME* IN SINGLE COMBAT?
I THINK WE WILL NEVER SEE HER AGAIN.
WOULD YOU LIKE A WAGER ON THAT?
YOU CAN'T TRUST THE WORD OF A PIRATE.
SEARCH YOUR FILES, MOSES. DOESN'T KONGRE ALWAYS KEEP HIS WORD?
BESIDES, IF HE IS LYING...
... IT'S A BIT LATE TO CHANGE MY MIND, RIGHT?

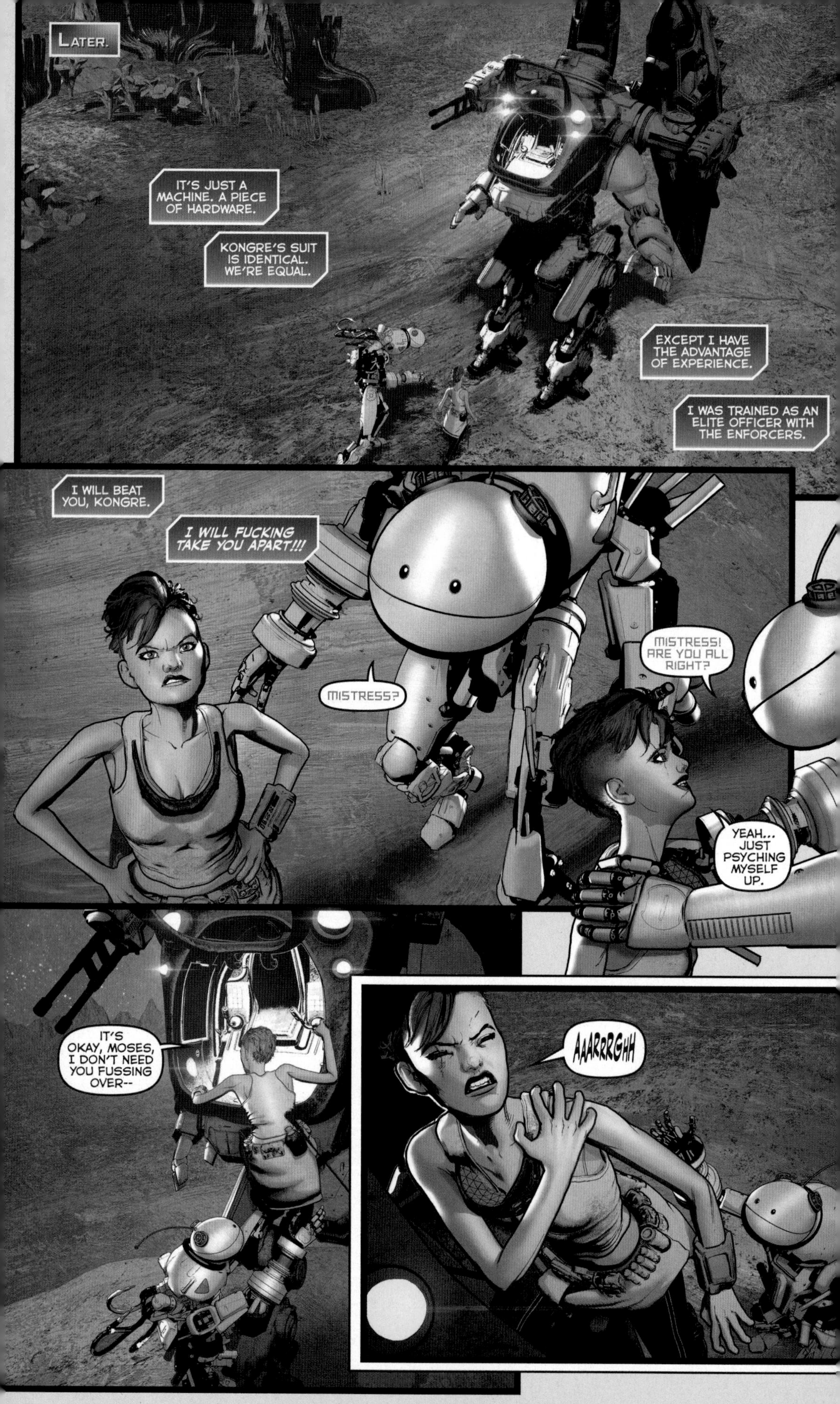
LATER.
IT'S JUST A MACHINE. A PIECE OF HARDWARE.
KONGRE'S SUIT IS IDENTICAL. WE'RE EQUAL.
EXCEPT I HAVE THE ADVANTAGE OF EXPERIENCE.
I WAS TRAINED AS AN ELITE OFFICER WITH THE ENFORCERS.
I WILL BEAT YOU, KONGRE.
I WILL FUCKING TAKE YOU APART!!!
MISTRESS?
MISTRESS! ARE YOU ALL RIGHT?
YEAH... JUST PSYCHING MYSELF UP.
IT'S OKAY, MOSES, I DON'T NEED YOU FUSSING OVER--
AAARRRGHH

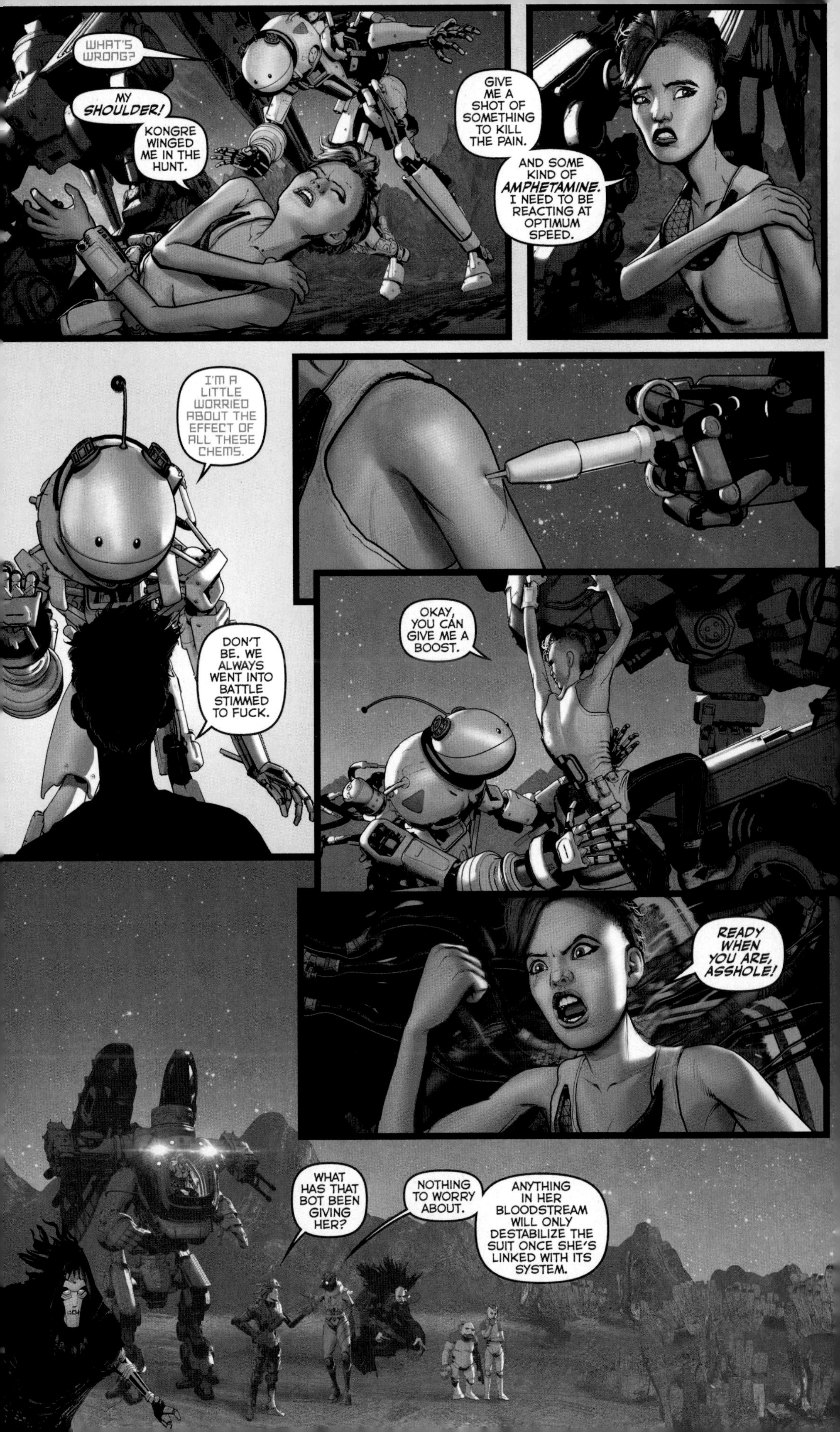
WHAT'S WRONG?
MY *SHOULDER!*
KONGRE WINGED ME IN THE HUNT.
GIVE ME A SHOT OF SOMETHING TO KILL THE PAIN.
AND SOME KIND OF *AMPHETAMINE.* I NEED TO BE REACTING AT OPTIMUM SPEED.
I'M A LITTLE WORRIED ABOUT THE EFFECT OF ALL THESE CHEMS.
DON'T BE. WE ALWAYS WENT INTO BATTLE STIMMED TO FUCK.
OKAY, YOU CAN GIVE ME A BOOST.
READY WHEN YOU ARE, ASSHOLE!
WHAT HAS THAT BOT BEEN GIVING HER?
NOTHING TO WORRY ABOUT.
ANYTHING IN HER BLOODSTREAM WILL ONLY DESTABILIZE THE SUIT ONCE SHE'S LINKED WITH ITS SYSTEM.

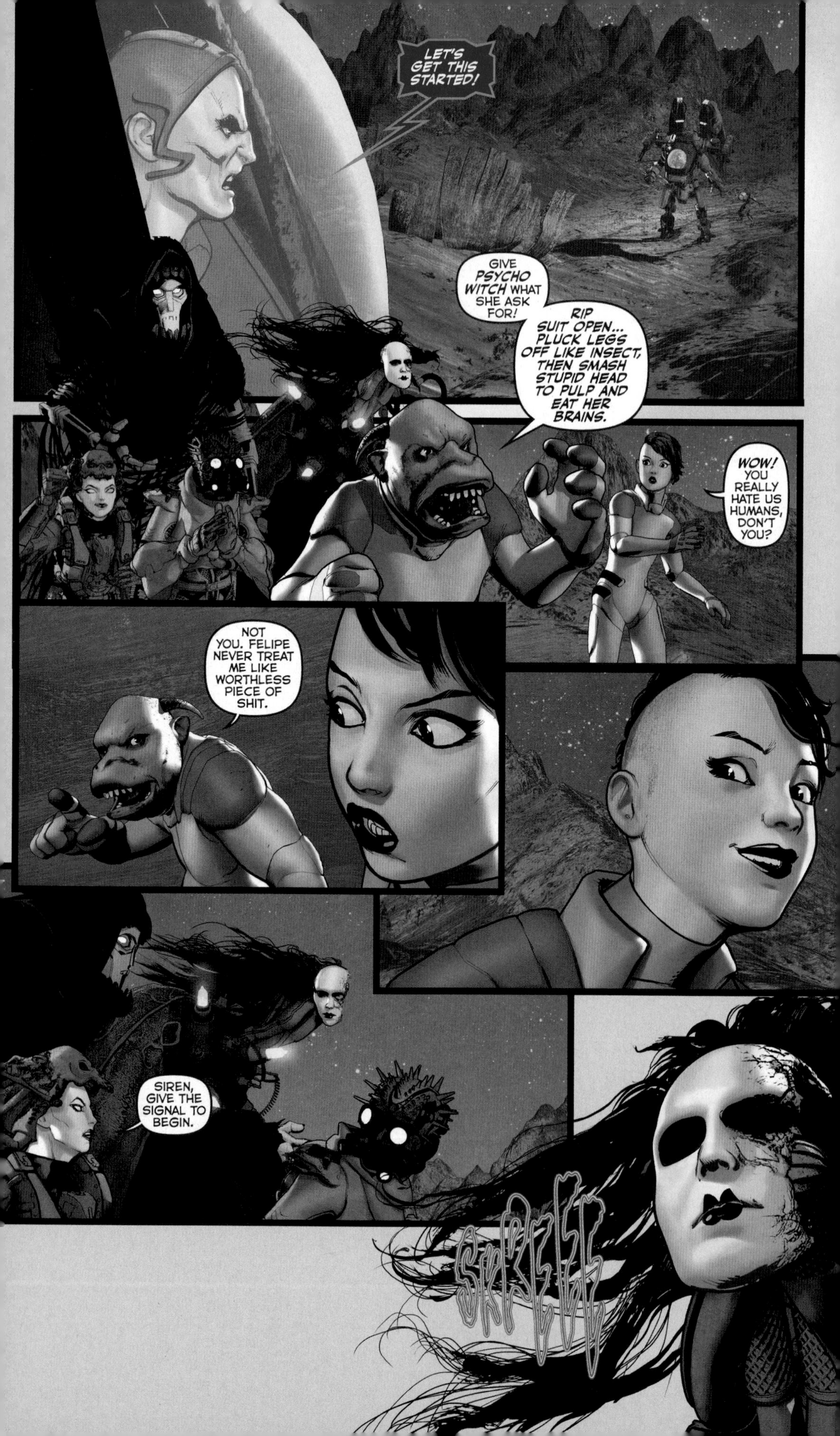
LET'S GET THIS STARTED!
GIVE PSYCHO WITCH WHAT SHE ASK FOR!
RIP SUIT OPEN... PLUCK LEGS OFF LIKE INSECT, THEN SMASH STUPID HEAD TO PULP AND EAT HER BRAINS.
WOW! YOU REALLY HATE US HUMANS, DON'T YOU?
NOT YOU. FELIPE NEVER TREAT ME LIKE WORTHLESS PIECE OF SHIT.
SIREN, GIVE THE SIGNAL TO BEGIN.
SKREEE

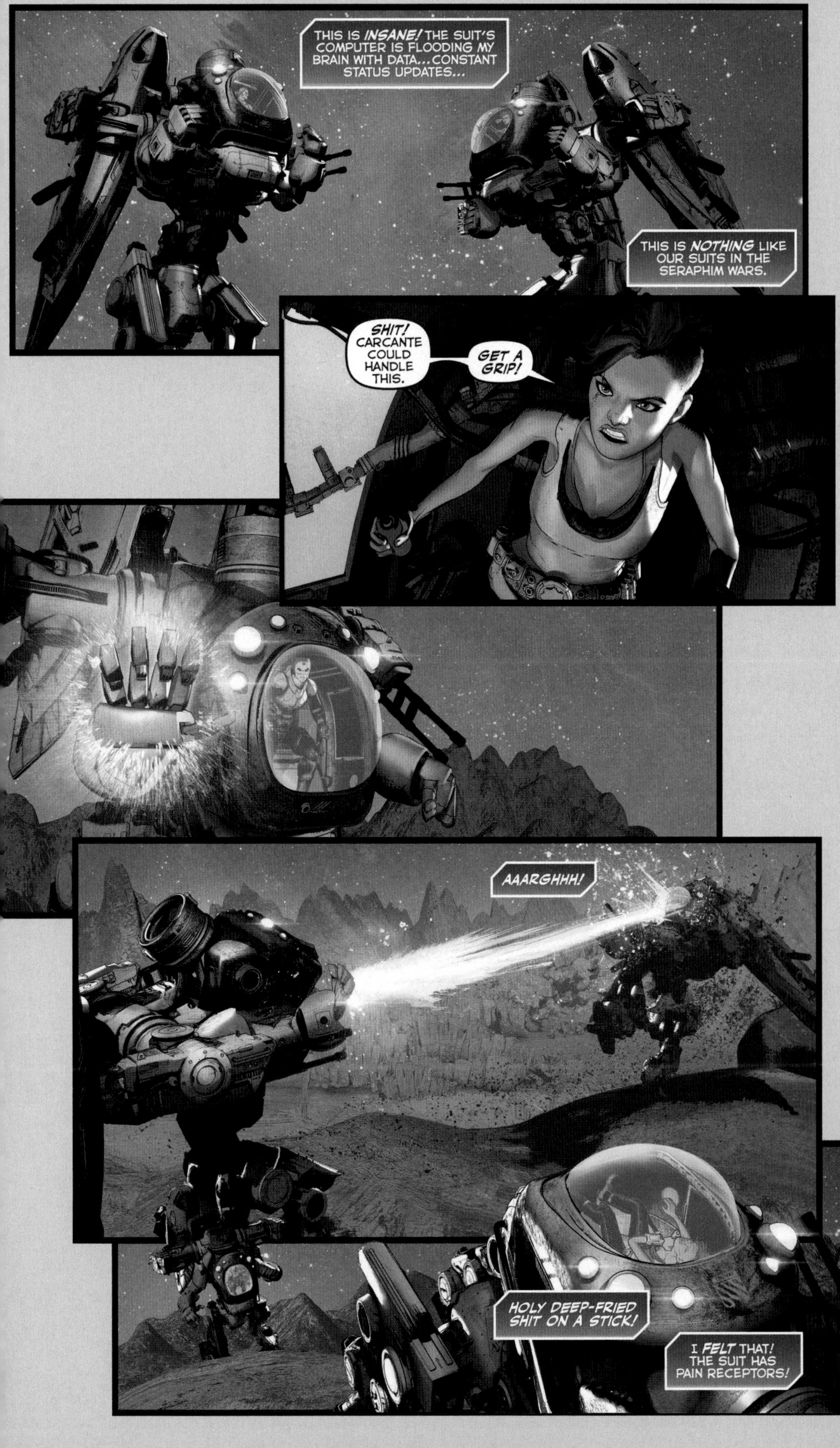
THIS IS *INSANE!* THE SUIT'S COMPUTER IS FLOODING MY BRAIN WITH DATA...CONSTANT STATUS UPDATES...
THIS IS *NOTHING* LIKE OUR SUITS IN THE SERAPHIM WARS.
SHIT! CARCANTE COULD HANDLE THIS.
GET A GRIP!
AAARGHHH!
HOLY DEEP-FRIED SHIT ON A STICK!
I *FELT* THAT! THE SUIT HAS PAIN RECEPTORS!

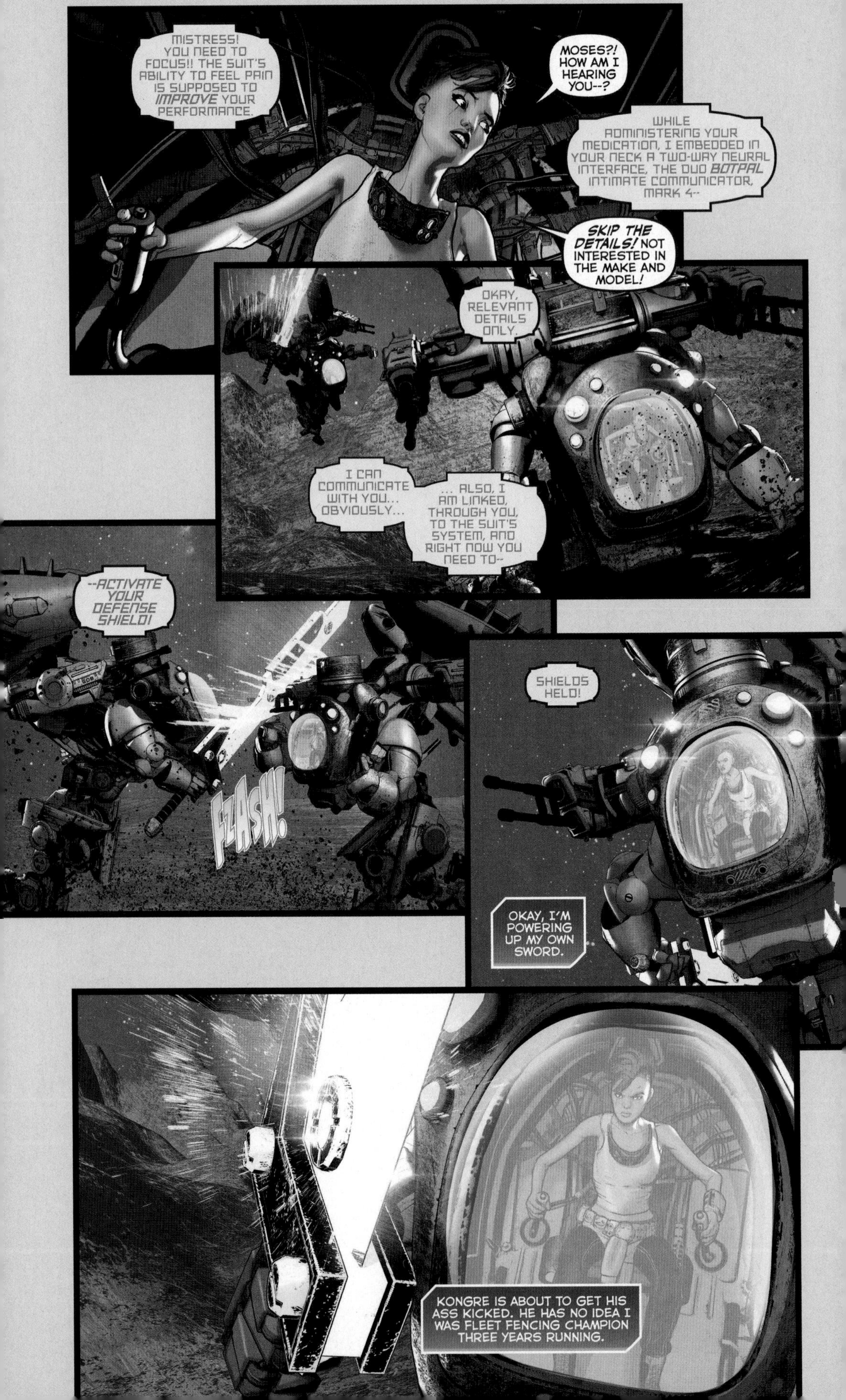
MISTRESS! YOU NEED TO FOCUS!! THE SUIT'S ABILITY TO FEEL PAIN IS SUPPOSED TO IMPROVE YOUR PERFORMANCE.
MOSES?! HOW AM I HEARING YOU--?
WHILE ADMINISTERING YOUR MEDICATION, I EMBEDDED IN YOUR NECK A TWO-WAY NEURAL INTERFACE, THE DUO BOTPAL INTIMATE COMMUNICATOR, MARK 4--
SKIP THE DETAILS! NOT INTERESTED IN THE MAKE AND MODEL!
OKAY, RELEVANT DETAILS ONLY.
I CAN COMMUNICATE WITH YOU... OBVIOUSLY...
... ALSO, I AM LINKED, THROUGH YOU, TO THE SUIT'S SYSTEM, AND RIGHT NOW YOU NEED TO--
--ACTIVATE YOUR DEFENSE SHIELD!
FZASH!
SHIELDS HELD!
OKAY, I'M POWERING UP MY OWN SWORD.
KONGRE IS ABOUT TO GET HIS ASS KICKED. HE HAS NO IDEA I WAS FLEET FENCING CHAMPION THREE YEARS RUNNING.

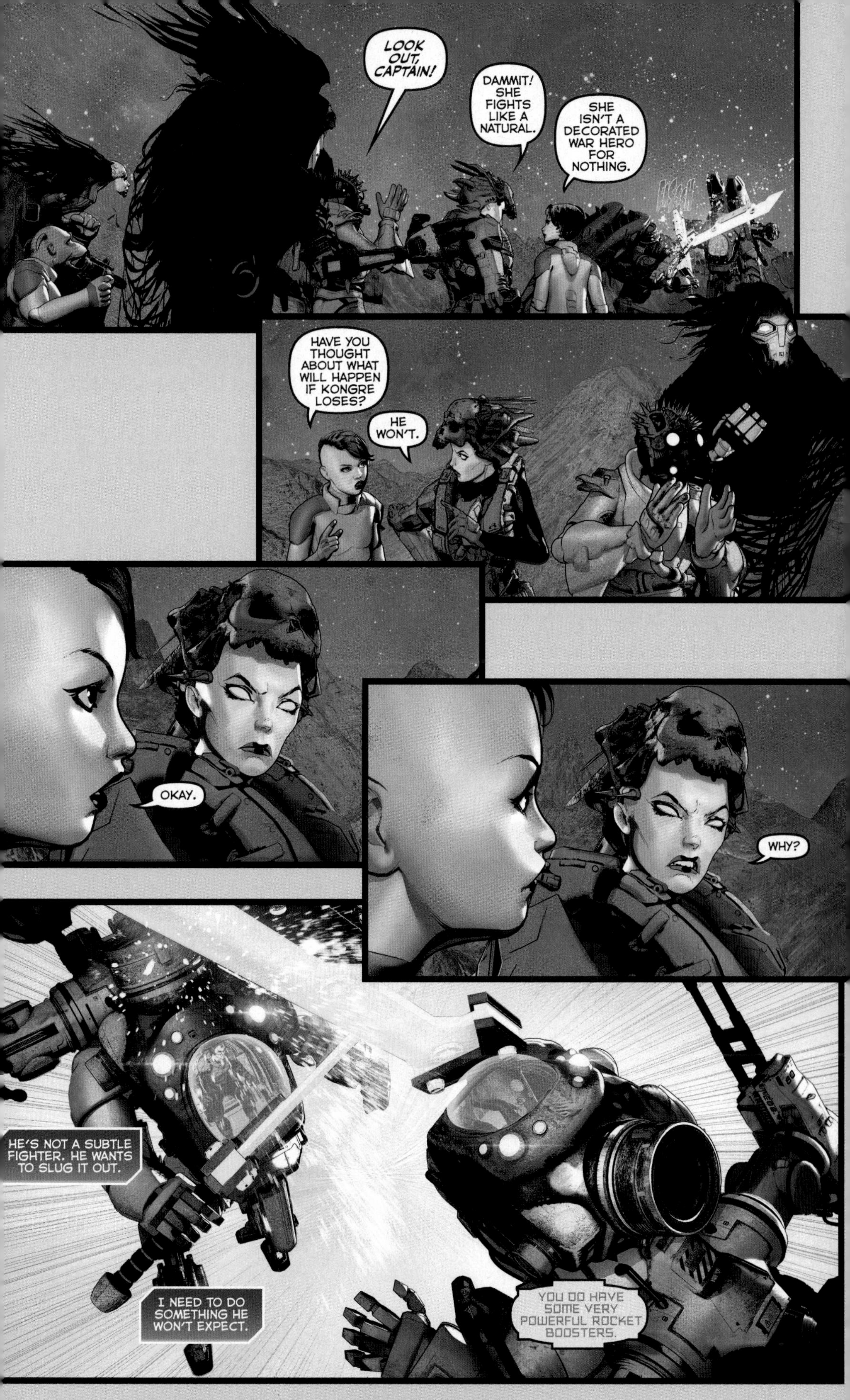
LOOK OUT, CAPTAIN!
DAMMIT! SHE FIGHTS LIKE A NATURAL.
SHE ISN'T A DECORATED WAR HERO FOR NOTHING.
HAVE YOU THOUGHT ABOUT WHAT WILL HAPPEN IF KONGRE LOSES?
HE WON'T.
OKAY.
WHY?
HE'S NOT A SUBTLE FIGHTER. HE WANTS TO SLUG IT OUT.
I NEED TO DO SOMETHING HE WON'T EXPECT.
YOU DO HAVE SOME VERY POWERFUL ROCKET BOOSTERS.

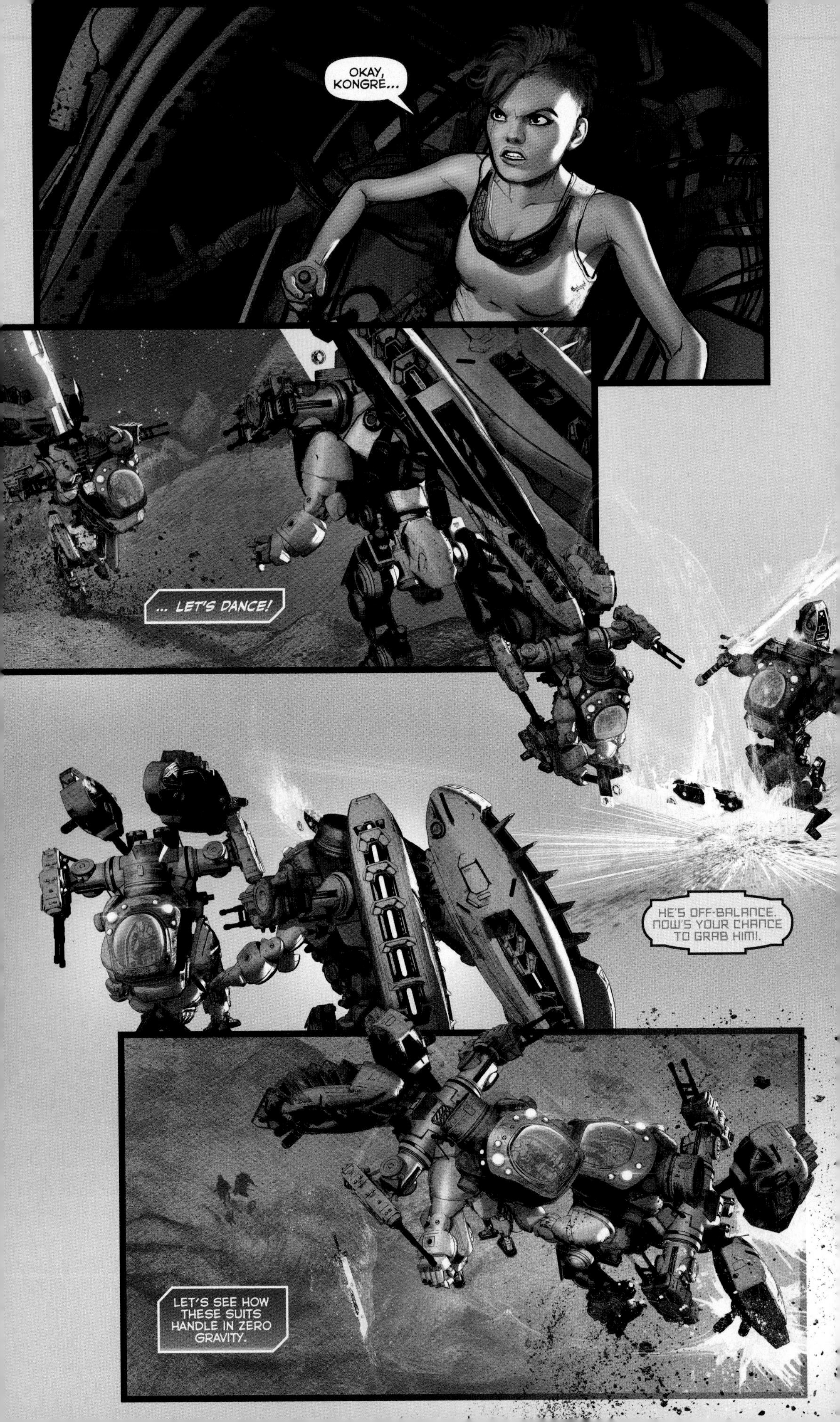
OKAY, KONGRE...
... LET'S DANCE!
HE'S OFF-BALANCE. NOW'S YOUR CHANCE TO GRAB HIM!.
LET'S SEE HOW THESE SUITS HANDLE IN ZERO GRAVITY.

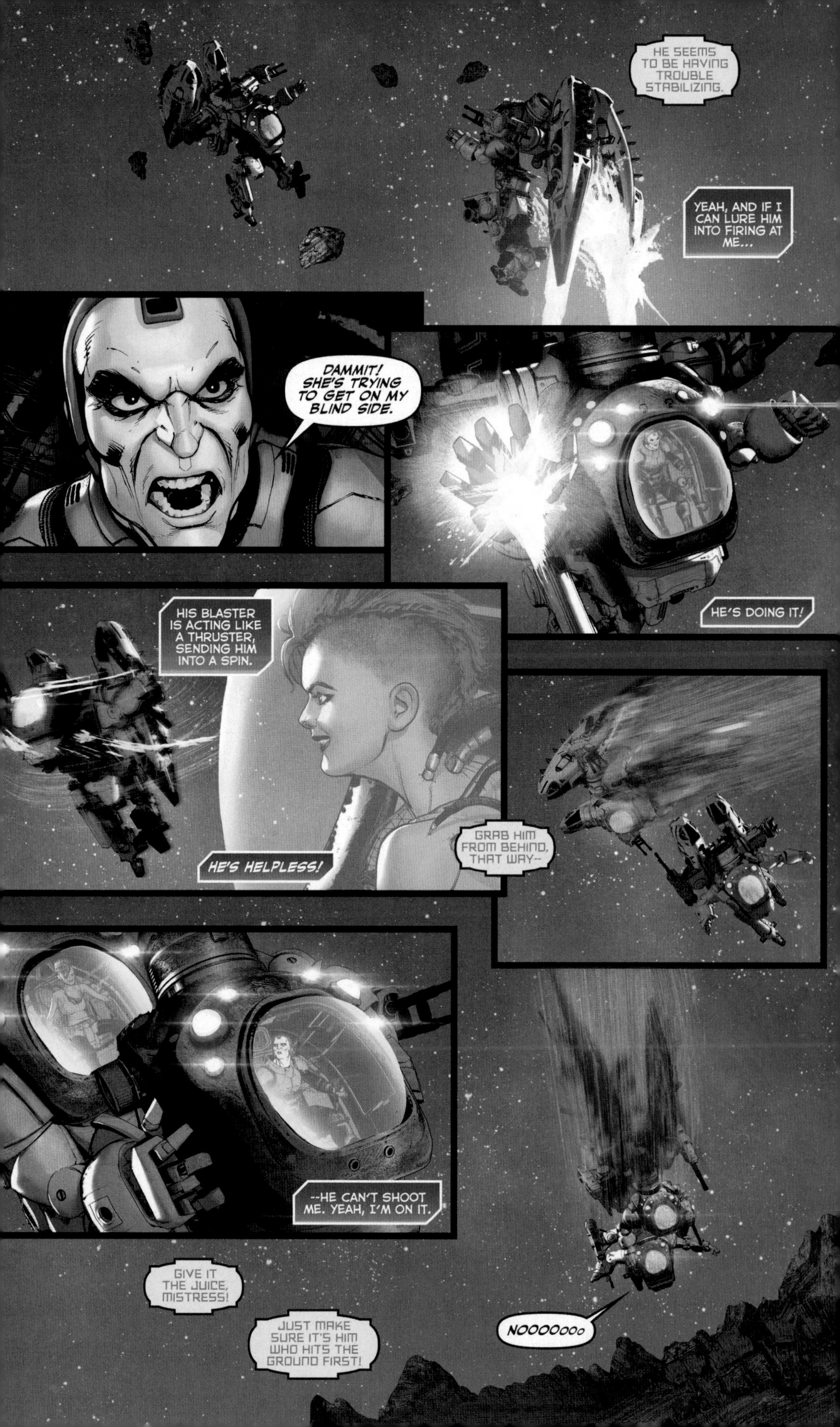
HE SEEMS TO BE HAVING TROUBLE STABILIZING.
YEAH, AND IF I CAN LURE HIM INTO FIRING AT ME...
DAMMIT! SHE'S TRYING TO GET ON MY BLIND SIDE.
HE'S DOING IT!
HIS BLASTER IS ACTING LIKE A THRUSTER, SENDING HIM INTO A SPIN.
HE'S HELPLESS!
GRAB HIM FROM BEHIND, THAT WAY--
--HE CAN'T SHOOT ME. YEAH, I'M ON IT.
GIVE IT THE JUICE, MISTRESS!
JUST MAKE SURE IT'S HIM WHO HITS THE GROUND FIRST!
NOOOOooo

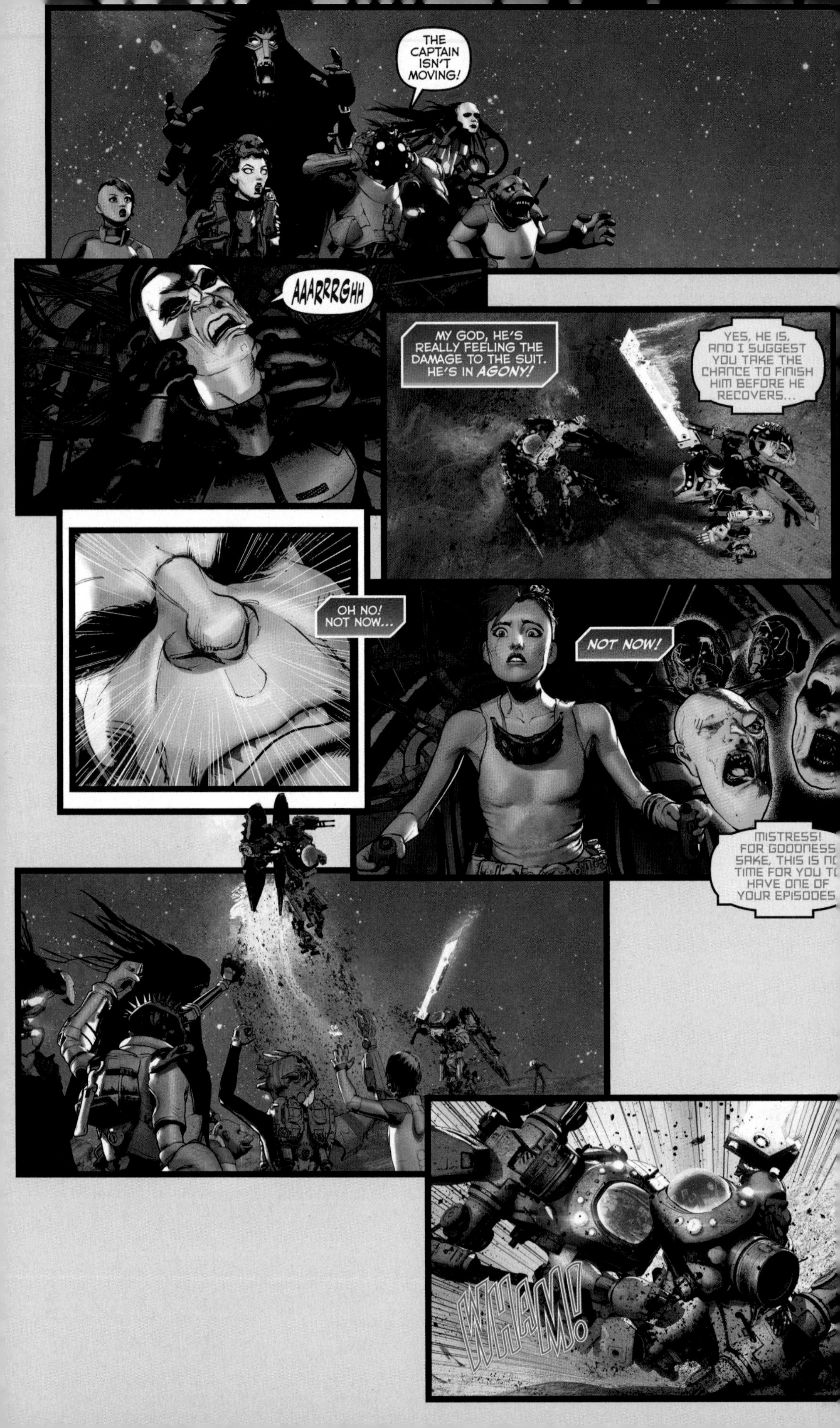
THE CAPTAIN ISN'T MOVING!
AAARRRGHH
MY GOD, HE'S REALLY FEELING THE DAMAGE TO THE SUIT. HE'S IN AGONY!
YES, HE IS, AND I SUGGEST YOU TAKE THE CHANCE TO FINISH HIM BEFORE HE RECOVERS...
OH NO! NOT NOW...
NOT NOW!
MISTRESS! FOR GOODNESS SAKE, THIS IS NO TIME FOR YOU TO HAVE ONE OF YOUR EPISODES
WHAM!

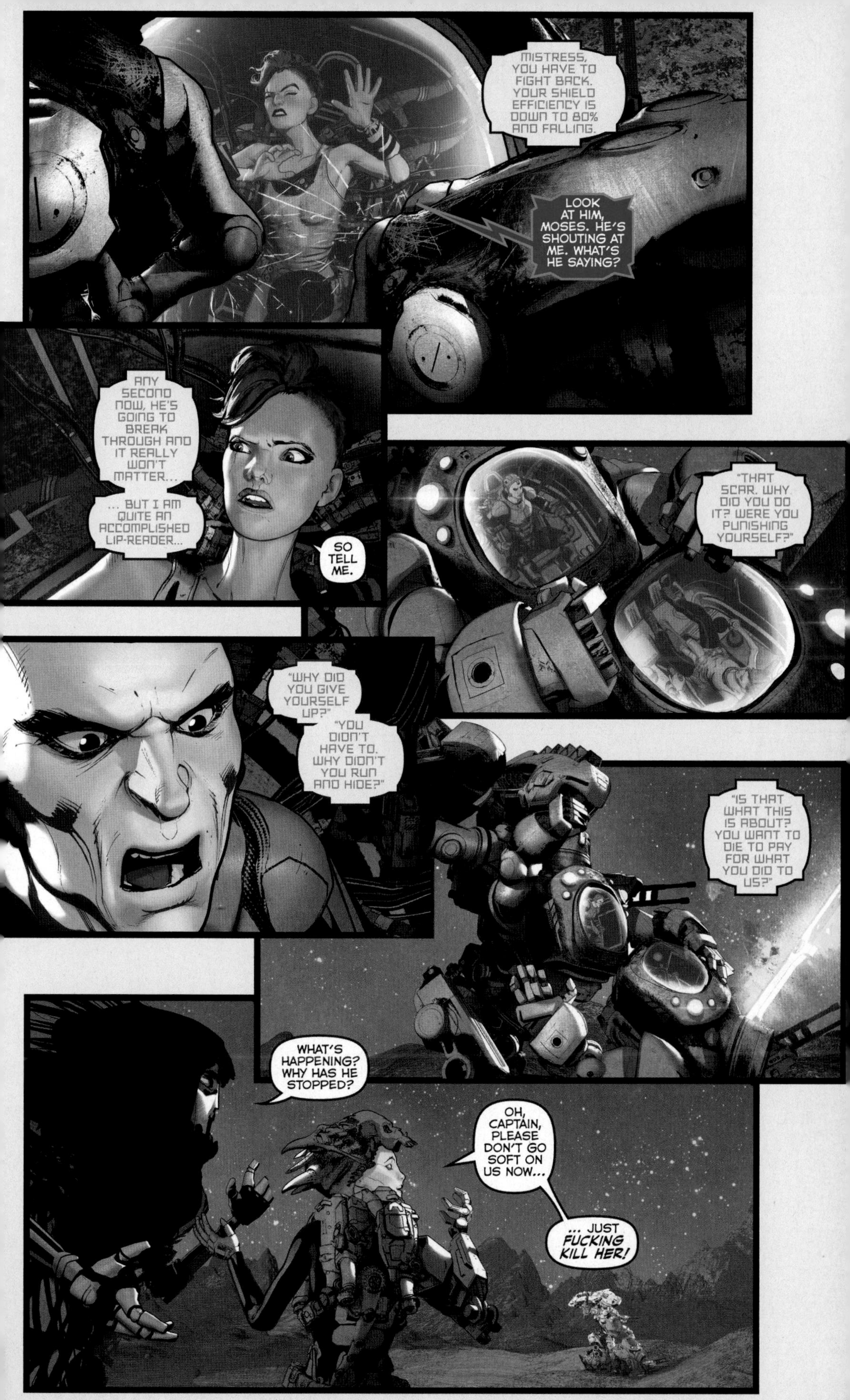
MISTRESS, YOU HAVE TO FIGHT BACK. YOUR SHIELD EFFICIENCY IS DOWN TO 80% AND FALLING.
LOOK AT HIM, MOSES. HE'S SHOUTING AT ME. WHAT'S HE SAYING?
ANY SECOND NOW, HE'S GOING TO BREAK THROUGH AND IT REALLY WON'T MATTER...
... BUT I AM QUITE AN ACCOMPLISHED LIP-READER...
SO TELL ME.
"THAT SCAR. WHY DID YOU DO IT? WERE YOU PUNISHING YOURSELF?"
"WHY DID YOU GIVE YOURSELF UP?"
"YOU DIDN'T HAVE TO. WHY DIDN'T YOU RUN AND HIDE?"
"IS THAT WHAT THIS IS ABOUT? YOU WANT TO DIE TO PAY FOR WHAT YOU DID TO US?"
WHAT'S HAPPENING? WHY HAS HE STOPPED?
OH, CAPTAIN, PLEASE DON'T GO SOFT ON US NOW...
... JUST *FUCKING* KILL HER!

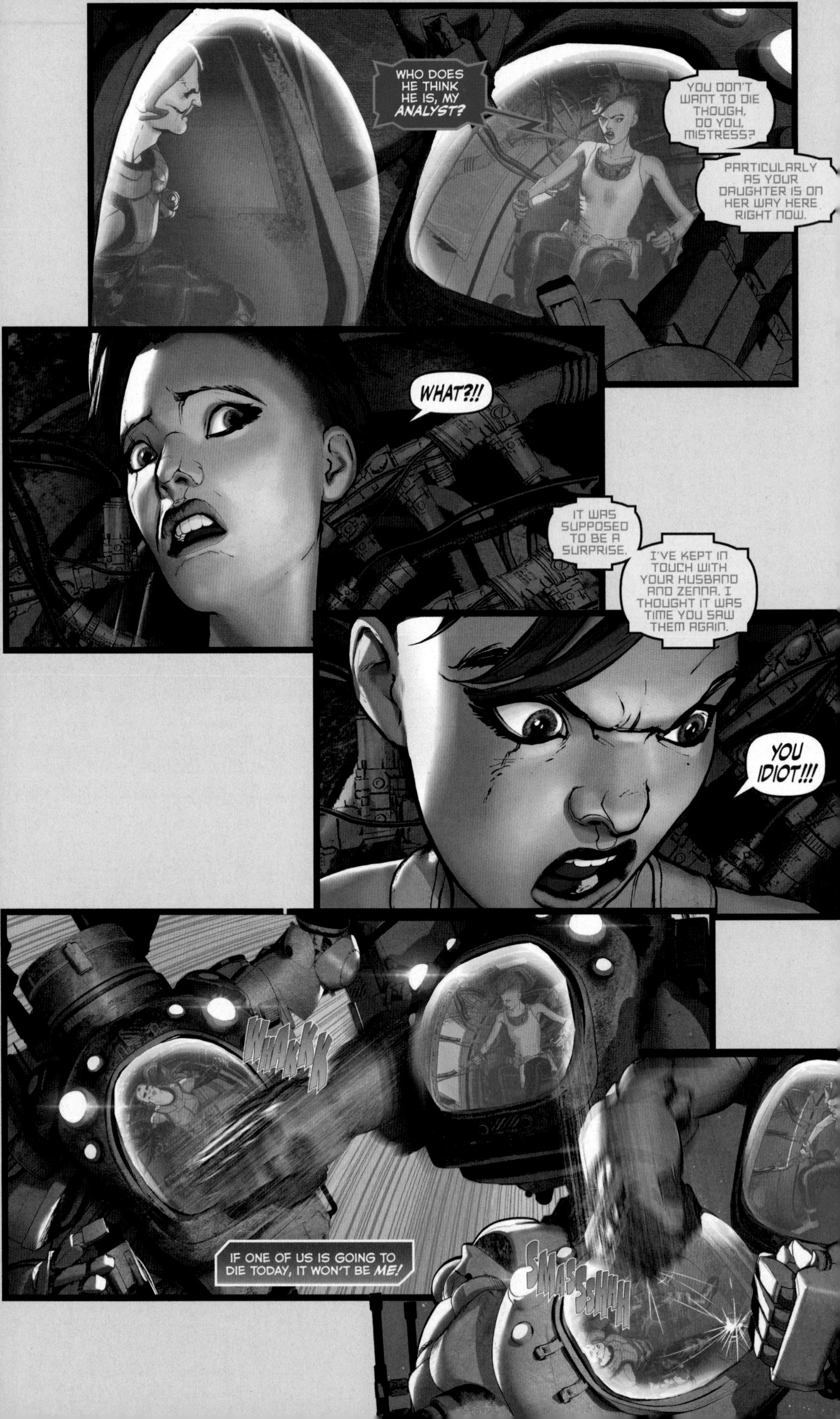

WHO DOES HE THINK HE IS, MY ANALYST?
YOU DON'T WANT TO DIE THOUGH, DO YOU, MISTRESS?
PARTICULARLY AS YOUR DAUGHTER IS ON HER WAY HERE RIGHT NOW.
WHAT?!!
IT WAS SUPPOSED TO BE A SURPRISE.
I'VE KEPT IN TOUCH WITH YOUR HUSBAND AND ZENNA. I THOUGHT IT WAS TIME YOU SAW THEM AGAIN.
YOU IDIOT!!!
WHAKKK
IF ONE OF US IS GOING TO DIE TODAY, IT WON'T BE ME!
SMASSSHHH

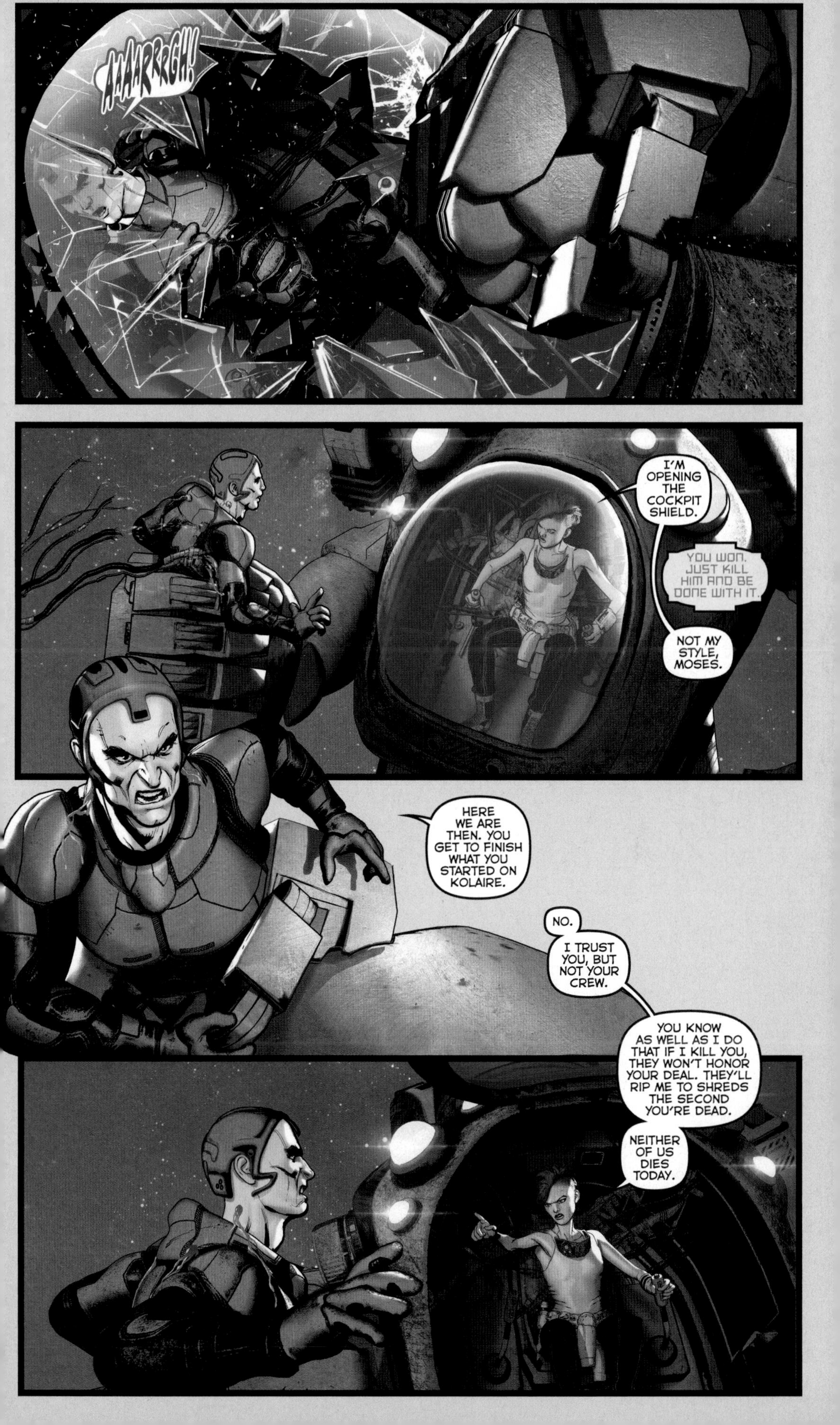
AAAARRRGH!
I'M OPENING THE COCKPIT SHIELD.
YOU WON. JUST KILL HIM AND BE DONE WITH IT.
NOT MY STYLE, MOSES.
HERE WE ARE THEN. YOU GET TO FINISH WHAT YOU STARTED ON KOLAIRE.
NO.
I TRUST YOU, BUT NOT YOUR CREW.
YOU KNOW AS WELL AS I DO THAT IF I KILL YOU, THEY WON'T HONOR YOUR DEAL. THEY'LL RIP ME TO SHREDS THE SECOND YOU'RE DEAD.
NEITHER OF US DIES TODAY.

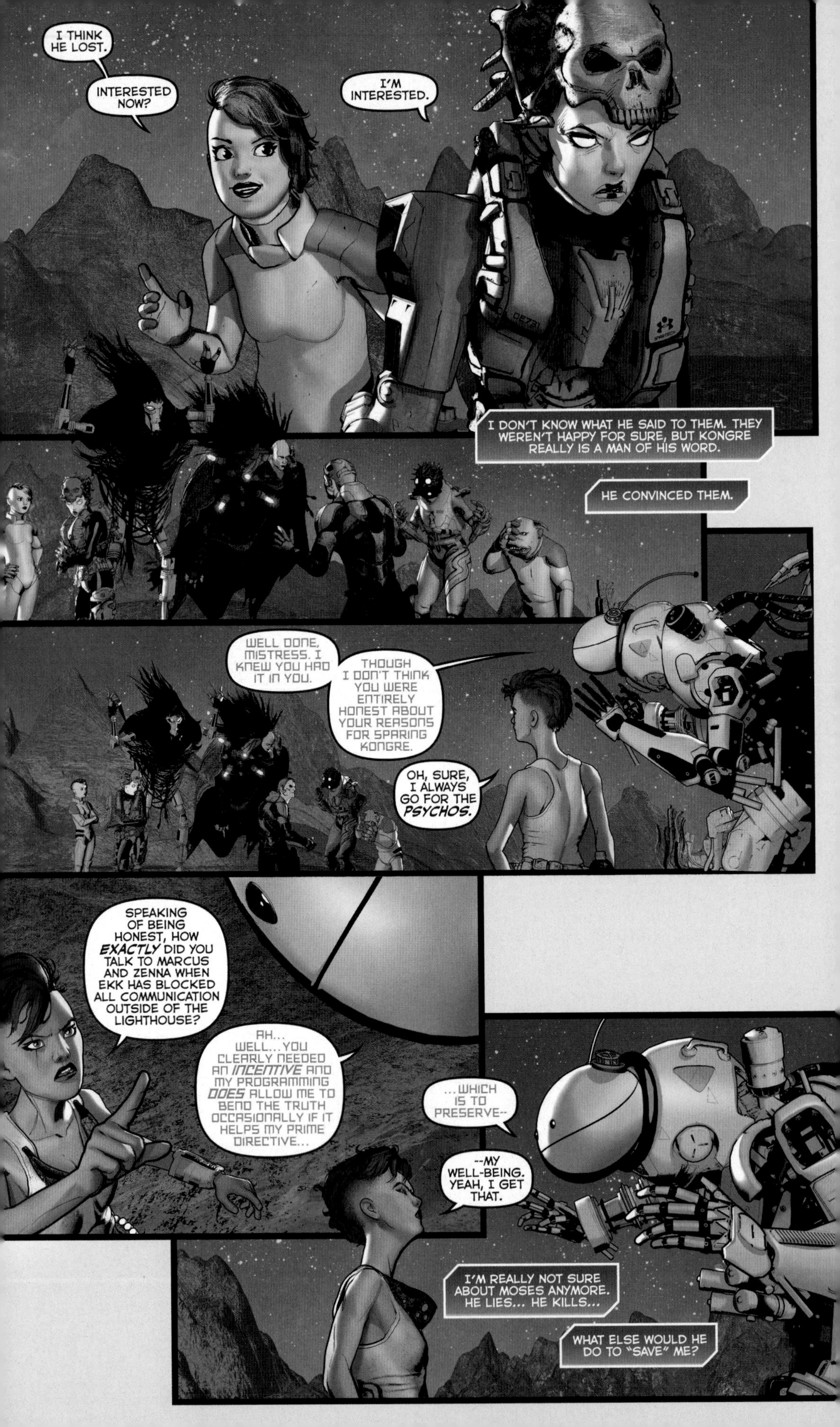
I THINK HE LOST.
INTERESTED NOW?
I'M INTERESTED.
I DON'T KNOW WHAT HE SAID TO THEM. THEY WEREN'T HAPPY FOR SURE, BUT KONGRE REALLY IS A MAN OF HIS WORD.
HE CONVINCED THEM.
WELL DONE, MISTRESS. I KNEW YOU HAD IT IN YOU.
THOUGH I DON'T THINK YOU WERE ENTIRELY HONEST ABOUT YOUR REASONS FOR SPARING KONGRE.
OH, SURE, I ALWAYS GO FOR THE PSYCHOS.
SPEAKING OF BEING HONEST, HOW EXACTLY DID YOU TALK TO MARCUS AND ZENNA WHEN EKK HAS BLOCKED ALL COMMUNICATION OUTSIDE OF THE LIGHTHOUSE?
AH... WELL... YOU CLEARLY NEEDED AN INCENTIVE AND MY PROGRAMMING DOES ALLOW ME TO BEND THE TRUTH OCCASIONALLY IF IT HELPS MY PRIME DIRECTIVE...
...WHICH IS TO PRESERVE--
--MY WELL-BEING. YEAH, I GET THAT.
I'M REALLY NOT SURE ABOUT MOSES ANYMORE. HE LIES... HE KILLS...
WHAT ELSE WOULD HE DO TO "SAVE" ME?

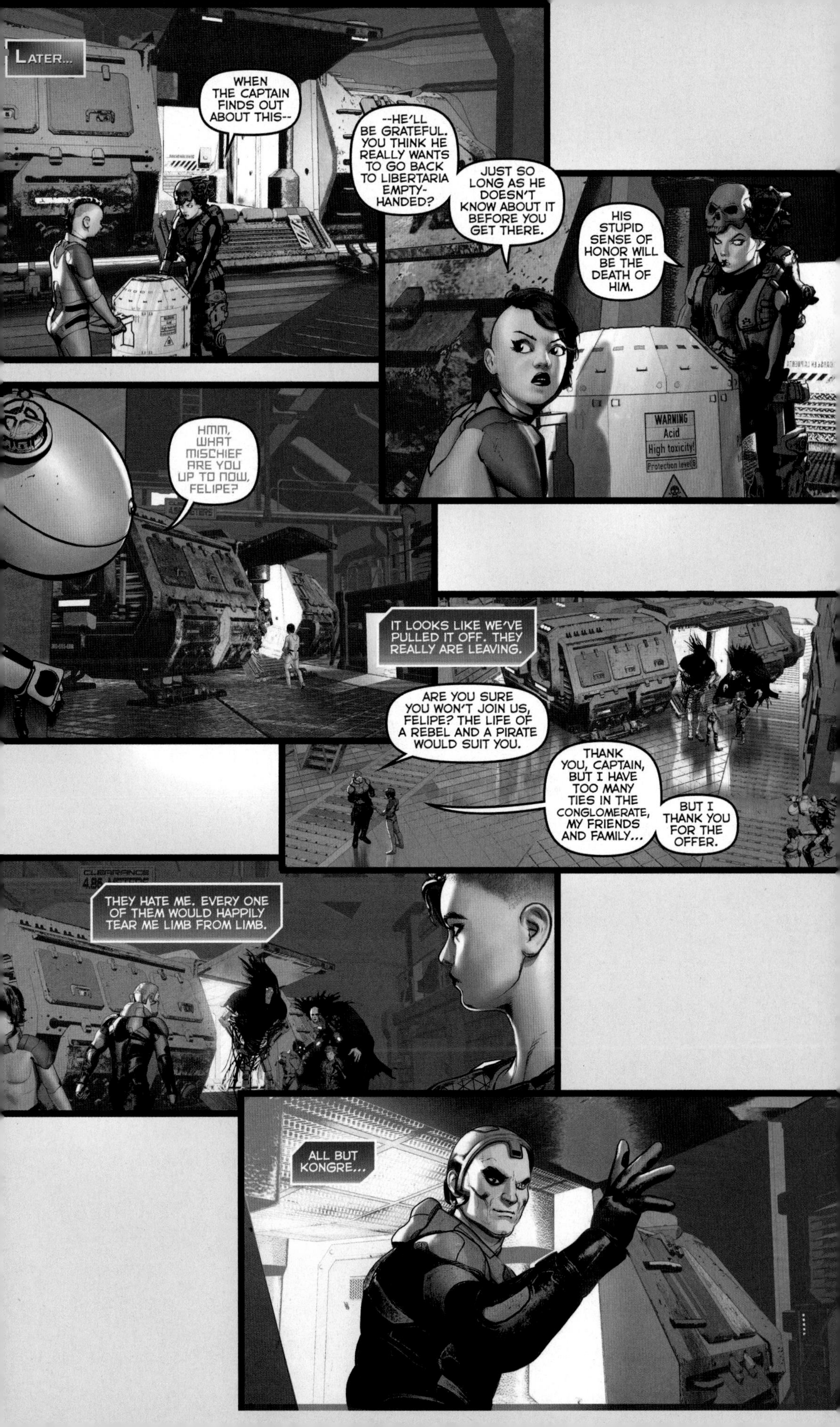
LATER...
WHEN THE CAPTAIN FINDS OUT ABOUT THIS--
--HE'LL BE GRATEFUL. YOU THINK HE REALLY WANTS TO GO BACK TO LIBERTARIA EMPTY-HANDED?
JUST SO LONG AS HE DOESN'T KNOW ABOUT IT BEFORE YOU GET THERE.
HIS STUPID SENSE OF HONOR WILL BE THE DEATH OF HIM.
WARNING
Acid
High toxicity!
HMM, WHAT MISCHIEF ARE YOU UP TO NOW, FELIPE?
IT LOOKS LIKE WE'VE PULLED IT OFF. THEY REALLY ARE LEAVING.
ARE YOU SURE YOU WON'T JOIN US, FELIPE? THE LIFE OF A REBEL AND A PIRATE WOULD SUIT YOU.
THANK YOU, CAPTAIN, BUT I HAVE TOO MANY TIES IN THE CONGLOMERATE, MY FRIENDS AND FAMILY...
BUT I THANK YOU FOR THE OFFER.
THEY HATE ME. EVERY ONE OF THEM WOULD HAPPILY TEAR ME LIMB FROM LIMB.
ALL BUT KONGRE...

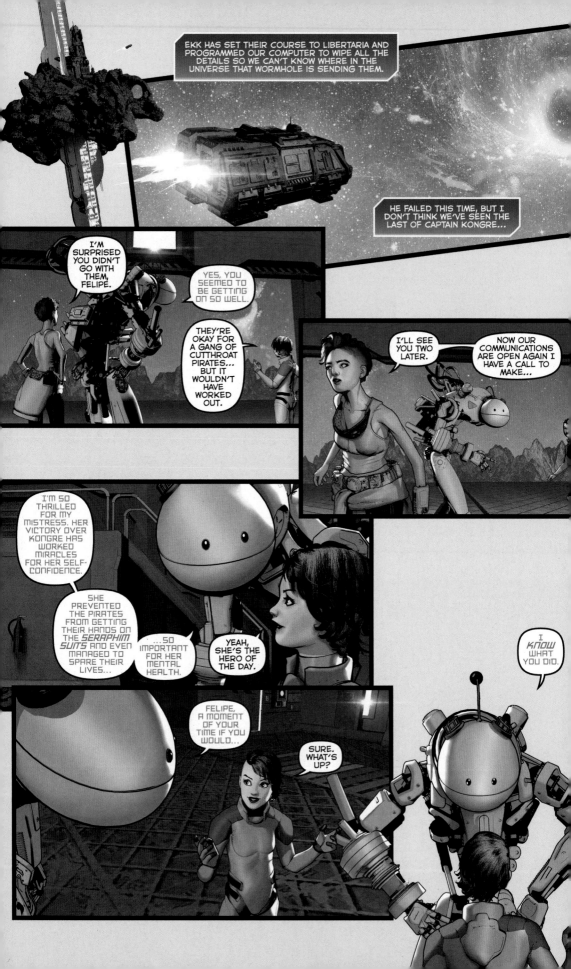

EKK HAS SET THEIR COURSE TO LIBERTARIA AND PROGRAMMED OUR COMPUTER TO WIPE ALL THE DETAILS SO WE CAN'T KNOW WHERE IN THE UNIVERSE THAT WORMHOLE IS SENDING THEM.

HE FAILED THIS TIME, BUT I DON'T THINK WE'VE SEEN THE LAST OF CAPTAIN KONGRE...

I'M SURPRISED YOU DIDN'T GO WITH THEM, FELIPE.

YES, YOU SEEMED TO BE GETTING ON SO WELL.

THEY'RE OKAY FOR A GANG OF CUTTHROAT PIRATES... BUT IT WOULDN'T HAVE WORKED OUT.

I'LL SEE YOU TWO LATER.

NOW OUR COMMUNICATIONS ARE OPEN AGAIN I HAVE A CALL TO MAKE...

I'M SO THRILLED FOR MY MISTRESS. HER VICTORY OVER KONGRE HAS WORKED MIRACLES FOR HER SELF-CONFIDENCE.

SHE PREVENTED THE PIRATES FROM GETTING THEIR HANDS ON THE *SERAPHIM SUITS* AND EVEN MANAGED TO SPARE THEIR LIVES...

...SO IMPORTANT FOR HER MENTAL HEALTH.

YEAH, SHE'S THE HERO OF THE DAY.

I *KNOW* WHAT YOU DID.

FELIPE, A MOMENT OF YOUR TIME IF YOU WOULD...

SURE. WHAT'S UP?

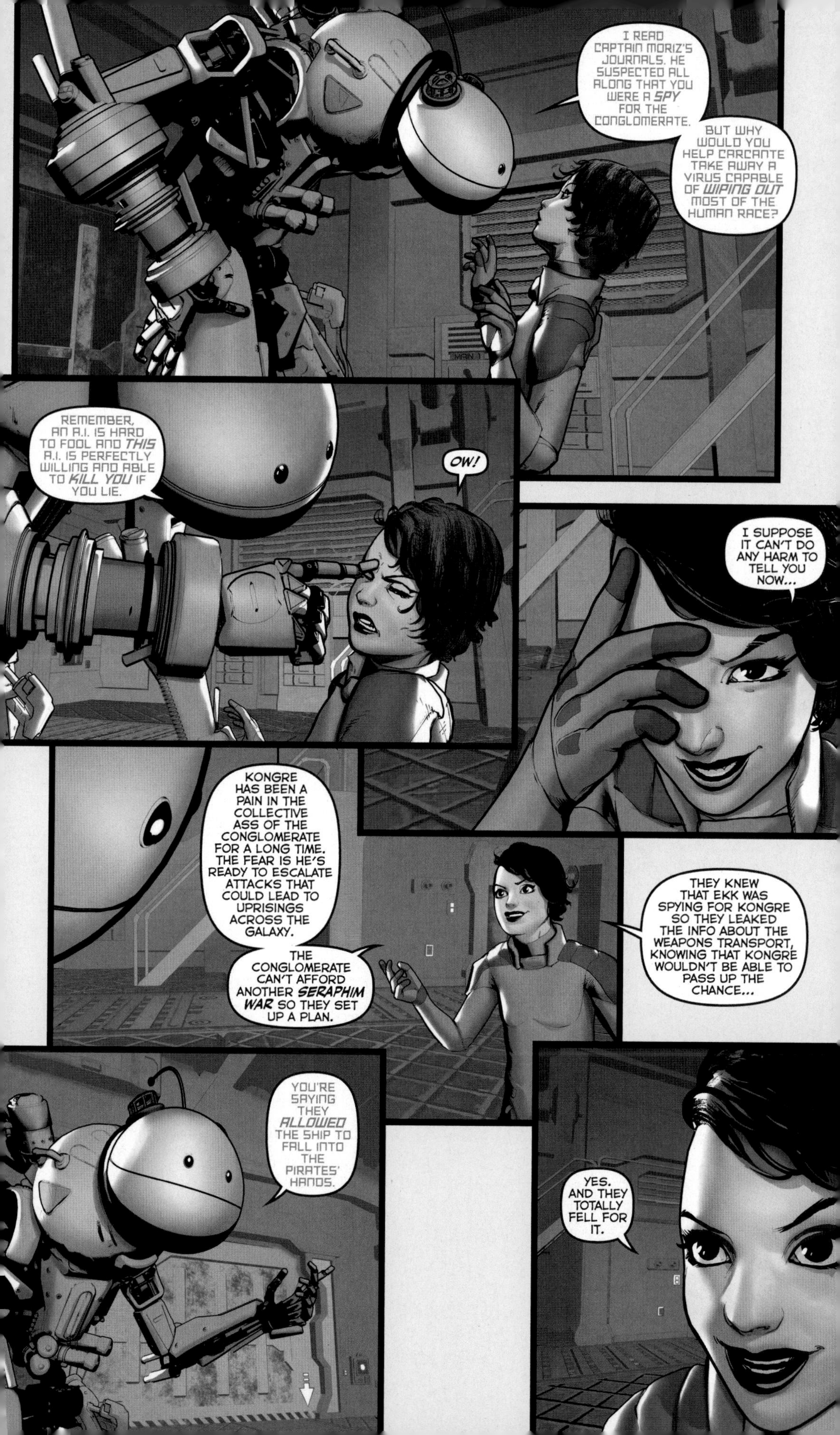
I READ CAPTAIN MORIZ'S JOURNALS. HE SUSPECTED ALL ALONG THAT YOU WERE A SPY FOR THE CONGLOMERATE.
BUT WHY WOULD YOU HELP CARCANTE TAKE AWAY A VIRUS CAPABLE OF WIPING OUT MOST OF THE HUMAN RACE?
REMEMBER, AN A.I. IS HARD TO FOOL AND THIS A.I. IS PERFECTLY WILLING AND ABLE TO KILL YOU IF YOU LIE.
OW!
I SUPPOSE IT CAN'T DO ANY HARM TO TELL YOU NOW...
KONGRE HAS BEEN A PAIN IN THE COLLECTIVE ASS OF THE CONGLOMERATE FOR A LONG TIME. THE FEAR IS HE'S READY TO ESCALATE ATTACKS THAT COULD LEAD TO UPRISINGS ACROSS THE GALAXY.
THE CONGLOMERATE CAN'T AFFORD ANOTHER SERAPHIM WAR SO THEY SET UP A PLAN.
THEY KNEW THAT EKK WAS SPYING FOR KONGRE SO THEY LEAKED THE INFO ABOUT THE WEAPONS TRANSPORT, KNOWING THAT KONGRE WOULDN'T BE ABLE TO PASS UP THE CHANCE...
YOU'RE SAYING THEY ALLOWED THE SHIP TO FALL INTO THE PIRATES' HANDS.
YES. AND THEY TOTALLY FELL FOR IT.

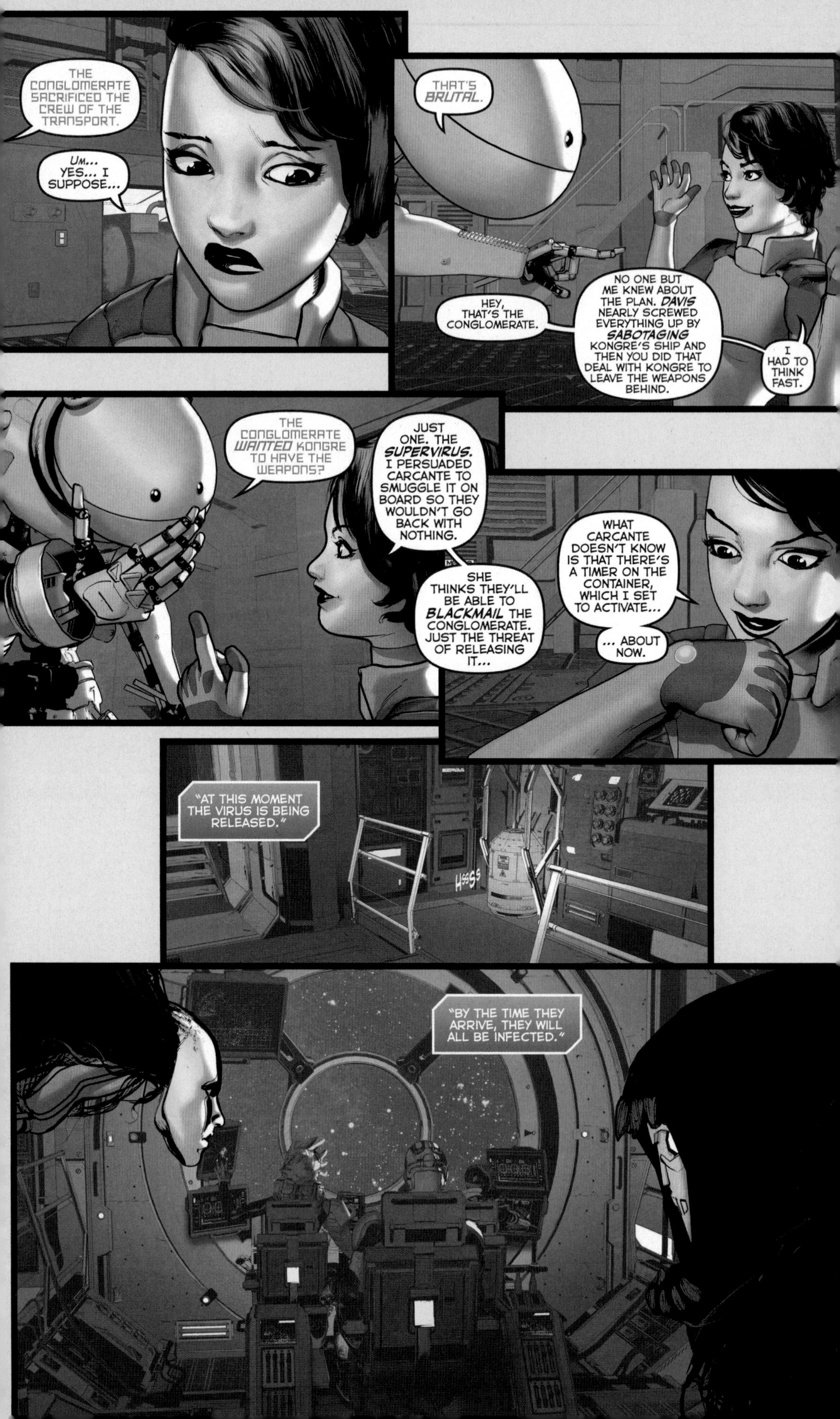
THE CONGLOMERATE SACRIFICED THE CREW OF THE TRANSPORT.
UM... YES... I SUPPOSE...
THAT'S BRUTAL.
HEY, THAT'S THE CONGLOMERATE.
NO ONE BUT ME KNEW ABOUT THE PLAN. DAVIS NEARLY SCREWED EVERYTHING UP BY SABOTAGING KONGRE'S SHIP AND THEN YOU DID THAT DEAL WITH KONGRE TO LEAVE THE WEAPONS BEHIND.
I HAD TO THINK FAST.
THE CONGLOMERATE WANTED KONGRE TO HAVE THE WEAPONS?
JUST ONE. THE SUPERVIRUS. I PERSUADED CARCANTE TO SMUGGLE IT ON BOARD SO THEY WOULDN'T GO BACK WITH NOTHING.
SHE THINKS THEY'LL BE ABLE TO BLACKMAIL THE CONGLOMERATE. JUST THE THREAT OF RELEASING IT...
WHAT CARCANTE DOESN'T KNOW IS THAT THERE'S A TIMER ON THE CONTAINER, WHICH I SET TO ACTIVATE...
... ABOUT NOW.
"AT THIS MOMENT THE VIRUS IS BEING RELEASED."
HSSSS
"BY THE TIME THEY ARRIVE, THEY WILL ALL BE INFECTED."

WITHIN DAYS THE VIRUS WILL SPREAD THROUGHOUT LIBERTARIA.

IN A WEEK EVERYONE ON THE PLANET WILL BE *DEAD.*

MY MISTRESS MUST NEVER KNOW ABOUT THIS. THE GUILT WOULD DRIVE HER *MAD!*

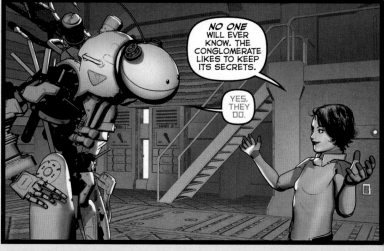

NO ONE WILL EVER KNOW. THE CONGLOMERATE LIKES TO KEEP ITS SECRETS.

YES, THEY DO.

HAS IT OCCURRED TO YOU THAT YOU ARE A LOOSE END?

WHAT?

MY SENSORS DETECT AN IMPLANT INSIDE YOUR BRAIN.

I KNOW. IT'S JUST A STANDARD TRACKER. THEY DON'T LIKE TO LOSE THEIR AGENTS.

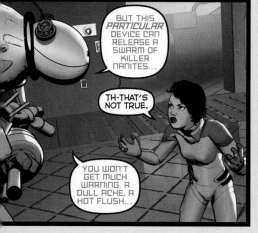

BUT THIS *PARTICULAR* DEVICE CAN RELEASE A SWARM OF KILLER NANITES...

TH-THAT'S NOT TRUE.

YOU WON'T GET MUCH WARNING. A DULL ACHE, A HOT FLUSH...

...IT'S FAST, BUT APPARENTLY QUITE *PAINFUL.*

YOU... YOU'RE MAKING THAT UP.

MOSES...?

MOSES?

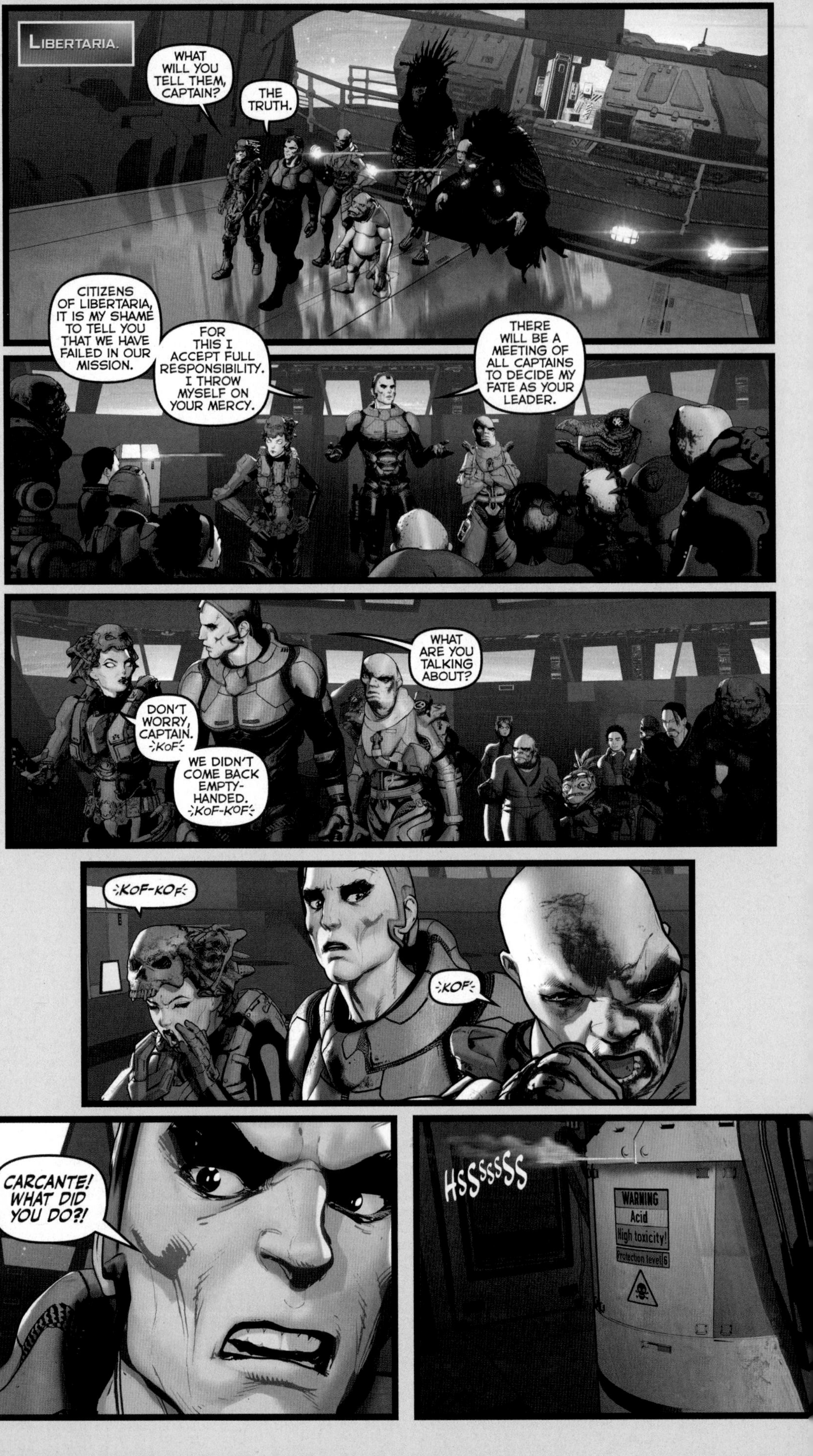
LIBERTARIA.
WHAT WILL YOU TELL THEM, CAPTAIN?
THE TRUTH.
CITIZENS OF LIBERTARIA, IT IS MY SHAME TO TELL YOU THAT WE HAVE FAILED IN OUR MISSION.
FOR THIS I ACCEPT FULL RESPONSIBILITY. I THROW MYSELF ON YOUR MERCY.
THERE WILL BE A MEETING OF ALL CAPTAINS TO DECIDE MY FATE AS YOUR LEADER.
WHAT ARE YOU TALKING ABOUT?
DON'T WORRY, CAPTAIN. KOF
WE DIDN'T COME BACK EMPTY-HANDED. KOF-KOF
KOF-KOF
KOF
CARCANTE! WHAT DID YOU DO?!
HSSSSSS
WARNING
Acid
High toxicity!
Protection level 6

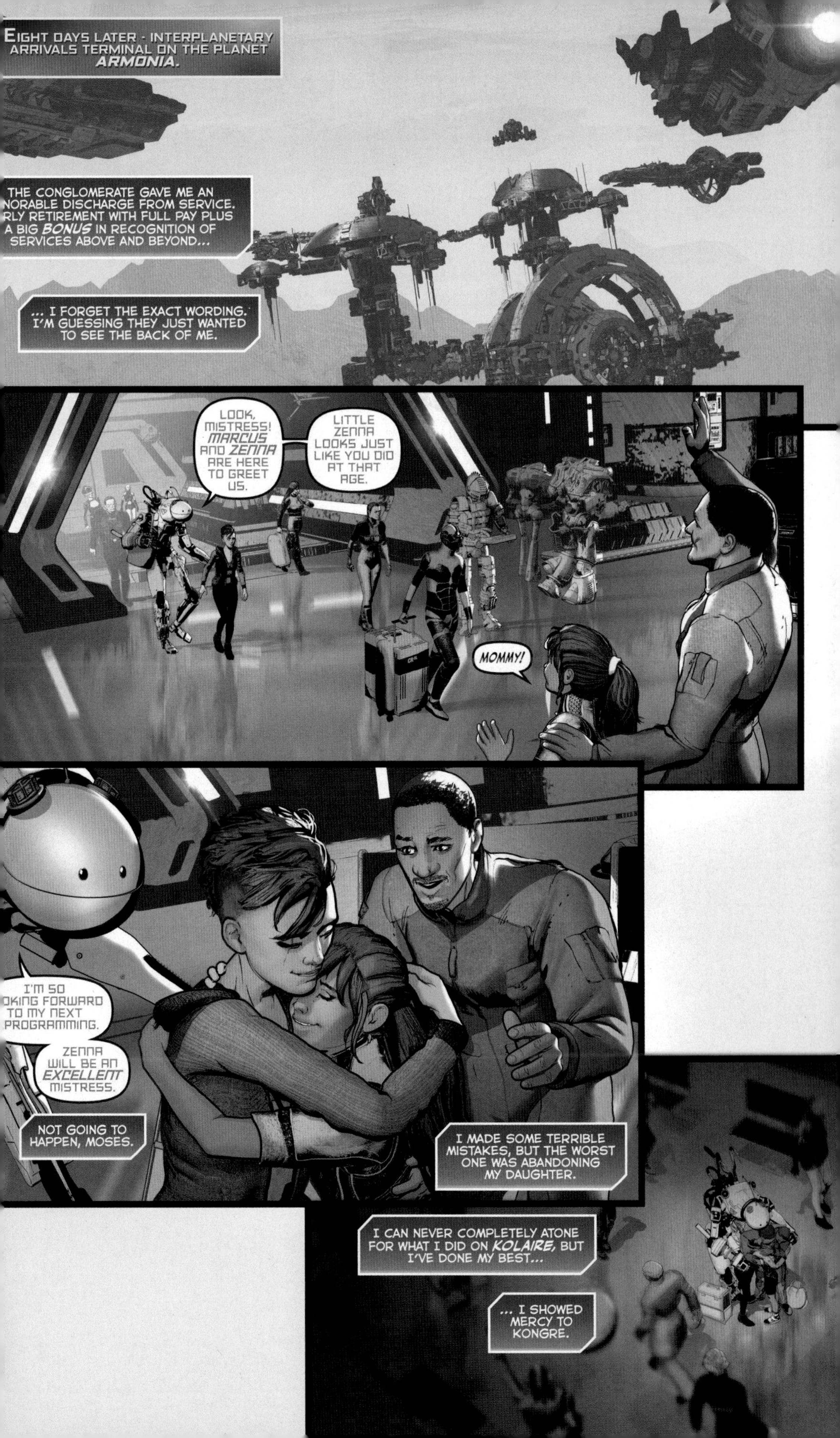
EIGHT DAYS LATER - INTERPLANETARY ARRIVALS TERMINAL ON THE PLANET ARMONIA.
THE CONGLOMERATE GAVE ME AN NORABLE DISCHARGE FROM SERVICE. RLY RETIREMENT WITH FULL PAY PLUS A BIG BONUS IN RECOGNITION OF SERVICES ABOVE AND BEYOND...
... I FORGET THE EXACT WORDING. I'M GUESSING THEY JUST WANTED TO SEE THE BACK OF ME.
LOOK, MISTRESS! MARCUS AND ZENNA ARE HERE TO GREET US.
LITTLE ZENNA LOOKS JUST LIKE YOU DID AT THAT AGE.
MOMMY!
I'M SO OKING FORWARD TO MY NEXT PROGRAMMING.
ZENNA WILL BE AN EXCELLENT MISTRESS.
NOT GOING TO HAPPEN, MOSES.
I MADE SOME TERRIBLE MISTAKES, BUT THE WORST ONE WAS ABANDONING MY DAUGHTER.
I CAN NEVER COMPLETELY ATONE FOR WHAT I DID ON KOLAIRE, BUT I'VE DONE MY BEST...
... I SHOWED MERCY TO KONGRE.

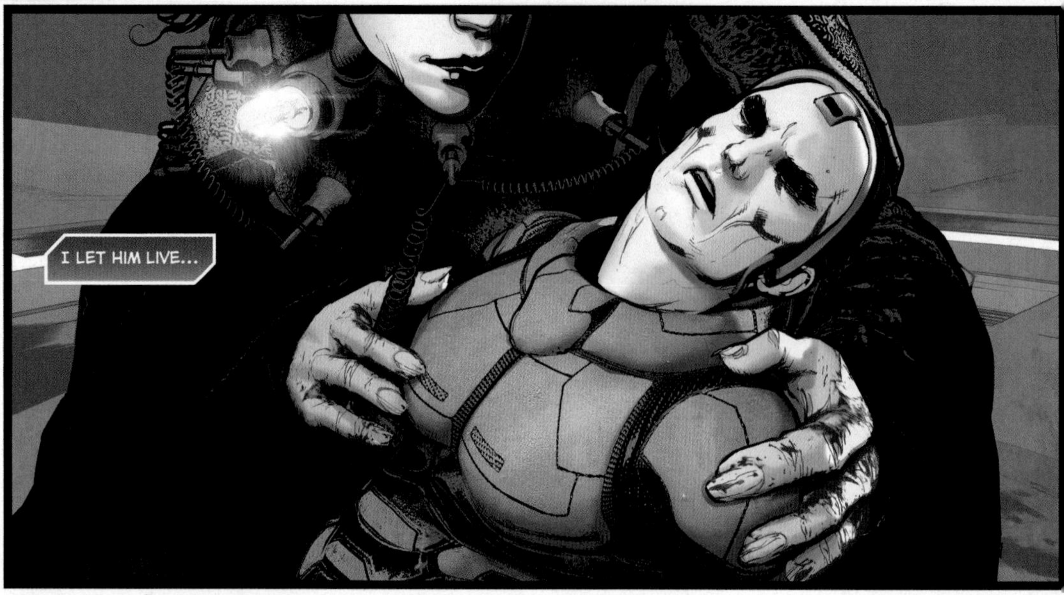
I LET HIM LIVE...

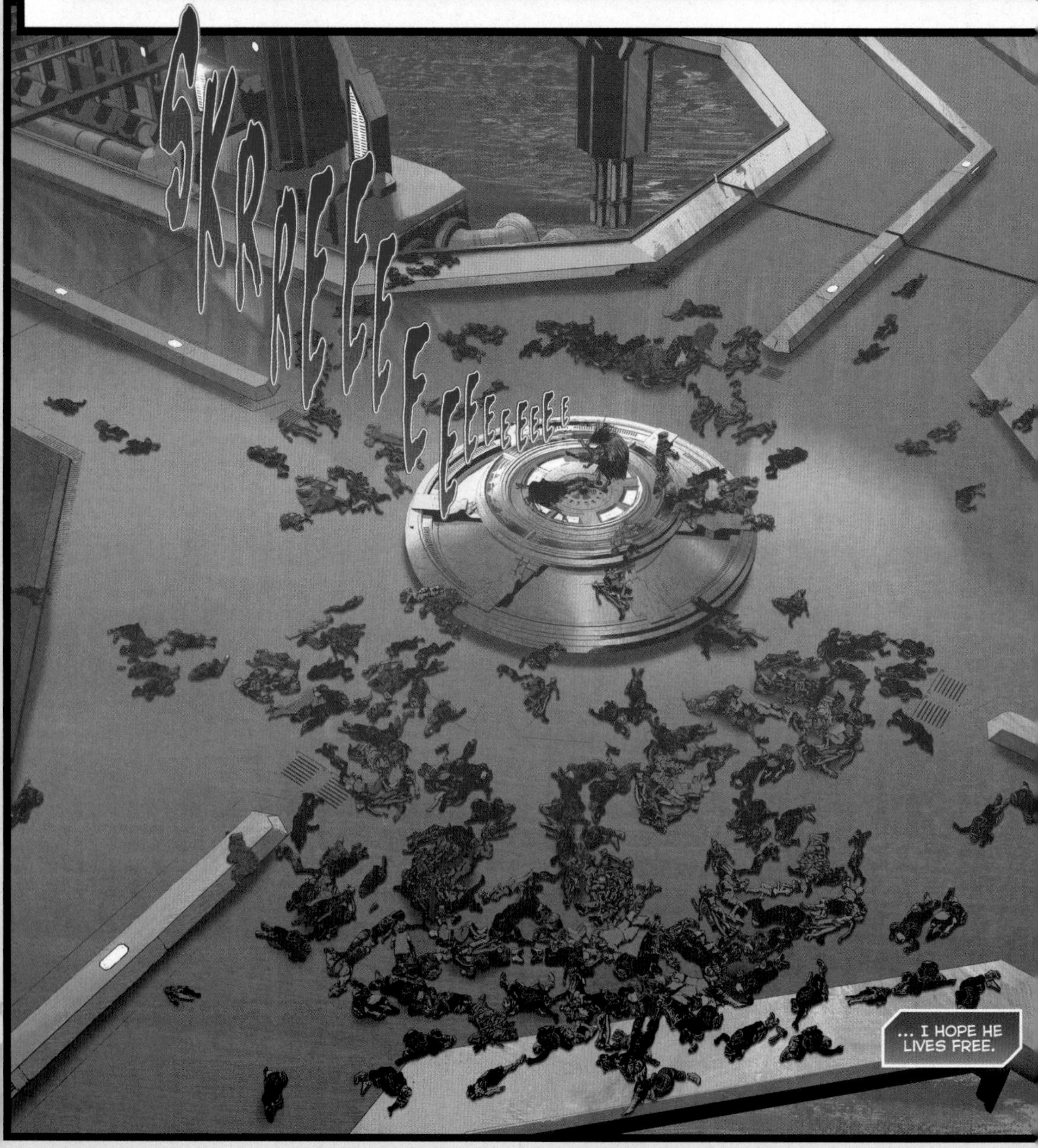
SKREEEEEEEEEEEE
... I HOPE HE LIVES FREE.

EXTRAS

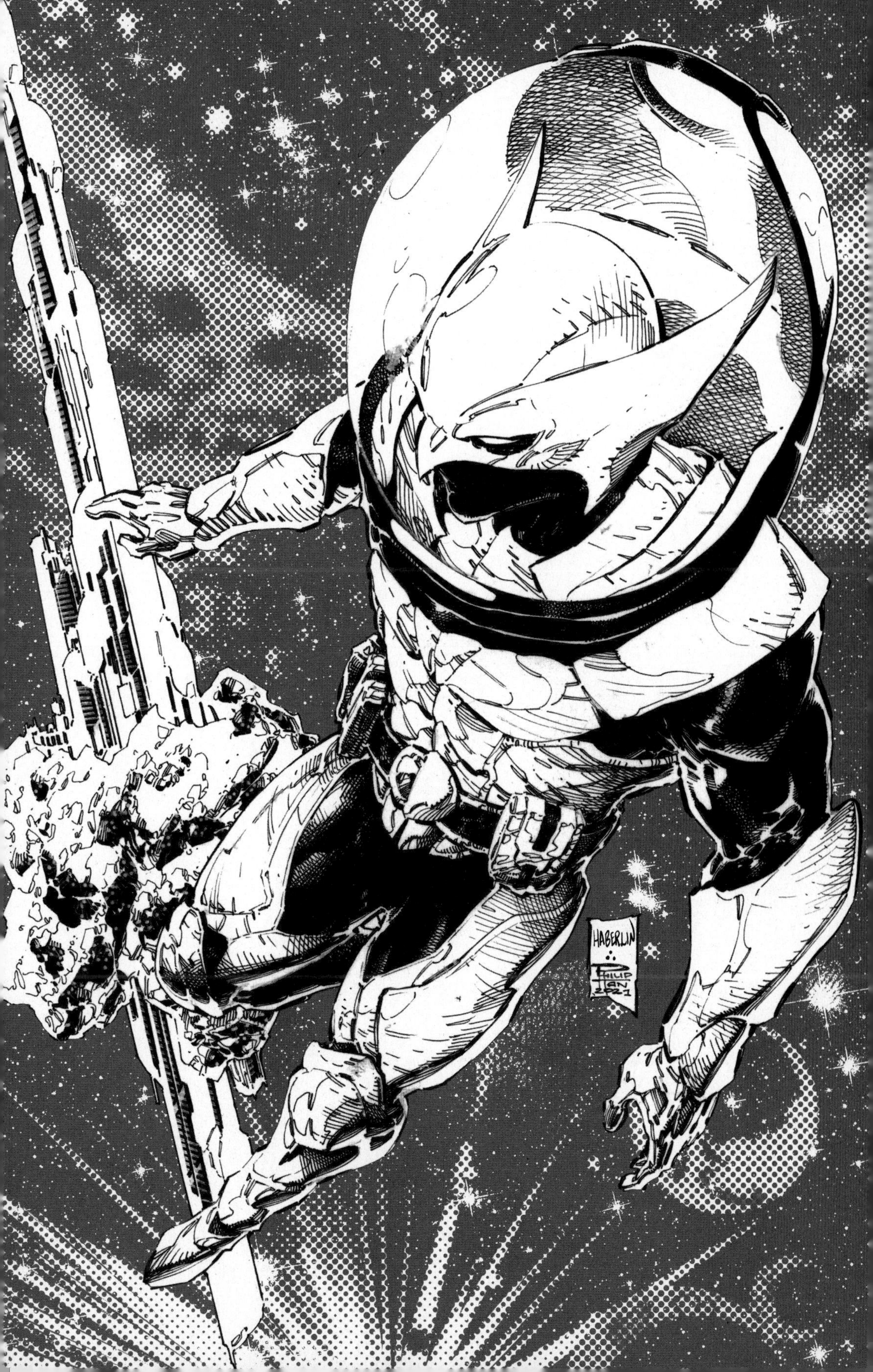
HABERLIN

Issue #2 Retailer Exclusive

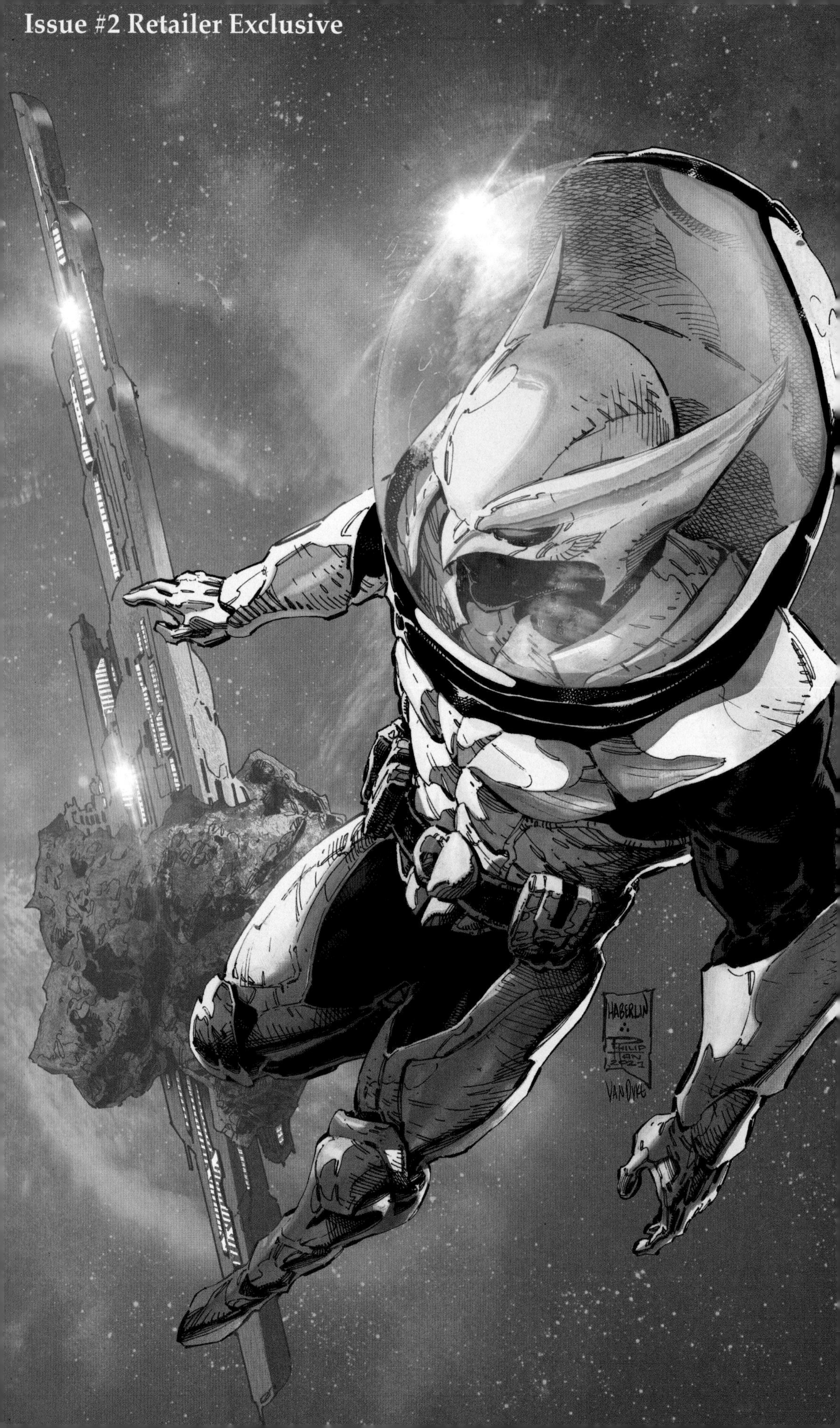
HABERLIN
PHILIP TAN 2021
VAN DYKE

Issue #2 Cover C

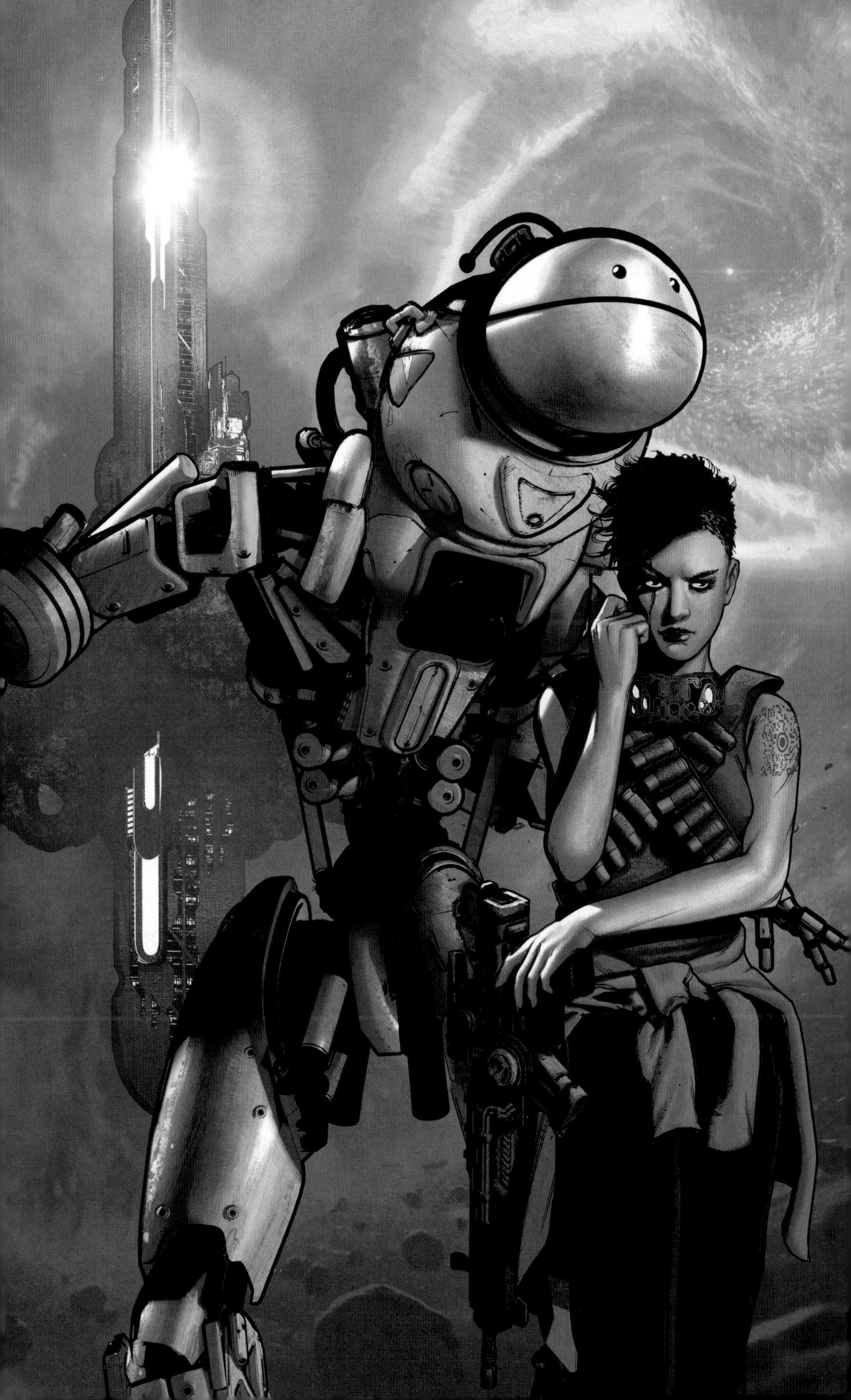

Issue #4 Cover C

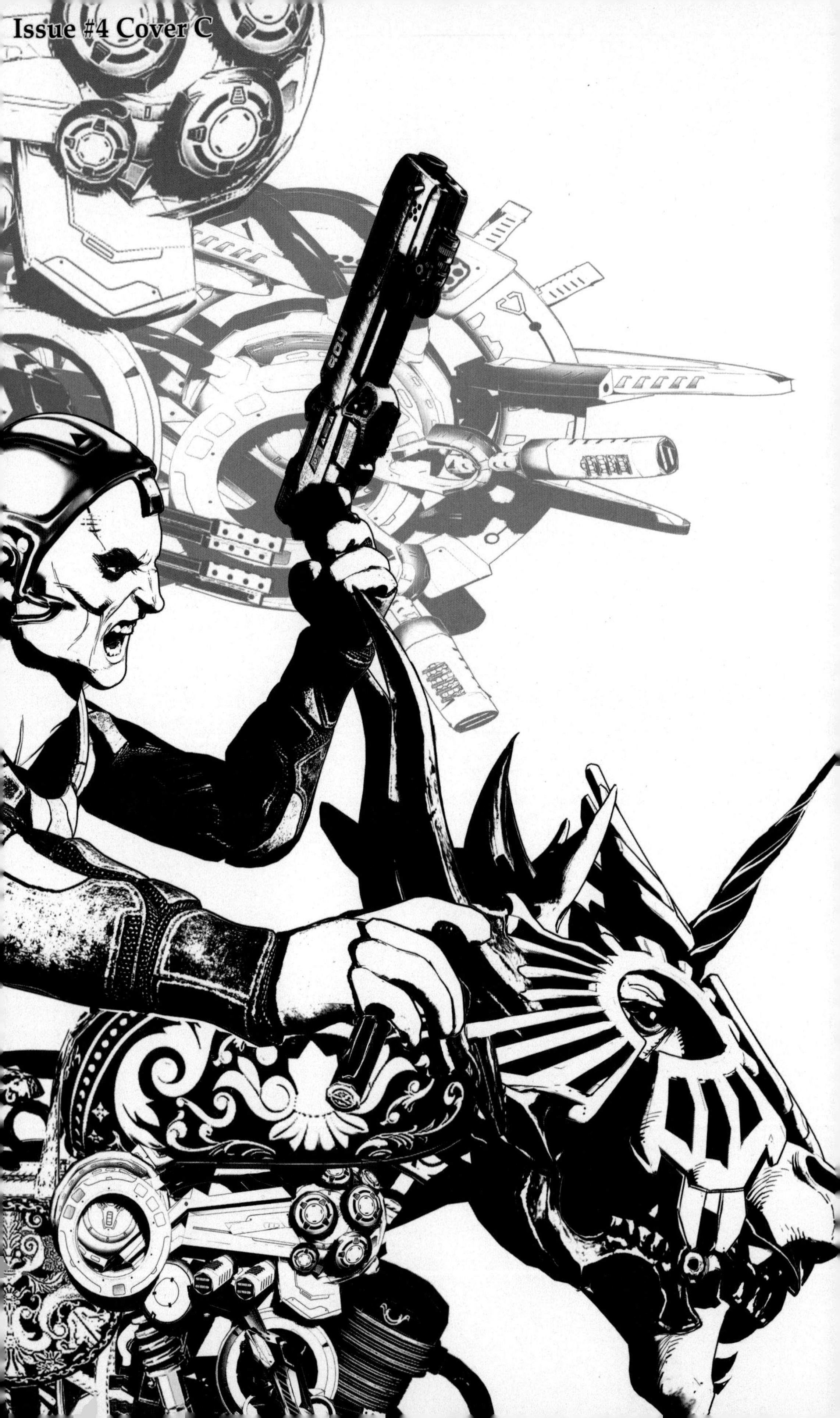

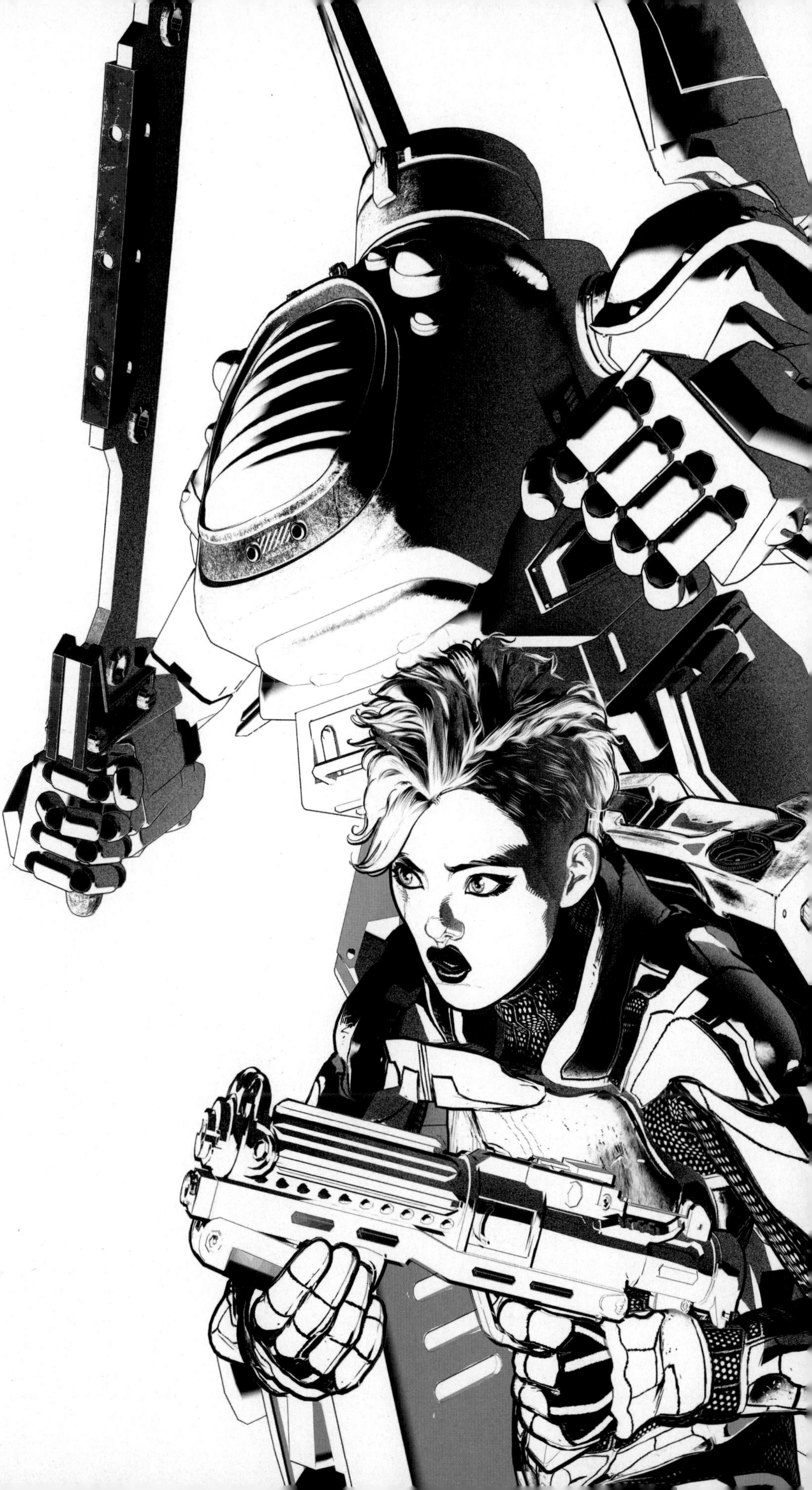

Issue #1 Retailer Exclusive Cover (Good Guys)

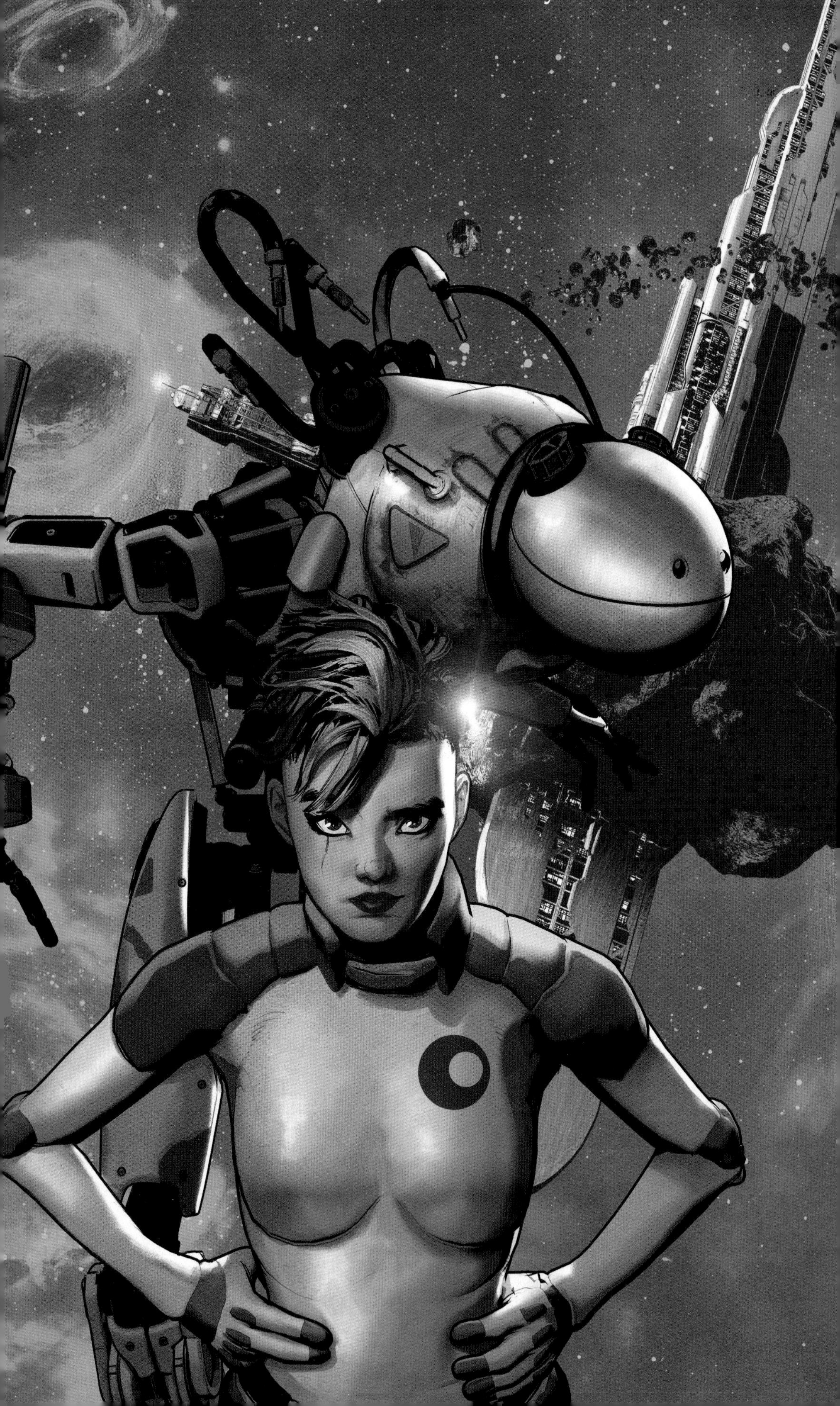